THE
OTHER
GUEST

About the Author

Helen Cooper is from Derby and lives in Leicester. She has taught English and Academic Writing in both Further and Higher Education and was Head of Learning Enhancement at the University of Birmingham. She has a MA in Creative Writing from Nottingham Trent University and has been published in Writers' Forum, Mslexia, the *Bath Short Story Prize Anthology* (2014) and the *Leicester Writes Short Story Prize Anthology* (2018).

Also by Helen Cooper

The Downstairs Neighbour

THE
OTHER
GUEST

HELEN COOPER

HODDER &
STOUGHTON

First published in Great Britain in 2022 by Hodder & Stoughton
An Hachette UK company

1

Copyright © Helen Cooper 2022

The right of Helen Cooper to be identified as the Author of the Work has been
asserted by her in accordance with the Copyright, Designs and Patents Act 1988.

A CIP catalogue record for this title is available from the British Library

Hardback ISBN 978 1 529 33013 7
Trade Paperback ISBN 978 1 529 33015 1
eBook ISBN 978 1 529 33014 4

Typeset in Plantin Light by Hewer Text UK Ltd, Edinburgh
Printed and bound in Great Britain by Clays Ltd, Elcograf S.p.A.

Hodder & Stoughton policy is to use papers that are natural, renewable
and recyclable products and made from wood grown in sustainable
forests. The logging and manufacturing processes are expected to
conform to the environmental regulations of the country of origin.

Hodder & Stoughton Ltd
Carmelite House
50 Victoria Embankment
London EC4Y 0DZ

www.hodder.co.uk

For Christine. This is a book about sisters and you're absolutely the best kind.

And for my friends who are like a gang of bonus sisters I'm lucky enough to have.

Prologue

I've seen so many storms rage over this lake. I know how the water blazes as if it's on fire, how the rain blows in huge pillars between the mountains. I've watched flaming arrows of lightning dive towards the surface, and I've felt my hands clench in recognition of all that anger and energy. Like the wildest punk anthem I've ever heard, like a band trashing their own instruments, swept up in the anarchy of the moment. I've even shouted at storms the way a fan might scream during a gig – the closest I can get to that kind of freedom.

But I've never been stupid enough, before tonight, to find myself on a tiny boat in the middle of it all.

I *did* feel this storm approaching. The thrum and taste of it in the air. But the day escalated faster than the weather – confusion, arguments, suspicion, panic. By the time the sun began to set and the rain closed in, I'd run out of choices. Now I try to see the storm as a transition, washing away all the bad moments, or even as my ally, my disguise, if I can just get through it – get *away* – and not look back.

Two lightning bolts rip downwards. The jagged shapes of the mountains are briefly backlit – and something else is illuminated at the edge of my eyeline, too. My heart thuds as I turn to squint at it. Another small boat looms out of the spray, like a mirror image of mine, lurching towards me with a silhouetted figure on board.

I

Joanna

Despite everything that had happened, there were times when Joanna loved living alone. When she woke to nothing but birdsong in the morning, and yellow light through her new curtains, and she could starfish across her bed into patches of coolness. Or when she came home after a busy day, poured a glass of wine, and sat in her shady little garden without having to talk or think. Nobody to gate-crash the quiet, to complicate that hard-earned sip of sauvignon blanc.

Then there were the other times, of course.

The nights when she would wake in chilly darkness to a house full of creaks and too much space in her bed. The weekends when all her friends were busy with their families or partners, and her Spotify kept landing on songs that were spiked with memories.

Or the evenings like this one, when a glass of wine and the last rays of June sun weren't enough to lift the darkness of a truly harrowing day.

Joanna burrowed her bare feet into the grass of her garden, trying to focus on the tickly sensation between her toes. But her head was too full of the awfulness, the guilt. The failings in her department that had almost caused something unthinkable.

Almost, she reminded herself, clenching the stem of her glass.

Still, the image blared again: a figure on the roof of the university's tallest building, on the wrong side of the safety barriers. The marks his palms had left behind on the railings from gripping so tight.

Joanna shook her head and reached for her phone, instinctively opening the WhatsApp group she had with her closest friends. She could write something and there would be a flood of compassion, reliable and lovely friends that they were. But then she'd feel guilty for attracting so much attention, and she'd start backtracking, saying oh it wasn't really that bad, and surely *they'd* all had much more stressful days with their teething babies and hectic school runs. Somehow, she felt she'd used up her quota of sympathy during her break-up with Luke. Her friends had been heroes throughout those hideous few months, but now she shied away from mentioning other troubles, even from admitting that Luke still plagued her thoughts. She'd had her unwanted limelight.

Pushing aside the phone, she took another cold gulp of wine. There were several sensible things she could do for her mental state. Things she'd recommended to many of the students she'd counselled over the years. But meditation and mindfulness now seemed much less appealing than going to a pub and getting drunk among strangers.

Joanna left her glass on the bench and ran to fetch her purse.

She had called into The Last Junction a few times since moving to this part of Derby. It was a red-brick pub next to the station, usually full of people who were either waiting for trains or had just got off one, their suitcases parked next to their tables as they drank. Part of its appeal was that there was never anybody she knew. Although Derby was a city, it felt tiny sometimes. Joanna had been part of the same crowd, hanging out in the same places, since she was sixteen. And almost every memory from those two decades circled back to Luke.

But in this pub, as usual, she didn't recognise a single person under the dim lighting. Even the barman wasn't somebody she'd seen working in here before – he was younger than the other staff, though he had a face that could've put him anywhere between late twenties and early forties. Boyish dimples but crinkly eyes. Curly, soft-looking hair, but a tinge of silver in his blond stubble. He blinked as if she'd startled him, then studied her face as though there was something strange about it. There probably was. Smears of mascara always transferred themselves to her upper eyelids when she was stressed, like two extra brows. There would be sweat patches under her arms and her long skirt would be crushed from hours sat in hot rooms chairing crisis meetings. She felt too tired to fix herself, though. Too tired even to drag a finger over her lids.

'Rum and coke please,' she said.

'Which rum?' the barman asked.

Joanna looked at him in surprise. She didn't want to have to make decisions; she'd spent all day doing that, or failing to. This wasn't the kind of pub where she expected to have to show knowledge or preference.

'Any's fine.'

'Shall I choose for you?'

'Please.' The idea of relinquishing responsibility, even for this minor thing, was a relief.

'Something with a bit of spice?'

'Something strong.'

He raised his eyebrows. Joanna flushed at how she must look, marching in alone and demanding strong alcohol. The barman scanned the shelves, swooped in on a bottle, and poured amber liquid into an ice-filled tumbler.

'You sure you want coke in it?' he asked.

She nodded, but then saw that he was grinning, that it was a joke. Joanna gave in to a small amount of banter: 'But only because neat rum on a Thursday teatime isn't socially acceptable.'

The bar man opened a miniature glass bottle of coke, surprising her again because she'd expected it from a pump. When he sloshed some into her drink before handing her the rest of the bottle, she couldn't help twirling it in her hands, a nostalgic feeling rising in her. Picnics when she was young. Being allowed a bottle of coke as a treat. Mum, before her illness, opening one at arm's length in case it had got fizzed up on the way there. That blue and yellow checked blanket they used to have, which they would shake out afterwards, sandwich and cake crumbs flying. What had happened to the blanket? It was exactly the kind of thing Joanna had been filling her new house with: artefacts from a pre- or post-Luke world, bracketing the chunk of her life that had been snipped out from the middle.

She realised the barman was waiting with the card machine. Not impatiently, though. He seemed to be watching her drift into a reverie about the coke bottle, as if he understood. Maybe everybody got nostalgic about those glass bottles. That was probably the idea.

'Sorry,' she said, tapping her card.

'No problem.' He smiled at her again. 'Enjoy.'

The only spare table was so close to the toilets it got bumped every time somebody passed in or out, so she decided to perch on a bar stool instead. The spicy warmth of the rum flooded her mouth, and the barman made a thumbs-up-or-down gesture, checking whether she liked his choice. She gave him a quick thumbs up. Because she'd hardly eaten all day, and rarely drank spirits, the alcohol surged through her, blurring and softening the evening's edges.

'Make sure I don't have more than two,' she found herself calling to him. 'I've got work tomorrow, and I have to be . . . can't be . . .'

'Two.' He nodded. 'Bad day?'

'Is it that obvious?'

He came back towards her. 'What happened?'

At some point, the pub had almost emptied. It was another thing she'd liked about the place, the handful of times she'd been: the way a proportion of the customers would abruptly leave, en masse, presumably all catching the same train. Then there'd be another influx, but hardly anybody would stay for more than a couple of drinks. The transience was refreshing. So different from the bars she and Luke used to go to with their friends at weekends, where everybody knew one another, and the nights would follow a well-worn pattern. She had loved that at the time, of course. In the aftershock of separation, she'd grieved for the routines of their life almost as much as for him.

'I don't really want to talk about it,' she told the barman. 'Thanks, though.'

But he continued to hover, drying glasses with a squeaky cloth, the quiet of the pub beginning to feel like a loaded pause in a conversation.

'Work?' he prompted, and she nodded. 'What do you do?'

'I'm Head of Counselling Services at the uni. I used to be a student counsellor but now I run the department and it's—'

'Tough, I'd imagine.'

'Yep.' Joanna's eyes fuzzed with tears. That poor student, whose name she'd spoken and written and read countless times today. The student they'd almost failed – except *they* really meant *her*, Joanna, because she was in charge, it was her responsibility. And *almost* wasn't accurate either, because the young man *had* been failed, even though he was alive.

Joanna had only ever wanted to help students cope with the stresses of university. Of struggling to fit in, keep up, keep going. Being a counsellor had been hard at times, too, but every day she had felt she'd achieved something, listened to someone. Since her promotion, she'd barely spoken to a student in weeks. Her job had become a treadmill of meetings and spreadsheets and frustrations. There was never enough money or staff; there were always too many students in need. How had she never realised how much strain their services were under, as she'd sat in a little pod with tissues and privacy blinds, focusing on each individual without panicking that there were a hundred more on a waiting list?

All she did now was think about that waiting list.

'A student who should've had a counselling appointment weeks ago –' Joanna tried to swallow her tears along with another gulp of rum – 'attempted to . . .' She stopped before it all avalanched out; she could lose her job for disclosing it to a stranger in a pub. 'Sorry, I can't actually tell you.'

The barman's smile had faded now. 'Sounds like you've got a lot on your plate,' he said, letting her off the hook of explaining fully.

Joanna swirled her drink so the ice cubes clinked, a sound that reminded her of summer barbecues and weddings. Of Luke, because he'd always been with her at those things.

'I'm too aware of the bigger picture, now. All the people who have to wait for help, the ones who don't get it at all. Turns out I'm the kind of person who can help someone who's sitting in front of me, but not the kind who can make important decisions about—'

'*Impossible* decisions,' he said. 'Seems to me?'

Joanna paused for a moment. She thought of the medical student who'd reached the limit of what he could cope with alone. The lecturer who'd talked him down, her own brilliant staff stepping in afterwards. The enquiry that had been launched and the meetings she'd had to manage, while all she'd wanted was to talk to that student herself.

She didn't tell the barman any of this. But she did talk more generally about her job – the most she'd spoken about herself in months. At intervals she thought, *what are you doing? Shut up!* But she couldn't once she'd started. There was something in his manner that invited confidence – an attentiveness, a stillness – as the pub got even quieter and its small windows darkened.

He kept his word, refusing to serve her a third rum. The second had seemed stronger, though, bringing a welcome anaesthesia to her brain. When she realised they'd reached closing time, and that her tongue felt almost tender from over-sharing, she snapped back to herself. He flicked on the lights and she was suddenly sober and exposed.

'Get some sleep,' he said as she left. 'Tomorrow's a new day.'

It was what her mum used to say when Joanna was upset. Maybe she had told the barman that, during the course of their conversation, and he was simply echoing it now? She murmured it as she made her way home through the dark. The streets were deserted and she kept jumping at shadows and sounds. More than once, she was convinced she heard footsteps behind her, but each time she turned, there was nobody there. She hugged her elbows and walked quickly, wishing she'd left the lights on in her empty house.

2

Leah

The final stretch of Leah's journey had to be taken by boat. Small ferries, exclusive to guests of *Il Mandarino* Luxury Holiday Village, departed every hour from 'the dock with the golden railings'. The smartest, shiniest dock on this part of Lake Garda.

Leah was the only person waiting there that afternoon, anxious and sweating in her weather-inappropriate black jeans. The glaring blue of the lake surrounded her on all sides. A rocky mountain reared out of the water to the north, looking almost muscular as the sun rippled over its curves and planes. Behind it, out of sight, lay the resort. Waiting to reveal itself to those who were privileged enough to be staying there.

Would her sister come on the ferry to meet her? Leah had told Charlotte what time she expected to arrive, but Charlotte had been typically vague about her intentions. Since landing, Leah had been on tenterhooks. Might she meet her at the airport? she'd wondered first. No, but there *had* been a man in mirrored sunglasses, holding a sign with Leah's name on, who'd whisked her into a plush, air-conditioned car and driven her to the small town of Malcesine, the last stop in reality before *Il Mandarino*.

Stepping out into blinding sunlight, Leah had looked around for Charlotte again, before assuming she should head to the dock and hope for a ferry. It was unsettling, not knowing at what point she would clap eyes on her sister, after two years apart. It wouldn't have occurred to Charlotte that Leah might be nervous, that most people – *especially* Leah – liked to have schedules and plans. 'Charlottetime', their dad used to call it, laughing fondly at his eldest daughter's ability to be hours late and not even appear to realise. Since moving to Italy, and immersing herself in *Il Mandarino*, Charlotte seemed to exist even more in her own unfathomable world.

At least, she had done when Leah had last visited. To her shame, she didn't know who her sister might be now. How grief might have changed her. Leah reminded herself she was here to build bridges, to assess with her own eyes whether Charlotte was 'coping fine', as her strange, brief emails always claimed she was.

Her gaze was tugged towards the centre of the lake, where the blue was darker and denser, where the water seemed to swallow the sunlight rather than bounce it into her eyes. Something dragged at her stomach, like a weight trying to pull her in. She gripped the golden railings of the dock but they were scalding hot and she jolted back. At that moment, she spotted the ferry cutting a frothy path towards her, an orange and gold *Il Mandarino* flag streaming from its top deck.

At the front stood a familiar figure, with long dark hair bannering in the breeze. Not Charlotte, as Leah misidentified her for a moment, but her daughter, Olivia, Leah's niece.

Leah's *other* niece, as she couldn't help thinking of her now.

The boat drew up, gleaming with water droplets and polished chrome, its tapered prow giving it the look of a miniature yacht. It was empty apart from the man driving it – also in reflective shades – and Olivia, wearing a pale orange shift dress and high strappy sandals. She stepped down carefully, her heavily made-up face composed in a smile. Again, if Leah squinted, she could've been looking at a younger clone of Charlotte. The mother–daughter resemblance was even more pronounced than the last time she'd been here.

'Auntie Lee!' Olivia brushed Leah's cheek with a cool, perfumey kiss. 'Welcome back.'

Leah swallowed, unable to speak. Her niece was greeting her as she'd been trained to welcome all guests of *Il Mandarino*: as if they were a temporary member of a special family.

Except Leah *was* one of the family. It was just that only Amy had ever made her feel that way.

As they sped away from Malcesine, Leah gripped the damp edges of her leather seat and stared around. She'd forgotten the gasping freshness of the air out on the water, compared to the heat of the shore. How the lake narrowed and then dramatically widened, so that the villages on opposite shores seemed flung apart. And she'd forgotten how, as you began to sail around the huge rocky outcrop that hid *Il Mandarino* from the rest of Lake Garda, there was the sense of a curtain being slowly drawn back.

There was no mention of Amy during their journey. Olivia gushed about *Il Mandarino*, how much it had grown, a prestigious award they'd recently won. Silently, Leah counted the months since Amy's death. Nine. To her, it was still savagely raw. She'd only just emerged from a paralysis of shock and finally felt able to come to Italy. But perhaps she shouldn't have expected everyone here to be constantly talking about Amy. Maybe life had to resume at some point, especially for a seventeen-year-old.

'I'm pretty much in charge of customer relations now,' Olivia said, pinning down her hair against the wind.

'What about school?' Leah asked, feeling like the killjoy aunt. 'Or did you—'

'Well, that's over for the summer. My tutor won't be back for eight weeks, thank God! I can be all about *Il Mandarino* for the whole peak season!'

Leah felt a deep, uneasy pang. Even since her last visit, there was a ramped-up corporateness to Olivia's turns of phrase, her measured smile, the fact that her dress was the same shade of orange as the flag flying from the boat.

'Aren't you hot, Auntie Lee?' she asked, eyeing Leah's standard outfit of black jeans and black T-shirt, as if she was a dark smear on the sunny landscape.

'I'm fine,' Leah lied.

The boat lurched and she slipped in her seat. She'd forgotten this bit, too: the sudden direction change as the ferry cleared the outcrop and angled itself to approach the resort. At last, *Il Mandarino* dazzled into view. A dozen or so white buildings climbing one side of a lush mountain, fanning upwards from a private bay. Castle-like villas rose on stilts out of the greenery of the slope, and the sun flashing off their pools gave the impression that the whole place was glittering. It was hard to squint at it for any length of time, yet looking away wasn't easy, either; *Il Mandarino* demanded your gaze. Leah's eyes travelled upwards. At the very top of the resort the trees gave way to a craggy ridge, naked and almost brutal in contrast. A single cloud hovered like something that should've been airbrushed out.

As the ferry pulled up to a twin of the dock they'd just left, the wind carried down the scent of the place. The thick sweetness of the olive groves was undercut by hints of rich coffee and cologne. Leah stalled as she disembarked. Olivia gave her a curious look and offered her a hand off the boat, as if she were a doddery relative come to stay rather than a fell runner, a climber, activities she never spoke about with her family because she didn't think they'd understand why she needed them. Leah shook herself, leaping to shore. Why did this place always chip away at her pride?

A chauffeured golf buggy whizzed them up the path that snaked through the middle of the resort. Even as they rose, and the lake dropped away behind them, the villas were always taller, their white turrets shimmering in a haze of heat. Lemon and olive trees were planted strategically in between, for perfect aesthetics and shade, while sprinklers rotated in a constant dance. Leah glimpsed some guests sat out on their balconies, sipping drinks beneath gold-trimmed umbrellas, their faces shrouded by sunglasses. Beside her, Olivia smiled and waved and scrutinised everything.

'That hedge needs trimming,' she murmured, whipping an iPad from her handbag and tapping frantically. 'And,

God, that laundry really needs collecting from outside *Casa del Fico*.' She put a hand up to her mouth, as if a canvas bag of dirty laundry was a shocking eyesore, and immediately made a call.

All Leah could see was Amy, incongruous among the perfection. Resisting it. She pictured her climbing a tree to see the world beyond her boundaries. Running up the mountain in her frayed shorts and Bikini Kill T-shirt, shaking her head at each golf buggy that offered to pick her up.

The family's large villa was at the top, overlooking the resort and the lake at its feet. Leah's eyes went straight to the first-floor balcony, where Amy used to sit with her headphones on, music crashing in her ears, her parents barking at her to 'get changed or get inside' if she wasn't wearing acceptable clothes. She would often text Leah from that spot, describing clouds and birds, the music she was listening to, whether the lake looked choppy or calm. Now the balcony was deserted. Even the orange deckchair she used to sit in was gone. Leah battled to get a grip as they left the buggy and Olivia exchanged a few words with the driver. Then they were walking between the thick white pillars of the villa's entrance, stepping into the abrupt coolness of its terracotta hallway. Passing from sun into shade, Leah was momentarily blind. It was only as her vision adjusted that the tall, slim figure of her sister took shape.

Charlotte flung out her arms, bracelets clinking. '*Lee!*'

Her hug was so effusive that Leah stiffened inside it – then, seconds later, was overwhelmed by guilt. How could she not have come sooner? The scent of her sister's skin and hair bombarded her. Exotic fruits, wild flowers. She used to have a theory that Charlotte's bouts of flightiness were a side effect of too much heady perfume, but that felt unkind now. Charlotte was just Charlotte. Her ability to detach from the world and then snap back was enviable, in a way. Necessary, perhaps. And Leah had failed to be there when she'd needed her most.

'How have you been?' she asked tentatively, drawing back.

'Busy!' Charlotte twirled her manicured hands. 'Summer season madness. Aren't you *boiling*, Lee? All covered up as usual!'

Leah blinked and didn't respond. Charlotte floated into the main part of the villa with Olivia in her wake. Taking a breath, Leah followed. At some point, without her even noticing, her luggage had been taken from her and presumably – hopefully – deposited inside. She felt naked without her laptop bag – repurposed as hand luggage – bumping its familiar weight against her hip. She was used to being laden down with client notes, hefty contracts, articles on copyright law that were interesting to almost nobody but her.

Now she watched her sister's natural sashay and well-cut linen dress, her fluttering necktie in orange and gold *Il Mandarino* stripes. They passed through several high-ceilinged rooms that never seemed to get used, into the heart of the villa. Even there it was almost magazine-centre-fold tidy, with neutral colours and hard glossy surfaces, but there were signs of couches having been sat on, coasters having hosted drinks. As Charlotte and Olivia went to fetch refreshments, Leah glanced around, wary of Gordon emerging from a side room and taking her by surprise.

Her gaze was drawn to a family photograph on the wall, one she hadn't seen before. Charlotte and Olivia's swept-back hairstyles were near-identical, as were their pearly smiles, their caramel tans. Gordon stood between them, broad-chested in a cream shirt with gold cufflinks and an orange tie. In the background, the resort framed them as if it had been arranged around their shoulders. The picture must've been taken from a boat, to get the whole of *Il Mandarino* in the shot, but the impression was that the three of them were an island, levitating just off their private shore.

Amy was absent from the photo. In fact, as Leah glanced around, she couldn't see a single picture of her.

Goosebumps broke out on her skin. Her eyes zigzagged, desperate to land on one trace of Amy, one thing she didn't have to conjure from her memories. There was a framed photo of Olivia holding a glass trophy, and a picture of the family pug who'd died a few years back. But no Amy. For a few panicked seconds, Leah couldn't even bring her niece's face to mind. It became blurred and formless, when Amy had always been, to her, the only one with any solidity.

Charlotte burst back into the room holding a bottle of champagne. 'To celebrate your arrival, Lee!'

Olivia followed with three crystal flutes, arranging them on the table while Charlotte removed the cork with a pop like a gunshot. Leah's mouth dried up. *Champagne?* For a moment she was convinced none of this was real. That she would jerk awake in her London flat to the roar of the traffic and the fade of a bad dream.

'Oh . . .' Charlotte said. 'Fetch another glass for Daddy, Olivia.'

Leah startled as she clocked what Charlotte had seemed to sense with her back turned: Gordon's materialisation in the doorway.

'Hello, Leah.'

Leah lifted her chin – the closest thing to a greeting she could muster. Gordon looked much older than the last time she'd seen him, much older than in the touched-up photo on the wall. He was the only one whose ageing seemed to have accelerated since his twenty-one-year-old daughter had drowned. He still carried himself with confidence, but his hair was thinner – though raven black, surely dyed – and there were new shadows and grooves in his face.

'None for me,' Gordon said to Charlotte.

'It's the good stuff,' Charlotte rushed to assure him. 'Not the case you were going to send back.'

'I've got things to do. I just stopped by to say welcome to Leah.'

Charlotte wavered over the rim of a glass. 'Perhaps it is a little . . .' Leah thought she was going to say inappropriate, but instead she said, 'early,' and glanced at the thin gold watch on her wrist.

'Don't let me stop you,' Gordon said, striding away.

Charlotte hesitated for another few moments before resuming her pouring. The bubbles seemed to die in the flutes rather than frothing to the top. When Charlotte raised her glass towards Leah's, there was something collapsed about her mouth, and her toast appeared to have deserted her.

3

Joanna

Dear all, Joanna typed, then deleted it.

Dear colleagues, she tried instead, then stopped.

What could she say to all the staff who'd been affected by the horror of a young student's suicide attempt?

Actually, she *did* know what to say, but not how to express it in the soulless manager-speak she'd been encouraged to adopt since her promotion. Apparently, you couldn't just write, I've cried every day since it happened, even though I don't know Rohan, and I suspect some of you have too, and I'm sorry, I feel like it's my fault.

Joanna closed down the screen and kneaded her temples. Her eyes fell to her diary open on her desk, crammed so full of appointments she'd had to add in extra bits of paper. At 1 p.m. she had a meeting with Rohan's personal tutor; at 2 p.m. a review of the triage procedure for counselling appointments. Both were important but her mind was a fog. Was she hungover from two rum and cokes, or was her brain just yelling, *Overload, overload, please let me rest?* She remembered the barman saying, *Sounds like you've got a lot on your plate.* It had been a welcome acknowledgement, even if it was just something people said.

A rush of embarrassment followed. How she'd gone on about herself last night! It wasn't like her – not these days – and she wished she could tell him that now. She didn't even know his name. Why was she thinking about him when there were so many other things demanding her attention?

She sighed at a knock on her office door. It was another thing that saddened her about her new job: that visitors made her groan. That any interactions with her colleagues, whom she'd previously loved chatting to in the staffroom while making tea and scoffing biscuits, now just seemed to result in more things to worry about.

The sigh expanded inside her when Mandy stuck her head round the door.

'We made it to Friday, Jo! Got a min?'

Joanna forced a smile. 'Course!'

Interactions with Mandy were a different beast again. Minor work-related quibbles were usually a thin veil for the fact that she wanted to tell Joanna something about Luke. Mandy had been determined that she and Joanna would stay friends after the break-up, even though they were no longer destined to become sisters-in-law, and Joanna had wanted that, too, especially because they worked together. But she hadn't anticipated how hard it would be. Hearing the casual familiarity with which Mandy talked about her brother. Being thrown titbits of information about what Luke was up to, when Joanna had once known pretty much everything about him. Worse than that was how Mandy seemed to assume Joanna and Luke would be getting back together at some point. Sometimes she even talked as if they were still a couple, consulting Joanna on whether he might prefer 'trendy beer' or 'a nice bottle of red' for his birthday.

Now, Mandy rattled off a few inconsequential points about a meeting that was over a week away, before finally coming round to what she really wanted to discuss.

'I don't agree with it,' she said. 'It isn't right, and I *did* tell him so.'

Joanna struggled to understand. In her head she was planning her meeting with Rohan's tutor, while simultaneously imagining what she would say to Rohan when she finally got to talk to him, or his parents. On another level, she was composing an apology-slash-thank-you for the barman at The Last Junction, remembering how his eyes had fixed on her as she'd talked.

'The thing is, he's got a date.'

'What?' For a second Joanna connected this to the barman. Then, with a jolt, she understood. *Luke.* He had a date with another woman and Mandy had felt the need to come here, in the middle of a stressful working day, to tell Joanna.

Questions went off like bombs in her head. Who was she? Was this the first date? Where had they met?

And could Luke really be moving on so soon? Luke who had seemed as broken as her when they'd split, even though he'd been the one doing the leaving.

Joanna knew she had to push the questions away, end the conversation. Knew she wouldn't be able to get through the rest of the afternoon if she didn't.

She pressed her palms into the soft leather of her chair. Mandy kept talking, not revealing much, just eager to assure

Joanna that she did *not* support this turn of events. Even more than usual, she seemed to share Luke's mannerisms. That habit of touching his neck when he got worked up.

'Sorry Mandy,' Joanna cut in. 'I've got a meeting soon. Could we talk another time?'

Mandy looked put out, but slicked it over with a smile. 'Oh, of course!'

Just before she left, Mandy spun back and added, in a stage whisper: 'It's just a rebound date, Jo. Everybody knows you and Luke belong together.'

Joanna ground her nails deeper into the armrests. 'Well, I'm not sure that's true anymore,' she said, her jaw clenched painfully tight.

By the end of the day, somehow, Joanna had drafted a support plan with Rohan's personal tutor, signed off on three changes to their triage system, and spoken to Rohan's dad on the phone, allowing him to use her as a sounding board for all his anger and bewilderment and sadness.

She had managed to do all this *without* picturing Luke on a date, without obsessing over what the woman looked like or whether they would go to one of her and Luke's once-favourite restaurants. As soon as she stepped out of work, though, the thoughts were unleashed. They multiplied as she cycled home along the river, her impractically flowy skirt almost catching on the pedals, back to her small house which would've once been a railway worker's cottage. The sight of it always calmed her. Its dark red door and leaning chimney stack. Bricks of all different shades, which appealed to her own inability to stick to one colour when it came to outfits, décor or even pens (she loved those biros with blue, black, green and red ink in one).

She had tried so hard to make this house feel like a sanctuary rather than a backwards step, after she and Luke had sold their three-bedroom semi ('a forever house', Mandy had called it excitedly when they'd bought it), and Joanna had found herself, for the first time ever, choosing somewhere to live on her own. She'd avoided the pricey suburbs that Luke had seemed so taken with, and found she liked being in town, near the bustle of the station and the pubs but with a little garden where she could hide away and attempt to grow tomatoes. And inside her house, all those things that affirmed who she was. A gallery of crazy, crayoned pictures, drawn by the many friends' children who called her Auntie Jo. Old photos of her mum, dad and brothers: before and after Mum's stroke, before and after her recovery. The Young Carer award Joanna had got at school, aged seven, after she'd devoted her summer to her mum's rehabilitation, sharing her spelling cards with her as she'd learned to speak and write again, holding her hand as she'd taken wobbly steps across their living room.

Joanna stood among her things now, trying to reground herself, as her tabby cat, Roxy, rubbed herself against her ankles. All she could see was Luke sitting opposite a woman with skinny arms and a slinky dress. Brunette to Joanna's strawberry-blonde, size eight to Joanna's fourteen, understated style to Joanna's overkill of colour. He'd be clinking his wine glass against hers, telling her about the highs and lows of starting his own business, maybe about his addiction to TED talks and that one time he skydived. Joanna placed them in the little Thai restaurant she and Luke always claimed they'd 'discovered', sitting in *their* corner under the sloped ceiling, sharing a starter, tasting each other's mains.

She shook her head as the scene spiralled. For the second evening in a row, she knew she had to get out of the house.

He was there again. Standing behind the bar as she approached, frowning at his phone. It was a very old model, Joanna saw, the kind even her dad had recently given up on and finally upgraded to an iPhone. The barman's didn't look particularly worn or well-used, though. The idea of someone choosing to buy a basic phone in modern times struck her as interesting. Did it say something about who he was?

'Oh, hi!' He spotted her and shoved the phone into his pocket. Although there was somebody else already waiting to be served, he came straight towards Joanna, taking her by surprise. 'Sorry, I was miles away. Nice to see you again. What can I get you?'

'I think this guy was first . . .' But the other customer threw up his hands, mumbled 'forget it' and stalked away dragging an enormous suitcase.

The barman didn't seem to care. His attention was on Joanna, turning her flustered and flattered all at once. He wore the same clothes as yesterday, a crinkly blue shirt and combat shorts. As a shaft of light fell across him, she noticed for the first time how tanned his hands and face were. The deep, freckly tan of someone with a much more outdoorsy job than his.

'Oh, I haven't really come for a drink,' she said, then blushed at the implied admission: that she'd come to see him.

'That's strange, because this is a pub,' he said with a small grin.

Joanna tucked her hair behind her ears. 'I just came to say sorry about last night, and thanks for listening.'

'You don't need to apologise.'

'I think I—'

'No, no. I'll accept the thanks, if you insist, but not the apology.'

'Well, okay.' She tried to stop fidgeting. 'Thanks for letting me ramble on. I feel a bit embarrassed.'

He shook his head. 'Seriously, there's no need. I just hope you had a better day today?'

She weighed it up. Better in some ways, awful in others. She decided not to say this, but he clearly read it in her face.

'Oh,' he said, reaching for a glass. 'Right, I'm getting you that drink. And it's Friday, so a double this time?'

He remembered which rum, and how much ice. Pressed the coke bottle into her hands as if also recalling how she'd twirled it last time, thinking of her mum. Was this what good bartenders did – memorised their punters' quirks? As the chill of the bottle seeped into her palms, she felt his gaze on her again, and glanced up just as he averted it. Goosepimples rose on her skin and she released the bottle, reaching for her rum.

'Cheers, Joanna,' he said, lifting his glass of water.

She jolted. Despite all her ramblings about her job, she didn't remember telling him her name last night, just as she hadn't learned his.

'Bartender's trick,' he said, nodding at her debit card, which she'd got out ready to pay.

'Ah.' She traced the letters of her name with her finger. Had he noted the 'Miss' as well, her unmarried status? What else had her card told him, which she hadn't?

She did a quick scan for something equivalent on him – a name badge or lanyard she might've missed the previous evening – but found nothing, and he let her do it for a beat too long before he smiled and said, 'I'm Callum.'

'Guess I'll have to take your word for that,' she said, half-joking but also sliding her card out of sight once she'd tapped it, and gulping her rum to feel the sing of it in her head.

4

Leah

Surely they weren't going to put her in Amy's room?

The possibility crept up on Leah as she followed the housekeeper, Matilde, through the vanilla-scented upstairs corridors of the family villa. On previous visits, she had stayed in the guest annex that sat to the side of the house, next to the pool. It was like a self-contained chalet, separate enough from the main villa to provide a bit of privacy and calm. Leah had expected to be led there again, but found herself on route to Amy's old bedroom, her heart thumping at the very idea of seeing it, facing it, let alone unpacking and sleeping in there.

Partway along the L-shaped landing, the temperature dropped. Leah realised it was air-con blasting out of Gordon's large office. She saw him through the half-open door, stretching back in a chair with one chino-clad leg crossed over the other. An aerial photograph of *Il Mandarino* hung behind him in a gold frame. From above, it looked like an art installation, a perfect balance of white geometric shapes and strokes of green and blue. Two other men were also in the room: the pair of business advisors who'd worked for Gordon and Charlotte since they'd launched *Il Mandarino* eighteen years ago, as nothing but two villas and an expensive restaurant. All three were staring at a screen of CCTV images – the resort rolling past, caught at strange angles, glimpses of guests unaware of being watched. Leah snapped her eyes away and hurried to catch up with Matilde.

To her relief, she was shown into the room next to Amy's. It was much smaller than the annex – not that Leah minded, she was used to cramped London living, after all – and oddly bare, though the pale wooden furniture and cream bedding looked expensive.

'It was the tutor's room,' Matilde said, as if detecting Leah's surprise. 'She moved out a week ago, at the end of term. I have cleaned it thoroughly, of course.'

'Oh, of course,' Leah said. 'No problem.'

Matilde gave her a pile of soft towels and, unexpectedly, squeezed one of her hands before hurrying off. Leah was left staring after her, half-wishing she'd lingered. She had almost forgotten how kind Matilde had always been. How 'normal', compared to most people here. She'd worked for her sister's family for as long as those two business advisors, and she'd had a soft spot for Amy.

Leah yearned for a shower and a lie-down but restlessness coursed through her, stopping her from peeling off her jeans and collapsing on the bed. Her thoughts flitted to what she would usually be doing on a Friday evening. Dragging herself away from the office and thinking about where she could escape to. Out of the city to find a hill to sprint up, a rockface to tackle, anything that would make her heart pump, her head clear. That would strain her muscles and bruise her limbs.

She hadn't yet adjusted to being here instead. And, evidently, she hadn't yet accepted the fact that, even if she'd still been in London, she wouldn't have been welcome at work. She'd probably have been roaming around her flat feeling as displaced as she did now.

At least you came. Even if it took a semi-public meltdown to finally push you to it.

She laid her palms on the wall and thought about Amy's room on the other side. She wouldn't be able to settle until she had confronted it.

Edging into the hall, Leah stood for a moment at her niece's door. There were no sounds of muffled music, turning pages. No smell of damp trainers, which Amy had so often got in trouble for. She stepped inside and her breath disappeared. The room looked as if Amy had just popped out. Books and pens were strewn across the desk. There were blue sheets on her bed, faded by the sunlight that persisted in streaming through the window. Leah felt tears pushing again, blocking her sinuses but refusing, as always, to burst. She hadn't realised what the small details would do to her. Amy's potted cacti on the windowsill, outliving her. Her cherry-red Converse sticking out from beneath her bed.

None of these things was coated in a layer of dust, she noticed. Somebody had been cleaning this room but keeping it intact. Why had Amy been erased from the rest of the villa, yet preserved here, in what looked almost like a freeze-frame of her final day alive?

Leah turned towards Amy's collage of Blu-Tacked photos, sprawled across one wall like an explosion of life at the centre of the tableaux. There she was with her many friends, her 'lifesavers', hanging out in the dusty piazzas of the nearest villages whenever she could get away. Leah was touched to see one of her and Amy eating melting gelato cones, the resemblance between them plucking at her heart. But none, she noticed, of the rest of the family. In over half the pictures, Amy was on a boat, hand raised in a peace sign, or wading in the lake with soaking wet clothes.

Happiest in the water. Liberated by it. That was what seemed so unfair, so tragically wrong.

Then something caught Leah's eye. In the very corner, half-obscured, was a photo of a man she didn't recognise, older than Amy and with curly, tied-back hair. She lifted an overlapping picture to see it in full. While many of the others were of groups of mates, this one showed the man and Amy alone, taken in darkness rather than bright sunshine like the rest. It was over-exposed, their close-up faces blanched by a flash. And it seemed more recent than the others. Leah realised the sunny shots of Amy and her other friends were from a time when they were all a little more baby-faced.

'Who are you?' she found herself saying out loud. The boom of her voice in the silent room spooked her. She backed towards the door with a sudden, desperate need for air.

She could breathe again a few minutes later, standing out on the front balcony where Amy used to sit. But a feeling still haunted her: that sense of suspension in her niece's room, of things hanging unsaid. Leah focused on the distant mountains, understanding why Amy had favoured this spot, with its sense of vast, elevated perspective. From here, you felt connected to the rest of Lake Garda in a way that disappeared once you got down into the heart of the resort. You could peek over the ridges that penned the place in, see birds circling the faraway cliffs.

Amy used to weather-watch from up here. She'd loved the violent storms that would electrify the lake when the heat peaked. They'd exhilarated her, but she'd also respected them. So why had she ventured out in one, just to get to a friend's party in Malcesine? She'd often ranted about tourists who took silly risks and had to be rescued, draining the emergency services' resources. Now it struck Leah, as she confronted the blaze of sunlit water: would Amy have done that for the sake of a *party*?

Her chest retightened. Suddenly she wanted to call out to the miniature boats in the middle of the lake, even though there was no hint of bad weather rolling in. Instead, she stared at the resort cascading directly below her. A huge white yurt contained the spa, which Amy used to call 'Tinkly Music Hell'. Beyond it was the glass-roofed restaurant, its obsession with edible flowers another thing Leah and Amy would often joke about. Leah also spotted a cluster of orange umbrellas about halfway down the mountain, surrounding what looked like a circular bar. Was that the new cocktail place Amy had mentioned a few times in her texts?

And something else new, too. Right on the perimeter, a large villa that hadn't existed the last time she'd visited. It was set apart from – and even bigger than – all the others, and surrounded by tall, densely planted conifers. Leah stepped to the edge of the balcony, leaning to see better, but jumped at a voice from behind her.

'Auntie Lee?'

Leah turned. It was Olivia, of course, holding an iPad and a large bunch of keys. Her make-up looked slightly melted, as if she'd been out and busy since they'd finished their champagne.

'Everything okay?'

Leah nodded. 'Just . . . reacquainting myself with the view.' She felt light-headed, and held onto the warm railings at her back. 'Everything okay with you? You look tired!'

'Everything's perfect.' And Olivia's smile was too, except for the small red smear where her lipstick had bled. 'Dinner at seven on the terrace, okay?'

The terrace was on the more private side of the family villa, overlooking the pool and the presumably empty annex. A low wall enclosed it, topped with several white busts, which had always creeped Leah out with their truncated necks and blank stone eyes.

Leah, Charlotte and Olivia had been there for fifteen minutes, staring at a table spread with glazed prawns, giant balls of mozzarella, sundried tomatoes basking in oil. Olivia, now showered and make-up-less, was beginning to show her teenage side for once, asking her mum why they couldn't just get on with the meal.

'Without Daddy?' Charlotte asked, something sharp in her voice. 'That's not nice, Olivia.'

Olivia looked abashed. 'Where is he?'

'He's coming. He's busy. And we'll wait.'

Leah sipped her white wine. It was the first time she'd felt like eating all day, and the feast called to her from the untouched plates. Glancing at Olivia, she was struck again by how much younger her niece looked without her mask of foundation, and with her hair hanging damp, natural curls revealing themselves. Her bare feet overlapped beneath the table and she scratched at a mosquito bite on her neck.

'Put some cream on that,' Charlotte said, frowning. 'It's going to look dreadful by morning.'

Olivia flattened her palm over the bite. Then both Charlotte and Olivia looked in unison towards the terrace steps. Gordon had arrived.

'Evening.' As he sat down, Leah noticed him doing an appraising sweep: of the food, the clean white tablecloth, his family gazing towards him. He took a sip of his waiting glass of wine and plucked a slice of prosciutto from the nearest plate. After a beat, Olivia and Charlotte began to help themselves too, and Leah followed suit.

'Good of you to dress for dinner, Olivia,' Gordon said.

Olivia glanced down at her vest top and linen shorts, which looked infinitely more comfortable than the dress she'd been wearing. 'I—'

'I'm kidding, sweetheart!' Gordon barked out a laugh. 'What's that on your neck, though?'

Olivia's hand flew back to the bite.

'I've told her to put some cream on it,' Charlotte said.

Gordon returned to his food. For a few moments the only sounds were cutlery scraping plates and the background hum of cicadas.

'So how does it feel being back here, Leah?' Gordon asked.

She froze. She had no idea how to answer. How did it feel now Amy was dead, and nobody was even mentioning it? Now everything and nothing had changed?

'You've really grown the place,' she said through clenched teeth.

'And you know how?' Gordon said.

Out of the corner of her eye, Leah saw Olivia straighten with expectation. Gordon looked at his daughter and she straightened further. The desire for praise was so naked on her face that Leah ached for her.

'Reputation,' Gordon said, and Olivia seemed to deflate. 'It's all about controlling your reputation.'

'I've been doing our social media,' Olivia said.

'And you've been doing it well,' Gordon conceded.

Olivia twinkled. She reached for another chunk of mozzarella, as if to reward herself, but Charlotte made a subtle gesture and Olivia withdrew. Leah frowned, wondering what she had seen. Why couldn't Olivia have one more piece? Did it mean Leah shouldn't continue to eat?

Actually, her appetite was gone. But she scooped up a large slice of cheese anyway, in pathetic protest, spearing it hard with her fork.

'Sometimes you get carried away, though,' Gordon said, pointing his knife at his daughter. 'Keep it classy, remember.'

Olivia folded her hands in her lap, as if to curtail the urge to reach for more food. Only Gordon was still picking from the plates, dabbing theatrically at his mouth with a cloth napkin.

Leah felt her frustration mounting. This place, this family, the whole dynamic. She'd hoped tragedy might've transformed things, that Amy's loss might've done some good at least. But how could it, if it wasn't even being acknowledged?

She glanced towards the lake, then quickly away: it was becoming shadowy and depthless as the sun disappeared. Amy had died at sunset. *In a storm she wouldn't normally have gone anywhere near.* Leah stared around at her family, questions rising as a chill inched up her spine.

She was diverted by the sight of Charlotte pushing her wine aside and pressing her fingertips against her eyebrows.

'Char?' Leah said, concern breaking through. 'You okay?'

Charlotte closed her eyes. 'Migraine,' she said, her voice strained. 'I can always feel them coming on.'

Leah frowned. She didn't remember her sister suffering from migraines before. 'Do you want some water?' As she reached for the jug, she caught sight of Gordon's expression. He looked unconcerned, unsurprised. Leah would've gone as far as to say irritated.

Charlotte took a sip and winced. 'I think I'd better go and lie down until it passes. I'm so sorry, Lee, when you've only just arrived.'

'It's okay,' Leah said. 'Should we bring you anything?' She glanced at Olivia to see how she was reacting, and saw her looking away into the distance, as if embarrassed.

'No, no. I'll be fine in a while.' Charlotte stood up, gesturing for Leah to stay seated.

'I'll send Matilde with some tablets,' Gordon said.

Charlotte nodded and wandered away. Leah noticed she didn't head back into the main villa, but went down towards the pool area – to the guest annex, perhaps, though Leah would've had to crane her neck to keep watching.

An awkward silence descended. Olivia began scratching her bite again, until Gordon shot her a look and she whipped her hand away. Laughter and music floated up from the holiday village, and the low honk of a ferry from the lake.

Gordon checked his watch. 'I have a phone meeting, I'm afraid. But please help yourself to more wine, Leah. And Matilde will bring you some of her excellent tiramisu.'

'Tell her I don't want any,' Olivia said. 'I'm full.'

Gordon nodded, standing and tossing down his napkin. 'I'll leave you two to catch up.'

After he was gone, Leah eyed Olivia as she closed her knife and fork neatly on her plate, wishing she knew what to say. Olivia stared down at her cutlery as if examining her distorted reflection in the metal. Then calmly, without seeming to notice she was being watched, she pressed her finger against the sharp tip of her knife. Just as Leah opened her mouth to say, 'Careful!', Olivia blinked and snatched her hand away, looking at Leah with a polite but distant smile back in place.

5

Amy

Last September
Eight hours before sunset

Normally, September is a month of relief and despair. As
the guest numbers start to tail off, I feel a loosening in my
chest – I can bear to lift my head again as I move around
the resort, to take normal-sized breaths of its air. But that
isn't enough to counterbalance the other side to it. The
wrench of seeing friends going off to uni, out into the world,
the blooming of new lives that can't be mine.

This September, though, is different. Even if I'm the only
one who knows. Just as *Il Mandarino* is winding down,
reaching the end of its most 'triumphant' season yet, I am
coming alive.

Since I woke this morning, my whole body has been fizzing. With nerves, with anticipation, with the knowledge of
what I'm going to do, the desperation to pull it off. A count-
down to tonight ticks in my head, a checklist of things to do
and people to avoid. As I pace my room, suddenly all my
belongings seem different. Some more precious than
before, some less. I ripple my fingers over my photo wall,
brimming with love for all the friends who've stuck by me,

even as the things that once connected us – school, sleepovers, sports clubs – were gradually taken away from me. Faces seem to burst out of the pictures, their corners bending from the wall as if returning my touch.

You've kept me sane. Kept my faith in people alive.

But I've reached the end of the line.

I jump at the rumble of my dad's voice further down the landing. Is he coming this way? Patrolling, seeing what I'm up to? My muscles unclench as I realise he's still in his office, talking heatedly on the phone. The more *Il Mandarino* expands, the more stressed he gets, yet the more he pushes to expand it even further, to attract bigger and better guests. I think of the new grotesquely huge villa enclosed by pines. The cold feeling it gives me when I look down on it from my balcony spot. I think of *Segreto*, the new cocktail bar, and silently call myself a hypocrite – because this time it's a warm sensation that spreads through me, like the first sip of one of Nate's creations.

My eyes move to a photo at the edge of my wall, almost completely overlapped by another. Nate's face is hidden, but his curly hair is visible if you know it's there, mingling with my untidy mane as our heads lean in.

My heart speeds up and I check my watch. His shift will be starting about now. I could slip out while Dad's on the phone, head to *Segreto* unchecked. I fling open my wardrobe: what to wear on this day I must pretend is ordinary? I pull out my white Banksy T-shirt with the drawing of a young girl letting go of a red balloon. I can never decide if she looks happy or sad to watch it float away, if she's released it accidentally or on purpose. The balloon is a vibrant crimson heart. Mum always tuts that it looks like a blood-stain, 'off-putting' for the guests, but that just makes me want to wear it all the more.

Today, it seems extra blood-red. Right where my heart is. I glance briefly at the mirror, then step out of my room to face this final day.

Though the high season is coming to an end, there are still strangers everywhere as I make my way through the resort. The air is hot and close, and there is still a sense of eyes following me wherever I go. Eyes from the high white balconies of the villas, where guests eat breakfast or silently smoke. The eyes of the staff rushing around with laundry and room service; the pool cleaners and garden-ers forever sweeping and raking. But most of all, eyes from the many CCTV cameras attached to the buildings and trees. My dad's eyes. I know where the blind spots are by now, though. I duck and weave, imagining myself invisible, like a ghost.

Segreto isn't open yet, but Nate is in the middle of the circular, roofless bar, polishing martini glasses and slicing limes. The usual soft jazz music is already playing; I think he must like it really, despite claiming the endless loop of it drives him mad. I pause to register the smell of fruit and vermouth, the flutter of the orange umbrellas that shade the tables. Taking in the details, as if I'll never return.

'Stop lurking,' Nate says without looking up.

I laugh. I should've known he would sense my presence. He's always aware of who's around, waiting to be served, wanting his attention. He can sense when Mum or Dad arrive at *Segreto* and are subtly watching his performance, or even if one of the guests is a reviewer in disguise.

And he knows when it's safe for us to exchange a coded smile or touch fingers as he passes me a drink.

We're completely alone, now. The breeze drops and the air stills. He emerges from behind the bar, to where I'm waiting in another CCTV blind spot, and puts his arms around me. His hands are cold from cleaning out the ice machine and he smells sharp and citrusy.

'How do you feel?' he whispers into my ear. 'All ready?'

I nod and my stomach corkscrews.

6

Joanna

In an unexpected and unnerving turn of events, now Joanna was the one with the date.

She was the one doing what she hadn't in sixteen years: choosing a first-date outfit, twirling in front of the mirror, changing too many times until a heap of rejected dresses covered her bed and Roxy settled in their midst. There was something thrilling about the ritual, though. Something that made her skin tingle in a way she had almost forgotten.

Earlier, as she had got towards the bottom of her double rum, Callum had told her he was finishing at 8 p.m. and asked if she fancied meeting at a different pub. He had wrapped it in a joke about needing a change of scene but wanting to hear more about her team member who kept calling her 'chief', so it had taken a moment to sink in: he was asking her out. Moving things on from two strangers chatting over a bar to two strangers deliberately meeting for a drink.

Joanna had almost said no, like a reflex. But that image had flashed back at her: Luke in the Thai restaurant she could no longer even walk past without a twinge, leaning towards the woman she had constructed as the opposite of herself. Joanna had drained her rum, sat tall on her bar stool and thought, *I can do this.*

Now her hands shook as she fumbled with her necklace. On her dressing table, her phone was constantly lighting up. Her mum was texting about their weekly brunch, whether Saturday or Sunday would be best, and a conversation full of gifs and laughing-face emojis was unfolding on her friends' WhatsApp group, enlivened by the beckoning weekend. She knew that if she announced she was about to have a drink with a man, a tsunami of excitement would flood in her direction. But she was reluctant to mention it, even to her best friends. She needed to figure out how she felt about going on a date, her first since Luke, before she made it real by telling anybody else.

It's GREAT that you're getting out there, she imagined them saying.

You don't owe Luke anything.

They would want to know exactly where she was going and when, for safety; they'd give her a code word to post on the group chat if she needed rescuing. Unease prickled her spine as she wondered whether she was being irresponsible, meeting a man she barely knew and not making anybody aware. Yet still, she couldn't quite bring herself to type the words and set off the inevitable flurry of surprise and questions.

As she approached the riverside pub where they'd arranged to meet, she told herself it was pointless being nervous. She had nothing to lose, nothing invested. She couldn't work out whether her nerves betrayed the fact that she really liked Callum, or whether it was everything the date represented that was whipping up an emotional storm.

When she'd first started dating Luke, sixteen years ago, they had already been friends. Part of a big crowd who would hang out after college, drink cider in each other's bedrooms, listen to dance music and quote their favourite TV shows. There had been no pressure to prove to him what kind of person she was; they'd already known that they could banter and laugh. Now, the idea of being assessed and scrutinised by a new potential partner – the idea of even *considering* a new partner – was terrifying. She had to force herself to step through the door into the hot, beer-scented bustle.

The inside was dark and wood-panelled, but at the rear was a huge garden, from which you could see families of geese paddling down the River Derwent. Joanna spotted Callum at a small table by the back fence. He was fiddling with his old-school phone, eyes darting, raking a hand through his curls in a way that suggested he was nervous, too.

When he noticed her, he smiled and stood up for an awkward half-hug. He smelled different from Luke: less designer, more natural. The first Luke comparison already kicking in.

'You look nice,' he said.

'So do you,' she replied, although he was wearing the same as earlier, probably not having been home since the end of his shift. In the evening light, his sun-kissed appearance struck her again. He reminded her of the surfers on Newquay beach, whom she used to watch for hours on family holidays, entranced by the way they took flight. Callum would've looked more at home in a Cornish beach bar than a station pub in Derby with only two windows. She got a sudden sense of him as somebody displaced.

He insisted on going to get the drinks, shoving his phone into his pocket and fishing out a crumple of loose cash. As Joanna watched him walk away, more Luke comparisons swooped in. Callum was much taller than Luke, who had always had a hang-up about the fact that he and Joanna were the same height, not that it had bothered her in the slightest. Callum was quieter, too, more of a listener than a talker, not as vocal and opinionated as Luke had sometimes been. Luke *could* be a little arrogant, but he'd had other traits that had balanced it out, like intelligence, ambition—

'I had to make an executive decision about *which* sauvignon blanc you'd prefer,' Callum said, returning with the drinks.

It was a relief to slip back into an undemanding conversation. 'Choice of sauvignons? That's granular.'

'I went for the New Zealand.'

She sipped the cool, crisp wine. 'Lovely.'

He did a mock *phew* gesture, swiping his brow.

'Are you into wine?' she asked, cursing herself for the boringness of the question.

'Not especially, but I know a bit about it from work, I guess.'

'You get wine connoisseurs in The Last Junction?' Joanna raised a sceptical eyebrow, then cursed herself again for mocking his workplace.

He grinned, though. 'If we did, they'd be disappointed. No, it's more from previous places I've worked, places where you *did* have to be prepared to be cross-examined about the Chateau-du-whatever.'

'Ah, like where?' Joanna asked. 'Are you from round here?'

He blinked as if wondering which question to respond to, then shook his head. 'I haven't lived here very long.'

'I thought I hadn't seen you working in the pub before. I was going to ask if you were new, but you didn't *seem* new. You seemed to know what you were doing.'

'Well, I've worked in a lot of bars. Are *you* from Derby?'

'Very much so. Always lived here, apart from when I went to uni . . .' Joanna was drinking a bit too fast, talking a bit too fast as well. She was aware of Callum's feet under the table; if she crossed her legs, she would bump against them. 'I did a beginners' Italian class a couple of years ago, but when we were learning to say simple sentences about ourselves, mine were all the same – I'm from Derby, I live in Derby, I work in Derby!'

He laughed. 'Nothing wrong with that.'

'No, I know. I do love Derby. There's more to it than meets the eye.'

'So I'm discovering.' He smiled at her, his cheeks colouring.

Was that flirting? Joanna had no idea how to recognise it anymore. But she knew she was flushing too, dipping her face to her glass.

'So . . .' He moved hastily on. 'Italian, hey?'

Now Joanna wished she'd let the flirtation progress. Or maybe it wasn't flirtation? Maybe he'd been referring to Derby's history, or music scene, or its art gallery with all the huge, candlelit Joseph Wright paintings . . . She took another sip, trying to pull herself together.

'We get discount on the languages classes at work,' she said. 'So, I know endless ways to talk about being from Derby in *Italiano*. And, more importantly, how to order a drink.'

'Speaking of which . . .' He gestured at her glass. Joanna looked down and was shocked to find it almost empty. His was too, though, and a fleck of beer froth glistened in his stubble.

He moved as if to stand, but Joanna leapt up. 'My round!'

She felt her skirt clinging to the backs of her thighs as she made her way towards the pub's rear door. Her face glowed with a combination of summer-night warmth, mild tipsiness, and something like adrenaline. She got the sense, yet again, that she'd spoken a lot, while Callum had questioned and prompted.

That's a GOOD thing, she imagined her friends saying. *He's interested in you! Don't apologise for it!*

At the bar, her mood nose-dived when she spotted a familiar face. One of Luke's best friends, Dev, was waiting to be served. Dev had slept on her and Luke's sofa after countless nights out in the past. He'd been lined up to be the best man at their wedding, and had been speechless when they'd split. Right now, though, he was almost the last person Joanna wanted to see.

She hung back, letting several people get served in front of her. The temperature was soaring: she fanned herself with her hand as she performed a series of manoeuvres to stay out of Dev's eyeline. Her own eyes roamed across the busy pub, fearing that Luke was here too, until at last Dev walked away, pint in hand.

Joanna got her drinks and elbowed her way out towards the garden. She felt off-kilter now, kept spilling drops of beer and wine. Just as the back door was in her sights, she almost collided with a man coming out of the toilets. The froth slipped off Callum's beer, slopping down her arm. Her chin jerked up as the man apologised in an immediately familiar voice.

There was something so inevitable about it. Of *course* it was him.

'Jo!'

'Luke . . .'

They froze in awkward silence, caught in the cramped space between the toilets and the garden door. She could smell his favourite aftershave, an instant blast of sensory memory, and something less familiar, a different laundry powder perhaps. He was wearing the salmon-pink Mr Porter shirt he'd treated himself to when he'd signed his first ever freelance client, which Joanna had secretly thought was shockingly overpriced. But it seemed to hang differently on his body now, as if it was the same shirt and yet not. It took her a few moments to work out what had changed: not the shirt, but the body. Luke had lost a lot of weight. His cheeks were hollow where they used to be chiselled, and his chest – once her favourite part of him, solid and comforting to lay her head on – seemed concave beneath the billows of expensive, slightly faded material.

'How are you?' he asked.

'Fine,' she stuttered, trying not to stare at his thin arms, or meet his eyes. 'You?'

There was a tiny pause. 'Yes, fine.'

'It's been a while,' she said.

'Has it?'

She shrugged and looked at her feet. The last time they'd seen each other seemed at once painfully recent and a life-time ago. It had been at the estate agent's, signing away their 'forever home'. *Also overpriced,* Joanna told herself. Maybe the life they'd planned would hang wrongly on them, now, like Luke's shirt, even if they could somehow turn back the clock.

Silence fell again. It wasn't like Luke to be stuck for conversation; he'd become a master of it while he'd been building up his marketing connections. But small talk between the two of them felt as awful as screaming at one another, she realised. Neither could bring themselves to do it.

'Who are you here with?' he asked.

Joanna glanced at the half-open door to the garden. She could see Callum at their table, his back turned. Luke followed her gaze and Joanna pulled hers away. 'A work friend.'

'Anyone I know?' His eyes panned the garden and Joanna fought an urge to block his view. *Probably not, you never paid much attention to my work,* she almost snapped, but bit her tongue and shook her head. Already, she was imagining Mandy's interrogation on Monday, once word reached her that Joanna had been out with an unnamed colleague.

'I better get back,' she said.

Luke was still peering outside. Had he figured out that Callum must be Joanna's companion, as the only one sitting by himself? Well, what did it matter? Hadn't Luke got a date planned, too? Wasn't that what had propelled Joanna here in the first place, as if she was trying to compete?

Ironic, really. Luke had always been the competitive one.

She shook herself. 'Right. Bye, then. Have fun!' The words came out flimsy and fake. Luke seemed rooted to the spot, lost in thought.

He stirred at last. 'See you, Jo. Oh, and sorry about the spillage . . .'

The beer was a sticky film on her bare arm, but she shrugged off his apology.

'I *am* sorry,' he said again, with more weight this time. Joanna blinked in confusion, then turned away, diving for the fresh air. She felt Luke watching her go, and kicked the door shut behind her as subtly as she could manage.

As she returned to Callum, everything seemed distorted. Seeing Luke had destroyed her social skills. She was monosyllabic, unable even to hold the right expressions on her face. She felt Callum observing her, like he had in The Last Junction, only this time maybe trying to work out what had changed.

'Are you okay?' he asked.

'Sorry, yes!'

'Have I done something to offend you?'

'No! No, honestly, I'm fine.'

Still the flow of their conversation was blocked, and Joanna knew she was the one doing the blocking. She opened her mouth to offer another feeble apology, but instead, almost at the last second, decided to come clean.

'This is embarrassing . . .' She laced her fingers around her wine glass. 'I've just seen my ex, and it's really thrown me. It's not the kind of thing you're supposed to admit on a first date, I know . . .'

Callum's shoulders visibly relaxed. 'Ah,' he said. 'I thought you'd decided I was terrible company and you needed to abort.'

Joanna winced. 'No. Sorry. Definitely not.'

'We could go somewhere else?'

'You don't mind?'

'Course not.' He began glugging his pint to finish it. 'We've all been there. And I promise I'll wait at least ten minutes before interrogating you about the ex.'

Joanna laughed faintly and scooped up her handbag, clutching it to her chest as if she could hide behind the tiny, pointless thing. As they made their way back through the pub, she kept a lookout for Luke and Dev, but there was no sign of them now in the thickening crowd. She startled at a hand on her back – Callum's hand – steering her towards the exit, gentle but slightly territorial, as if prompted by the mention of an ex.

As soon as they were out, she began to feel more like herself again. Callum dropped his hand and changed the subject, asking her about Derby as they strolled through its streets. Joanna led him across the marketplace, pointing out the registry office where her brother had got married, the concrete waterfall where she and friends used to soak themselves during hot summers in their early teens. Every corner of Derby was inseparable from her memories. She omitted all the Luke associations, though they seemed to jump out from every shadow, along with the new memory of his thin face and the way he'd said, *I* am *sorry*.

'Do your family still live in Derby?' Callum asked.

'My mum and dad do.'

'You must be close.'

She nodded. Then, emboldened by the fact that they were walking side by side, rather than sitting staring at one another, she elaborated: 'I think it's one of the reasons I've stayed in Derby all these years. My mum had a stroke when I was seven – a reaction to some tablets she was on – so I never like to be too far away from her.'

'God, I'm sorry. How is she now?'

'Oh, much better, thanks. It was strange, though, as a kid, watching her relearn to walk and talk and write. I was teaching her for a while – or attempting to – rather than the other way around.'

'You're a natural carer,' he said, as if it was a fact he was sure of rather than a question.

Joanna's face warmed and she shrugged. Their forearms brushed as they turned down Irongate, where the setting sun was rippling over the cobbles in shades of pink and gold.

'Gorgeous sunset,' she commented.

Callum ducked his head as if the mellow light was too dazzling. Joanna noticed him focusing on his shoes as they walked on.

'Not a fan of sunsets?' she asked jokingly. Somehow, she'd thought he'd be into them, with his surfer vibe.

He looked surprised, almost annoyed for a split-second, but then he laughed and said, 'Course I do. Everyone likes sunsets!'

'I love the idea that they're easing you into night,' she said. 'Saying goodbye to the day with a display of all the nicest colours.'

'Sometimes they drop quickly, though,' he said. 'Especially abroad. The darkness doesn't always ease in, it's just suddenly there and pitch black.'

Joanna shivered. They'd passed into the shadow of a large old building as the street curved round.

'Cold?' Callum said, drawing closer so his arm touched hers again, with a tiny static-electric shock. 'We should probably find a pub.'

She nodded. The sky seemed much darker now, as if Callum's observation had sped up the drawing-in of night.

7

Leah

When Leah woke, she didn't know where she was. The light was strong and warm, and a distant clink of crockery made her think of hotel breakfast rooms. At first she assumed she was away with work, at one of those legal conferences that would lurch between serious and raucous. But the sheets were never this soft, and the sunshine—

Of course.

She covered her face, the light suddenly offensive, her sadness a dead weight on her chest. Memories of last night came back: Charlotte's sudden migraine, Olivia pressing her fingertip against the point of her knife. Leah cursed herself for the excruciating small talk they had made after that. She was known at work for having guts – mainly because word had got round about her 'hardcore' hobbies, and because she was like a dog with a bone once she got on a case – yet in this place, and in all the ways that really mattered, she was weak. Each time she'd come close to broaching the topic of Amy, her throat had narrowed and she'd asked Olivia about her studies instead.

All Olivia had wanted to talk about was *Il Mandarino*. Nothing else seemed to exist to her anymore. Leah remembered her as a little girl: she'd loved playing shops and pretending to be on the catwalk. Her dressing-up box had overflowed with tulle skirts and plastic strings of pearls. Was it her or Charlotte who'd had a childhood obsession with coloured berets? Leah's memories of her sister and her niece were getting weirdly mixed up, as if everybody was blurring except Amy.

Amy had been strong-willed since she was tiny. Leah thought of her first ever visit here, when Amy was almost three, and *Il Mandarino* was still being built. She and Charlotte had spent the whole time chasing Amy as she'd acquainted herself with stray cats, open doorways, spiky plants she was determined to taste. And the water. Always the water. If she glimpsed the shimmering blue she would hurtle towards it, plunging into the shallows.

A little girl who'd thought she was growing up in the land of adventure. What had gone so wrong in her relationship with her home?

Leah forced herself out of bed, contemplating the bundle of creased clothes she could barely remember packing. Catching sight of her reflection in the full-length mirror, she paused and frowned. Charlotte used to tease her about her 'mannish' figure when they were younger, and now it seemed exacerbated, seemed to matter when normally it didn't. Her legs were scratched and bruised and had got even more muscular in the last few months. Leah rejected several pairs of shorts and a jersey dress, ending up back in her stifling black jeans.

It was 7.45 a.m. Saturday morning. She pictured herself leaning against her kitchen counter at home, with a protein shake and a Sudoku, her laptop and emails open at her elbow. Wondering what to do with the weekend hours yawning ahead; knowing she should see friends, make an effort, but unable to summon much enthusiasm for any of it anymore.

There would be even more spare hours when she got back. Part of her wanted to run from *Il Mandarino*, from everything that was too much to bear, but another part was more afraid of the emptiness she'd be returning to. And the shame – mostly the shame of losing it like that, letting herself down in front of people who'd assumed she was as unemotional as the contracts she drew up.

I'd have taken compassionate leave when my niece first died, if I'd felt I needed it, she had insisted to her boss last week, when she'd pulled Leah into her office for 'a little chat about your recent conduct'.

Well, maybe you should've done, her boss had said, not unkindly, but not in a voice that invited arguments, either. *Then maybe this wouldn't have happened. And perhaps I should've insisted on it – which I am now, Leah, I'm afraid.*

She'd asked Leah to explain herself, but she hadn't been able to. It would've sounded insane. A missed call. All because of an erased missed call.

Now here she was. Edging out onto the sun-swathed landing of her sister's villa, listening for signs that her family were awake. She caught Gordon's voice, carrying from the other end of the corridor, where his and Charlotte's master bedroom took up most of the shorter side of the L-shape.

'Are you recovered?' It was the way he said it that caught her attention. The snap of the word *recovered*.

She inched closer, wincing as her foot hit a creaky floor-board hidden beneath a plush rug. She wanted to hear her sister's response, but there was only Gordon again: 'You need to rest, Charlotte. Stop doing this to yourself.' The words should've been tender, yet his tone didn't match.

And still no audible reply. It wasn't like her sister to stay silent if she and Gordon argued. Usually, she would either placate him or divert him; she had a whole toolkit for smoothing things over, which she also used on demanding guests. Then later, after they'd made up, Leah would notice how she and Gordon couldn't stop touching each other, exchanging smiles over dinner like smitten teenagers.

The tone of this one-sided argument felt different, though. Less of a sense that they were teetering between fall-out and foreplay. Only a cold impatience from Gordon.

'You'd better tell Leah, then,' he said. 'I'm too busy to play the host today, if you're not up to it.'

Leah flushed at the sound of her name, spoken as if she was a nuisance, and in the same moment realised Gordon was on the phone. So where was Charlotte? The annex?

She panicked when she heard the bedroom door opening, and Gordon's brisk footsteps down the corridor. Leah dived into the nearest room – Amy's – holding still as she heard the rattle of Gordon unlocking his office and going inside. Exhaling, she sank against Amy's door. Being in here was no less affecting than the first time, but now she realised something was changing in the way she was seeing Amy's things. She wanted them to tell her about her niece's last days, weeks, months. And why something didn't sit right. Something about Amy drowning in a storm on her way to a party.

On the desk there was an Oxfam calendar, stuck heartbreakingly on September, and a postcard with a panorama of Florence. Leah turned the postcard over to read a message from Amy's friend Melina, mostly in Italian and seeming to describe her travels, but ending in English with the sign-off, *Wish you could have come.* In the desk drawer, she found a book called *Essays on Social Justice*, gasping out dust as she fanned its pages. At the front was a handwritten note: *Plenty to get you fired up in here! N x*

Leah stood thumbing through the book, reading snippets from chapters on social privilege and the distribution of wealth. Amy had wanted to go to university and study sociology, but she hadn't been allowed. Apparently, Gordon had deemed it a waste of money and time, given that Amy had a guaranteed career at *Il Mandarino*. Amy had surmised that he didn't want her to break away and learn things that would make her hate their lifestyle even more. He'd probably known she would never have come back, leaving a messy hole in the family's public image. Amy had appealed to her mum, Leah knew, and Charlotte had seemed to waver, but had ultimately backed Gordon.

Even having me here embarrassing them is better than letting me go off to develop a mind of my own, she had written in a text to Leah. The message had made Leah throw her phone across her flat in fury. But she hadn't acted on it, hadn't done anything – except continue to feel angry, and silently thankful for her own education, her career, her encouraging parents.

All the things she was currently failing to deserve.

Leah gazed at the postcard, with its domes and spires stretching to a blue horizon, then ran her finger down the embossed spine of the book. Her eyes moved back to Amy's photo wall. Back to the curly-haired man in the corner.

'Are you okay, Leah?'

Leah whipped around, pulse flying. She was relieved that it was Matilde peering from the doorway, but still she flushed. 'Yes, I was just . . .'

Matilde nodded solemnly. 'You loved her very much.' Then she flushed too, as if she'd overstepped a mark.

'So did you, I think,' Leah said.

The housekeeper ventured into the room. She was tall, probably in her mid-fifties, with broad limbs, thick black hair, and a warm, attractive face. Despite her size, she would move unobtrusively around the villa, always seeming to perform multiple jobs at once. How much did she pick up on? Leah wondered. How much did she understand about the family?

'She made me laugh,' Matilde said.

Leah grinned in surprise. 'Yes, she was hilarious!' Talking about her was like releasing a breath she'd been holding since she'd arrived.

She turned to the photos and pointed at the curly-haired man. 'Who is this?'

Matilde barely looked. 'Nate,' she said, her accent lengthening the name, bouncing off the 't'. Something about the way she answered, as if she'd already anticipated the question, made the hairs bristle on Leah's arms.

'Was he one of Amy's friends?' Leah tried to remember whether her niece had ever mentioned him. She didn't recall so. How could this name be new to her, when she and Amy had supposedly been close?

Matilde paused. 'He worked in the cocktail bar here.'

'He doesn't anymore?'

'He left. After . . . after she died.'

'Really? Why?'

'I think . . .' Matilde hesitated again. 'Too many rumours.'

Leah's heart boomed. '*Rumours?*'

Matilde shuffled in her flat shoes. 'It was just the internet. Twitter, I don't know. Nothing official. But enough to make him disappear.' She blinked on the final word, as if thrown by her own phrasing.

Nausea bloomed in Leah's stomach. She didn't remember reading anything about a man called Nate – or *any* man – in relation to Amy's death. But admittedly, she had started turning away from any news coverage after the first couple of weeks. Even from the information her dad would forward to her about the inquest. She'd closed her eyes, tried to close her heart. Her then boyfriend, Josh, had ended things not long after. It seemed she'd accidentally closed her heart to him instead of the grief. The grief had only been hiding, and growing, preparing to make itself brutally felt.

'Did people think he had something to do with it?' she asked, breathless. 'Amy's accident?'

Matilde gazed at the photo. Now Leah noticed the edge of a martini glass in the corner of the shot – and what looked like two sets of hands wrapped around it, fingers overlapping. Amy *had* started mentioning cocktail hour in some of her messages last year. Leah remembered thinking it was out of character – **gotta go, Auntie Lee, cocktail hour's calling!** She'd wondered if she was the only one who didn't really get the whole cocktail craze. Not a patch on a well-poured, no-frills beer in her book. But maybe she was uncool, unfun – just as Josh had once blurted out, as things had soured between them. His remark had upset her more than it should've done. She wished she hadn't wasted any emotion on him, wished every drop had been devoted to Amy.

'People said he was Amy's boyfriend,' Matilde said. 'But I am not so sure. He was older. And she was never boy crazy – not like her sister, with her posters, you remember?' She half-smiled, then her gaze dropped. Leah nodded. Olivia's room used to be covered in posters of male movie stars, the ones she'd thought were the most sophisticated, dressed up for the Oscars. They'd all been gone last time Leah had been here, though. She'd grown up and so had her bedroom.

There was a clatter down the corridor, and Gordon's voice could be heard from his office, raised in Italian.

Matilde clasped her hands against her chest. 'I should . . .' She looked quickly around the room, almost in a panic, then turned to go.

Seeing her appraise Amy's space reminded Leah of something. She blurted: 'Is it you who dusts her things?'

The housekeeper paused with one hand on the door-frame. Her arm was spattered with dark sunspots. 'I would do, but they are always clean.'

She closed the door and her footsteps hurried away. Leah's eyes went back to Nate. Now his smile seemed full of secrecy, and she had a violent urge to rip it from the wall. She noticed something else as the morning light glimmered on the picture. It was dotted with fingerprints. Much more so than any of the others. Somebody else had touched this photo often – and recently? – leaving marks all over their two faces, the one who had drowned and the one who had disappeared.

8

Joanna

'What have you been doing over the weekend, Jo?'

Joanna hesitated as she leaned across for the scrambled eggs. Her mum's question was innocent, and she'd be expecting nothing more than the usual, *did some gardening, ate too much pizza, went round to Farrah's and chatted over the top of a bad film.* But Joanna felt her face glowing hot as she wondered whether to tell the whole truth. Her mind rolled back to walking through the streets in the pink evening sun. Ending up in Derby's oldest pub, an ancient timber-framed building with four tiny rooms, perfect for squirrelling away in. Hugging goodnight as they'd waited for separate taxis (he lived the opposite side of town, it turned out, nowhere near where he worked). A brief kiss before she'd got into hers.

She'd replayed it all several times already. There was no denying the trill of excitement in her belly, mingling with something less comfortable, maybe the disquiet of her encounter with Luke or the weirdness of getting to know somebody new. But she wasn't yet prepared to share it with her parents over Sunday brunch in their conservatory, where Luke's chair still seemed conspicuously empty, and the quantities of bacon and eggs hadn't yet been adjusted in his absence. Her mum and dad were grieving the new gap in their family, too. Swinging between pretending Luke hadn't been such a big part of their lives, and turning, without thinking, to ask him a question about their computer.

'Nothing much,' Joanna said, heaping eggs onto her plate. 'You?'

'Spag bol both nights, we made too much! A documentary about the Victorians – also both nights, actually, 'cause we fell asleep halfway through on Friday. So, a non-stop rave.'

Joanna smiled. 'Sounds similar to my weekend.'

'Oh, did you see the documentary?'

'No, I just meant—'

But her mum was off, talking about prime ministers and workhouses. Joanna drowned her brunch in ketchup, indulging in a moment of contentedness. Her mum looked well, which always made her happy. The eggs were a buttery cloud and she was managing to keep her post-date anxieties under control. And she liked him. She could admit that to herself, at least. She liked Callum, despite her hesitancy, and that was enough to bring a shine to her Sunday.

At home, she surrendered to the inevitable googling. She'd learned his full name on Friday night – Callum Foley – and was surprised she'd lasted so long without looking him up. The last time she'd been in a dating situation, social media hadn't been widespread, plus she'd already known most things about Luke. Later, of course, Luke's career as a brand manager had come to revolve around 'the socials', and suddenly he'd had a double-screened PC, the fanciest of phones, TweetDeck permanently open on both. There had been another side to his work, though – a creative side that saw him surrounded by mood boards and sketches, trying to breathe life into a brand. Joanna had loved him most in *that* mode. She'd never been very interested in social media, beyond liking friends' photos or following bits of education news. If she'd been more up on it, she'd surely have googled her current date much sooner, and probably more effectively.

Right now, curled into her sofa, she was getting no relevant results. People with Callum's name, but none that were him. Didn't everybody pop up *somewhere* on the internet?

Callum had mentioned that he wasn't much of a social media person, either. In fact, he'd pulled a face, seemed even less keen than her. Joanna felt her anxiety creeping back up, that sense of Callum as a question mark. She still didn't know a lot about him, aside from the fact that he was a good listener, a long-term bartender, that he'd travelled a lot and liked sailing and walking. There was a rootlessness to him with his unironed clothes, his internet-less phone, the crumpled bank notes plucked from the pockets of his shorts each time he'd bought a round. They'd talked about her family but very little about his, apart from the fact that he'd moved around a fair bit when he was young.

Well, you can't cover everything on a first date, her friends would say, if she ever came clean. *You've got to save some material for the second, third, fourth . . .*

Joanna abandoned her search and distracted herself with the memory of that soft kiss just before she'd jumped into her taxi. Their lips had barely brushed, but it was the most intimate contact she'd had with anybody in eight months, and she could still feel it now. The surprising difference between his mouth and Luke's. She'd realised how much she missed being kissed and touched. Hugs from friends had got her through the last few months, but he'd reawakened a slightly scary yearning for something else.

A message popped up on her phone.

Thanks again for introducing me to some Derby pubs that aren't 30 per cent luggage. Would love to do it again soon? X

She never slept well on a Sunday. Thoughts of the week ahead would start to play in her mind from around 6 p.m., and by bedtime they'd have reached a crescendo. Mental to-do lists would be drawn up. Worst-case scenarios enacted.

Tonight, thoughts of Callum snaked their way between the usual worries, making her toss and turn in fits of energy and exhaustion. There were flashes of Luke's face, thinner each time, and returning images of the medical student, Rohan, on the roof of that building. She hadn't even been there, only had 'the incident' recounted to her afterwards, but she could picture it vividly; she saw his high-up silhouette every time she walked through that part of campus now.

She had finally dropped off when her mobile rang, jarring her awake. She never turned it off, always fearful of her mum having a second stroke or a relapse. Even though it had been almost thirty years, it was still Joanna's first, terrified thought whenever her phone rang at unexpected times.

She'd never forgive herself if she missed the call, missed a chance to help, to be there.

'Hello?' she answered, bolt up in bed.

'Is that Joanna Greenfield?'

It was a stranger's voice, a woman's, with an air of formality that quickened Joanna's pulse.

'Yes . . .'

'I'm calling from Derby Royal Hospital.'

No, no, no. Joanna's throat closed. She scrunched a handful of duvet in her fist.

'On behalf of Callum Foley,' the woman added.

Joanna was thrown. 'What?' For a second, the name was so incongruous that she thought, *It's a wrong number, thank God.*

Then the date and yesterday's googling resurfaced through her fear.

'Are you his partner?'

'No.' Joanna almost laughed, almost said, *we've been on one date,* before she remembered she was on the phone to someone from the hospital. Someone who had called her in the middle of the night.

'I'm a friend,' she said awkwardly. 'Is he okay?'

'He was brought into A&E this evening. He gave us your details as an emergency contact. I'm calling you because, unfortunately, his condition has worsened. We're having to operate.'

'What?' Joanna's eyes roamed the darkness of her room. 'What happened?'

'We're not entirely sure yet. He's sustained some injuries. The doctors will explain when you get here.'

Her head reeled. Emergency contact? Injuries?

When you get here?

'I . . .' Concern and confusion were swathed in a floaty sense that she was dreaming. 'Is he going to be alright?'

'The doctors are hopeful they can stabilise him. As I said, they can talk you through it when—'

'But I'm not sure I'm the best person to come. What about his family?'

'He gave us your name and number before he fell unconscious.'

'*Unconscious?*'

'He's being taken down to theatre now. It would be good for him to have a friendly face to come back up to.'

Joanna blinked several times, struck by an image of Callum lying motionless on an operating table. Callum whom she'd drunk with and kissed only two nights before.

She hung up and scrambled out of bed. It was half past midnight. She had no idea which clothes she was dragging on, where her car keys were, or what on earth she was doing, rushing to the bedside of a man she hardly knew. Callum had given the hospital *her* name. A warning sounded faintly, seeming to whisper out of the darkness: the dangers of leaping into an unknown situation with a near-stranger in the middle of the night. But another thought shouted louder: *He has nobody else.* And unexpectedly, as she found her keys and stumbled outside, it was Rohan's face that was in her mind, with Callum's hovering somewhere behind.

9

Leah

Leah hadn't seen her sister for over thirty-six hours. Somehow, it felt stranger than not seeing her for two years before this trip. Because she was here now. She'd come wanting to make things better between them. And she could feel that slipping through her fingers as Charlotte remained shut away with a migraine, and Leah was alone, full of new questions about Amy – and Nate – that had nowhere to go but round in dizzying circles.

She walked down the steps at the side of the villa, watched by the busts on the terrace wall, past the family pool that seemed to get cleaned more often than swam in. The guest annex stood before her like an *Il Mandarino* villa in miniature. Matilde had confirmed that Charlotte tended to stay in there when she got her migraines, to have peace and quiet while they passed. *Her migraines.* As though they were part of Charlotte now.

Leah knocked softly on the door, then a little louder, calling through: 'Charlotte? It's me. Just checking you're okay?'

There was still no response. Leah went to the window, but could see only the slats of the shutters and the gauze of the curtains. She remembered staying in there during past visits, opening the windows wide at night and smelling the chlorine from the pool. Sometimes she would peer up at the family villa and glimpse Gordon and Charlotte's silhouettes, unable to tell whether they were laughing or arguing.

Now she retreated, with a stab of loneliness that might've been an echo from those other times. She didn't even have Amy anymore, to text with the suggestion of a walk or a lakeside game of Uno. No Amy to text from London, either, or play never-ending online Scrabble against – so Leah had fallen out of the habit of texting anybody at all.

She thought again of the call she had failed to pick up. Could still see Amy's name in red with the 'missed' symbol beside it. A final chance to talk to her, squandered. If Leah had answered, would it have made any difference? To anything?

Guilt fired again, but with it came a blast of determination. She could use this time alone to look for answers. Try to understand what had happened that night, to lead Amy to the water in the storm.

Leah propelled herself down the mountain, joining the path that snaked between the towering villas. The ground was hot beneath her battered old sliders, sloped enough that she had to grip the tops of her shoes with her toes. Once she was in among the buildings and olive groves, she lost her bearings. Where was the cocktail bar she'd seen from above? A woman in a midnight-blue bikini and gold sarong stared at her from a balcony; a golf buggy whirred past and she felt its driver staring, too. 'Need a ride, *signora?*' he called out, and she instinctively shook her head.

Leah took a fork to the right, past a tennis court where she could hear a ball thumping and a male voice swearing, then stopped dead when she couldn't get any further. She had reached a dense wall of dark green pines. Peering between their trunks, she saw glimpses of iron railings, and tyre tracks across white gravel. She inched along, peeking through gaps until she realised: this was the new villa she had spotted from Amy's favourite balcony. She could make out the curve of a stone entranceway, the black doors of a garage, the diamond sparkle of a pool.

A high-pitched whine made her jump. Goosebumps flew up her arms and she was amazed to find herself cold: the shadows cast by these trees gobbled up the heat. Leaves were moving, rustling, as a set of part-camouflaged gates creaked open to her left.

Leah half-expected a limousine with blacked-out windows to come slinking out, so was surprised when Olivia emerged, dressed in a gold silk blouse and a fitted skirt, her hair pinned in a neat chignon. She aimed a remote control at the gates and they swung closed. Then she put her hand on a tree trunk and leaned for a moment, seeming to catch her breath. A lock of hair came loose and fell into her face. She flapped her blouse as if to cool herself, though Leah still felt chilled in the thick shade.

'Olivia?' Leah said. 'You okay?'

Olivia shot upright. 'Auntie Lee! What are you *doing* here?'

'I was out for a walk, I took a wrong turn . . .'

Olivia began straightening her blouse, fixing her hair, snapping out of what had looked like a moment of recuperation. 'Right, well, you shouldn't really be hanging around here. There are important guests. I'll show you the way back.'

'But . . . are you alright?'

'I'm fine! Just didn't eat breakfast, so went a bit light-headed.'

'You shouldn't skip breakfast,' Leah said, though she knew she didn't necessarily follow this advice herself when she was obsessed with a case at work, or had forgotten to shop. 'Matilde said you headed out really early this morning.'

'Well, there's even more to do while Mum's *incapacitated*.' Olivia put her hand on Leah's elbow and steered her away. Her palm was sticky and Leah noticed sweat trickles at her hairline, too.

'I don't remember that villa from before?'

'It was only built last year.'

'Why is it surrounded by so many huge trees?'

Olivia picked up her pace, urging Leah along. They turned a corner and the path opened into sunlight, the shadows shrinking away.

'The guests who stay there value privacy,' Olivia said. Her voice became a little stronger as she added: 'That's part of our package.'

'Package?'

'Well, it's not *just* a villa. We provide a whole range of services.' Her 'we' was pronounced and proud. She was back to being the perfect *Il Mandarino* rep.

Leah frowned. 'Such as?'

'Every package is bespoke. I can't give you a typical example.'

Leah tried to steal one last look at the villa's tall gates, but they were no longer in sight. She and Olivia were immersed once again in the white, shiny heat of the main part of the resort.

Olivia paused to pull a compact mirror out of her bag. As she blotted her forehead with powder, her expression was identical to Charlotte's when she was putting on make-up. Leah thought of the times back home in their twenties, when she would sit on Charlotte's bed, flicking through her postgrad coursework, watching her sister get ready for drinks with clients of the events company where she worked. Perfume in the air, jewellery box open and spilling its treasure. Part of Leah had yearned to be gorgeous and sociable, like her sister, but she'd also been aware of her own freedom, even then, freedom from always having to present a shined-up version of herself. She'd deliberately chosen an area of law where you could hide among words, figures and detail, rather than having to network and schmooze.

Charlotte had met Gordon at a work event. He was a property developer then, living between London and Lake Garda ('His roots are here but his soul is in Italy,' Charlotte used to say, clearly quoting his chat-up line), and he'd been in the early stages of ambitious plans for *Il Mandarino.* Leah was convinced he'd been on the lookout for a woman who would add the beauty, the charm. Who would help him create a perfect family to build his dream resort around. The girls had been so cute in all the early publicity photos, and Charlotte so good at beguiling the guests. Her social skills were almost magical when she was on form – she knew when to shake hands, kiss cheeks, how to pay the right compliments, make people feel special. Perhaps it was all the drama classes she had taken when she was younger.

Charlotte would come alive in front of an audience, in a costume, losing herself in a role.

Leah stirred, remembering what she'd set out to do. 'Can you point me towards the cocktail bar?' she asked Olivia.

'Cocktails before lunch, Auntie Lee?'

Leah tried to laugh. 'Well, I am on holiday.' It felt wrong as soon as she'd said it. This wasn't a holiday. It was a trip she should've had the guts to make months ago.

Olivia gestured with a mascara wand: 'Further down the hill, turn left after the fountain.'

'I haven't been before,' Leah said. 'Do you tend to oversee things there, too?'

A flicker crossed Olivia's face. 'That's more Mum's area, these days.' She dropped her make-up into her bag. 'I've got some errands to run – but I'll see you later? Hopefully Mum will be recovered by dinner.' There was the hint of an eyeroll, but Leah thought she detected something else beneath it: maybe worry or frustration.

She watched her niece stride away, calling out instructions to a gardener pruning a rose bush. Orange roses, of course. After a few moments, Olivia glanced back and stalled, as if she hadn't expected Leah to still be standing there. Leah waved and moved on. A guest passed by in a cream satin jumpsuit and high wedges, shooting an amused glance at Leah's jeans. She was carrying a flute of champagne. Just strolling around with it, flicking froth off her fingers where it had spilled.

The fountain that Olivia had referred to was a scaled-down replica of the Trevi Fountain in Rome. Leah stopped in front of it, unable to decide if it was tacky or beautiful. It didn't seem like Charlotte or Gordon's style to have a blatant copy. And yet, as water fell past Pegasuses and gods, it was inescapably striking. Perhaps it *was* typical of this place. The arrogance of having their own Trevi, dotted with coins that people had thrown in to make a wish.

Around the next bend, two palm trees flanked a large gold sign.

SEGRETO.

A unique cocktail experience.

Beyond it was a sparkling patio filled with umbrella-shaded tables, and a circular mahogany bar ringed by leather stools in alternating black and white. There were no customers, but a man in a white shirt and apron was slicing a vast array of fruit behind the bar, his back turned to Leah. She stood watching the chopping motion of his elbow, the sun winking off his knife. The air smelled of mango and polish.

He turned suddenly. 'Oh, hello!' He had a Dutch accent, a slightly forced-looking smile. 'So sorry, madam. I didn't realise you were there. Please, take a seat . . .'

Leah perched at the bar, doing an automatic comparison with the photo of Nate. His replacement was older, maybe in his late forties. Clean-shaven, average height, and lacking the instant charisma that a lot of the customer-facing staff here tended to have. Leah couldn't put her finger on it exactly, but he didn't strike her as '*Il Mandarino* material' – a phrase she'd once heard Gordon use.

He handed her a menu of breakfast cocktails, but told her they were only a 'starting point', *Segreto*'s approach was to 'build a drink around *you*'. It sounded like a script he'd recently learned. Just as Leah was debating asking for a beer instead, something rose out of her memory: Amy mentioning a particular cocktail in one of their text conversations.

'Could I have a Dark and Stormy?'

He looked surprised, then he seemed to don his professionalism like an extra apron, and launched into making the drink. His preparations were like a choreographed routine: stretching up for a glass, bending for a scoop of ice, grabbing two bottles from parallel shelves and tossing all his ingredients into the shaker in a climactic note. But there was something robotic about the way he performed it, as if he wasn't yet comfortable with his moves.

He strained his concoction into a tall glass. Leah took a sip and winced. Of course Amy would like the drink with the moody name and dark, cloudy appearance, rather than the ones that looked like a sunrise and tasted of pick 'n' mix.

'Are you staying here, madam?' the bartender asked, now standing with his hands behind his back.

'With the family,' Leah said. 'I'm Charlotte's sister, Leah.'

'Ah, Charlotte mentioned you were coming!'

'She did?'

'She's been looking forward to it. Especially the party.'

Leah spluttered out her drink. '*Party?*'

'Oh.' His hand went to his mouth. 'Maybe it's a surprise. I wasn't thinking . . .'

'I'll act shocked,' Leah assured him, with a drop in her stomach. 'When should I expect this . . . surprise?'

'Friday. Here at *Segreto*. I'm so sorry.' He shook his head, seeming genuinely distressed. 'I should be more careful. I hope you won't . . . I hope I haven't spoiled things.'

'Don't worry about it. You've done me a favour.' She took another glug of her drink, wondering, yet again, about the workings of her sister's mind. Surely the last thing anybody wanted, in the circumstances, was a cock-tail party.

Leah tried to recover her focus. Tried to channel some-thing akin to being in the flow of negotiation at work: a single-mindedness, overriding her emotions. 'How long have you worked here?' she asked.

He was clearly trying to recover his composure, too. 'Six months.' He smiled awkwardly, smoothing his collar. 'I'm Bram.'

'Did you know the guy before you?' She let her eyes flick up as she added: 'Nate?'

'Oh . . .' He frowned. 'No. He left before I started.'

'Suddenly?'

'I don't know all the circumstances. Can I get you anything else, Leah? Some water, perhaps?'

She shook her head, impatient now. 'Did you know my niece, Amy?'

Her directness seemed to fluster him. 'No, but of course I . . . I am so very sorry . . .' He lowered his voice, reverent: 'She sounded like an amazing person.'

'She was.' Leah swallowed, craning forward. 'Were you living in this area when she died?'

'Yes . . . in Malcesine. I never met her, though.'

'But you knew of her?'

'Everyone knows who the family are. Everyone knows *Il Mandarino*.' He seemed to offer this as a compliment, but the phrase sent a shudder down Leah's spine, like being back in the shade of the conifers.

'Were there rumours?' she pressed.

He took a tiny step backwards. 'What do you mean?'

'What did people think about her death? Outside of this place . . .' Leah waved her arms around as if to indicate the very air of *Il Mandarino*.

'Nobody . . . I'm not aware that anybody thought anything.' Bram's neck flushed and he looked as if he thought he was being tested. 'It was a terrible accident. A storm, wasn't it? Tragic.'

Abruptly, Leah's flow was punctured. Her hands sank, her chin dropping. 'Yes. Tragic. It *was* tragic.'

Silence fell. She covered her face and could hear Bram shifting from foot to foot.

'I really am sorry for your loss,' he said, eventually.

'It's the first time I've been back here since it happened,' she said into her palms. 'I didn't even come to her funeral.'

'Well.' He coughed quietly. 'It is a long way.'

'Not really.' She thought of the pathetic excuses she'd made to her family. To herself. Work commitments. A 'big deal' copyright case. Pathetic, pathetic, pathetic.

Bram seemed to struggle for what to say. After another pause, he ventured: 'There was a memorial in Malcesine, too.'

Leah's head lifted. 'Was there?'

'Her friends held one.' He seemed buoyed to be able to share this. 'There were white poppies everywhere, all around the streets.'

Leah retrieved the napkin from under her drink and pressed it against her burning eyes. There was an image behind her lids: a shower of white petals falling onto the sun-baked cobbles of an Italian street, and friends lining the road, the ones from Amy's photos.

An image of Nate pushed forward, with a poppy pinched between his finger and thumb – a red one for him, though, blood red. He was the clearest figure in her imagined crowd, but when she zoomed in, he broke into pieces.

She turned back to Bram. 'His surname,' she said, too abruptly. 'Nate's,' she clarified, seeing his confusion, and trying to keep her cool. 'Do you know it?'

'I . . .' He seemed thrown again by her swing back to this topic. Perturbed, even: frown lines settling between his brows. 'Fraser, I believe. Is there—'

'Thank you.' Leah cut him off with a polite smile. But when she pulled out her phone, and saw that her mobile signal had disappeared again, she realised she needed one more thing from Bram. 'Actually, do you have the WiFi password? It seems to have been changed since my last visit here. And there's no signal to use my data.'

He hesitated, then reeled off the password, eyeing her as she tapped it into her phone. Leah tried to keep her expression blank as she pulled up Google.

Nate Fraser Il Mandarino, she typed, moving her phone into her lap.

Bram returned to his array of fruit. A chopping sound resumed, softer than before, faltering occasionally as he seemed to shoot glances her way. Leah drummed her fingers on her knee. The top search result said: *Police dismiss*

leaked eyewitness account of argument between Nate Fras ...
The remainder of the headline wasn't visible, so Leah clicked into it.

She stared down at her phone. An error message had appeared. *This website is inaccessible on your network.*

She frowned and clicked back, trying again. Same message. She tested some of the other search results – from Twitter and Facebook, appearing to make accusations against Nate – but they were all blocked when she tried to read them in full. As an experiment, she searched for something different, and innocuous – ice cream flavours, the distance to Verona – and had no problems.

Inaccessible on your network? What exactly did that mean?

She pinched the corners of her phone, feeling as if she'd just run into an invisible wall.

10

Amy

Last September
Seven and a half hours before sunset

Nate and I barely have a chance to talk before Olivia appears. We both hear her coming, both recognise the click of her heeled sandals, and we jump apart.

She whirls in, busy and urgent, and somehow the martini glasses rattle and the sun umbrellas tremble, even though she's not exactly heavy-footed. She's wearing an orange sleeveless blouse and a long white skirt with a slit, one tanned leg emerging with every hurried stride. Olivia spends Dad's 'wardrobe budget' impeccably, whereas I gave mine away when he first forced the allowance on me. They all thought I was doing it to be difficult, but Dad wouldn't accept it back and I didn't know what else to do that wouldn't make me feel crap. I donated it to the local women's refuge; Olivia saw their thank-you card and took it straight to Dad.

Today, though, none of it matters. I don't feel any anger or resentment – though Olivia seems to radiate both those things lately, whenever she's in my company. Instead, I find myself wanting to touch her, smile at her. To close the distance between us before I go. It hasn't always been there, after all. We used to stick together, stick up for each other, before we somehow ended up on opposing teams.

'Nate,' Olivia says, not even looking at me. 'Could you fix a large pitcher of a *really* refreshing drink for the two guests at the new villa? They've been working half the night on this merger they've got going on, and they're hoping to finalise it today, so I'd love to surprise them with some refreshments. Something a bit special.'

'Alcoholic?'

'Oh, no. I think they had enough while they were working last night, judging by the empties I had cleared away this morning! They'll be on the champagne once the deal is closed, though . . .' She's all wink-wink with her insider knowledge. Irritation grumbles at me, but I try to hold on to that feeling of love, of already missing her. For just a moment, I see her from a distance, as if through the wrong end of a telescope.

'I've still got some homemade lemonade from yesterday,' Nate says, heading for the huge fridge behind the bar. 'I could add some lime, fresh mint. Maybe some ginger if they need reviving.'

He's amazing, the way he can mask what he thinks and feels. Look how enthusiastic he appears, how willing to help Olivia suck up to these people, who are quite likely to be the antithesis of everything he and I believe in, everything we discuss when nobody else is around. Then again, he does love concocting drinks, combining ingredients. He reads people by their favourite tipples, even the way they hold their glass. The customers at *Segreto* shower him with applause and insanely big tips, but they don't know his real judgments of them. His true talent is making them feel as if he's listening. Most people here want someone to hang off their every greedy word.

I watch him rub mint leaves between his fingers and inhale their scent. And I suppress a dash of jealousy as he holds the mint out for Olivia to sniff, and she leans across the bar, blouse gaping. 'Smells so good!' She beams at him. 'Thank you, Nate, that sounds *perfect*.'

As he sets about preparing the drink, Olivia finally looks at me. I make myself smile and it turns into genuine emotion, almost choking me up. 'Morning, Liffer,' I say, using her old nickname – I couldn't pronounce 'Olivia' when she was first born.

She arches her plucked eyebrows. 'You've got a mark on your top.'

At first I think she's referring to the 'bloodstain' balloon in the Banksy picture, mimicking Mum's hatred of the design. But as she points with one of her dark red acrylic nails, I realise there's a blemish of lime juice near my waist. Nate must've smeared it there when we hugged. My cheeks heat and I catch Nate's eye as he clocks it, too. Then I realise Olivia is watching us both intently. I fold my arms and mumble something sarcastic about dissolving Alka-Seltzer into the guests' drink, while Nate busies himself chopping mint. We have to be careful. If Olivia suspects there is anything between us, even so much as an atmosphere, I can't trust her not to go running to Dad. And he wouldn't stand for it. Not his golden-boy cocktail artist with the daughter who ruins everything.

Nate adds the finishing flourishes to the lemonade, then presents it to Olivia in a tall jug shaped like an hourglass, clinking with ice.

'That should set them up for the day!' She claps her hands in delight. I know she'll be imagining their gratitude when she delivers it to them. She won't send a maid or a waiter; she'll want this small moment of glory for herself.

And why not, I think, finding some generosity. I try to smile at her one last time, but she's absorbed in carrying the jug without sloshing any liquid. Her skirt flaps open, revealing her perfect leg – and I see Nate's eye drawn there before he snatches it away. I dismiss another burn of jealousy and focus on the sweet expression of concentration on Olivia's face as she holds the pitcher level. The way her tongue sticks out like it used to when we were little, our heads dipped to our colouring books.

I notice the woman at the same time Olivia seems to. She is standing beneath the leafy trellis that marks the back entrance to *Segreto*, peering around as if she doesn't quite know where she is. She must be around my age, but that's where the resemblance ends. This woman looks like a model. Tall and willowy, with a pale pink sundress, delicate limbs and butter-blonde hair. Her nails are painted jet black, a weird contrast to all the pastel shades, but somehow it works, gives her an edge.

We all stare at her. I'm not sure why. It isn't as if we're not used to supremely beautiful people; Dad makes sure *Il Mandarino* is full of them. But there is something about the way she's standing there, beneath the arch of climbing plants, exuding both confidence and a measure of uncertainty.

Olivia recovers first. 'Hello! Welcome to *Segreto*!'

'I may be in the wrong place,' the woman says. 'I'm here for a meeting with Gordon Wynne.'

I see Olivia's face change. 'Oh! Of course! Yes, you are in the wrong place. But no problem. Let me take you . . .' She seems flustered, still holding the jug. She goes to put it down on a table then changes her mind. 'Actually, I just need to deliver this. Could you wait here for five minutes? I'll send Mr Wynne down to collect you. Nate, could you make a coffee for—'

'Hanna,' the woman supplies, and seems to do a double-take as she catches sight of Nate.

'Of course,' Olivia says again, nodding. 'Please, take a seat. Dad – Mr Wynne – won't be long.'

She hesitates once more, as if she doesn't want to leave this woman in our care. I try to catch Nate's eye but he's staring at Hanna, his brow knitted, as though he's troubled by her presence. Does he know her? Or is he just disappointed that we won't get any more time to talk? She's an intrusion, and I feel it too, a sense that this day is already coming off its tracks.

Hanna chooses a table on the far side, under the shade of a palm. I watch her arrange the hem of her dress and the fall of her hair, as if she's expecting somebody to take a photo of her.

And suddenly, with a sinking feeling, I think I know why she's here.

11

Joanna

Joanna knew her way around the hospital. She'd accompanied her mum to her appointments lots of times. Yet tonight the dark car park seemed back-to-front, the corridors were a labyrinth, the lift plummeted to the basement when she was sure she'd pressed 'Up'. She was soaked in sweat by the time she found the ICU.

She had to press a buzzer because it was well outside of standard visiting hours. For a guilty moment, she hoped they wouldn't let her in, but a nurse appeared and showed her inside once Joanna had mumbled her name. She glimpsed other visitors sitting quietly beside beds, their loved ones sleeping in nests of tubes and wires. Clearly, different visiting rules applied here. The realisation made her swallow. *This is the ICU. This is serious.*

'Mr Foley is out of theatre, but in recovery,' the nurse told her in a whisper, showing her to a deserted waiting room. 'The operation to control his internal bleeding was a success. He also has fractured ribs, a fractured jaw, and extensive bruising. The neurologist will assess for any brain injuries tomorrow.'

Joanna baulked at this summary. 'What *happened* to him?'

The nurse looked surprised, as if she'd expected her to already know. 'He was hit by a car.'

'Really?' Joanna tried to take this in. 'Where?'

The nurse checked her notes. 'Near the railway station.'

'He works close to there,' Joanna said, her thoughts tumbling.

'We're not yet sure of all the circumstances. We're hoping Mr Foley can tell us more when he wakes.'

Left alone, Joanna flipped through a year-old magazine without reading it. She noticed she was wearing odd ballet pumps: one white, one pale grey. Her mouth was middle-of-the-night dry and she still felt as if she was dreaming.

Internal bleeding. Assessment for brain injuries.

Hit by a car.

Then she heard the squeak of trolley wheels, and looked up to recognise Callum's curly hair sailing past. He had an oxygen mask over his face – that was all she could make out as he was pushed around the corner.

Joanna stood up, bending the unread magazine into a scroll against her chest.

'Miss Greenfield?'

Then she was being led into the hushed heart of the ICU, the beeps of the machines all fractionally out of sync. She stood a wary distance from Callum's bed. His eyes were slits inside pillows of blue-black skin. There was a huge bruise across his jaw, too, and a deep-looking gash in his cheek. Joanna swayed on the spot, then made herself shuffle closer.

'Callum?'

His eyelids moved inside the black swelling.

'Can you hear me?'

'You came.' The words were squeezed out, his jaw rigid. 'Didn't know who else . . .'

'It's okay.' Joanna felt a sharp pang of sympathy. She touched his hand and his fingers gripped hers, then slackened. His skin was cold, with rough patches of dried blood.

'What happened, Callum?' she asked.

He shook his head and let it fall to one side, away from her gaze.

At 7.30 a.m., Joanna called her PA and told her she wouldn't be coming in. She hadn't had a sick day in years, let alone a fake one – not since she'd worked at Boots when she was eighteen and skived off to go to a festival with her friends. Her hands were shaking once she'd got off the phone, guilt heavy in her stomach. All the meetings that would have to be rearranged. The report about Rohan that was sitting, unfinished, on her computer.

Would her guilt have been stronger or weaker if she'd left Callum to go and deal with those things instead? His need was visible, unavoidable: the injuries re-shaping his face, the spurts of agony darting across. Heading back to his bay after making the call, Joanna saw that a doctor had arrived and was closing the curtain around Callum's bed. She paused when she noticed Joanna. 'Ah, hello, are you . . .?'

'Joanna. Callum's friend.'

'You're the next of kin?'

She wished people would stop calling her that. 'Not exactly, but I'm . . . here for Callum.'

'I'm Dr Khalifa. Please . . .' The doctor ushered her inside the oval of the curtain as she swept it around the bed. Joanna stood awkwardly in the tent-like space, feeling claustrophobic, and like an imposter.

Dr Khalifa slid a stethoscope under the neck of Callum's hospital gown, revealing more purple bruising along his collarbone. Callum stared up at the ceiling as the doctor checked his temperature, shone a light into his eyes, asked him if he knew who the prime minister was. It felt intimate to see his body and brain examined. Joanna breathed out once it was over, the curtain rolled halfway back.

'The police want to talk to you about what happened,' Dr Khalifa said to Callum.

'Not now,' Callum said. The restricted movement of his jaw gave everything a curt, clipped tone that was at odds with his usual manner.

Dr Khalifa glanced at Joanna, then back to Callum. 'They're very keen to—'

'Not yet,' Callum said more forcefully, and an uncomfortable silence fell. He exhaled and mumbled in a softer tone: 'Don't feel up to it.'

'Okay,' Dr Khalifa relented. 'I'll hold them off for now.'

'How much do you remember?' Joanna asked him, tentatively.

His eyes shifted to her, but only briefly, wavering past her and seeming to glaze. 'I was leaving the pub. Walked behind a car that was reversing.' There was a pause before he added: 'My fault.'

Joanna blinked at his injuries, trying to picture a reversing car hitting him hard enough to cause them. 'Did you see who was driving? Did they stop?'

He shook his head. 'Not sure they even knew they'd hit me.'

Joanna struggled to imagine this. How could they not know? Why was Callum absorbing all the blame?

Dr Khalifa frowned. 'Could the driver have been under the influence?'

'Maybe,' he said.

'Do you reckon they'd been drinking in your pub?' Joanna asked. 'You might even have served them.'

'I don't know. It was dark. It happened quickly.' He closed his eyes. 'I walked into the road. Wasn't paying attention.'

'But they didn't stop!' Joanna said.

'No.'

'You *have* to talk to the police. If they were over the limit, or if they knew they'd hit you, and just left you . . . And look how hurt you are! They must've hit you at speed, hit you bloody *hard* . . .' Joanna was surprised by the passion flowing into her voice. Regardless of how well she did or didn't know Callum, she was suddenly enraged. Who could do this to another person, then drive away?

He nodded, finally opening his eyes. 'You're right.'

'I'm really sorry this happened to you.' She took his hand again, feeling bad for her earlier awkwardness. An echo of her conversation with Rohan's dad came unexpectedly into her head. She'd said sorry to him as well, lots of times, knowing it wasn't enough.

After Dr Khalifa had gone, Joanna sat down beside Callum's bed. An image of a fast-reversing car streaked through her mind, then dissolved. She was a naturally visual person, seeing reels of action when people told her stories or she was reading a book. She'd reconstructed Rohan's almost-leap from the top of that building in startling detail . . . and yet she couldn't fully envision Callum's ordeal. All she could see was the blur of a moving car, and a freeze-frame of him lying on a road.

'Is there anyone you want me to contact?' she asked. 'Your family, another friend?'

He shook his head. 'They'd worry.'

'Well, of course, but—'

'Thanks for being here. I know it's a big ask.'

'I'm happy to. I just think your family would want to know.'

'There's only my mum. I don't want to upset her.'

There didn't seem anything else Joanna could say. She felt responsibility falling hard onto her shoulders. But she was used to that, wasn't she? It just wasn't usually this confusing.

This frightening.

Her phone vibrated in her pocket. It was a text from Mandy: **Just heard you're poorly. Take care hon. Luke says get well soon too xx**

Joanna sighed. Why had Mandy told her brother she was off sick? And she doubted he'd asked her to pass on a message; Mandy had clearly made a leap there. Sometimes her constant Luke references seemed deliberately taunting. This pantomime of everything being the same and yet obviously not.

She imagined how Mandy would react if she told her where she really was. How quickly would it get back to Luke? How would he feel about it?

Nobody knows you're here.

The thought struck her again. She'd been called Callum's 'next of kin' several times in the last few hours, while her own friends and family were oblivious to his existence.

Out of the corner of her eye, she saw two police officers hovering at the door of the ward, peering over at her and Callum, before Dr Khalifa turned them away.

12

Leah

'Saffron risotto! Isn't it the most *gorgeous* colour?'

Leah nodded, looking down into her bowl of luminous yellow rice. 'Hardly even looks like food.'

Charlotte laughed. 'You say some funny things, Lee.'

'Do I?'

It was Monday lunchtime, and Leah was finally alone with her sister. Charlotte sat across from her at the table on the terrace, burgundy nails curved around a goblet of white wine, dark hair frothing around her shoulders. For all her marvelling at its colour, she ate her risotto in the tiniest bites, with a teaspoon, while Leah had been given a bigger portion and a normal-sized spoon. She couldn't stop staring at her sister's thin wrists, wondering how they were bearing the weight of the oversized glass and the chunky silver bangles that clanged along her arm. Her own hands were suddenly huge. The nails ragged and bitten. She remembered arm-wrestling with Amy once, collapsing into laughter, while Charlotte and Olivia had watched with bemusement.

Charlotte had dismissed all questions and concerns about the migraines. But her brief absence made it feel as if they were being reunited a second time, piling on the pressure of another new start. Leah grappled for things to say, biting back everything she desperately wanted to ask. The incident with the websites had made her feel as if she had to tread carefully. Last night, she had emailed one of the IT staff from work to ask what the message 'inaccessible on your network' could mean. He'd seemed surprised to hear from her (did even the IT team know she'd been forced to take time off?), but had replied: It usually means the network administrators have blocked certain websites or key words from their WiFi network.

Network administrators? Leah had checked.

Whoever's in control, he'd replied, unaware how much his phrasing had disturbed her. It was as if *Il Mandarino* was its own state, restricting web access and information. But why block content about Nate?

Leah looked cautiously at her sister. 'Have you spoken to Mum and Dad?' she asked.

'They call once a week,' Charlotte said. 'Same day, same time . . . It's like they're calling from prison! Or maybe they think I'm the one in prison?' She laughed dryly and the teaspoon trembled in her hand.

Leah didn't feel like laughing. She knew how much her parents worried about Charlotte and Olivia. How helpless they felt.

'I know they'd like to visit again,' she said, 'but Dad can't really fly anymore, with his heart . . .' She was unsure why she'd nominated herself as their spokesperson. It wasn't as if she saw them that often either. Nowhere near as much as she should.

'It's not that,' Charlotte said, unexpectedly. 'I don't think that's the reason.'

Leah held a spoonful of rice in her mouth, not wanting to jeopardise the moment by chewing and swallowing.

Her sister broke the silence just as it began to seem unending. 'Last time they were here, Gordon and I weren't . . . ourselves,' she said, staring at some distant point over the top of Leah's head. 'I think we might've scared them off.'

Leah swallowed her food, but was mute. There seemed so much to untangle in her sister's words. *Last time they were here*, meant for Amy's funeral. *Weren't ourselves . . . scared them off* . . . The admissions were like fragile particles drifting across the terrace; she wanted to grab them, examine them, but she was afraid they would disintegrate.

'Of course you weren't yourselves,' she said. 'It must've been . . .' She inched her hand forward but they were too far apart, her fingertips barely making it halfway. And Leah, as ever, gave up too easily.

Charlotte had a misty look about her now. She took a long drink of wine, and when she plonked her glass down onto the table, colour flooded back into her cheeks. 'Perfect pinot, that. Dry as they come.' She pushed her quarter-eaten lunch aside and rubbed her stomach as if she'd never been so full.

Leah kept eating, making a point of finishing it. For what purpose, she wasn't sure, and now the rice seemed to plaster the roof of her mouth. Charlotte was coiling a lock of hair around her finger, closing one eye against the sun.

'Charlotte, I . . .' Leah's words came out strangled. 'I'm sorry I didn't come to the funeral.'

Charlotte stopped twisting. The strand stuck in place, rigid with product. 'I barely even remember it. You could've told me you'd come and I would've believed you.' She laughed again but there was not a shred of humour in it. 'I suppose a triple dose of diazepam will do that.'

'I hear there was a memorial for her in Malcesine, too.'

Charlotte jerked her head to toss back the rogue lock. 'Oh, yes. Her friends' little *alternative* funeral.'

'You didn't go?'

'How could I? I was at the *actual* funeral. Burying my—' She broke off, taking another gulp of wine.

'You mean the other memorial was on the same day?'

'At *exactly* the same time. I suppose they were making some kind of statement.' Her voice crackled with sudden anger. 'They wanted people to choose.'

Leah thought of the white poppies Bram had described. Pictured Charlotte all in black, with big dark glasses, drugged and vacant in a draughty church. She imagined a celebration of Amy's life on the colourful streets of Malcesine, at the same time as her coffin was being carried into a room full of Gordon's associates and the few bemused, distraught relatives – none more so than her grandparents – who had flown in.

And she thought of herself, alone in her flat, watching the clock until she knew it was over. Until the decision about whether to go had slipped from dilemma to regret.

That night was humid, the air sultry and charged. Over dinner, Olivia mentioned that maybe a storm was coming, and there was a perceptible tremor around the table, like a light dimming. Gordon scowled at a ragu stain on the white tablecloth and Charlotte pushed away her plate just as she had done at lunch.

It was the closest thing Leah had seen to a moment of shared grief. Yet, as she looked around, she saw it wasn't really shared. They each seemed to be responding to the same trigger, but they were self-enclosed, not even looking at one another.

Gordon glanced at his watch and Leah recognised the signs that he was about to make his excuses. Before he could, she blurted out: 'I've been having a bit of trouble with the WiFi.'

'The connection?' he said. 'I'll have it looked at immediately. I hope no other guests have experienced problems.' He glanced at Olivia as if she should've somehow spotted this blip.

'Not the connection,' Leah said. 'Just certain websites being inaccessible. I get an error message . . .'

'Which websites?' Gordon's eyes narrowed.

'Some research I was doing for a work case. It's not important, I just wondered why—'

'We do block some sites on the *Il Mandarino* network,' Gordon said. 'Anything that might make our guests' experience less than ideal. We want them to feel nothing but relaxed while they're here.'

'Oh.' Leah fell silent. She could feel Gordon's eyes still on her. When she glanced up again, all three of them were gazing her way.

'Did you find *Segreto* okay yesterday?' Olivia asked, in such a sudden and pointed way that Leah felt as if she was being grassed up.

'*Segreto?*' Charlotte said, 'You went?'

'Yes. It's . . .' Leah couldn't think of an appropriate adjective and her voice trailed off.

'So you met Bram?' Charlotte said.

'Boring Bram,' Olivia chimed in, then flushed as her parents both frowned at her.

'He's not boring,' Charlotte tutted. 'He's . . . reliable.' She held her wine glass with both hands. 'He's exactly what we need.'

Afterwards, in her room, Leah couldn't sleep. The heat sat on top of the air-con's current, like a layer of sweat over shivery skin. She was aware of the night creeping by, the darkness thickening behind the shutters, her mind dipping in and out of worries and dreams.

Something isn't right here, her nightmares whispered. *You have to find out what.*

Sometime in the early hours, she stiffened in her bed, thinking she'd heard a noise from Amy's room. Keeping as still as possible, she held her breath and listened. There was a definite shuffling. Footsteps. When the noises failed to stop, she slid out of bed and tiptoed onto the landing.

Amy's door was ajar. Through the gap, Leah could make out a figure in a dark robe. As her eyes adjusted, she saw the tumble of dark hair, the slim elegance of the person's shape. Charlotte? Or Olivia?

Leah cleared her throat to alert the person to her presence. It was Charlotte, she saw now. Her sister didn't turn as Leah edged forward to stand in the doorway. She was bending over the cacti on Amy's windowsill, wiping the rims of their pots with the wide sleeve of her dressing gown. Leah heard her gasp as if she'd pricked herself, but she carried on, dusting the sill underneath.

'Char?' Leah whispered.

Charlotte turned and came towards her. Her eyes shone blindly in the moonlit room. *She's sleepwalking,* Leah realised, remembering that her sister used to do that sometimes when they were young. Charlotte halted when they were almost nose to nose, then reached sideways to swipe her sleeve across a mirror. Leah jumped back as she drifted out of the room, a silver veil of dust motes pirouetting around her.

Slipping back into Amy's room, Leah looked around. There was a tiny drop of blood on the windowsill where Charlotte had pricked herself. And on the wall, the photo of Nate jutted out slightly further than before, as if it had been prodded or tugged.

13

Joanna

'On what date did the student first contact your department for support?'

'Rohan,' Joanna said, instinctively. She wanted them to use his name. Couldn't bear to spend this whole meeting with her superiors, which was already tense and formal enough, referring to 'the student'.

Her boss blinked, and glanced at his printout of Joanna's report, which she had come in at 6 a.m. to finish. She felt as if she *was* ill now, after her sickie on Monday. Was it exhaustion, or karma?

'Yes. Rohan. What date did he enter the system?'

Joanna cringed at the clinical phrase, but knew her answer was worse than her boss's wording. Too long ago.

'Who assessed him?' This was her manager's manager, now, somebody Joanna only tended to see in a crisis. She was flipping pages of the report, removing and replacing her glasses.

Joanna wanted to stand up and open a window. The room was airless and she hadn't brought her water bottle. But she felt pinned to her seat, her own copy of the report heavy in her lap. It didn't say what she really wanted it to. She'd almost veered into an alternative narrative, about how lost

Rohan's dad had sounded on the phone, and how two of her counselling staff were now off with stress, and how Joanna felt in awe of the lecturer who'd talked Rohan down, and irrationally guilty that it hadn't been her. But in the end, of course, the report was full of the facts and none of the story.

The questions kept coming. *Who judged him to be a 'green' in the traffic-light waiting system, not an amber or a red alert? What self-help resources was he sent in the interim? Did anybody check on him?*

Joanna felt herself getting lower in her chair, while the room got hotter and the swish of pages got louder, brisker. When it was over, she fell out of the room and stumbled to the nearest exit from the building. The sky spun and she wheezed in the fresh air, pulling off the suit jacket she'd worn to make a good impression.

Then she ran towards her car. An urge to get to the hospital for lunchtime visiting hours was suddenly fizzing over her. An urge to be useful to *somebody*.

Callum had now been moved from the ICU to a ward. The swelling in his face was subsiding and he was able to walk with crutches. And Joanna had developed a surreal new routine, running in parallel to her normal life. Driving to work instead of cycling so she could nip to the hospital on her breaks. Keeping a secret from her colleagues, escaping to a different kind of responsibility.

Today, she threw herself into carer mode extra vehemently – fussing with Callum's pillows, pouring more water than he could drink. Determined to be up to this, since it seemed she was failing elsewhere.

'You okay, Jo?' Callum asked, as she refilled his plastic beaker to the point of overflowing.

Joanna deflated into a chair. She was reminded of the first day they'd met, how he'd seemed to know her head was a mess and had nudged her into talking. But now *she* should be asking *him* if he was okay, nudging *him* into talking – wasn't that supposedly her forte? Yet he never seemed to want to talk much about what had happened to him.

'I'm . . . fine,' she said, shaking away the memory of the meeting, the guilt-inducing questions. 'Are you? Did the police come back this morning?'

He pulled at the collar of his hospital gown. 'I made my statement.'

Joanna felt a flutter of relief. It had been bothering her, the way he'd declined to talk to the police at first. She hadn't realised quite how much.

'They weren't hopeful about identifying the driver, though,' Callum added.

'Seriously? Didn't anybody see anything?'

'They'll knock on doors. But it was late.'

'Maybe it was picked up on CCTV, though. Or maybe your colleagues have information?'

'I locked up by myself that night.'

'And you don't remember anything? Not the make of the car, the colour?'

'*Nothing*—' He stopped and winced, shifting position on the bed as if the recollection had given him a physical twinge.

Joanna fell silent, aware of pushing him again. Could she blame him for not wanting to relive what had happened? And was it really any of her business?

Well maybe it was, since she was the one holding a straw to his lips when he was thirsty, fetching the nurses when he needed extra pain relief. She'd never even done anything like this for Luke, in all their years together – though not because she'd shied away from it. Luke didn't really 'do' illnesses, something he used to declare with pride, as if it showed strength of character. And yet, the way he had been in the last few months of their relationship . . . Joanna had become convinced he was suffering from depression. He had dismissed it when she'd broached the subject, said he was just tired and snowed-under at work. He'd even accused her of going all 'counsellor Joanna' on him, snapping that not everybody needed saving.

The memory of his words still landed with a sting. Dr Khalifa appeared then, pulling Joanna back into the present.

'I've got good news, Callum!' she said. 'I've just had a meeting with the rest of your care team. You've made great progress and we think you're well enough to go home. Perhaps as early as today, if we can get everything organised!'

'That's great,' he said hoarsely.

Joanna echoed him, feeling an odd clash of relief and disappointment that her role here was about to be over.

She could walk away, now. No more strange, secretive hospital visits.

No more distractions from the rest of her life, either.

'We need to make sure you're going to be able to continue your recovery safely, though,' the doctor said, glancing from Callum to Joanna. 'Do you two live together?'

'Oh, no,' they said at the same time. Joanna's cheeks heated in the way they had done on their date, when Callum had said something borderline flirtatious. How trivial it now seemed, the way she'd obsessed over whether he'd meant to flirt with her or not. And yet there had been little moments, over the last three crazy days, when they'd veered close to flirtation again, even with him in a hospital bed.

'No, we're . . .' Joanna regretted the beginning of her sentence.

'We only just . . .' He let his explanation trail off, too.

'We don't live together,' Joanna finished weakly.

'Do you live alone?' Dr Khalifa asked Callum.

He nodded.

'A house? A flat? I'm just trying to ascertain whether we can discharge you without concern. We've got you on some very strong painkillers, which can cause severe dizziness.'

Joanna listened with curiosity. She'd seen the pattern of Callum's heartbeat on a monitor, but not the inside of his living room. She knew the quantities of his daily drugs but still so little about his life outside their hospital bubble.

'It's a flat,' he said, not giving her much to go on.

'Upstairs?' Dr Khalifa asked.

'Third floor.'

'Do other people live in the building? People who could check on you, or help with shopping and things?'

Callum paused. 'The flat next to me is empty at the moment. I don't know about the people downstairs. I barely see them. I only moved in recently.'

'Hmm.' Dr Khalifa tapped her pen against her lip. 'Do you have somewhere else you could stay? I'm not sure I can discharge you to an upstairs flat, by yourself, while you're taking high doses of tramadol. Plus, you might struggle with mobility at first, while your ribs heal.'

Joanna felt Dr Khalifa looking at her. On a delay, she realised where the conversation was going, what the doctor was hoping she would say. The magic words that would allow Callum to be discharged.

'Not really,' Callum mumbled, glancing at her too. 'I don't know many people nearby.'

There was a pause which, to Joanna, felt excruciating. How must it look that she wasn't offering Callum a place to recuperate? Dr Khalifa didn't know they'd only just met, that it would be a big deal to open her home to him, the home she'd worked so hard to make her own.

A tug-of-war played out inside her. On one side was her personal safety gauge, wailing like a siren along with the imaginary, warning voices of her friends. The knowledge that she had done enough for Callum, she wasn't obliged to take him in as well. But on the other side was her guilt about Rohan, the permanent crush of it in her chest, and all those other students languishing on her department's waiting list. Callum was someone she could actually, *immediately* help. She pictured him falling down the stairs when she might've prevented it. How she would think back to this moment and wish she'd made a different decision, just as she'd done a hundred times in the case of Rohan.

For some reason, she didn't address Callum directly, but murmured to the doctor, 'He could . . . stay with me for a bit. I have a sofa bed downstairs. I'd be at work during the day but I could pop back if he needed me.'

'Perfect! Could I take a discharge address?'

Joanna hesitated again.

'You don't have to do this, Jo,' Callum said. 'I'll manage at home.' But there was no conviction in his words, and she could sense he was worried about the prospect of being alone, too.

'I really wouldn't recommend that,' Dr Khalifa said, 'I can only discharge you if—'

'Honestly, it's no problem,' Joanna cut in. 'Just stay with me for a few days.'

Dr Khalifa beamed. 'The address, then?'

'16 Railway Terrace . . .' Joanna focused on the familiar rhythm of her address and postcode, telling herself this was the right thing to do. 'Don't worry,' she said to Callum, aiming to strike a jokey note. 'I'm an experienced carer.'

She thought of gripping her mum's soft hand as she'd struggled to coordinate her footsteps. How proud she'd felt as they'd made it to the other side of their living room. This situation was nothing like that, of course. Her dad wouldn't be near, making sure they were safe. She wouldn't get hugs from her parents, or a certificate at school, or the bursting relief of watching her mum get slowly better. But still, Joanna felt a tingle of warmth at the thought of looking after somebody again. She caught Callum's eye and tried to smile as if all of this was normal.

Everything seemed to accelerate after that, almost as if the hospital staff knew Joanna was unsure and wanted to usher Callum out before she changed her mind. She worked on her laptop from a waiting room for an hour, dodging her colleagues' calls and sending vague replies to Mandy's emails asking where she was. Then Callum appeared on crutches, with a bag of medication and a slightly agitated air.

'Let's go!' Joanna said with forced brightness.

Waves of nerves crashed over her as she drove them towards home. She was hyper-conscious of the cereal bar wrappers littering her car; the high frequency of Madonna tracks in her driving playlist; the need to steer smoothly so as not to keep jolting Callum's injuries.

Then something else occurred to her. 'Hey, do you want to swing by your place and get some clothes? I could nip in, collect whatever you need?'

'Oh, no.' He knocked the crutch that was tucked between his legs as he answered, and it clattered against the passenger door. 'No, it's okay thanks.'

'You're sure? It's no trouble. You only have what you're wearing . . .' She decided not to point out the obvious: that his current outfit was ripped and dirty, bearing the stains of his accident.

'No, honestly.' His voice got a little louder. 'I don't want to put you out further. I'll ask my landlady to send some things over.'

'Well . . . okay.' Joanna glanced at him as the traffic paused. He had righted the crutch and his hands were clamped around it. 'If you're sure.'

She parked up, as close to her house as she could get on the car-clogged street, and helped him out of the passenger seat. The sudden revving of a car further down the road swivelled his head, and she glimpsed a flash of panic in his face. He turned quickly back and Joanna pretended not to have noticed. Callum glanced all around him, then hobbled towards her front gate.

'How did you guess which house it was?' she asked him, as she followed with his meds.

'You said your address at the hospital.'

'Oh, yes . . .' She felt flustered, overtaking him to unlock the door.

Inside, she couldn't help seeing her home through his eyes. Wondering what it smelled like to him, if he was registering the number of kids' finger-paintings stuck to the fridge and questioning whether she had a not-yet-mentioned child. The living room was a mess. One of the perks of living alone was allowing yourself to be a slob when you wanted to, but now she snatched up hair bobbles and mugs under Callum's curious gaze.

'I've got to nip back to work,' she said. 'Will you be okay?'

He blinked, as if he hadn't expected her to leave him alone so soon. 'Of course. Is there anything I can do to make myself useful?'

'No, you should rest!' Joanna grabbed the TV remote and indicated which buttons to press.

Then she handed him a key. The key to her house. A man she'd known for less than a week. As if sensing her unease, he smiled and touched her arm. 'Jo, I don't know how to thank you. Don't know what I would've done . . .'

She swallowed, told him she'd be back around seven, and turned to go.

One last pause in her hall. One last chance to change her mind. From behind, she heard her TV blare on, and a triumphant little cheer from her guest. Joanna walked out, closing the door on the sound of an afternoon quiz show, rather than the silence she'd become accustomed to.

14

Leah

Leah rolled up her jeans and thrust her toes into the cool, numbing shallows of the lake.

It was early, the air ripe with building heat, *Il Mandarino* still quiet, stirring – whereas she had been wide awake since 4 a.m., a plan shaping in her mind.

She was sitting on the small strip of beach that ran underneath the dock, waiting for the first ferry of the day. There was a secretive feel to this spot, especially at this hour – nestled at the foot of the resort, level with the flat expanse of the lake rather than gazing down on it. With one hand Leah churned at the sand, pausing every few seconds to check the vital piece of paper was still in her pocket. Her other hand clutched her mobile, where flickers of signal would occasionally appear and then die.

A message from her dad was on its screen. He was acting casual about her trip – **how's it going?** – but was clearly worried about his distant, bereaved family. He'd seemed so diminished since they'd lost Amy, his heart problems worsening, his whole body seeming to shrink, to age. Charlotte's words came back to Leah: *Gordon and I weren't ourselves . . . think we scared them off.* Might her dad have further insight? Instead of replying to his message, Leah pressed 'call using

WiFi'. Briefly, she wondered whether any phone numbers were blocked by the *Il Mandarino* network, too.

Her dad usually answered within a few rings these days. He would joke that he was a retiree with nothing else to do, but Leah knew it was more about anxiety, the constant fear of further bad news. She'd become obsessive about answering her phone, too. Would she ever forgive herself for being too busy to pick up Amy's call that afternoon? For assuming she'd have infinite other chances to speak to her? In the months afterwards, she'd kept looking at the record of it on her phone, determined to keep reminding herself, punishing herself – or sometimes just aching to see Amy's name, fantasising that she could tap it and ring her straight back. The day it had disappeared from her call list, pushed off the end by one from a client, had been the day – only last week – that Leah had melted down. Realising the record had been erased had snapped something in her brain. She hadn't cried – still hadn't, not properly – but a curtain of rage had fallen over her.

She'd yelled at a client. The ultimate professional crime. In a meeting, in front of three of her colleagues, including her boss. The same client whose call had elbowed Amy's off the list. He'd been difficult in the meeting, but clients often were, and Leah was normally able to handle them coolly. Not once the fury had swept in, though. It had been a powerful force, and she'd felt the rumble of it again since arriving in Italy, letting her know it was there to be used. But in the right way this time. For the right purpose. Her fist clenched, sand running through her fingers as if through an egg timer, counting her down to something unknown.

'Hello, sweetheart!' her dad answered. 'A pleasant surprise on a rainy Wednesday!' He always named the day of the week when she rang, and usually either the weather or the state of the country. (*On this political disaster of a morning/on this dismal news day . . .*)

'How are you, Dad?'

'Can't complain.' It was a standard phrase. '*E tu?*'

She smiled faintly. He had started learning Italian when Charlotte and Gordon had moved out here, but his pronunciation was terrible.

'I'm . . . well, not exactly . . . not great . . .'

He paused before replying, and when he spoke his voice was gentler. 'Why's that, love?'

Leah recognised his tone with a small jolt. It was the way *she* had spoken to Charlotte during their lunch, when she'd hoped she would open up and had been concerned about frightening her out of it. Was Leah no better at talking about her feelings than her sister? Did she need careful handling, too?

She knew the answer was yes. Maybe the one thing she and Charlotte had in common.

'It's just, being here,' she said, self-consciously. 'It's bringing up a lot of . . . stuff.'

'It's bound to, Lee. Have you been talking to Charlotte about it?'

Leah blinked the film from her eyes. It had never fully occurred to her that her dad was the most open, empathetic one of their family. Such a contrast to Gordon, as a husband and a father. *You're hard on him,* her dad had even said to Leah, once. *He's not so bad, he loves them all, he just doesn't*

always know how to show it. Leah wished she had his ability
to give people the benefit of the doubt.

'We haven't talked much,' she admitted. 'Dad, what was
she like when you came over for Amy's funeral? And
Gordon? I never asked you much about it.'

There was another pause, and what sounded like her
dad's footsteps, as if he was taking the phone into another
room. Leah imagined her mum glancing up from her morning green tea, Dad trying to cushion her from hearing all
this recounted.

'In all honesty, love, it was hard to watch. We were all torn
up, but your sister and Gordon . . . well, each day, we never
quite knew what we were going to get. Some days Mum
and I didn't even see them. We weren't sure whether they
just stayed in their room, not able to face things, or went off
somewhere. They'd reappear the next day and nothing
would be said. Other days, they had these *huge* arguments.'

'What about?'

'Oh, the catering for the funeral. And the "invitation list",
as Gordon kept calling it. How long *Il Mandarino* should
remain closed. Unimportant things, but so volatile. I've
never heard them like that before.'

'Was there a police enquiry going on?'

'They came to talk to Charlotte and Gordon a couple of
times. Why do you ask?'

Leah hesitated, wondering how much to say. What might
it do to her mum and dad, this can of worms she was inch-
ing open? 'No reason. I – I only just learned about Nate . . .'
She left a pause to see if her dad knew the name.

'Ah. The supposed boyfriend.'

Her stomach tightened and she kept running sand through her fingers, faster and faster until the slip of it made her shudder. 'Were the police interested in him?'

'Only briefly. And Charlotte seemed fixated on him at first, too. But Gordon said she had to stop doing it to herself, that it was just an accident, nobody to blame. Charlotte was more settled once she'd accepted that. Of course you look for a scapegoat, even when there isn't one, except . . . well, except *nature* . . .' His voice splintered, and Leah glanced up at the sky, as if challenging it to react to being blamed. Her eyes fell to the small, swaying motorboats that were moored near to the jetty for use by staff, imagining Amy setting out in one that night. She wanted to say: *What if nature wasn't the culprit?* But how could she drop that idea on her dad, from hundreds of miles away?

'I'm sorry I wasn't there to help you cope, Dad.'

'You had some coping of your own to do, Lee. We all do it in different ways.'

Her eyes filled. She scrunched them closed as she asked one last question: 'What about Olivia?'

'What about her?'

'How did *she* cope?'

Leah heard her dad exhale through his nose.

'She was almost silent,' he said, his voice a little thinner. 'And she hardly ate. Mum and I were very worried. But one thing Charlotte and Gordon *did* do, I think, was try their best to protect her. They kept her out of the police's enquiries, never spoke about anything upsetting in front of her. They even sent her to stay with a friend for a few days. Mum and I were unsure about that, we wanted her with us, but we could see the logic of it. Things were very intense at *Il Mandarino* at the time.'

Leah stared at a seagull that had landed near to her, letting it all sink in. Then she heard a foghorn, and looked up to see a ferry creasing the stillness of the lake. She jumped up and dusted sand off her jeans, glancing around to check none of her family had realised she was gone and come rushing down. Leah had asked Matilde to tell Charlotte she was having a lie-in and would catch her at lunch.

Another favour she owed the housekeeper, along with the folded-up address in her pocket, which she touched the corners of again now.

'I've got to go, Dad,' Leah said, 'I'm sorry to rake over all this.'

'I'm glad you're there, Leah. Please give everybody my love. Mum and I are thinking about you all, all of the time.'

'I know,' Leah said, her voice disappearing in the narrowness of her throat.

As the ferry steamed away from the dock, Leah felt as if she was escaping. Just before they rounded the outcrop, the boat accelerated and the wind gushed through her hair, and it was like a moment of release. The square turret of Malcesine's castle poked up on the other side, beckoning her towards it.

Leah eyed her fellow passengers, wondering whether any of them were the guests staying in the big, tree-surrounded villa. Maybe the woman with the linen jacket and slick, cropped hair, whose face was mostly hidden by enormous sunglasses, so that Leah couldn't tell if she was staring back at her or into the distance. Or the young, tanned couple sitting together in silence – her gazing at *Il Mandarino* as it receded, him with his head back and eyes closed, as if he'd had a heavy night.

They all swayed in unison as the ferry did its swerve around the ridge. Then they were clear of its shadow, out onto the main part of the lake where a flurry of other boats appeared. Ahead, the small town of Malcesine was a tumble of multicoloured roofs. Leah had been there a few times with Amy, who had shown her the gelato bars the locals preferred, introducing her to people as they'd eaten the creamiest pistachio ice cream. And once, around eight years ago, Leah and Charlotte had had an unexpectedly lovely day trip there while the girls were still in school. They had climbed up to the castle and sat looking over the sparkling water. *I always used to think if you lived somewhere beautiful you would stop seeing it,* Charlotte had said, *Or that you'd discover all the cracks.* But she hadn't confirmed whether that had proven true.

The ferry docked and the captain tipped his hat at every guest as they disembarked. A few hopeful tourists surged forward to try to board, but were firmly told that the boat was for *Il Mandarino* guests. Only those who could prove they were staying at the resort were ushered on.

Leah drew the piece of paper from her pocket. Matilde had seemed concerned when Leah had caught her alone earlier that morning, and asked whether she knew the address of the party Amy had been heading to on her last night alive. Leah had said she was just trying to make sense of it all, and Matilde had nodded sympathetically, but her brow had wrinkled. Half an hour later, though, she had knocked on Leah's door, handed her the folded note, and scurried away.

Now, as Leah opened it to tap the address into her phone, she noticed something written in faint, tiny writing at the bottom.

Be careful.

Leah's heart juddered. She thought again of the worry in Matilde's eyes as she'd given it to her, folded up tight. Her sudden exit from Amy's room when they'd heard Gordon's raised voice the other day.

She wiped sweat from her forehead, breathed deeply, and keyed in the address. She couldn't turn back, now.

The blue GPS dot came to land on a street near the top of the mountain, round the back of the castle. Leah began the climb upwards, through the morning crowds shuffling in and out of the bakeries; the locals drinking coffee and chattering in the small piazzas. Such a different atmosphere from *Il Mandarino*, yet she still couldn't relax. She climbed faster, soothed by the familiar strain in her calves and lungs.

The map guided her down a cobbled backstreet to a tall house of mustard-coloured stone. Washing hung from the balconies on the top two storeys, flapping in a breeze that Leah couldn't even feel down in the hot, narrow street. She buzzed the third-floor apartment, imagining Amy, in a parallel version of events, pressing this buzzer on the night of the party she'd never reached.

'*Buongiorno?*' came an Italian woman's voice through the intercom.

Leah floundered. Stupidly, despite all her mental preparations, she hadn't considered that the person who lived here was likely to be Italian.

'*Lei parla inglese?*' she asked.

'I do,' came the reply.

'I'm Amy Wynne's aunt,' Leah said into the speaker. 'Do . . . did you know her?'

There was a pause. Then, to her surprise: 'Are you . . . Leah?'

She blinked. 'I am.'

'Leah! I knew you would come!'

'You—?'

The voice became quieter. 'Is it just you? Are you on your own?'

'Yes . . .' Before Leah could fully digest the unexpected greeting, there was a humming noise and the main door was released, to reveal a dim staircase twisting steeply upward.

15

Amy

Last September
Seven hours before sunset

It's hard to explain how I feel about the women I call the Mannequins. On the one hand, of course, the very idea of women hired just to sit around and make a resort look more beautiful appals me. Made even worse by the images I can't get out of my head: my dad, examining their photos, deciding which ones to invite for an interview or a trial. Sometimes he recruits them from modelling agencies; other times he spots them working in restaurants or shops, headhunts them with the promise of easy work, good money, and the prestige of *Il Mandarino*.

I wouldn't find it easy work, and I'm not sure they do, either, once they start. They're positioned around *Il Mandarino* like ornaments or plants, and they sit sipping champagne or the latest signature cocktail, creating the impression that everyone here is stunning. When I was younger, I thought they were all genuine guests. But then I noticed how static they were, and how there always seemed to be more of them whenever a journalist was being shown around or a particularly significant guest was staying.

When I was fourteen, I overheard two of them discussing me. I was wearing a pair of Francesca's dungarees with the shirt from my school football kit underneath. I couldn't stand the clothes Mum bought me anymore. The dresses so uncomfortable, so restrictive, with their tailored shapes and suffocating necklines. I was still going to school, then, so I started changing into clothes my friends would smuggle in for me. I had joined the girls' football team, playing at lunchtimes without telling my parents, and I felt so free running around in the kit, I wondered why I hadn't worn shorts and T-shirts all my life. One day, I decided to test the water by coming home in a red football shirt and Francesca's hand-sewn dungarees. I got some odd looks on the ferry and my confidence diminished with every step along *Il Mandarino*'s white paths. Just before I headed up the last part of the slope towards our villa, I paused to pull myself together. What was the big deal? Why was I so nervous? It was only clothes, only football. Wasn't I old enough to make these choices for myself?

That was when I heard them. Two of the Mannequins passed by, their eyes snagging on my outfit. As they walked off down the hill, I heard one of them whispering, 'I didn't get the memo about Dress Down Day.'

The other hissed back: 'Dress Weird Day, more like. You know she's Gordon's daughter?'

'No way!' I didn't hear anything more, but their scandalised laughter trailed behind them.

Then I saw my mum. She'd appeared from our villa and was standing at the top of the slope. She must've clocked it all: my outfit, my flushed face, the two women's reaction.

As I got closer, her eyebrows were low and her nostrils were flared. Anger, I thought at first. Anger that two employees had made fun of me.

But, no. Quite quickly, I realised it wasn't that.

'What are you *wearing?*' Her voice was shrill. She glanced around and I'm not sure what she was scanning for: Dad? Other guests? Or maybe just reassuring herself that everything else was untainted.

'Come inside, Amy. Whose dungarees are they? Why do you have a football shirt? We've talked about this! When you're moving around the resort, you're representing the family. Come on, quick, before your dad catches you . . .'

I wanted to cry at the time. Especially when, the next morning, the dungarees were gone from my room. The football shirt, too – and then I was off the team because I'd lost my kit. I went back to the uncomfortable dresses in *Il Mandarino* colours for a while. Until my courage crept back, fuelled by a growing anger. I wasn't a kid anymore. Didn't have to be who they wanted me to be. I gritted my teeth against their disapproval, decided I would do my thing and suffer the consequences.

And there have been consequences, sometimes. Big and small.

Occasionally, in the early days, I used to try to talk to the Mannequins. I asked them questions about themselves, wanting to make them three-dimensional, wanting to understand. Some of them seemed to like chatting to me, as long as my parents weren't around. Some edged away or stared past me with their frozen smiles.

Now, it appears that a new recruit has arrived. Hanna. She's still sitting at her table, waiting for Dad, looking increasingly nervous. My heart is heavy because I thought Dad had stopped hiring them. Since *Segreto* opened, Nate's cocktails have created such a buzz that other marketing tactics have shrunk in importance.

'She's a Mannequin, isn't she?' I whisper to Nate. He's the only person who knows I call them that. It's not a nice nickname, I realise. It popped into my head the first time I understood what they were employed to do, and I haven't been able to shake it. I've even dreamed about the Mannequins before. Dreamed they all turned into statues, like the busts on the terrace wall.

Nate doesn't seem to hear me. He's supposed to be making Hanna a coffee but he's just standing with his hand on the plunger of the cafetiere, staring in her direction.

'*Nate*,' I say, and he turns.

'Sorry. What?'

'Do you think she's a new—'

'Yes. I think so.' His eyes dart towards her again.

'Do you know her or something?'

He pulls his attention back to the coffee. 'What? No. I'm just feeling the same thing as you, Aimes. Disappointed that this . . . approach seems to be back on.'

I nod, trying to console myself with the knowledge that I'll be gone from this place by sunset tonight. Nate takes Hanna her coffee and I watch her look up at him through her lashes. He speaks and her smile wavers, then her lips move briefly, but I can't tell what's being said. Something cold and bitter swirls inside me. I can't tell if it's jealousy again, or anxiety, or just that familiar, pervading sense of wrongness, like a low dose of toxicity in the air.

Whatever it is, it makes the pressure rise inside my skull. Sometimes, when I feel this way, I sail out onto the lake and yell. Sometimes I drink a Dark and Stormy so fast it makes my head whirl. Once – just once – I got into the water fully clothed, put my face under the surface and imagined what it would feel like to flood my lungs.

Right now, I vault onto the bar, spin across the polished wood on my bum, and land behind it with a satisfying thud. I unplug the company iPad from the sound system and the jazz cuts out. Attaching my phone instead, I scroll for the right song to blast apart the tension between my ears.

'Amy!' Nate reappears, looking concerned. 'What are you doing?'

'I want to dance.'

'*Now?*'

'Yes. I just need to . . .' I raise my hands and shake them in the air, hoping he'll understand.

'You're going to land me in trouble.' He's trying to sound playful but I can tell he's worried. He glances over his shoulder towards where Hanna is sitting, drinking her coffee. I pull him around to the other side of the bar, shielded from her view.

'Just one song,' I promise, hitting play and feeling the rush of a Patti Smith intro, its instant intensity.

I grab Nate's hands and urge him to dance with me. He shifts us away from the CCTV camera and then gives in, head-banging to the fast chorus with his curly mop. I flail my limbs and feel breathless, released, but I also get a surge of frustration that this is as far as our relationship ever goes. Conversation and music; swapping books and debating them over texts, or over the bar when it's quiet; contenting ourselves with an exchange of private smiles when it's busy. Even on Nate's days off, when we manage to sneak away for hikes in the mountains, there's a charge between us but nothing ever happens. And I'm never sure whether it's me or him who's hesitating.

As the music sweeps me up and spins me round, a sense of recklessness blooms. Why not make something happen, today, before I go? A goodbye kiss, or more . . . something we can both think about when I'm in Edinburgh studying and Nate is still here. My blood flares at the thought. I have almost no experience with men. He's the first one who's ever interested me, or understood me. Who doesn't just find my politics 'endearing' or my hot-headedness 'cute' – who actually cares what I think.

When he first started working here, I avoided him. People employed by my parents make me uneasy. But one day, I'd had a fight with Olivia and I wanted a drink, so I came to *Segreto* and sat morosely at the bar, reading a sociology book called *The Fear of Freedom*. An apt name, maybe, but also an intriguing one, it seems, because Nate sidled over during a quiet spell and asked me about it. Looking back, I'm sure he sensed I was unhappy. Asking about the book was a way to get me talking, and it set a precedent for our friendship: book chat leads the way, while more personal topics creep in around the sides.

Halfway through Patti's last chorus, I come over light-headed, and wobble into a shelf of champagne glasses.

'Shit!' I say, as one flies over the bar and shatters on the flagstones beyond. Nate starts hunting around for a sweeping brush and I realise I've cut my finger, that blood is running down my arm. He dives back towards me, wrapping my hand in a tea towel, his arm around my shoulders like a concerned big brother.

Then a shout cuts through the confusion: 'WHAT ON EARTH ARE YOU DOING?'

Nate drops my hand and springs back. I turn, clutching the red-stained tea towel. My dad is weaving through the tables and chairs, but the umbrellas aren't shaking like they did when Olivia rushed among them. Everything is still. The song tails off into silence. Dad stares at the smashed glass on the ground, then brings his gaze up to settle on us.

'That *isn't* on the approved playlist.'

He looks at my cut, still oozing blood. I've spattered scarlet onto the mahogany bar and onto the sliced limes that are lying, glistening, on a chopping board.

Dad steps closer. I notice he's holding a slim, black box, like a jewellery or a watch box, embossed with the word BROOKMYRE in elegant silver letters.

He jabs a finger at Nate with his other hand. 'I shouldn't need to remind you that there is important stuff happening here today. Everything needs to be in perfect, *professional* order. And *you* . . .' He stares at me as if he can't even summarise all the shoulds and should-nots that I'm associated with.

I want to grab Nate's hand defiantly. Want to keep dancing, and kiss him right in front of my dad, just to see his reaction. The only thing that stops me is how much I care about Nate. I know he needs this job, needs the money, feels settled here in Lake Garda for the first time in his life. He said once, on one of our hikes: *Money isn't everything, Aimes, but after some of the wages I've survived on in the past, it's nice to be able to afford my own apartment, rather than just a grotty room.* Something unspoken wedged between us: an awareness that *I* could have real luxury and comfort if I wanted. I could have the lifestyle of my parents, or the people Nate serves at *Segreto*, but I'm choosing to shun it. For a second, then, I wondered whether he resents me just a little, for the fact that I do have an alternative option.

It doesn't feel like an option, though. Not for me. And Nate gets that, I know he does. In return, I can't ruin the life he's made his peace with.

So I catch my breath, stare back at my dad, and wait for the rush of fondness and forgiveness that I've felt towards everybody else today. Wait to be reminded of the better times, the boat trips and beach days when Olivia and I were small, how he tried to get us excited about this place, tried to make it something we could share. But the feeling doesn't come, and I'm left with a rock in my stomach. All I remember is sensing, even then – even as he flew kites with us and taught us Italian words – that we weren't living up to whatever he'd envisaged.

He was trying to recreate his own summers in Italy from when he was younger, I think. He used to get packed off to stay with some professor friend of his dad's – 'sent out from under my parents' feet,' I've heard him say, but actually, from what I can make out, he became obsessed with this other family he used to spend the holidays with. Sometimes he gets the photos out: the pristine kids and the pearl-draped mum and the pin-striped father. It's as if he built *Il Mandarino* as a shrine to those people, those summers, a life he glimpsed and coveted. And it snowballed from there: higher standards and loftier ambitions.

'Get that cleaned up, Amy,' he says now, and I can't tell if he means my cut or the smashed glass. 'Are you badly injured?' For a second there's a dent in his anger, a softening, but then he's distracted again, looking around. 'Where's Hanna?'

I shuffle to the other side of the circular bar, frowning at the table where she was sitting. Empty, now. Just an abandoned coffee cup. 'She . . .'

'The girl who was waiting for me,' Dad says, two spots of angry puce reappearing in his cheeks. '*Where* is she?'

I look to Nate. He's come out from behind the bar and is sweeping up the broken glass, eyes fixed to the floor as the shards clink.

'She was sitting there . . .' I say, pointing.

'Well, she's not there, now, is she?' Dad says. 'Why did you let her leave?'

'*Let* her?'

'Did you say something to her?'

'No!' I think of Nate murmuring to her as he delivered her coffee. At what point did she leave?

'I'll have to check the CCTV.' Dad pushes a hand through his waxy black hair, then looks down at the box he's holding. 'Bloody hell. This *cannot* happen today.'

The thought of him checking the cameras for Hanna's whereabouts makes me twitch.

'Just let her go, if she wants to leave,' I say. 'Who can blame her?'

Dad glares at me. Nate stops sweeping and stands with the dustpan full of sparkly glass.

Then Dad lets out a strange little laugh. 'What would you know about what she wants?' he says to me, 'Or who to *blame*?'

His eyes move to Nate and linger there, while Nate shifts uncomfortably, unable to meet the directness of his gaze. Without even dropping his eyes, Dad points out a rogue sliver of glass on the bar top before striding away.

16

Joanna

Joanna smelled curry as she was chaining up her bike. She automatically assumed it was coming from a neighbour's house, but as she walked towards her red front door, the scent of onions and spices got stronger. For once, hers was the house with the lights on, the dinner already cooking.

The unfamiliar silhouette at the kitchen window.

Bracing herself, she walked in. The curry smell pervaded the whole house, her taste buds stirring reflexively. It was both welcome and disconcerting, a comfort and an invasion.

'Hello!' sailed out Callum's voice, as she leafed through the post he'd stacked on the hall table. She called back a greeting and imagined the neighbours hearing conversation from her side of the wall for once, not just the sound of Absolute Radio 90s.

Her small kitchen sizzled with cooking. Callum was turning naans under the grill with one hand, supporting his ribs with the other.

'Wow,' she said. 'Are you . . . do you want me to do that?'

He straightened up stiffly. 'Done! Hope you don't mind. I saw you had spices and stuff in the cupboard, and I managed to hobble to the corner shop for some other bits.'

'Smells good,' she said, dismissing a fleeting worry about whether he should be cooking on strong drugs.

'Least I could do. It's just soft vegetables in the curry, though – don't think my jaw can handle meat yet.'

Joanna kicked off her shoes and poured herself a glass of water. They moved around each other in the suddenly narrowed space, a scene of tentative domesticity. He'd used all the wrong pans, she saw. The ones she never used. He'd dug out spices from the very back of her cupboard that were probably years out of date.

For something to do, she got out plates and cutlery. Should they sit at the table or eat in front of the TV? A laid table would create the atmosphere of a date. Would that only ramp up the strangeness?

'How are you feeling?' she asked him, looking sidelong at his healing bruises.

'Not too bad. A bit sore. Sometimes woozy from the pills.'

'Did you speak to your landlady about your things?'

'Yeah, she's going to send them over tomorrow.'

'I can go and pick them up.'

'No,' he said firmly. 'Thanks, Jo. You've done plenty already. I feel like I'm taking advantage of the fact that you're probably the kindest person I've ever met.'

Despite everything, warmth unfurled in her belly. It wasn't the words exactly, but the way he had said them. As if being kind genuinely *was* a positive quality. Sometimes, she felt kindness became equated with weakness. And maybe it was true, maybe that was why she'd ended up with a man she hardly knew in her house. But she could stand up for herself when she needed to. She liked helping people, what was wrong with that? And seeing the best in people: another charge that had been lobbied at her in the past, like an accusation.

During her reverie, she realised she had laid the table. Two plates, two sets of cutlery, two of her favourite wine glasses – checking for the ones without chips in the rim. So, decision made, it seemed.

'I'm just going to get changed,' she said, flustered again.

She ran upstairs to her bedroom. Without quite knowing why, she looked around to check whether anything had been moved, and opened her jewellery box to confirm that the emerald earrings she'd inherited from her grandma were still there. *So much for seeing the best in people,* she thought, feeling like a fraud.

She wiped her face, changed into her favourite stripy shirt dress, put on some fresh deodorant and a slick of lip gloss. All her actions were contrary. Wanting to look nice for him in almost the same instant as she was checking if he had stolen from her. She headed back down to find him still in the kitchen, leaning on her worktop. His clothes appeared almost clean. He must have attempted to scrub out the stains that afternoon. The remaining patches of dirt and blood strummed her sympathy, made her feel protective towards him all over again.

Then she noticed he was looking at her phone, which she'd dropped habitually onto the side when she'd got in from work. The screen was lit and she could see the grinning faces of her nephews, her screensaver. As she approached, he swung away from it, moving to drain the rice.

'Sorry, I was just checking the time,' he said. 'Cute kids, though – are they your brother's? The one who lives in Leeds?'

'Uh . . . that's right.' Joanna snatched it up and imagined her nephews, beaming out, somehow able to see the unfamiliar face peering back. She tried to consider whether she would prod her friends' phones like that. Even she and Luke had generally left each other's mobiles alone, like some unspoken rule of privacy.

There were message notifications on the screen. She unlocked it and scanned a text from her mum – **just checking in, was your day okay? Xxx** – then jolted as she saw Luke's name underneath. The name that used to pop up daily, asking if they needed anything from the shop, suggesting evening plans, sending her memes and kisses. Now it was like a small bomb in her inbox. Three words: **Can we talk?**

She tapped sharply back to the home screen. She couldn't deal with it now. Her temples ached as if they agreed: *At capacity. Don't let this in.*

She poured some wine and sat down. Then she realised Callum was struggling with the wok full of curry, and sprang up to take it from him. She helped him get comfortable at his seat at the table, both of them laughing as she pushed him in as if he was one of her nephews.

Callum raised his glass. 'Well, this is all a bit weird,' he said, 'but kind of . . . nice?'

If only he knew how many times she had swung between those two perspectives.

★   ★   ★

After dinner, emboldened by wine, Joanna shoved their plates into the sink and spun back to face her house guest.

'I have an idea,' she said.

He looked at her with raised eyebrows.

'Let's find out a bit more about each other,' she went on, secretly thinking, *let me find out a bit more about you.* 'I get to ask you a question, you ask me one, and so on. And we have to be honest.'

'That . . . sounds interesting.'

Deciding they needed another drink for this, Joanna grabbed a bottle of gin out of the cupboard, and two little cans of tonic from the fridge.

'Have you got any limes?' Callum piped up over her shoulder. 'Sorry, it's the barman in me.'

'I think I have . . .' Joanna peered into the fridge.

'Ice?' He moved towards the freezer.

'Yes, there's some in there,' she said, and he opened it and got out a bag.

Before she knew it he was slicing the limes, squeezing juice over the ice cubes, measuring out the perfect amounts of tonic and gin. She stepped back to leave him to it, and he apologised for taking over, for treating it like an art form.

'Not a problem,' she said, trying a sip. It was, in fact, the best gin and tonic she'd ever had, but she resisted a second gulp too soon. She needed to be the right balance of sober and tipsy. Courageous but in control. Callum wasn't drinking much because of his medication, so she'd had twice as much wine as him at dinner, her nerves causing her to reach too often for her glass.

They sat at the table, facing each other like chess opponents.

'What were you doing before you came to Derby?' she asked.

He paused.

'You have to answer straight away,' she said, attempting to sound light-hearted. 'That's one of the rules of the game.'

'Are there forfeits if we hesitate?'

She forced a laugh. 'Maybe. I'm making up the rules as I go along.'

'I was bartending in Italy.'

'Why did you leave?'

'Isn't it my turn to ask a question now?'

She nodded, conceding, though it felt agonising to wait for her next turn.

'Have *you* ever been to Italy?' he asked.

The mundane question was a relief. And the answer was easy – Joanna shook her head. 'I always wanted to. That's why I started learning Italian. But I've still never been.'

He looked surprised. 'I'd say we should go, but . . .' He trailed off, and Joanna was left unsure what the 'but' signified.

She edged forward. 'What made you leave?'

'A . . . misunderstanding.'

Though prompt, his answer was exasperatingly brief. But she hadn't laid down any rules about comprehensive replies, after all.

'Where was the last place you went abroad?' he asked.

'Are all your questions going to be on this theme?'

He laughed. 'I'm just saying them as they occur to me. And you haven't answered!'

Her grin faded. 'Croatia. I got engaged there. We broke up a few months ago.'

'I'm sorry.'

She shrugged, pressing her lips together and thinking of the transparent Croatian sea. They'd swum in it one night, bellies full from dinner, shoulders sunburnt from a lazy day. Joanna had touched her new engagement ring under the water and felt so happy it had made her guilty, like she was being greedy with too much joy.

Blinking back into the room, she saw Callum watching her with interest, as if trying to tap into her memory.

'Did you have . . . someone?' she deflected, 'in Italy?'

He stared at the table. 'Sort of. I suppose, if I'm being truthful—'

'Which is the whole point!'

He nodded, swirling his drink. 'I suppose she was the real reason I left.'

'So, we're both kind of in the same boat,' Joanna murmured.

'Yes.' Now he was the one who seemed to go elsewhere, staring into his clinking ice cubes and the riled-up whirlpool of tonic.

Joanna was on her second gin – Callum still on his first – by the time the 'game' started to fizzle out. She could hardly tell whether she knew much more about him than when they'd started. She *felt* closer to him, but perhaps the alcohol was creating that illusion. Or the fact that they had moved onto the living room sofa, their legs almost touching, Callum making shy jokes about how this was actually his bed, and could she be careful not to slosh gin onto his pillows?

She'd learned this much: his life in Italy had fallen to pieces. He was picking himself up and putting himself back together, just as she'd been doing these last few months. And it seemed to make sense, all of a sudden, that he'd ended up in her home. They'd been drawn towards one another because they were both a bit lost. Callum's accident had only made him more so. A little voice in her head warned her not to get carried away with this line of thought – she had a tendency to romanticise things when she'd had a drink.

'One last question each,' Joanna said.

'It's your go, I think.'

She tapped her chin in thought. It was tempting to ask something playful, almost flirtatious. The mood seemed to be teetering between light and heavy, and part of her wanted to tip it towards the former. But a sober part remembered why she was doing this. 'Do you really believe it was your own fault you got hit by that car?'

At the mention of his accident, the atmosphere sank.

There was a long pause as he rolled his glass in his hands. 'What's the alternative?'

'The alternative?' She thought he was requesting an alternative question, and was about to drunkenly reinforce her made-up rules.

'The alternative is thinking someone ran me over deliberately.'

'Oh.' She shivered a little. Callum's jaw looked clamped, reminding her of when he'd been in the ICU and could hardly move it.

'I'd rather blame my carelessness than someone else's . . . malice?' The word landed between them, making Joanna flinch. He let out a small laugh, clearly trying to break the tension that had descended, but the noise was brittle. 'I don't want to be reminded that not everyone's as nice as you!'

Joanna laughed along, but unease budded inside her. His references to her kindness were starting to feel like a diversion tactic. 'I'm no angel.'

'Okay, well, you've just walked straight into my final question.'

'Which is?'

'Have you ever done anything you regret?'

She was caught off guard. He arched one eyebrow like an extra question mark, but there was something shuttered about his face. Where had that question come from? It was different from all the others they'd been asking. Less specific but somehow more personal.

'Everybody has regrets,' she said.

'True.'

'Have you?'

'I'm in the question seat!'

She held up her palms. 'Well, of course I've done things I wish I hadn't. Fibs here and there. Putting my foot in it . . .' She was aware of saying generic things, while an alternative reel of answers ran through her head. Did she regret not fighting harder for her and Luke? Or the opposite

– letting him get away with walking out on her, leaving her doubting everything about her life. What about regrets at work? Different decisions she should have made?

Callum was watching her again. Then he looked away and drained his gin. 'That was a mean question,' he said, allowing her to stop babbling. 'Sorry.' He grinned and she smiled back uncertainly, glad of the reprieve yet wishing she could've heard him answer the same thing.

'Bedtime,' she said, rubbing her goose-pimpled arms. Neither of them moved for a moment, then she hauled herself to her feet.

He stood up, too, and she wrestled with the sofa to extend it into a low bed.

'Thanks,' he said. 'Well . . . goodnight.'

There was a charge in the air as they looked at each other over the top of Callum's temporary bed. They caught each other's eyes as if to say, *Are we definitely going to part ways?* Joanna's heart quickened. Some potent combination of alcohol, confusion and attraction was trying to convince her that the whole situation was more exciting than unnerving. That it had all been leading up to something that might be on the cusp of going ahead.

But the sensible voice in her head spoke up.

Yes, we are going to part ways. We should.

She felt Callum's eyes on her as she locked the front door and slid the chain across, sealing the night out and the two of them in.

17

Leah

Francesca had vivid pink hair cut into a blunt bob with a fringe. Her tortoiseshell glasses dominated her freckled face, and she wore sky blue dungarees. She kissed Leah on both cheeks, then pulled her into the apartment at the top of the stairs as if drawing her into a private club. It had lime green walls and pale floorboards made up of tessellating chevrons. Francesca invited Leah to sit on the wood-framed sofa while she poured glasses of orange juice in the kitchen.

'My parents are at work and my sister is out with her friends,' she said, joining Leah. 'Which is good. We can talk.' She glanced at the window as if somebody might still be listening in, then handed Leah her drink.

'Sorry to intrude,' Leah said.

'Not at all. Amy talked about you often. And I have been desperately wanting to talk to you, too, since – since what happened. It has been so confusing. I even tried to track you down, but I didn't know your last name, didn't know where to start.'

Yet again, guilt sank through Leah's core. For not being around. Not realising that Amy needed her in death as well as in life. So far, she had failed her in both.

'Confusing?'

'*Nobody* wanted to listen,' Francesca said. 'Even her parents . . .' She glanced at Leah, as if to gauge how much she could say.

'It's okay. My relationship with them . . . it's complicated.' There was a pang in her chest as she admitted it aloud.

Francesca nodded, her pink hair falling from behind her ears.

'Were you the one who organised the alternative memorial for Amy?' Leah asked.

'I helped.'

'Weren't Amy's friends invited to the actual funeral?'

'We were. But we did not feel *encouraged* to go. And we knew she would not have wanted something so . . . what is the word in English . . .?' She mimed an uptight posture, lifting her nose into the air.

'Stuffy?' Leah suggested.

Francesca smiled. 'Maybe. I don't know this word either.'

'The opposite of Amy.'

'Yes!' Francesca clapped her palms onto her knees. 'Exactly. We had her favourite foods and music. People from the cafes and shops gave things. I have photos, you can have them if you like.'

'Thank you,' Leah said, glad that Amy had had a friend like Francesca. She reminded her of one of her own colleagues, Katya, whom Leah often thought she should make more effort to get to know outside of work, without ever doing anything about it. She'd become even more anti-social since Amy had died, and sometimes wondered if she used it as an excuse, even to herself, a reason to duck out of parties and dates.

It had been Katya who'd encouraged her to come here, in fact, when she'd spotted Leah in their staff lounge, head in hands, after being put on enforced compassionate leave. Leah's guard had been down – as much as it ever was – and she'd ended up telling Katya almost everything. About Amy's death, about not attending the funeral, about the unanswered call that still haunted her. And the anger she'd unleashed on that client – how good it had felt in the moment; how horrified she'd been straight afterwards.

If Katya had judged her, she'd done a good job of hiding it.

Well, now you have the chance to go to Italy, see your family, she'd said. *Use this time off to make things right, then come back and be the awesome, rarely-yells-at-clients lawyer that you are!*

Leah had laughed, in spite of everything. Katya had made it sound so simple. Now it felt as if her whole reason for being here was changing, spiralling.

She leaned towards Francesca. 'You said you didn't feel listened to after Amy died?'

Francesca looked down. 'It was as if everybody had already decided what happened to her.'

Leah's heart began to thump. 'Do *you* know what happened to her?'

'I wish I did.'

'You think it was different from the official version?'

'There are things wrong with that story.'

Leah sat forward, her pulse jumping through her like a bassline. Such a simple sentence, but it was the first time anybody had articulated it, admitted it outright. *There are things wrong with that story.* Yes, there were, there really were.

'Tell me everything. Please. You can trust me.'

Francesca took a long drink of her juice. 'Well. The first thing is, Amy was not coming to my party.'

'*Was* there a party?'

'A small one, for my birthday.'

'Amy died on your birthday?'

'Yes,' Francesca said, the corners of her mouth turning downward. 'I won't celebrate it again. Not the same, anyway.'

'Why wasn't Amy coming?'

'She was going to. But then she called me . . . to say goodbye.'

'Goodbye?' A high ringing began in Leah's ears, triggered by the word, its finality.

'She was . . .' Francesca drummed her chin, searching for the right vocab. 'Vague? She said she was sorry, she could not come to my party. She wanted to say goodbye and she loved me. And not to worry. I could not get her to say any more.'

'What the hell?' Leah found herself on her feet, glancing agitatedly around the room. 'What do you think she meant? Goodbye . . .' Its connotations rose up on all sides, closing her in. Had Amy been wanting to say goodbye to her, too? Was that what the call had been about? Not just one of their regular chats, which would've turned out to be their last if Leah had answered. That idea had tortured her enough, but now there was another possibility, a horrifying one . . . Had Amy somehow known she was going to die?

'She tried to call me too, that afternoon,' Leah choked

out. 'I just thought it was a normal call. I was busy at work. I felt so guilty, later. But you don't think she meant . . . She wasn't going to . . .?'

'Kill herself?' Francesca dropped to a whisper, briefly closing her eyes. 'I did think of that, of course, afterwards. But I don't believe that was what she was trying to say.'

Leah covered her face. Hiding again. Wanting the truth but not, apparently, if it was too unpalatable. She sat down and brought her hands down, too, trapping them between her knees.

'I think she was going away,' Francesca said. 'She had wanted to for so long.'

'Really?' This theory seemed almost as crushing. That Amy had planned a future for herself, planned to launch it on the night she'd died. 'Where?'

'I don't know. I thought maybe to stay with our friend Melina in Florence, but Melina says not.'

'Did you tell this to the police?'

'Yes. And to Gordon and Charlotte.'

'You told them Amy wasn't coming here? That she called you?'

Francesca nodded, her eyes huge. 'They came to see me, separately, asking about that day. I told them everything I told the police. Then *Il Mandarino* released a . . . a statement?' She glanced at Leah to check it was the correct word, and Leah nodded, breathless. 'It said Amy was coming to my party and got caught in the storm. The verdict was accidental drowning. The investigation was closed.'

'That's crazy.' Leah sat back, stunned. 'Why would they discount what you said?'

'Discount?'

'Ignore. Dismiss . . .' Leah grew panicked, angry, as she grappled for more synonyms.

Francesca's shrug was heavy. 'I tried to speak to Charlotte and Gordon again, but they told me I'd got it wrong. Even Olivia would not listen. She used to be good friends with my younger sister, but she seems different, now. Very . . .' She made a tunnel-vision gesture with her hands either side of her face.

Leah couldn't speak. A whole new pitch of alarm was vibrating inside her skull, shaking up her already whirling thoughts. Her eyes moved to a framed photo on top of a nearby cabinet: Francesca and a younger girl who must've been her sister. She looked around the same age as Olivia, yet worlds apart: wearing a floppy hat, face streaked with white sun cream, linking her sister's arm and grinning. Leah was caught by another blast of sadness, though she didn't know if it was for Olivia and Amy, or for Charlotte and herself. As if both sisterly relationships had become something to grieve.

She whipped back to Francesca. 'What about Nate?' His curly ponytail and tanned face loomed back into her mind. The photo of him and Amy, covered in the smudges of fingerprints.

Francesca sighed as if she'd agonised over this. 'Witnesses said they saw him and Amy that night, arguing at *Il Mandarino*. I don't know who, or whether it was true, but social media went *crazy* with it. Trolls, hashtags, everything. But he was never arrested. It all went away after a while, but Nate had already gone.'

'Did you like him?'

'I didn't know him, really. He was Amy's friend, separate from the rest of us. Sometimes we would go to the cocktail bar, and he was polite, friendly. A bit distant, but maybe because he was working. We did not go very often – Gordon didn't like us gathering, being loud around the guests . . . We *can* be kind of loud.' She smiled mistily. 'So, we never got to know him much. But I could tell Amy liked him.'

'Just as a friend?'

'I was never sure. It was not like Amy to be secretive, but she was a little, about him. But honestly, Leah . . . most days I do not know *what* to believe. I drive myself crazy.'

Leah stared at the chevrons in the floor. 'I don't know what to think, either. For the last few months I've been trying not to think about it all. Like a total coward.'

'You're not leaving soon, are you?'

'Well, I . . .' Leah raised her head. Her flight home was less than three days away.

Francesca grabbed her hand. 'Please stay. Help me.'

'I – I don't know if . . . I don't know how much help I can be.'

'A lot. I know it.'

Leah felt so many things as Francesca's fingers gripped hers. Guilty. Afraid. Desperately sad and yet ignited, determination flickering higher inside her.

She *could* extend her trip. After all, she had no job to rush back to for another fortnight, at least – even though, when she'd first told Charlotte she was coming, she'd implied they couldn't spare her for long. She'd been reluctant to stay for more than a week, reluctant to admit what had happened at work. Now the idea of a prolonged visit was even more daunting. Yet how could she leave?

'I'll stay,' she said to Francesca. 'I'll stay.'

Francesca's other palm went to her chest. 'Thank you.'

'We'll keep in touch.' Leah glanced at the clock on the wall. 'But now I'd better get back. They'll be wondering where I've gone.'

Francesca stood, pushing her glasses up her nose. 'I will fetch the photos of the memorial for you. And . . .' She paused, biting her lip, her face suddenly pinched, frightened.

Leah straightened in her seat. 'What is it? Francesca?'

'There's something else.'

Francesca hurried out of the room and Leah waited in the silence, retrieving her orange juice to flood the dryness of her mouth. Her mind was reeling. Why would Amy's own family – *Leah*'s family – ignore or suppress the full facts? Why would the police not follow up on discrepancies in the reported events? It all brought a rising sense of dread, like water creeping up around her neck.

It took her a moment to realise Francesca was back. She'd taken off her glasses and her eyes looked small.

'Are you okay?' Leah asked.

Francesca held up a white envelope. Leah could see the colours and outlines of photographs inside.

'There's a SIM card in here, too,' Francesca said, her voice low. 'My old SIM card. Listen to the voicemail on it.' Her words stalled and the envelope quivered. 'I can't bear to hear it again. I listened to it over and over when she first . . .'

'Is it from Amy?'

Francesca nodded. 'She tried to call me again. Later that night.'

'To say what?'

'Just listen to it.' Tears pooled in Francesca's eyes, shining in the light. 'But don't show anybody else. I don't think they know I kept it. I think they thought I'd given up. But I didn't give up, I just didn't know what else to do. But now . . . now you're here.' She stepped forward, pressing the envelope into Leah's hands.

Leah tried to nod, to say something, but her head was floating and her mouth was seized up with fear.

18

Joanna

In the midst of everything, Joanna had forgotten she had a drink with Mandy scheduled for Thursday evening. By the time she noticed it in her diary, it was too late to wriggle out of it.

She could hear Callum watching TV downstairs as she was getting ready. Her mind kept going back over last night's 'game', back over that charged moment when they'd said goodnight. She was glad of her restraint, now. She'd woken under a shadow of renewed doubt, with Callum's final question on repeat inside her brain. *Have you ever done anything you regret?*

Now her phone glowed with a message from Mandy.

Tim's giving me a lift into town before the kids' bedtime. We can pick you up.

Joanna panicked. She didn't want Mandy to see that she had a man living with her, a man she hadn't mentioned to anybody in her life. It wasn't worth the interrogation that would follow. *And it would definitely get back to Luke,* a small voice in her head added, unsure whether that was a good or a bad thing. Joanna still hadn't replied to his can-we-talk text. She'd been shoving it out of her thoughts every time it tried to invade.

No don't worry, she replied to Mandy, **I feel like walking.**

The reply came instantly: **In this heat! We'll get you at 7. Xx**

Joanna tapped frantically, making several mistakes which took her longer to correct than if she'd just typed at normal speed. **Honestly, it's fine, it's out of your way. Xx**

Not really! The kids would love to see you briefly too! x

Joanna swore under her breath. She would just have to be outside when they arrived, make sure Mandy didn't come into the house.

Downstairs, she found Callum sitting on the sofa, frowning at his mobile. She remembered catching him peering at hers and felt another echo of unease. His had a crack across its screen, now – another casualty of his hit and run. Joanna wondered about the network of his life outside of here. Was he texting his mum? The woman he'd left behind in Italy?

He put it away as he noticed her. 'Wow, you look great!'

Joanna smiled self-consciously. Her perfume seemed too strong now she was down here, without the diluting smells of her shower products and candles. She felt too dressed up, all wrong. Unsure again about leaving Callum here alone.

Realising it was almost seven o'clock, she grabbed her handbag. 'I'm going to wait outside for my lift.'

He looked surprised. The standard behaviour, of course, was to wait *inside* for a knock, a text, a friendly horn-beep. But Joanna didn't want to risk it. Mandy's well-trained eyes would spot Callum's Converse in the hall – sent over by his

landlady while Joanna had been at work, along with a small
bag of clean clothes. Her nose would detect a male scent,
like a tracker dog.

'Have a good time!' Callum called.

Hearing a car engine, she dived outside and tugged the
door shut behind her.

'Someone's desperate for a drink,' Mandy said, as Joanna
reached the car before Tim had even finished parking.

Luke's niece and nephew grinned at her from the back
seat, dressed in onesies, excited to see her.

Nights with Mandy were never relaxing. She had intense
opinions about everything, and always wanted Joanna to
share more than she felt comfortable with, as if to force a
confidence between them. Tonight felt even more so.
Joanna spent the whole time swerving certain subjects,
trying to answer Mandy's questions without directly telling lies.

'Have you been dating?' Mandy asked at one point. When
Joanna said no, Mandy's expression was a study of
understanding.

There was no mention of Luke's text, which surprised
Joanna. Mandy usually knew what was going on where her
brother was concerned – somehow she wheedled things out
of him. The fact that he hadn't told her he'd been in touch
with Joanna gave his text extra gravitas. Luke tended to
keep the big things to himself. He'd even kept them from
Joanna, sometimes, when they'd been together. Part of the
shock of breaking up had been the realisation that she
hadn't known him as well as she'd thought.

There were hints from Mandy that Luke wasn't doing too well. She mentioned that his date had been a non-starter, which Joanna was guiltily glad to hear, but also that he'd 'gone a bit quiet'. Joanna's concern was piqued. She remembered Luke's withdrawal in the last few months of their relationship. He'd always been such a sociable person that it had been a marked change, but one he'd brushed off with claims of needing to focus on his work and doing up their new house. What would be his excuse now? Was his business still hectic, did he still fill his life with projects and plans, or had his deflation continued?

He's not yours to worry about anymore, she told herself, with a pang, summoning the willpower to change the subject.

At the end of the night, they got separate taxis home. Mandy hugged her tightly, making her promise they would never stop being friends, and Joanna felt a rush of affection for her, even though she'd spent most of the evening willing it to be over.

'Of course we'll always be friends,' she said recklessly, not knowing whether it was a promise she could stick to.

In the taxi, her mind swung between Luke and Callum, as if they were the two men in her life – which she supposed they were, in a warped kind of way. She thought again about the conversation she and Callum had had last night. *I'd rather blame my carelessness than someone else's malice,* she remembered him saying, when she'd questioned whether he truly thought the accident was his fault.

Something still didn't feel right to her. Something about the police having no leads, Callum not wanting to dwell on the details, the fact that everybody except her seemed happy to write it off as an unfortunate incident.

Impulsively, as her taxi passed The Last Junction, she leaned forward to the driver: 'Please could you drop me here?'

Then she was standing on the pavement in front of the pub, half-surprised to find herself there.

Okay. Right. What now?

She stepped inside. It was 11.15 and the place was unexpectedly full. She'd imagined it lifeless after commuter hour. It was mostly men over fifty, she noticed, feeling conspicuous as she wove through the drinking crowds in her wrap-around skirt and bright pink camisole top.

She recognised the man behind the bar from previous visits, before she'd met Callum. He gave off an air of authority, as if he was the manager or the owner. Joanna pushed down her nerves as she walked towards him.

'Yes please, love?'

She faltered, but he didn't bat an eyelid, clearly used to people approaching the bar without having decided what they wanted to drink. His expression changed when she said, 'Could I talk to you about Callum Foley's hit and run?'

'Sorry, what?'

She regretted launching in with such a dramatic phrase, attracting glances from people nearby. She lowered her voice, flattening her palms on the sticky bar. 'Callum Foley, one of your bar staff?'

'I know Callum, yeah. The new guy.'

'The police haven't got very far in investigating who ran him over,' Joanna said. 'I thought I'd just check what they've said to you? It might've been someone who'd been drinking in here that night. Do you have cameras outside?'

His face was a cloud of bafflement. She realised he must be wondering who she was and why the hell she was doing the questioning. As she tried to explain, the man cut her off.

'Sorry, love – you said *hit and run*?'

She felt the first chills of unease. A sense that she'd made a faux pas or a misstep, but without a clue what it was. 'Yes . . . after his shift last Sunday?'

He stared at her. Joanna wondered if her expression mirrored his.

'I knew he'd been in some kind of car accident,' the man eventually said, 'but he didn't say anything about a hit and run. I didn't realise it was that serious.'

Shit. She hadn't even considered the possibility that Callum might've kept the details of his accident from his employer. Why would he? And how?

'And as far as I know,' the man added, 'he wasn't even working on Sunday.'

Joanna reeled at that. 'Are you sure? He must've been.'

The man turned around and peered at what looked like a rota, pinned up behind the bar. 'He worked Friday and Saturday last weekend. Not Sunday. Then he phoned on Monday and said he'd had a prang in a car, needed some time off but he was okay.' He frowned, looking closely at her. 'Is there something more I should know?'

'No . . .' Joanna's head swam. 'He *is* okay. Sort of. And it *was* a car accident . . .' Again she was going to add 'sort of', but her confusion made her trail off.

'What's all this about a hit and run? Outside here? Wouldn't the police have spoken to me?'

'So, they haven't?'

'No.' The man's frown was deep. Other customers were left hanging, waiting to be served.

'Ignore me,' Joanna said, starting to back away. 'I got mixed up.'

'Maybe I should speak to him.'

'No, no, it's my mistake. Honestly, forget I said anything.'

She turned and rushed out of the pub. As the night air hit her skin, she was racked with shivers. She rubbed her arms, replaying the conversation, thinking of the man in her house down the road, with the fading imprints of two black eyes. Who had he lied to, and why?

19

Leah

The heat was even more oppressive as Leah left Francesca's flat. It steamed off the cobbles and seemed to coil around her in the narrowness of the street. Two women chatted on opposite balconies, their lively Italian voices criss-crossing above her head. Leah walked as quickly as her hot, swollen feet would allow, feeling as if her brain was on fire.

She slipped her hand inside her shoulder bag and pulled out the envelope containing the photos of Amy's memorial. She could feel the outline of the SIM card nestled beside them. Should she put it into her phone and listen right now?

'Ah, Leah!'

She jumped, almost dropping the envelope as her chin reared up.

'*Gordon?*'

'Sorry to startle you.'

Leah shoved the envelope into her bag, seeing his eyes flicker to it. What was he doing here? In this backstreet – in the same backstreet as her? He seemed out of breath. There was a gleam of sweat on his forehead and his shirt was open at his broad neck.

'Would you allow me to escort you back to *Il Mandarino*, please?' he said.

She stared at him. 'Escort me?'

'There's a storm on its way. It's best you come back with me now, before it becomes unsafe.'

Leah peered up at the sky, acknowledging that it was, indeed, turning darker. Bruised, bloated clouds were starting to cluster, and the air had a smell like a crowded steam room.

'But . . .' She looked back to Gordon. 'How did you know I was here?' She thought about the excuse she'd asked Matilde to pass onto Charlotte, about her having a lie-in. It seemed foolish, now. Leah had never been one for lie-ins; her mind was overactive from the second she woke. But she'd hoped her sister might've forgotten that.

'We can see which guests are on which ferries.' Gordon eyed her steadily. 'We have CCTV.'

'On the boats?' Leah had never noticed cameras on board before. She imagined herself on film, sitting upright on the top deck, alternating between watching the water and darting glances at her fellow passengers.

'Of course. Security is very important to us. I sent some of my staff to round up the other guests, but when I saw *you* were here, I wanted to ensure your safety myself.'

'Very generous.' Leah couldn't stop a sarcastic note from creeping in. She had never been good at hiding her dislike of her sister's husband, but it had always seemed to slide off him, even to amuse him. Today, though, he was unreadable. And it had been that way since she'd got here. She had even less sense of what he was thinking and feeling than ever.

'Why are you here?' he asked, and for a moment she thought he meant in Italy, in his home, until she saw his eyes flicker in the direction of Francesca's building. 'Matilde told us you were *lying* in.'

'I decided I needed some fresh air. Thought I'd come and buy some postcards.'

'I don't remember any postcard shops this far up.'

'Well, I was exploring.'

Gordon studied her for a long pause, and she was reminded of how uncomfortable he could make her, how at times he seemed to choose to do so, while at others he showered her with almost aggressive levels of hospitality. The best wines and foods for her visits; the hot and cold flashes of interest in her life. He would poke fun at her addiction to puzzles one minute, then suddenly he'd be pulling up a chair, asking her to hit him with a crossword clue. Maybe it was this unpredictability that had attracted Charlotte. The challenge of hooking and keeping his interest. Being drawn into his grand vision for the resort but also, in a way, competing with it for Gordon's attention.

'We should go.' He moved to touch her arm, but Leah sidestepped. For an odd moment they stared at each other, a stand-off, until he strode away, as if confident she would follow. Gritting her teeth, Leah did. She held her bag tight against her, conscious of the envelope inside.

As they spiralled down the mountain, she noticed shop owners and restaurant staff nodding at Gordon. Everybody seemed to know him, but they didn't call out '*ciao!*' or '*bella giornata!*' as they used to with Amy. Leah had once joked that it was like a scene from a musical when Amy walked these streets. People swinging out of doorways to plant double kisses on her cheeks. Gordon appeared to cherry-pick who he engaged more closely with – he stopped to shake two or three hands, but mostly it was chin jerks of acknowledgement.

The person who got the most of his time wore a black uniform with red strips across the chest. *Carabinieri.* The Italian police force. He and Gordon spoke in Italian, laughed and clapped each other's backs, while Leah watched through narrowed eyes.

On the ferry, there was only herself, Gordon, and a smartly dressed man and woman with suit jackets held carefully in their laps. She didn't detect any urgency from them, no worried glances at the sky. Leah couldn't shake the feeling that she was the only one who had been rounded up and escorted away. Even that the gathering thunder-clouds had been engineered by Gordon – which was insane, of course, but right now anything seemed possible, as Malcesine's darkening blue-green shore got further away.

Half an hour later, Leah stood on Amy's favourite balcony at the front of the family villa, absorbing the energy of the building storm. She felt it in the sky above her, which seemed low and weighted, and in the lake below, like water heating in a vast saucepan. And she felt it as a drumroll of nerves inside herself.

She had to listen to the voicemail. Could she do it now? Was she alone in the villa?

She felt alone in the whole resort, in fact. Marooned. The ferries were all moored at the dock, going nowhere, and the paths and terraces were deserted. Her eyes were drawn to the private villa on the far edge of the resort. The dense trees that surrounded it had no space in which to thrash and sway in the wind. The olive trees elsewhere were beginning to twist and bend, dancing to an intensifying song.

She hurried inside. The villa was silent and dim. Gordon had disappeared to 'check on a few things' when they'd disembarked the boat – but not before he'd urged her into a golf buggy and watched it whisk her back up the slope. Charlotte wasn't in her bedroom and neither was Olivia. Leah peeked into Olivia's room, which was dominated by a large cream dressing table with an enormous oval mirror. On it was a vast collection of make-up and lotions, like a window display in an expensive salon. But Leah also saw a crocheted sheep leaning up against the mirror – a favourite toy from when Olivia had been small.

She considered creeping into the room for a closer look. An insight into her 'other' niece's world. *She seems different,* she recalled Francesca saying about Olivia, with that tunnel-vision gesture. But Leah pulled herself away. It was time to hear what might have been Amy's last words, however painful.

She shut herself in her room and dug the envelope out of her bag. Tipping the SIM card into her palm, she stared at it for a moment. Such a light, innocuous thing, yet the skin of her hand prickled beneath it. She removed her phone case and her existing SIM, slotting in Francesca's.

Then she heard a loud creak from outside in the corridor. Leah jumped up, covering her phone with her bag. There was another creak, and a thud. She went to her door and peeked out.

'Hello?' she called, edging onto the landing.

Rain was spattering the windows, now, and the sky was a false kind of dark, blurring all sense of time. Shutters flapped and banged further down the corridor. She hurried to close them, the wind trying to wrestle them out of her grip. As she made her way back to her room, a flash of lightning illuminated the corridor and then thunder rattled the floor. Leah trailed her fingertips along the walls as if to help her balance.

In her room, she secured her own shutters as they swung on their hinges. Back on her bed, phone in hand, she felt as if she was starting all over again. Even less ready than before, even more agitated.

Movement caught her eye. She was sure a shadow had just passed beneath her door. *Was* somebody there? She sat rigid, listening, then poked her head out of the room again. 'Hello?'

The sounds seemed to come from the other direction, this time. And they were decidedly human – footsteps, objects being moved, the faint jangle of keys. Gordon's office. There was someone in there. A hinge whined and the office door opened, a figure stepping out.

'Oh!' They blinked at each other in mutual surprise. It was Matilde. She was wearing a plastic rain poncho over the top of her uniform, her wet hair flattened to her head. Her mobile was in her hand – the first time Leah had seen her with one – and she lowered it by her side, looking anxious. 'Leah,' she said. 'I didn't know anybody was here.'

'It's just me, I think.' Leah's voice came out wheezy

and she realised how much her pulse had climbed during the last few minutes. 'Do you know where everybody is?'

'Gordon's at the restaurant, organising meals for guests who would rather dine in their villas tonight. He has asked me to help . . .' Matilde glanced at his office door behind her, then down at her phone. 'Charlotte is at *Segreto*, helping Bram with the rain shields. I don't know about Olivia. Also dealing with the storm, I would think . . .' She looked towards the window and her mouth twisted to one side. Leah recalled those tiny, faint words beneath Francesca's address: *Be careful.* When Matilde's eyes swung back to her, there seemed a similar warning in them, especially as she stepped forward and touched Leah's wrist. 'Are you alright here by yourself?'

'I . . . yes,' Leah said.

'Because I have to get back . . .'

'It's fine. I'm okay.'

There was a flash of lightning. The shadows of the landing seemed to deepen in its wake. Matilde excused herself and hurried to the stairs, glancing back just before she descended. Leah returned to her room and closed the door, determined she wouldn't get spooked or interrupted again.

Her phone was full of Francesca's contacts. But the inbox was empty and there was only one voicemail saved. From Amy's mobile number, timed 19.21 on the day she had died. Leah breathed in hard and pressed 'play' with the phone held flat against her ear.

For the first few seconds, it was difficult to make anything out. There was an indistinct roar of noise. Leah pushed the phone even closer, afraid to miss anything, though the cacophony of sound felt like an assault. A storm in her ears to match the one battering the windows of the villa. Her free hand stretched into the air, as if she could reach back through time, grab Amy and haul her out of danger.

Then she heard Amy's voice and almost dropped the handset. It had been so long since she'd been privy to her niece's distinct way of speaking, direct yet melodic. But there was something else this time – an urgency. The rise and fall of it behind the peaks and troughs of the weather.

Gone wrong, Leah could just about hear. Or maybe, *got it wrong?*

Then more fuzz, drowning out whole blocks of words.

Was trying to . . . don't know if I . . . there's someone . . .

Please tell someone . . .

It was so frustrating, only being able to grasp at fragments. Leah's heavy breathing was interfering even further with her ability to listen. The storm grew louder inside the phone – and outside, too, as if competing – swallowing up Amy's plea so that only odd words now made it through.

Watch . . . bad . . . whole . . . thing . . .

Then Amy's voice became louder, too, somehow soaring over the top: *CAN'T LET THEM . . .*

Or was it, *HIM?* The final word was dwarfed by a bang, like a collision, or something falling. Then the line went dead, and Leah shouted 'No!' into the silence, sinking forward onto her bed.

20

Amy

Last September
Five hours until sunset

I'm still seething, my cheeks hot with humiliation, as I leave Nate and march back up the mountain. How dare my dad talk to us like that? We're adults. We were just dancing. How can Nate stand to be barked at by his employer, just for letting his hair down the tiniest bit? And why did Dad hold us responsible for Hanna, acting as if we should've tied her to a table until he arrived?

I keep my head down as I pass cameras and guests. My finger aches under the dressing Nate taped around it before I left. There was an embarrassment between us as he cleaned and bandaged the cut – like two kids who'd made a scene and been told off – and now the wound throbs like a swollen heartbeat, making me feel queasy and strange.

Golf buggies whizz past, their drivers' eyes gliding over me, knowing not to offer me a lift anymore. Olivia loves zooming around in those things – we both used to, actually, when we were younger, giggling and clinging to one another – but these days they turn me dizzy. It's when I look down and see the mountain dropping away, then twist back and the heat shimmers across my vision. Give me a stretch of cool, blue water anytime. The lake is the thing I'll miss most. But I'll have Scottish lochs to explore, a new culture to lap up. Tentative excitement returns, and I hurry to my room to prepare.

I can't take much with me. I don't want anyone to realise I've left until I'm far enough away that they might not follow. Dad did that, once. When I'd turned eighteen and finally cast off my dreary tutor, I fled to stay with Melina, who was on her gap year in Venice. I was going to figure out what to do from there, but I hadn't even got on the coach in Malcesine before Dad caught up with me.

The scene at the bus stop still makes my nerve endings curl when I remember. I was waiting, listening to all my favourite songs to keep my courage up, clutching a book but unable to concentrate. Then I saw him coming. Recognised his angry stride. I had prepared to fight, to resist, but by the time he reached me, he was calm. There was a line of people at the bus stop and some of them probably knew who we were. Dad wouldn't risk exposing that all was not perfect at the famous resort around the bay.

He walked up to me and, to my surprise, handed me a folded piece of paper.

I glanced around as I opened it. People were darting curious looks, then averting their eyes. I still remember the texture of Dad's thick, embossed notepaper between my fingers.

Your mother is very ill, it said, in his looping script, the double 'l' slightly smeared.

It was like something from a Jane Austen novel. My mouth fell open and I stared up into his grave expression.

'Is this real?' I said in a loud voice, not caring what the onlookers thought.

Dad's jaw set rigid: his 'not up for discussion' face. Then I saw his throat move in a large swallow, as if he was holding back some other emotion. I faltered. *Was* this real? What if it was? How would I feel if I went ahead and left?

'What's wrong with—'

'Amy,' he hissed, leaning in close. 'Not here. Please. Come on.'

Mum's health was often up and down, like her moods. She seemed feisty and unbreakable at times, distant and vague at others. Occasionally silly and warm, even affectionate, but more often tired and stressed. So, it *was* believable. And if I got on that coach, I had a strong feeling I wouldn't find out either way. That I'd be punished with silence, left to wonder. I touched the word 'ill', imagining that the smudge was a teardrop, though I knew it was just the fountain pen Dad always used.

He had a ferry already waiting at the dock. It was only the two of us on the journey home, plus the captain who kept his eyes firmly on the water. As soon as we cast out, Dad's face changed, and I knew. Mum wasn't sick. I watched the receding, colourful houses of Malcesine, and the road that should've carried me away, and felt as if we were being dragged back to *Il Mandarino* by a system of powerful pulleys.

He called me ungrateful and foolish. Laid it on thick about how lucky I was, how I had no idea what the real world was like. But as we rounded the outcrop, he took my hand, softened his tone. 'I'm sorry, Amy. The stunt with the note was extreme, I know.' He had the decency to look ashamed, at least. 'But I had to get your attention, somehow. We all just want you around. You can do great things here, too, you know. With your family. *For* your family. Give it a chance?' He chucked my chin like he used to when I was little, usually when he was giving me a pep talk as I tried to hide from the guests.

My escape attempt was never mentioned again. But I sensed, from then on, that I was being more carefully watched. Mum hovered whenever she saw me talking on the phone. Dad asked questions if I went anywhere, and I know he often tracked me on CCTV. The more they tried to manage me, the more I found small ways to rebel. My T-shirts. My boycotts of the 'family photo shoots' or 'together moments' that were blatant marketing ploys. The time I cancelled a big order from the unethical coffee supplier they used to use, and it caused a huge row because Dad thought they'd messed up.

But I never had the guts or the means to try to run away again. I always knew that, when I did, everything had to be perfectly planned.

Now, I tuck my passport into the front pocket of my rucksack, along with the acceptance letter from Edinburgh University I've been hiding under my mattress. Part of me still can't believe I'm going. That I managed to capitalise on everybody's obsession with the new developments at *Il Mandarino*, and applied and got a place – even some funding – while my family's attention was elsewhere. Plus, there was all of Nate's help, all those forms he downloaded or printed for me from his flat.

What else should I take? Only the bare minimum of clothes and toiletries. I've saved up some money doing odd jobs for locals in Malcesine, and every time Nate gets an over-the-top tip from a wealthy guest, he insists on giving me a share. So, I'll be able to buy some supplies when I get to Scotland, then hopefully I'll find a job. I'll sever my dependency on this place if it kills me.

The one extra thing I do pack is a book that was a present from Nate. I can't take all the books he's ever passed on to me, but I choose my favourite, *Women Who Rocked the Boat*, with an 'N' scrawled in pencil at the front, and a sketch of a boat cresting a wave. I slide my plaited leather bracelet into my pocket, intending to give it to him as a gift to remember me by.

My cheeks simmer as I recall my earlier plan for a different kind of 'remember me'. It doesn't seem such a good idea anymore. The weirdness with Hanna and my dad's yelling has cast a cloud. I check the time on my phone again: 2 p.m. I *could* run back and catch Nate between his lunch shift and the pre-dinner rush. Clear the air between us, at least, before it's too late.

Looking at my phone reminds me of something else. Shit, it's Francesca's birthday. I find her number and, as my phone rings, let my eyes drift over the photos of her and me. She can still rock a pair of dungarees. Has them in every colour. She's a fantastic singer too, though she's shy about it, only really sings when we're on the lake. I wonder if it would freak her out if I asked her to sing down the phone to me now, for old times' sake. It's like I'm already thinking of our friendship in the past tense.

Instead, when she answers, I'm the one who launches into song – 'Happy Birthday' of course. I hear her laughing. '*Grazie.* That was exquisite.' The word sounds great in her accent. I wish I could see her face.

'Sorry I didn't call earlier,' I say. 'And I'm *really* sorry, but I won't make your party tonight.'

'Oh no!' she says. 'I was looking forward to seeing you.'

Guilt hits me as I realise it's been weeks. I've been so wrapped up in my plans. And in Nate, I admit to myself, though I never thought I'd be *that* person.

'I'm sorry,' I say again. 'Something's come up . . .' I'm talking in clichés. 'There's something I've got to do.'

She pauses. 'Now I *am* intrigued. *Stai bene?*'

'Yes, I'm fine! Sorry to be weird. I just wanted to say happy birthday . . . and bye.'

'Goodbye?'

I try to laugh it off, knowing I've said too much but also too little, confusing her. 'Ignore me! Just have a brilliant party tonight, okay? Love you.'

'Love you too . . .' She sounds bewildered. I close my eyes against welling tears and hear her start to say, 'Amy, are you—' before I hastily hang up.

I stare at the phone in silent apology. *Speak to you later,* I promise her, and myself. *After sunset, when you'll be tipsy-happy and I'll be free.*

Taking a shaky breath, I refocus on practical things. Double-checking my coach booking from Riva del Garda, my flight from Milan. One-way tickets stamped with a sense of momentousness. I call the taxi company to confirm, in a low voice, what we arranged: a car will pick me up at 7 p.m. from the craggy part of the mountaintop, a spot that's just outside the official *Il Mandarino* boundary but that can be reached via the rough mountain road. From there, it's possible to head further north to Riva without having to use the water. It takes ages, and it's kind of dicey, but I'm less likely to be seen or stopped than if I take a boat. And Nate will create a diversion as I'm going to meet the taxi. He's going to call my mum and dad to *Segreto* with some kind of fake emergency, make sure the coast is clear. We've got a code word I can text if I need him to divert them any earlier.

I can't do this without him.

Less than five hours to go.

When it's close to the time I know he'll be taking a break, I shove my rucksack under my bed and straighten my clothes. On this occasion, I allow myself longer in front of the mirror, but it only reminds me why I normally don't. My messy hair, peeling forehead, the blood spatters on my T-shirt to accompany the lime juice stain . . .

I freeze at footsteps along the landing. Mum and Dad's raised voices come sweeping along.

'Where would she have gone?' Mum is saying. 'Haven't you checked the cameras?'

For an odd moment, I think they're talking about me. As if I'm somehow seeing them after I've gone. Searching, realising.

'What do you think I'm doing?' Dad snaps, and I hear the jangle of his office keys. 'Bloody hell . . .' There's a clatter as if he's dropped them, and a low growl of frustration.

'Here . . .' Another jangle: keys being retrieved. 'Why are you so worked up, Gordon? Just hire another girl.'

'She's needed *today*. We can't disappoint. You know Brookmyre could make or break us.'

I think of the slim, black jewellery box Dad was carrying earlier. BROOKMYRE in silver letters. Who or what is it?

'Maybe she changed her mind,' Mum says. 'It happens all the time with recruiting, you know that.'

'Nate assured me she was keen.'

My body stiffens at the mention of his name. I stare at my door, unblinking, but my parents' voices fade into the office. Presumably they were talking about Hanna, the missing Mannequin.

Nate assured me she was keen?

21

Joanna

Joanna sat on the pavement outside The Last Junction, gulping lungfuls of night air, witnessing phantom car crashes on the stretch of dark road in front of her. Her buttocks were numb but she felt glued to the curb, counting her breaths in and out, as she'd advised so many panicking students to do in the past.

She was struggling to think straight. Why would Callum lie to his boss? Lie to her and the hospital about being at work? And the police – had he asked them not to pursue an investigation? She thought again of how reluctant he had been to talk about his accident. How reluctant to talk about himself, full stop. She'd mistaken his reticence for modesty, good listening skills. Even for vulnerability. Had she been completely stupid?

She considered calling Mandy and asking if she could stay at hers tonight, or one of her other friends – but they all had kids; it wasn't fair to disturb them. Maybe her mum and dad – but they'd only worry, and ask a million questions she wouldn't know how to answer.

Old instincts were bending her towards another possibility. The person she used to turn to when she was feeling lost. Who, despite his flaws, had usually made her feel better, and safe.

No, she really shouldn't. She was beyond that post-break-up phase of calling him late at night under some ruse of needing something. But the other options were to sit on this cold pavement as it got later and later, or go home to a man she couldn't trust.

She found Luke's number and dialled, wondering whether he would still be awake.

He picked up after two rings.

'Hi,' she said, 'You – you said you wanted to talk?'

She hadn't been to Luke's new house before. Although it wasn't far from hers, she'd avoided it when they'd split up, not wanting to see him in different surroundings, without her. He lived in a student area, in a house that reminded her of the first one they'd ever rented together, back when they'd felt as if they were only playing at being adults. And maybe Luke wanted to reinvoke that feeling, maybe that was why he'd put a stop to the onward march of their life. *He* was the one who'd been so keen to buy the grown-up house on the tree-lined street, though. He'd been the one to persuade her they could afford it, that they deserved it. The one obsessed with looking at aspirational properties on Rightmove, or comparing other people's LinkedIn profiles to his own.

There was nothing aspirational about his current place. Rubbish bags were piled up by the front wall and next door had a broken sofa in their front garden. When Luke opened the door, she was shocked again by his weight loss. His familiar blue pyjama bottoms hung off his hips, his fair hair looked greasy and he hadn't shaved.

'Come in, Jo,' Luke said. 'Are you okay?'

She didn't answer as she followed him into a featureless hallway. She glimpsed a study off it, his familiar double-screened computer surrounded by glossy brochures, pencil sketches, coffee cups and colourful Post-its. Signs of creativity and productivity that made her feel a little better. The rest of the house – the part she saw as he led her to the living room – was uncluttered and unadorned. He hadn't filled his home with self-affirming stuff, as Joanna had. Nor was it the bachelor pad she'd been dreading, although she wasn't quite sure what she'd anticipated: copies of *Playboy* and calendars of women? Not Luke's style, but how could she be sure anymore?

She perched in a hard-backed armchair as he went to make her some tea. Being here didn't put her at ease. She'd just swapped one complication for another. Suddenly, Luke felt as much a stranger as the man sleeping on her sofa, even though he didn't need to check how she took her tea.

'What did you want to talk about?' she made herself ask when he returned. 'Your text . . .?'

He was silent, looking down into his mug. When he raised his chin, his eyes were damp. 'I wanted to say sorry. Properly, this time.'

She thought of how he'd said it in the pub, pretending it was about the beer, blurring the lines. Exhaustion crashed over her. She wasn't sure she could do this now.

'For walking out on you,' he said. 'For being an utter coward.'

Joanna felt torn. Part of her wanted to hug him, kiss the wispy hair at his temples, tell him it was fine. Another part wanted to let out a giant sigh of frustration because this was all too late. And it wasn't fine.

Meanwhile, the tiniest part sang with hope, allowing the thought to wriggle in: *Maybe he wants to get back together.*

Her rational mind knew that wasn't what this was, though. Luke was just trying to offload some guilt. If she accepted his apology, would he regain his weight, the colour in his cheeks?

You don't even want to get back together with him. You're beyond that now. She'd finally kicked the habit of putting his favourite snacks into her trolley at the supermarket. Stopped bookmarking articles she knew he'd like. And she no longer cried on her cycle home from work, letting the wind blow the tears off her face.

'It's in the past, Luke,' she said, although it didn't always feel that way. Often didn't, in fact. 'No need for the big apology.'

'I let you down.' His voice was trembling. Joanna was stricken at the thought that he might break down completely, and so would she, probably, if she saw it. The steam from her tea felt suffocating. There were no tables on which to rest the mug. Hardly any furniture in the room at all, actually. Luke's dozens of non-fiction books sat in piles against the skirting board, autobiographies of inspirational figures slumped against faded wallpaper.

'I wouldn't have wanted you to just plod on, pretending to be happy.' As she said it, the old question bounced back: *For how long were you doing that before you left?*

She kind of knew the answer, really. She'd sensed him growing distant for a month or so before he'd finally ended it. He'd become less tactile, when they'd always been physically affectionate, and less talkative, no longer soundtracking their TV-watching with his commentary of opinions (which, admittedly, used to annoy her, before it had disappeared). He'd stopped suggesting they do the activities they'd always enjoyed, like going out for meals or to the cinema (it had been known for them to see two films back-to-back in the old days, with a quick pizza in between). He'd even started moving into the spare bed partway through the night, claiming he couldn't sleep and didn't want to keep her awake with his restlessness. The first few times she'd woken to find him gone, she had panicked, and shot up to check he was in the house. But after it had become a frequent occurrence, she would simply feel a pang, like a mini loss, then turn over and try to get back to sleep.

She remembered the first time he'd actually articulated that something was amiss. It was last autumn. They'd been in the car on the way back from Sunday lunch at Mandy's, and Joanna had been driving. She'd sensed something all afternoon: the way he'd watched her playing with his nephew and niece, lost in thought rather than joining in and making them laugh as he normally would. The way he'd hardly eaten, hardly spoken, his voice notably absent from the lively conversation around the table.

When they'd stopped at some traffic lights, Luke had declared, flatly, 'I don't think I ever want to have kids.'

Joanna could still remember the road sign she'd been looking at. Rather than register his announcement, she'd started trying to work out what it meant. A motorbike floating above a car, in a red circle. It had seemed to make no sense at all.

'I don't even think I want to get married,' Luke had continued. 'I don't . . .' His voice had cracked. 'I don't think I can do any of it. I haven't got it in me.'

It had been his final statement that had wrenched her eyes from the sign. *I haven't got it in me.* Luke rarely admitted to weakness. That was when she'd known something was really wrong.

Things had unravelled from there. Sometimes she had felt white-hot fury: since when did he not have it in him? What was so hard about building a future with her, the woman he loved and had made promises to? Other times she'd felt such sadness, for him as well as for herself, and guilt too, as if she must've done something to make him feel he couldn't go through with any of it.

'Don't let this consume you, Luke,' she said now. 'You made a decision, and I've accepted it. I still don't know if I understand it, but I'm getting on with my life.' She thought of Callum, and felt another shiver of misgiving, but tried not to let it show. Running to Luke for help had been a mistake. She had to leave.

Before you turn this situation on its head and convince yourself, all over again, that Luke needs you, too.

As she stood up, so did Luke. He rushed towards her unexpectedly, grabbing her hand. 'Listen, Jo . . .'

'Luke, I should go. I shouldn't have turned up here in the middle of the night.'

His eyes were intense. 'Everything's okay with you, isn't it?'

'What?' She took a small step back. 'Yes. Like I said, I'm getting on with things. It's you that seems—'

'But I mean, you're safe? You're being careful? You're not . . . There's nothing bad going on?'

'What do you mean?' Joanna felt a tremor behind her ribs. Did Luke somehow know about Callum? Had Mandy seen more than she'd let on?

'I just . . .' Luke dropped her hand and cast around him, as if for something he'd mislaid. His dishevelled appearance gave him the look of someone confused, almost unhinged. 'I worry about you,' he finished, locking his hands around the back of his neck. 'You'd tell me if there was anything, wouldn't you? If anyone tried to hurt you, or . . .?'

Joanna shook her head, bewildered and slightly disturbed. His words were scarily on-the-nose, yet at the same time had the ring of paranoia.

She had to get out of here. Had to sort her life out, be brave.

'I'm fine, Luke,' she said, with more conviction than she felt. 'You don't need to worry about me.'

Joanna stood outside her house, steeling herself, then feeling sad that she felt the need to do so. She'd dived through this red door so many times, thankful to be home. Now it seemed to take a lot of courage to step into her dark hall.

She paused inside, keys in hand. She couldn't hear any movement. The air had a stagnant feel, smelling of somebody else's sleep.

Tiptoeing into the living room, she saw Callum zonked out on the sofa bed, topless, with her spare sheets tangled

around him. He was breathing deeply, one shoulder twitch-
ing as if he was trying to shrug off his dreams. Roxy was
curled up at his feet, looking very cosy with the stranger
Joanna had brought into their previously all-female house.
Typical – she was anyone's if they gave her a bit of fuss.
Joanna wanted to scoop up her cat, carry her away, but she
didn't want Callum to wake.

She padded to the other side of the sofa bed and quietly
opened her old DVD cabinet where he was keeping his
belongings. The few T-shirts and pairs of shorts his landlady had sent were folded up on the bottom shelf. Joanna
wondered whether this was the full extent of his clothes,
vaguely comparing with the number of dresses she had in
her wardrobe upstairs. Underneath the pile was his paperwork from the hospital. She looked at his address and
scanned the details of his injuries, tucking it all away in her
mind.

There was an old-looking wallet on the top shelf. Joanna
didn't even know he owned one – she remembered his
pocketfuls of loose, crumpled cash on their date. The card
section was empty, which struck her as odd. But the wallet
was fat with notes, a wad of tens and twenties making the
cash section bulge. Checking again that Callum was still
sleeping, she moved on to the only other item in the cabinet, his wash bag. Inside were the dark shapes of the usual
things: soap, deodorant, nail clippers. A plaited leather
wristband that she hadn't noticed him wearing, but could
imagine him doing so; it matched his 'look'. There was also
a thin black notebook – perhaps a diary or address book.
Joanna carried something similar in her handbag, otherwise

she was forever forgetting appointments, but it surprised her, somehow, that Callum would have an organiser – and that he would keep it here.

As she touched it, Callum stirred. Joanna's heart kicked and she jerked back from the cabinet. Callum coughed and stirred again. Joanna pushed up from her crouch, but before she could get out of the room his eyes blinked open.

He squinted at her. 'Jo?'

Her pulse raced and her words scrambled. 'Sorry. I just got in . . . I was looking for my . . .' She petered off, watching him wriggle into a sitting position, hearing his sharp inhale as he seemed to jar his ribs. A blade of moonlight snuck through the curtains and cut across his bare chest.

'Callum,' Joanna said, before her courage could shrivel. 'I need to talk to you.'

He propped himself on a pillow, rubbing his eyes. His shoulders were broader-looking without a T-shirt, his face mostly in shadow. 'What about?'

'I went to your pub tonight. I wanted to see whether the police had talked to them yet. But the guy there – I think he's the manager – didn't seem to know anything about the hit and run.'

She saw his eyes widen, moonlight catching the whites. From outside came the purr of late-night traffic and the mewl of a fox.

'Ah,' Callum said. 'Shit. Yes.'

Joanna waited.

'I'm really sorry,' he continued. 'I should've told you. I . . . didn't give my boss the full story.'

'Why not?'

Callum sighed and dragged a hand across his stubble. 'He took a chance on me, giving me the job. Because I'd been travelling before I came here, my CV's a bit all over the place, and I haven't really got any references, but I persuaded him to give me a trial. He pays me cash, all a bit unofficial. So I didn't want him to think I was going to be trouble. Didn't want to draw the pub into a police inquiry within my first few weeks of working there.'

'But it happened outside the pub. Surely that would automatically involve him?'

'No, it happened on the road behind the station. I was on my way from the pub to the taxi rank.'

'Oh.' Joanna stalled. Had anybody actually said it was directly outside the pub? Or had she just assumed it because Callum had been leaving work, *apparently*, and the nurse at the ICU had said 'near the station'?

'But you *were* working on Sunday?' she asked. 'It did happen after your shift?'

'It happened exactly as I told you. I just didn't want to admit that to my boss. Rightly or wrongly. And . . . I played the whole thing down with the police, too. I'm sorry. I really just want to forget it and move on.'

'Your boss said you *didn't* work on Sunday.'

Callum's chin jerked. 'What?'

'He looked at the rota and said you worked Friday and Saturday only. Then phoned in sick on Monday.'

'He said . . .?' She saw his eyes widen once more. Then he nodded, his gaze darting down. 'I swapped shifts with a colleague. He asked me, as a favour. We just arranged it between ourselves, so it wouldn't have got recorded on the rota. I don't think Ged, the manager, even knew – he wasn't in over the weekend.'

Joanna tried to process this. Her instincts were fogged by exhaustion, but she could still hear what they were saying to her, what they'd been trying to say all along: *Protect yourself.*

'I'm really sorry for not putting you in the picture,' Callum said, shuffling towards her, the duvet bunched around his waist. 'After all you've done.'

She looked away, twisting one of her rings around her finger. 'It doesn't exactly put me at ease, Callum. Letting you into my house, an almost-stranger, then finding out you haven't told the whole truth.' Her voice grew louder as she added: 'It's a pretty shitty feeling.'

'I know,' he said. 'I never meant to ... I'll leave, Jo. My ribs are much better, and I've caused you enough disruption.'

'That's another lie,' she said, more softly. 'About your ribs being better.' She'd seen him only that evening, smarting in agony when he'd stretched up to get a mug from a shelf. Could she bring herself to throw him out, still injured, in the middle of the night?

She pressed the bridge of her nose. 'I'm too tired to make any decisions now.' And she meant it; suddenly she couldn't clarify a single thought in her brain.

He stayed where he was, sitting up, grimacing with apology and concern. She stared at the sofa bed taking up her living room, the shape of his legs underneath her covers. Her kitsch lamp with its fringed shade, looming like an alien over the scene.

She was so tired. So mixed up. She just wanted to shut the door to her bedroom, shut it all out.

'Plenty of people know you're here,' she said to him. 'If I have *any* more cause for doubt tonight . . .'

He nodded solemnly. She wasn't sure whether he could tell that the first part of her statement was frighteningly untrue.

22

Leah

I listened to it.

Leah had to try three times to get the text to send to Francesca because her signal and even the WiFi kept failing. Finally, a blue tick appeared and she waited, huddled on her bed. She considered swapping the SIM cards back and listening to Amy's voicemail for the fourth time. But it only got more distressing and confusing each time she heard it.

A reply came from Francesca: **I'm sorry if it upset you. I had to hear it. Do you think she was out on the water? She must have been.**

And the police heard this? Gordon, Charlotte?

Yes.

Leah let her head fall back, drawing her knees into her chest. How could anybody listen to Amy's frantic, fragmented words and still think there was no more to her death than an ill-judged boat journey? *Gone wrong. Can't let them.* Or, *him?* Or, *got it wrong?* Leah still didn't know, even after three replays.

A long message from Francesca appeared.

I kept playing it to people, at first. Charlotte went white when she heard it. Gordon got angry. But later they were dismissive. The police analysed the call and said Amy was just 'reacting to a realisation that

she was in danger from the storm'. It confirmed their verdict, not contradicted it.

Leah pressed her fingers against her eyes. There were strobes behind her lids. Before she could send anything back, a knock came on her door. She sat up from the wall, locking the screen of her phone. 'Come in?' she called, a catch in her voice transforming it into a question.

The door opened. Olivia's hair was plastered to her cheeks, her mascara like wet ink beneath her eyes. A damp smell came in with her and pervaded Leah's room.

'Olivia!' Leah scrambled off the bed to fetch her a towel. 'Are you okay?'

'Auntie Lee,' she said, without acknowledging how drenched she was. 'You're a lawyer, aren't you?'

Leah stalled, halfway to her en suite. 'Yes. Why?'

'I need your help with something. A guest.'

Leah's mind was still with Amy. Stranded on the lake, trapped inside a SIM card. She tried to focus on her other niece. 'What kind of help?'

'He needs a contract looking over. Nothing complicated, but he's on a deadline, and can't get through to his usual lawyer. We can normally provide our own, but she's stuck in Bardolino because of the weather.'

'But I'm not that kind of lawyer. I do intellectual property.' When Olivia looked blank, Leah reeled off: 'Copyright, patents, licences . . .'

'It'll be fine. It's just a box that needs ticking. Please, I need to come up with something! We're supposed to be able to provide whatever our guests need.'

'But surely, in the circumstances, they'd understand . . .'

'Understand?' Olivia looked at Leah as if she hadn't grasped the situation at all. 'I doubt it.' She reached for Leah's arm to urge her towards the door.

Outside, the darkness had a blue glow. Palm trees were bent double, their fringed leaves all forced in one direction, like windswept hair. The lake below had turned from a gleaming mirror into a choppy sea with new tides and waves.

Things Leah wanted to say to Olivia kept forming on her lips, then fading into the storm. It took her longer than it might've done to realise where they were walking to. The tall gates loomed black and glossy, the thicket of pines almost misty in their dampness, emitting a smell of wet bark. They were at the largest villa. Olivia was aiming her remote control at the gates as rain lashed into their faces.

There was another set of gates inside the main ones. These were made of ornate twists of wrought iron, but they were fingerprint-operated, the technology a contrast to their appearance. Olivia pressed her finger onto a pad beneath a waterproof shield and they creaked open.

The villa was starkly lit from the ground upwards by spotlights in the drive. Its bone-coloured walls glowed at the bottom but disappeared into darkness towards the top. There were six tall shuttered windows, a double-peaked roof, and a frontage of multiple pillars, coiled with climbing plants. Rain pocked the surface of a floodlit pool, which wrapped itself around one side of the villa like half of a moat.

Under the shelter of the front terrace – which was almost the size of Leah's entire flat, and better furnished, despite being basically a porch – Olivia drew an iPad out of her handbag. It was different from the one Leah had seen her with before, making notes and taking bookings. This one was a mini iPad inside a dark leather sleeve.

'Could you sign this, Auntie Lee?'

Leah frowned at the screen full of tiny words. Olivia held a stylus towards her with a surprisingly unsteady hand. Was she shivering in her soaked clothes? Leah should've offered her some dry ones, or huddled a towel around her shoulders as they'd set out. Where were her nurturing instincts? She met Olivia's eyes over the top of the iPad: they were like glinting pebbles in the combination of flashes from the storm and the glow of the ground-level spotlights.

'What is this?' Leah asked.

'Just a standard NDA.'

Leah knew the acronym, of course. Non-disclosure agreement. She recoiled a little. 'What for?'

'It's no biggie. Like I said before, our guests at this villa expect privacy. Our current guest is quite famous in certain circles. He just wants to make sure you're not going to brag online that you advised him, or leak any confidential details. He's trying to have a quiet few days doing business.'

'Who is he?'

'The CEO of *Sunshine Juice*.'

Leah was blank.

'The smoothie bar franchise?' Olivia prompted. 'It's huge?'

Leah shrugged. The uncool aunt again. 'Oh.'

'He's been in *Time* magazine,' Olivia said, and there was something else in her eyes now, nervous excitement or pride.

Leah scanned the small print, and felt another tingle of misgiving as she scribbled in the box. The large interior doors to the villa swung open, as if her signature had triggered them.

23

Amy

Last September
Four hours before sunset

I hurry back to *Segreto*, questions writhing in my head. Images, too: Olivia's tanned leg peeping from the slit in her skirt, Hanna's chin lifting towards Nate as he brought her coffee. The shards of glass sparkling on the bar top, and their two faces – Dad's and Nate's, one livid, one indecipherable – as we realised Hanna had disappeared.

I hear echoes of Dad's urgent tone as he talked to Mum about finding Hanna.

She's needed today. We can't disappoint. You know Brookmyre could make or break us.

Nate assured me she was keen.

I still can't understand it. Nate said he didn't know Hanna. Did he help to recruit her? That can't be true, it just can't. After all he's ever said about the Mannequins and my dad's misogyny. Was he just humouring me? The possibility hurts so much I have to pause, holding my fist against my breastbone.

When I get there, I see the last of the lunch crowd drifting away, and I lurk under a tree to make myself invisible again. A man in a dinner jacket – at lunch time! – frowns at my T-shirt but doesn't look at my face, as if he thinks the Banksy picture is floating in the shadows by itself. Nate begins loading the dishwasher behind the bar. There's a whiff of burning, maybe the aftermath of one of his showpiece cocktails where he sets the alcohol alight. Somebody's left a purple pashmina over the back of a chair and it twitches in the breeze like the feathers of a dying bird.

I hover out of Nate's eyeline. He doesn't seem to sense my presence as he often does. The connection between us, which has sustained me these last few months – was it ever genuine? Maybe he's duped and charmed me in the same way he does his customers, and his employers, everybody who wants a piece of him. Who's to say *I've* been getting the real Nate?

A memory plagues me. It's been dancing at the edges of my mind and I can't shove it away anymore. I once saw Dad behind the bar at *Segreto*, showing Nate headshots of three women. None of them was Hanna; this must've been about six months ago. Dad was business-like, as if he was asking Nate for his opinion on designs for a new logo. He would never approach it as a blokey thing, only ever as a commercial decision, like everything else in his life. But in a way, that disturbed me more. Those women could've been glassware, or tables, or paint shades in a colour chart.

'Aren't you going to ask *me* what I think?' I spoke up. 'Why don't we pass them round the bar, have a vote?'

They both turned, startled. Nate seemed horrified that I'd seen what they were doing. Dad looked discomfited for a split-second, then he said, 'That won't be necessary.' He tucked one photo inside his suit jacket and tossed the other two into the bin.

Into the bin.

I tried to fish them out later. It seemed wrong to leave them there among the rubbish. But they were too deep inside, staring up at me as if from the bottom of a well.

Nate assured me he'd found the whole conversation uncomfortable. That he hadn't given Gordon any kind of opinion on the women – but, admittedly, he hadn't told him what he really thought of the whole Mannequin approach, either. Caught, as ever, between needing to keep his job and hating so much of what it stands for.

Or so he said. So he always says.

Now I feel as if I'm observing a stranger. His careful movements. The methodical tidying up. His occasional glances around the now-empty bar – but still not noticing me, as I stay in shadow. I see him pause with a coffee cup in his hand, hovering over the dishwasher. Even from here, I can see a smear of pink lipstick on its rim: it's Hanna's coffee cup from earlier. Nate finally places it in the dishwasher, then slams it shut and I hear the beep and hum of it roaring into action.

He stalls as he realises he's left something out. The hourglass jug, which he used for the lemonade for the guests in the new villa, is sitting on the bar. Empty now, apart from a sheen of moisture and a mulch of mint leaves at the bottom. Nate runs his finger over the lip, examines it as if there's a crack or an imperfection, then plonks it heavily in the sink.

I step forward: 'Nate?'

He whirls around and his pupils dilate in surprise.

'Amy!' He dries his hands quickly on some kitchen roll. 'I didn't know if I'd see you again. Today, I mean. Before you . . .' He trails off as he seems to notice I'm not smiling or responding. The dishwasher rattles and I think of Hanna's cup inside, her lipstick being cleaned away. Maybe she came to her senses, got out of this place. Which is what I should be focusing on doing. Less than five hours to go, but everything is messy and strange.

'Nate,' I say again. 'What's the deal with Hanna?'

He goes very still. 'Hanna?'

'The woman from earlier. Do you know her?'

'No.' He seems to catch my sceptical expression. 'Well, not really . . .'

'Not really? What does that mean?'

He dabs at his face with the screwed-up kitchen roll.

'She's . . . my friend's sister,' he eventually says. 'She's travelling. She arrived in Lake Garda a few weeks ago.'

'Did you recommend her for a job here?'

'No.' His chin comes up but he can't look me in the eye. 'Hanna knew about *Il Mandarino* through me. But I didn't recommend her. Certainly not for—'

'I heard my dad say "Nate assured me she was keen".'

His mouth drops. 'When?'

'Does it matter? Just now. He's still looking for her. He said she's needed today. What's so special about today?'

'I don't know,' Nate says, and his eyes flick to the left. I try to remember which way is supposed to mean a person is lying.

He slips out from behind the bar and comes towards me, glancing at the CCTV camera and then around *Segreto*, which is still deserted, that pashmina still flapping on the back of the chair. The fairy lights looped around the palm trees have come on, even though it isn't anywhere near dark. There is a dullness to the sky, though. Clouds have swept in and veiled the sun.

'This isn't what you think,' he says.

The cliché brings a swell of nausea. I feel tears blocking my throat, burning my eyes, and I start to back away. I don't want him to see me cry right now. I tell myself that this is all just stupid *Il Mandarino* stuff, and it'll soon be a distant memory, if I can just keep my focus on my escape. But the air feels more toxic than ever, exacerbated by the tang of humidity, as if it wants to rain but can't, as if the clouds are taut with it, like the pressure in my throat and head.

'Amy, where are you going?'

Nate follows me as I move towards the exit. Instinct makes me speed up. This is my friend, a man I thought I might be in love with, the only one who knows my plans for today and can help me pull them off. But now I don't know if I can trust him, so when he appears to chase me, I run. That makes him run, too. On one level I'm aware of how ridiculous this is: me fleeing, him pursuing, up through the resort and in among the taller, denser trees. But on another level, it seems the only thing to do, and I'm pumped with adrenaline, as if I could run faster than I ever have before. As if I could take off, catapult away, no need for the taxi or the coach or the train. No need to worry about anyone following me because I'd be soaring beyond their reach.

'Amy, stop!' he shouts. 'Let me explain!'

Then I trip over a tree root – a rare imperfection in the *Il Mandarino* path – and crash to the floor.

24

Leah

The doors seemed to seal shut behind them. Olivia didn't turn on any lights in the villa's huge foyer, but Leah could see the sleek shapes of leather chairs and tall, empty vases. There was a coffee machine attached to one wall, a shelf of white espresso cups, a coat rack and a full-length mirror that seemed, somehow, to reflect the colours of the storm. Leah felt conscious of the rain running off her clothes and onto the marble floor.

'This way,' Olivia said in a hushed tone, leading her into the next room where the lights blared on automatically.

This one had the vibe of a networking lounge in a high-end conference centre, making Leah instinctively tense. Royal blue sofas dominated the space and glass coffee tables had been polished to a shine. In the far corner, two pairs of high-backed chairs faced each other conspiratorially, overflowing with plump velvet cushions, while a champagne fridge emitted a soft hum.

Olivia took her through yet another heavy door. It was dim again on the other side, but a computer screen cast a blue-white glow across a giant desk, and there was a fainter glow from what looked like a conference-call system embedded into the wall. Between the two, a man in his forties sat on the floor, legs splayed, leafing through a wad of papers. He was wearing a suit but his feet were bare, his shirt untucked. A pot of coffee sat next to him and he twirled a silver fountain pen between his teeth.

Leah didn't recognise him. Not that celebrities or smoothie bars were in any way her specialist subjects.

'Mr Huxley,' Olivia said. 'I've brought help. My aunt is a lawyer . . . Though not necessarily the kind that you—'

'You angel,' he cut her off, but flatly, without removing the pen from his mouth or taking his eyes off his papers. Leah thought he was talking about her for a second, until she realised he meant Olivia. 'And I told you to call me Alec.'

Olivia laughed skittishly, then went over to the desk and began shunting things around. 'Sorry, yes, Alec.' She didn't introduce Leah. Her usual professional charm seemed to have vanished.

Alec finally looked at Leah, and patted the floor next to him. 'You don't mind if we do it here? A villa full of million-euro furniture and I seem to be most comfortable on the floor.'

'We can bring other chairs for you to try,' Olivia said, but he waved the suggestion away.

Leah hesitated, then lowered herself onto the floor beside him, close enough to smell his unexpectedly sweet after-shave. It was strange to find herself back in work mode, yet so far out of her usual context. As Alec began talking her through the contract, her mind kept short-circuiting to Amy, the voicemail, Francesca, the police. Thunder growled outside, seeming distant from inside their blue-lit fort, but amplifying in Leah's head to remind her of the background roar from Amy's message.

A small cry and a thud made her look up in alarm. Olivia had dropped a folder from off the desk and documents were avalanching out.

'Careful!' Alec snapped.

'I'm so sorry . . .' Olivia's hands jittered as she scooped up the mess. 'So sorry.'

Her face was ashen, Leah saw. Why was she so nervy? Was it the weather? Olivia slid the folder back onto the desk, but held up a separate piece of paper. It had glossy headshots of various men and women on it, all in business dress, with captions underneath that Leah couldn't make out.

'Does this need to be filed somewhere?' Olivia asked. 'It was on the desk, underneath the folder . . .'

Alec gave it a cursory glance. 'Just leave it on the desk.'

But Olivia kept holding it, turning it over in her hands.

Leah was utterly confused. She blinked and then became brisk, wanting to get her task over with, get back to her room. What if Francesca had been trying to contact her? She pictured her phone lying on her bed, separated from her by numerous doors, gates, and winding paths. Still, she didn't want to put her signature to something she hadn't read, so she skimmed through the contract, masking her shock at the large sums of money involved in the new manufacturing facilities Alec was buying.

'That all looks pretty standard,' she told him, hoping it was true. She dashed out her signature, then looked back to Olivia. Her niece was at the window now, rearranging the long drapes with twitchy movements, the light and shade of the storm washing over her.

'Olivia?' Leah said. 'Shall we go?'

Olivia whipped around and for a moment she was a silhouette, dwarfed by the window. 'Yes,' came a small voice from her shadowed face. 'We should.' Then, as if remembering her role: 'That is, if there's nothing else you need, Mr Huxley?'

Before they left, Leah saw her throw one last glance at the desk, now in darkness because the computer had put itself to sleep.

Outside, Olivia broke into a jog through the rain, and Leah followed. The smell of the storm had become bitter and earthy, now, and the path underfoot was slimy with blown leaves. Olivia slowed as the hill got steeper. Leah finally asked her if everything was alright.

'I'm fine,' Olivia said, a little brusquely. Then, softer: 'Thanks for your help.'

Leah was going to leave it there, reverting to her habit of letting difficult subjects drop, but she knew she had to press it. 'You seemed a bit on edge in there. Did something make you anxious?'

There was a silence. The path swerved and the family home came into view, seeming almost small, cosy, compared to the place they'd just been in.

'It's just a bit . . . weird,' Olivia said, slowing further as they approached. 'The last time there was somebody staying in that villa was at the end of our last summer season . . . last September . . .' She paused, and the significance hung between them. 'I was at the villa for most of that day when Amy . . . So it just makes me think of it, I guess.'

'Oh,' Leah said, a sharp pain in her chest. 'Of course it would. It's totally understandable. Maybe you could talk to your parents, tell them you're finding it difficult to—'

'No!' Olivia cut her off. 'No, I just need to get used to it again. The villa's nothing to do with Amy, really! It's just a weird association that's formed in my mind. Don't say anything to Mum or Dad, please, Auntie Lee? They need me attending to things there. It's a big part of my job.'

'Well, okay . . .' Leah wanted to say more, but Olivia strode ahead towards the house.

The front door opened and a beam of warm light spilled out, revealing Charlotte in the entranceway.

'Olivia! Leah!' she shouted. 'Where have you *been*?'

Olivia ran inside, Leah behind, and to her surprise Charlotte threw her arms around them.

'I've been so worried. I got back from *Segreto* and found you both gone . . . and the storm . . .' Her face was drawn, her eyes huge.

'Mum, we're fine,' Olivia said. 'We just had to help a guest. Aren't you always telling me that should be my priority?'

'Yes, but . . .' Charlotte drew them both in for another wet hug. 'I was just worried. Silly, I know.' She kissed Olivia's cheek, then Leah's. Leah caught Olivia's shy smile, colour blooming where her mum had landed her lips.

They recovered themselves, stepping back from one another. Charlotte ushered them into a rarely used snug, fetched towels and hot chocolates and found three pairs of slippers. She seemed to revel, suddenly, in mothering them, and Leah was reminded of when they used to play with their toy kitchen when they were little, taking it in turns to be the mum or the child. Charlotte had loved playing the naughty kid, knocking the saucepans off the stove, but had thrown herself into the mum role too, buttering fake bread and sticking plasters all over Leah's forehead. Leah had been the weak link in the game; she never had her sister's imagination or dramatic skills. Now she wondered, as she gripped her hot chocolate, was Charlotte still acting a part? Or was she shedding a costume she usually wore?

At some point, Leah must've fallen asleep. She woke in the chair with a crick in her neck and a draught around her ankles. She was alone in the snug. The air smelled of chocolate and the sounds of the storm had faded to a whistle. Panic descended: she'd let herself relax, lowered her guard. Scrambling out of the armchair, she darted back upstairs to her room.

As soon as she stepped in, she felt it. An air of disturbance. Things had moved – subtly, almost imperceptibly – but enough to make her brain play Spot the Difference. Her suitcase at an angle. The bed pulled out by half an inch, revealing dents in the carpet where its legs had formerly been.

Leah stood motionless, listening. She checked under the bed and then, muscles braced, nudged the door to her en suite. Her shoulders dropped a fraction when she saw it was empty. Rushing back, she was relieved to find the envelope from Francesca still beneath her pillow. But as she slipped her hand into it, she knew something was wrong.

The SIM card wasn't in there. She rooted around, panic rising. The photos felt different, too. Flimsier. She switched on a lamp and tipped the contents of the envelope onto the bed.

Her heart stopped. The SIM card was missing and she was looking at a different set of photos altogether. Not of Amy's friends on the bright streets of Malcesine, but all of her, of Leah, in various places around *Il Mandarino*, looking oblivious yet haunted. There she was talking to Bram at *Segreto*; boarding an early-morning ferry to Malcesine; standing in the shadow of the conifers, peering between their trunks for glimpses of the big villa. She leafed through them, hairs rising on the back of her neck, then froze once again. Among them was a note, typed in plain black capitals.

WHATEVER IT IS YOU THINK YOU'RE LOOKING FOR, STOP.

BEFORE SOMEBODY ELSE GETS HURT.

25

Joanna

It had become a tradition on a Friday for Joanna to let her team finish a bit early, and for her to take them for a pitcher of sangria (why sangria, nobody was sure) at the campus bar before they all peeled away to their families and homes. So that afternoon, around 4 p.m., she could hear them in their shared office down the corridor from hers, switching off their computers and starting to chatter about the weekend. In a few minutes they would be milling in the corridor outside her door, waiting for her to emerge and declare the working week officially done, sangria hour officially started.

But tonight, even though it had been a hard week and they deserved it more than ever, she was going to let them down. She couldn't think about anything except the situation with Callum. That morning, she'd tiptoed out to work early. Avoidance and denial had seemed like the best approach at 6 a.m., after lying awake most of the night with her phone on her pillow and one eye on the door. But as the day had gone on, she'd known she would have to confront things.

She couldn't be Fun Friday Boss tonight. *I haven't got it in me,* she thought, inadvertently calling up the phrase that had killed her relationship with Luke.

She stepped out into the corridor where her team were shedding the stresses of the week, becoming their off-duty selves but also, inevitably, talking about work and students. They cheered when they saw her, as they did every Friday; it usually made the whole slog seem worth it. But now she felt all the more guilty as she said, 'I'm really sorry everyone, I'm going to have to leave you to it tonight.' Amid disappointed murmurs, she fished into her purse for thirty pounds. 'Obviously, the sangria's still on me.'

They protested, but she forced the money into the top pocket of Mandy's coat, making her promise to use it.

'You're not even coming for *one?*' she asked, as if Joanna had announced she was resigning and going to live in Nepal.

'Sorry,' Joanna said, sidestepping away. 'I'm expected somewhere.'

Mandy eyed her with suspicion – which she'd been doing all day, Joanna had noticed. Did she know Joanna had gone to Luke's after they'd parted ways last night? She would probably have mentioned it outright if she did. Joanna had got a text from him earlier, apologising for 'being intense' and telling her to ignore him. In a way, the message had smacked of his old self – embarrassed about seeming anything but composed. But his muddled, anxious questions continued to spin around her mind.

'Thanks for the hard work this week,' she said. 'All of you, as always.'

She meant it, too – her team had been getting on with it over the last few days, while she'd been useless and distracted. The sooner she could take back control of her life, the better.

When she opened her front door, no greeting came from within. In fact, as she wandered through to the kitchen, then the living room, she found both empty. Callum's coat was still hanging up and his trainers were there, but he was nowhere to be seen.

There was a creak above her head. Joanna froze. Was Callum *upstairs*?

She edged back into the hall and stood at the bottom of the staircase. There were a couple more creaks: unmistakably her ageing floorboards groaning under somebody's tread – and too heavy to be Roxy's. What was he doing up there? He hadn't left the ground floor since he'd arrived, as far as she knew. It hurt his ribs too much to climb the stairs.

Creeping halfway up, she tried to work out exactly where he was. Then she heard the burst of the shower coming on. It seemed he'd finally dragged himself up for a proper clean, rather than the sponge baths he'd been giving himself in her downstairs toilet, which they'd laughed about two evenings ago. Joanna felt her heart slow a little. But it still felt strange to have him upstairs, as if he'd crossed an invisible boundary.

As she retreated, the idea struck her: this was the perfect opportunity to have another look in his cabinet, and at the notebook. She cast off her doubts as she hurried into the living room. There was no time to think about the ethics or risks of further snooping.

She made another quick check of his wallet first. The money was still there and she remembered what he'd said about being paid in cash. Again, there were no debit cards, no driving licence – perhaps he kept them elsewhere? Men often had mysterious systems with their various pockets and wallets, in her limited experience. Luke had placed such confidence in his that he wouldn't even try looking in 'the wrong place' for a particular credit or business card if he couldn't find it. *I wouldn't have put it there, that's not where it goes!* Joanna used to laugh at his incredulity whenever the system did go awry.

She dismissed the distracting thoughts and moved on to Callum's washbag, briefly inspecting the plaited leather bracelet before discarding it and slipping out the book. It *was* a pocket diary. But when she flipped it open she saw he hadn't been using it that way; he'd been scrawling notes diagonally over the top of the dated boxes. And they were all written in Italian. She'd forgotten the majority of what she'd learned on her brief course at work, but she could pick out odd words: *pub, evening, man.*

Joanna took her phone from her pocket and snapped some quick photos of the contents of the diary to translate later. Turning a few more pages, she stopped in her tracks. Her name and address were written towards the middle of the book. It was disturbing to see her personal details in someone else's writing, someone else's diary. She told herself it wasn't so weird that Callum would note down the name and address of the person he was temporarily living with. But still she battled an impulse to rip the pages out, to reclaim them as her own.

She startled as the shower clicked off above. The jerk of her hands made something else slip out from the back of the diary: a small square of card with *Roundhouse Hostel* printed on the front, and a cartoonish logo featuring a train and a backpack. She turned it over. In black biro, it said: *FOLEY. Single bed, room 3. One month paid in cash, 1st June.*

Joanna sat back on her heels, staring at the words. Had Callum been staying in a hostel? That wasn't what he'd told her, or the hospital. She stared at the picture of the train, and the name Roundhouse Hostel, recognition dawning.

It was a place near the station, she was sure.

Near here. *Very* near here.

And he'd had a room there since the beginning of June?

From overhead came the loud clunk of her shower door opening. She dropped the diary back into the washbag and zipped it up, putting everything hastily back in place. Then she sprinted upstairs with her phone, to shut herself in the relative sanctuary of her bedroom. As an after-thought, and even though it made her feel slightly hysterical, she wedged a chair behind the door.

Sitting on her bed, she opened Google Translate on her phone.

The first of Callum's scribbled notes translated as: *Reservation code: 16092018 new.* For the hostel, possibly? Or some other booking? She moved on to the next, discovering that it said: *Try the pub near the station.* The obvious assumption was that he was jotting down notes about possible jobs. She felt her breath releasing in tense little huffs.

She swiped to the next picture, then pulled up Google Translate again, impatient that she had to keep flicking back and forth, forgetting how to spell words she'd only just read. Tiredness was slowing her brain. Across the landing, she heard the toilet flush in the bathroom, the taps gushing on.

The translation appeared and a tide of goosebumps swept her body.

She goes there some evenings.

26

Leah

The next morning dawned fresh and clear, as if Lake Garda had shed a layer of skin during the storm. The sky outside Leah's window was an unbroken blue, and a stirring of activity could be heard from down in the resort, like a hive of creatures emerging from hibernation.

Apart from her brief nap in the chair in the snug, Leah hadn't slept at all.

She'd searched her whole room for the SIM card. It was gone. Francesca had trusted her with it and it was gone. Leah had also stared endlessly at the printed-out photos, at the note, its threatening words. Who had put them there? Gordon? The thought made her sick to her stomach. She was afraid to leave her room, but she had to find out what was happening. Whether she was in danger, whether Amy had been, even before the storm. She texted Francesca: **Somebody's been in my room. The SIM card is missing. I'm so sorry. They left photos of me. And a note telling me to stop what I'm doing.**

The message was delivered but Francesca didn't respond. Leah picked at the already-shredded skin around her nails. She didn't expect Francesca to know what to do. Even telling her felt unfair, like putting a burden on Amy's friend. But Leah needed somebody to know. She felt completely alone on this mountain full of holiday-makers.

Gingerly, she pushed open the door to her room. The landing was flooded with sunlight and a smell like fresh laundry burst through the open windows. Leah was still wearing yesterday's clothes: they felt crispy from having got wet and then dried as she'd sat awake. She was a mess compared to her surroundings, which seemed cleansed and smoothed after the storm.

She took a few steps towards Gordon's office, listening outside, then seized the moment and tried the door. Locked. Of course. Her hand fell away and she inched towards the stairs, ears pricked. Nobody seemed to be up here. She made her way down, floating in a nauseating limbo between spaced-out and hyper-alert.

Charlotte was sitting at the table out on the terrace, picking at curls of croissant. She was wearing a red kimono, her glossy hair pinned up, Ray-Bans perched on her head. Ridiculously, Leah felt the familiar flutter of envy, like a reflex she couldn't switch off. She glanced down at the rumpled, wrung-out state of herself.

'Morning, Lee!' Charlotte's greeting was overly cheerful. Leah managed to croak something in return. She sat down and poured herself some coffee, burning her mouth as she swallowed it too fast. The table seemed to elongate between her and her sister, as if she was seeing her from the other side of a valley.

'Much calmer today,' Leah said, feeling the need to acknowledge last night's events.

A crease appeared between Charlotte's eyebrows. 'Mmmm.' She swatted at a wasp that was attempting to land on her croissant, and Leah got a feeling that it was the conversation she was really swatting away, the reminder of the storm.

'Sorry again if we worried you,' Leah pressed, watching her sister's face.

'Worried me?' Charlotte said. 'Not at all!'

As if it had all been a figment of Leah's imagination.

Leah closed her eyes, wondering why she was surprised. Her sister was a master of reframing or misremembering things. A few years ago, she had cried down the phone to Leah, confiding that she felt lonely in Italy now the girls were growing up, and all Gordon seemed to care about was the business. Leah had been on the verge of flying out there, concerned by her sister's rare admission that all was not rosy. But the next time they'd spoken, Charlotte had acted as if the conversation had never happened – she'd bubbled about new plans for expanding *Il Mandarino* and a business trip she and Gordon had taken to Rome. Was that why Leah had stopped trying to have honest conversations with her? Or might Charlotte reframe that too, as Leah never opening up in return – and maybe she'd have a point?

She spoke before she could change her mind. 'Do you know if anybody's been in my room?'

Charlotte eyed her sharply. 'What?'

'Last night, while I was out with Olivia . . . would anybody have gone in my room?'

'Of course not! We respect our guests' privacy here, Lee.'

Leah was reminded of Olivia talking about privacy and discretion, as if spouting lines from a brochure or a contract. Did those promises extend to Leah? Was she thought of as a guest, or an intruder?

'I've lost something,' she said.

Charlotte's lips parted but she said nothing. Leah was too sleep-deprived to be sure of the tone in which she was asking her questions. Whether she sounded aggressive, interrogatory.

Olivia arrived then, in a cream belted dress that Leah recognised as one of Charlotte's. She poured a black coffee and drank it standing up, scrolling on her iPad. 'Mum, three fences came down last night and there are loads of broken sun umbrellas scattered around.'

Charlotte pulled her shades down over her eyes. 'Well, log a job with the groundsmen.'

'What do you think I'm doing?' Olivia gestured at her iPad. 'I'm just letting you know, that's all. Dad's out there doing inspections.'

Charlotte seemed to snap back to herself, draining her own coffee and throwing her napkin over her barely touched croissant. 'Good. I'll be with you soon, if there's anything else to do.'

'All taken care of.' Olivia was pure efficiency, pure confidence this morning. Long acrylic nails typing with impressive speed.

'What about . . .' There was a tiny pause from Charlotte. 'The cameras?'

Olivia's eyes flickered to her mum. 'All fine this time. The lights on the dock got blown out, though.'

'Log a—'

'On it!' Olivia sang.

'And you need some concealer under your eyes,' Charlotte added. 'You look tired.'

Leah stared between the two of them in bewilderment. The chinks of realness she'd seen last night had been smoothed over again. Shadows plastered with concealer. As she tore off a piece of croissant, and held it without eating it, the exchange she'd just heard sank into her exhausted brain.

The cameras.

All fine this time.

'I'm thinking of staying a little longer,' she blurted without quite knowing why. Perhaps to create a wave, see their reactions.

Both turned towards her in surprise. Something crossed Charlotte's face, a dart of worry or wondering, but in the next instant she broke into a smile. 'Don't you have to rush back to work?'

'I've . . . got a bit of extra leave. And I should be able to move my flight.'

'Well, great!' Charlotte's initial concern had evaporated – if it had ever been there – and in its place was amazement that for once Leah wanted to prolong her stay. 'We'll celebrate with a drink later. A cocktail at *Segreto*.' She looked coy now, and Leah's stomach tensed as she remembered the surprise party Bram had let slip. It was tonight.

She looked down at her hands. Their tremor was a legacy of the long night that was being rapidly tidied away. She looked at her sister's perfect hands, and her niece's, still tap-tapping at the iPad, a silver ring winking. Who were these people? Who could Leah turn to, talk to, trust?

Perhaps nobody, now Amy was gone.

Gone wrong ... Please tell someone ...

But there had been no one there to listen to Amy, either, when it had mattered.

27

Joanna

Joanna sat paralysed on her bed. She was aware that Callum had been in the bathroom for what seemed like a while, and would surely emerge soon, but she was stuck, rigid, staring at the translated notes on her phone.

Try the pub next to the station.

She goes there some evenings.

Is she the right one?

She felt sick. Had Callum sought her out? It seemed farfetched, senseless, yet the dread that gripped her body was visceral and real. She ought to be doing something. Banging on the bathroom door? Running from the house? Calling the police?

Get out of my home, whoever you really are. Get out. Get out.

There were shuffling sounds from the bathroom. What was he doing in there, now, so long after he'd got out of the shower? She made sure the chair was firm against her bedroom door, and piled a few heavy books on top. Grabbing her phone, she debated who to call. Was this really a matter for the police? She'd invited this man to stay, after all. They'd had a couple of misunderstandings and he'd written some questionable things in a private diary. Maybe that was how the police would see it. What about her mum? She could phone her, but where would she even start to explain? Now Joanna saw how foolish she had been, clinging to her pride and not making somebody, *anybody*, aware of Callum's existence. Somebody who would immediately understand if Joanna dashed off an SOS text.

A lock clattered and she heard the bathroom door swing.

She froze, clutching her phone. Callum's footsteps paused on the landing.

'Jo?' he called. 'You home?'

Joanna stayed silent. She was home earlier than he would've expected, and maybe it was better to pretend she wasn't in the house, at least until she had decided what to do. She kept very still, pressing her hand over her mouth, her palm hot with her breath.

His footsteps advanced along the landing, rather than going back downstairs as she'd anticipated. Joanna's heartbeat filled her skull. She was sure he seemed to be walking more easily. She put her knee on the chair behind her door, to give it extra weight, and held her phone at the ready with her mum's number on the screen.

Callum went past her room. Where was he going? The spare room? Maybe he'd decided to set up camp in there, now he could make it upstairs. She imagined finding him all moved in, the room rearranged to suit him, his few clothes hanging up. And Joanna somehow unable to stop it, or reverse it, as if she was in a nightmare.

She inched open her bedroom door a tiny crack, shuffling back the chair so she could put her eye to the gap. Callum was in her spare room, moving in and out of her narrow field of vision. Bile rose into her throat as she realised he was opening drawers. Many of her most personal trinkets were stored in there: treasured gig tickets, letters from friends, shells from beaches she'd loved. It was also where she kept her birth certificate, passport, and dozens of bank statements she should've shredded by now. She could hear papers rustling, occasional pauses. A replay of what she'd been doing with his belongings.

There was a clunk and she saw the navy shine of her laptop as he drew it out of a drawer. Did he just want to steal her valuables? Was that what all this was about? If so, why had he waited until now? Theft would almost be a relief, Joanna thought. At least she could get her head around that, to an extent. What she was witnessing seemed more of a violation: him perching on her rarely used spare bed, legs stretched out in front of him, feet bare. And her laptop open on his knee. He began tapping the keys; she could hear the faint sound in short bursts, with lulls in between, as if he was trying to outwit the password screen.

Joanna jabbed at her phone. Her finger was so sweaty it didn't recognise her print to unlock it, then it slid out of her grasp and hit the floor. The typing outside the room stopped. She heard bed springs creak.

'Jo? Are you there?'

There was more shuffling, and the glide of a drawer being opened and shut.

'Jo?'

Footsteps on the landing. As Joanna stretched to retrieve her phone, the knock on her bedroom door seemed so close to her ear she almost overbalanced.

'You okay, Jo? You in there?'

She screwed her eyes shut, trying to stop the spinning in her head.

'I heard a bang. I'm worried – I'm coming in, okay?'

He tried the handle then pushed at her door. It gave way a couple of inches, the chair legs dancing against her floorboards. Joanna seized the chair and shoved back. 'Don't!'

'Oh . . . sorry.' Both the door and the handle stopped moving. 'I just wanted to make sure you're okay. Thought you might've fallen or something. I didn't even realise you were home.'

'I've got my phone in my hand and I'm going to call the police if you don't leave the house.'

There was a shocked silence. 'What?'

'Seriously.' She felt sweat moistening her upper lip, could taste its saltiness. 'Get out. Don't come back. Otherwise I'll call the police.'

'Jo? This is . . . Have I done something wrong?'

'You tell me.'

'Of course I'll leave if you want me to. But the police? Is that necessary?'

'Why were you trying to get into my laptop?'

'Oh, I'm sorry about that. The hospital sent me a form to fill out and I—'

'Stop lying! I'm dialling the police!' She bent and scooped up her phone. Her hands were shaking, struggling again to unlock it.

'No!' His voice rose. For the first time, he sounded rattled. 'No, you *really* don't want to do that, Joanna!' Then he shoved at the door, the chair toppling, and he was in her room, grabbing her by the arm so the phone shot out of her grasp.

28

Leah

Getting ready that evening, Leah found herself clammy with nerves. Her thick hair kept sticking to her neck as she tried to gather it up high, and she felt a desire, not for the first time, to hack it all off. Worse than that was the sapphire-blue dress she dragged up over her hips, the warm satin pawing at her skin.

Even if she hadn't already known that their 'one drink' at *Segreto* was a decoy for a party, she would've grown suspicious. Earlier, Charlotte had breezed into her room with this dress and thrust it against Leah's body, imploring her to wear it. Leah hadn't the energy to argue, even knowing she'd feel flashy and self-conscious and the sequins would bring her out in a rash.

As she was zipping it up, discovering that it was also entirely the wrong fit (of *course* it was), her phone illuminated from the bedside table. She left the dress half-fastened and grabbed it, hoping it would be Francesca. Leah had been waiting all day for a reply to the text she'd sent that morning, telling her the SIM card had gone missing. She wanted to ask her about CCTV from the night Amy had died, too, after what Olivia had said at breakfast – that the cameras had been unaffected by the weather *this time*. But

Leah pushed the phone away in disappointment: it was just a notification from the app she used to track her hill runs, prompting her because she hadn't used it in a week.

She jumped as Charlotte burst in again, giddy and glamorous in a plum-coloured dress, descending on her to force her zip the rest of the way. When she looked in the mirror, Leah saw how pale she was in the blue satin, any hint of a tan now drained from her face.

At least there was no holler of 'SURPRISE!' as they got to *Segreto*. But there were swaying gold balloons, champagne bottles in glinting coolers, and – strangely – an enlarged photograph of Leah and Charlotte from when they were little, wearing matching knitted cardigans and eighties ra-ra skirts, making Leah feel sad each time she glanced at it pinned behind the bar.

Olivia was waiting for them, halfway through a cocktail and wearing a short black dress, her long legs like polished bronze. Gordon emerged from behind a palm tree, as if he'd decided to do the 'surprise!' even if nobody else was. His own silent version: advancing towards Leah and pressing a cold champagne flute into her hand. Leah forced herself to meet his eyes. She imagined him printing off those photos, leaving them in her room with the note. It was hard to envisage, even from him.

Behind him, she glimpsed Matilde in a blouse embroidered with daisies: the first time Leah had ever seen her off-duty. Bram stood to attention beside a pyramid of glasses and another staff member was laying out an elaborate, basil-scented buffet. Leah checked for CCTV cameras, and immediately spotted one pointing at her like a spotlight.

'I thought this was going to be your send-off,' Charlotte told her, 'But if you're staying on, it's a celebration of that instead!' She raised her flute and clashed it against Leah's, causing an odd vibration all the way along her arm.

Gordon's head jerked. 'Staying on?'

'I thought I would,' Leah said, 'a few days.'

His eyebrows lifted. 'Can your clients spare you?'

'My colleagues will fill in until I get back. I hardly ever take all my holiday allowance, so it'll be fine this once.' Leah knew she sounded defensive, and felt her neck growing hot with the half lie.

She escaped to join Matilde at the bar. The party wasn't exclusive: other guests of *Il Mandarino* were starting to arrive in their swirling dresses and designer shirts, perfumes clashing in the evening air. As Leah pulled up a stool, Matilde jolted as if she'd given her a fright.

'Sorry,' Leah said. Matilde gave her a watery smile and Leah noticed how pale she looked. 'Are you alright?'

Matilde nodded, but her hands worried at the corner of napkin and her gaze flitted all around.

They sat without speaking for a while, watching Bram dashing about making cocktails, his fixed smile on the verge of cracking under the stress. Leah's mind kept reverting to its dream state, everything zooming in and out, her senses blunted one minute, heightened the next. When Bram lit a sparkler on top of a tall red drink, only just avoiding singeing his eyebrows, Leah had to avert her eyes from its fizzing brightness.

'Matilde,' she said, leaning towards her and dropping her voice. 'Can I ask you something?'

The housekeeper looked at her sideways. 'What?'

'The CCTV from the night Amy died . . .' Leah spoke as quietly as she could, checking who was nearby. 'Was it destroyed?'

'Destroyed?' Matilde stared at her.

'By the storm, or . . .' Leah let her sentence dangle.

'I don't know.' But there had been a pause there, a hesitation – Leah was sure of it.

'Did it come up in the inquest at all?' she pressed.

Matilde sprang off her stool, almost knocking over the glass of sparkling water she hadn't touched. 'Sorry, Leah, I have to go.'

'Oh, I didn't mean to—'

'It's okay. I just need to leave.'

They were diverted by Charlotte and Olivia swishing by, seeming to be in the middle of a hissed disagreement while holding tense smiles on their faces for the benefit of everybody else. Leah caught a snatch of Charlotte's words: 'not what I *meant* . . .' Then Olivia melted into a group of guests and her mother was forced to let their argument drop.

Leah and Matilde exchanged a glance.

'Do *you* have children?' Leah asked, desperate to keep Matilde with her.

Matilde nodded. 'A boy and a girl. Fourteen and sixteen.' Her eyes glimmered at the mention of them. 'They're my world.' She dipped her head and seemed choked for a moment. 'I'm sorry, I really do need to . . .'

Leah leaned towards her as if to kiss her cheek goodbye,

but instead whispered in her ear: 'Why did you tell me to be careful, Matilde? On the paper with Francesca's address?'

Matilde gripped her arm, drew her in closer. 'Because you should,' she whispered back. 'Please, Leah. Don't end up like Amy.'

Leah's skin turned icy, as Matilde released her and was gone.

Without Matilde, Leah hovered at the fringes of the party, near the buffet table, watching unknown people milling, laughing, drinking, flirting, bragging. She felt exposed and invisible all at once. Pulling at her dress and trying not to stare at the cameras. *Don't end up like Amy.* The words burrowed deeper and deeper into her consciousness.

She jumped as an arm slipped around her waist. It was Olivia, being unusually tactile, and reeking of alcohol.

'Hey, you okay?' Leah said, supporting her as she wobbled on her heels.

'I'm fine.' Olivia laughed at herself. 'Lightweight! I shouldn't have any more. Unprofessional.' There was a slur on the word.

'Have some food, that'll help.'

Olivia eyed the buffet, and seemed to inhale its aroma, which was only turning Leah's stomach. 'No, I'll leave it.' She patted her flat midriff but couldn't seem to wrench her gaze from the lobster salad.

'Olivia, you shouldn't starve yourself.'

'I don't starve myself! I just don't *stuff* myself.'

The phrase seemed strangely familiar to Leah. An echo of Charlotte saying something similar. Olivia looked away, and Leah followed her eyeline to where Charlotte was sitting at a high table, laughing with a male guest. Her legs were crossed beneath her chiffon hem, her bare shins catching the light. Leah moved her eyes back to Olivia, who was observing her mother, her face dark.

'See, I learned from the best.'

Leah blinked and Olivia's expression changed: she looked almost shocked by what had popped out of her own mouth.

'Perhaps I *should* eat a bit, after all,' she said, reaching for a plate and throwing a rocket leaf onto it.

Dark swept in and the lights glowing from the centre of the bar simmered from cool blue to blood orange. The night clogged with voices and body heat, and the smell of the tall, cream-laden cakes that had been brought out with great fanfare for dessert. At some point, to much excitement, a fire juggler had arrived. Flaming torches sailed up into the black sky, streaking across Leah's tired vision like little comets.

Charlotte continued to work the room, tossing back her head at guests' jokes or talking earnestly to them about their holiday plans. In the darkness, Leah couldn't see the pauses in her sister's performance, the tiny moments when her mask might slip. Only the glint of her pearls at her throat.

Meanwhile, Gordon sat deep in conversation with his two business advisors, always seeming to have one eye on his surroundings, which Leah kept accidentally catching. And Olivia became more and more unsteady, staggering from guest to guest and constantly touching them, flattering them, miming enthralment in a much less convincing way than her mum.

At the side of the bar nearest to Olivia, Bram added blocks of dry ice to a row of luminous martinis. A fog of white vapour poured from the drinks, clouds of it tumbling over the bar and rising into the faces of the guests who gathered around. Olivia burst through the middle and gasped in exaggerated awe, as if to enhance the spectacle. She led a round of applause, swaying behind the mist of dry ice, her clapping slowing as if she was sliding into a trance.

Leah made it around the bar just in time to catch Olivia's elbow, as she swayed too violently and almost fell.

'Olivia,' she said, gently. 'Do you think it might be time to call it a night?'

Ten minutes later, she was helping Olivia up the spiral staircase of the family villa, her niece's arm draped around her neck. Olivia had protested at first, not wanting to leave the party, but then she'd looked at Leah with unfocused eyes, and the fact of her own drunkenness had seemed to hit her. She'd allowed herself to be led away, pulling down her hem and glancing around as if painful self-awareness had returned.

As they staggered up the stairs, which were a hard black lacquer, lethal beneath Olivia's pointy heels, the kind of regrets that usually surfaced with a hangover were already pouring out of her. 'Oh God, I've let everyone down again, haven't I?' she kept saying, her words still slurred.

'Of course you haven't,' Leah told her. 'You were just having some fun, you're allowed! But it's time to sleep it off, now.'

'No, no, no. *I'm* not allowed. Not me. I've done it again, I've fucked up again.'

'It was a party. You overdid it a bit, that's all. You don't have to be ultra-composed all the time.'

'I do, though! I really, really do. I can't believe I've done this in front of everyone. It was seeing that face again . . .' She paused on the tightest bend, swaying against the polished banister. 'I didn't mean to get this drunk.'

Leah stopped as well. 'Seeing whose face again?'

Olivia hung her head and shook it. 'Nobody. I need sleep.'

'Olivia. *Whose* face?'

'Nobody!' Olivia tried to accelerate up the last few steps, but tripped and crashed down, her palms shooting out to break her fall. Leah hurried to catch her up, gripping her tiny waist and managing to half-lift her the rest of the way onto the landing. Olivia leaned against the wall and clutched her stomach.

'Are you going to be sick?' Leah asked.

'No.'

'You're sure? Shall we get you to a bathroom?'

'I'm sure.' But instead of heading into her own room, she lurched past it down the corridor.

'This way!' Leah said, catching her arm.

Olivia brushed her off and took two more wobbly steps in the wrong direction. Now Leah saw where she was going. Olivia stretched out her arms and grabbed the doorframe of Amy's room, then pitched through it. Within seconds she was collapsed on Amy's bed, curled up, crying. She scooped Amy's duvet into her arms and sobbed into the blue material, inking it with her mascara.

'Oh, Olivia.' Leah went to her, perching next to her on the bed. She gathered the curled-up form of her niece and the entwined, black-spattered duvet inside her own arms. Olivia sank against her, convulsing with crying.

'It should've been me. Look at me, I'm a fuck-up. It should've been me who died.'

'Don't say that!' Leah said, horrified.

'Don't you wish it had been me, not her?'

'No!' Olivia's words touched a deep nerve, but Leah's reaction was fierce, and real: *of course* she didn't wish that. 'I wish it had been neither of you!' She smoothed back Olivia's dampened hair, heat radiating off her face. 'I love you both so much. Survivor's guilt is a common thing, Olivia. It's natural to—'

'I don't have survivor's guilt!' Olivia almost shouted, pushing back from Leah and sprawling across the bed. 'I just think . . .' She seemed muddled now, blinking through messy tears. 'She never understood anything.'

'Amy didn't?'

Olivia closed her eyes, mascara tracks running horizontally from the corners. 'It should've been me, but she was always the special one,' she whispered, before she fell asleep with her mouth hanging open and her hair glued to the side of her face.

Leah lay with her for a while, her body exhausted but her mind a carousel she couldn't leap off. Who had Olivia meant by, *seeing that face again*? Leah tried to run through all the people she had seen at the party, but they were just blurry shapes in the carousel, smudging as they rotated past. Even more faces watched from Amy's photo wall, brushed in moonlight, Nate leering from the corner. The cacti on the windowsill formed a fence of barbed wire in the dark.

She looked at Olivia, faintly snoring, her stale booze-breath clouding the room. She remembered putting her and Amy to bed, sometimes, when they were little. Charlotte and Gordon went to a lot of events when *Il Mandarino* was new, so Leah would often end up babysitting when she visited. She'd tuck the girls in and they'd both want different things from her. Amy would ask a dozen in-depth questions about what she'd seen during the day, while Olivia wanted fairy stories, and for Leah to cuddle her while they watched her nightlight casting butterfly shapes across her ceiling.

Tears prickled her eyes. Why couldn't things have stayed as simple as they'd felt, at least some of the time, in those early years?

She reached down the side of the bed and rooted around in her clutch bag – *Charlotte*'s clutch bag – for her phone to check the time. 2.20 a.m. And still no reply from Francesca. Leah's eyes ached for sleep and she was desperate to claw herself out of this dress. She ought to get Olivia back into her own room, too, so she didn't wake up hungover and confused in Amy's bed. Olivia stirred as Leah sat her up and propped an arm around her waist. She opened her eyes but didn't seem fully aware, reminding Leah of Charlotte's sleepwalking.

They staggered to Olivia's room, where Leah lowered her into bed. Olivia writhed in the white sheets, then stilled and began to snore again. Leah filled a glass with water, put it next to her and waited a minute, checking Olivia seemed okay.

As she turned to leave, a glint from the dressing table drew her attention. There was a small bowl of keys beside Olivia's jewellery box. Including one with a blue plastic tag, labelled 'Office'.

Leah paused.

It was right there. Nothing to stop her taking it.

Francesca's SIM card might be hidden in the office. CCTV records. Other things, other answers.

But what would happen if she got caught?

Before she could change her mind or lose her opportunity, Leah darted forward and grabbed the key. There were two attached to the 'Office' tag, in fact: one smaller and lighter, perhaps for the cabinets. She clasped them in her fist and slipped from the room.

Out on the landing, she froze. Gordon was emerging from the staircase. He came towards her, passing through stripes of moonlight and shadow.

'Leah,' he said. 'Glad I caught you.'

Leah balled her fist tighter, the sharp edges of the key cutting into her palm. 'I was just helping Olivia to bed.'

Gordon glanced at his daughter's room, but didn't ask how she was. 'I need to make a request of you. A *firm* request, I'm afraid.'

She imagined this was how he spoke to his employees. Imagined responding, *I need to make some firm requests of you, too. Give me back the SIM card. Stop watching me. Tell me what happened to my niece.*

Before she had a chance to say anything, he stepped closer: 'Go home on Sunday morning, as you were supposed to. Don't prolong your trip.'

She stared at him. 'Why?'

'Charlotte will never say this to you, because you're her sister, but visitors exhaust her. You saw how a migraine came on as soon as you got here.'

'Her whole life is full of visitors. She lives in a resort!'

'*Family* visitors exhaust her. Especially now. They take an emotional toll. I'm sure she's loved seeing you, but let's not drag it out.'

Leah felt a surge of anger, undercut by another bolt of fear. He was so confident, yet there was something else in his face, too – either a reflection of Leah's fear, or an apprehension of his own.

'Don't change your flight,' he reinforced. 'You're an intelligent woman. You know what's in everyone's best interests.'

He dropped his eyes and strode past her towards Olivia's room. Opening the door, he stared in at his daughter, as Leah backed away towards the stairs.

29

Joanna

Joanna stumbled away from Callum, colliding with her bed. He followed her into the room, holding his ribs after the exertion of forcing open the door, but with something in his eyes that suggested adrenaline was overriding pain. She told herself he wasn't much of a threat with his fractured ribs. *If anything happens, I know exactly where I can hurt him.* Yet the idea of having to resort to that made her stomach churn.

'Don't call the police,' he said again, as she eyed her phone on the floor. 'I'm not going to hurt you.'

But he didn't make any kind of surrendering gesture. Instead, he angled his foot to kick her phone further away. She watched it spin across the varnished floorboards and crash into a flaky bit of skirting board, followed by a heavy silence.

For a moment, Joanna saw them as if from the outside. Her little room with the dusty black fireplace, the lumpy walls she'd painted a fresh powder blue, the yellow curtains that let in the light. But signs of something wrong: the bookshelf half bare because her favourite novels were in a spilled heap on the floor. The chair on its side. And the altered lens of her thoughts: would she be able to climb out of the sash window? Which of her belongings could be used in defence?

She lifted her eyes to meet his. 'You've been lying to me.'

'I explained that last night.'

'This isn't just about your accident.' Joanna was surprised by the strength she managed to force into her voice, belying the fact that the only thing stopping her legs from crumpling was the bedpost she was clinging to. 'You've been staying in a hostel right near here, even though you said you lived across town. And I saw the notes in your book. I think they were about me. I think you wrote them before we even met.' Her final sentence sent a chill through her body. The idea of him watching her before they'd had their apparently casual first conversation. The idea that all of it – the chats at the bar, the date, the moving in – had been orchestrated by him.

She waited for his excuses. Hoped for them, really, if they could wipe her fears away.

Instead, he said, 'Well, I think you've lied, too.'

Her breath stopped. '*What?*'

His irises were a darker blue than usual, merging with his pupils. He watched her steadily but intently, so different from the gentle way he'd kept his eyes on her face during their first encounter, encouraging her to keep talking about herself.

He came closer. Joanna slipped behind the bedpost – not much of a barrier, but something, if only psychological. There was nowhere else for her to go to put any more distance between them. Her gaze flicked between Callum and her exit and her phone.

'You said you'd never been to Italy.'

She was thrown. 'I haven't. What has that got to do with anything?'

'You've never been to Lake Garda?'

'No.'

'Never stayed at a place called *Il Mandarino*?'

'No, what is that?'

'Did you know a woman called Amy Wynne?'

'No! I don't understand—'

'Tell the truth!' His hand was on the bedpost now, too. The whole situation seemed to have spun on its axis. Him snooping through *her* things, accusing *her* of something – of *what*? Joanna's brain and body seemed to have separated, one scrabbling to understand while the other was shifting into fight or flight mode, primed to act.

'You tell the truth, then so will I,' said Callum. 'For real this time, not some bullshit game.'

'I *am* telling the truth. I've never been there, I don't know her. What are you talking about?'

'I'm sure it's you. You're the guest.'

'*You're* the guest. You're a guest in my house and I don't know who you are or why you're here.'

'I'm here because of Amy. My friend. I think you know what I'm talking about. Can we stop pretending you were never there?'

30

Amy

Last September
Three hours before sunset

I lie sprawled and panting, my face against the path, the smell of pine needles in my nose. My trip has knocked the wind out of me. I feel muddled and deflated, no longer sure why I was running.

Nate reaches me and crouches down, also out of breath. 'Amy? You okay?'

I heave into a kneeling position and brush dust off my Banksy T-shirt, gently cleaning the girl's face and her red balloon. The conifers form a canopy over our heads, pencils of light slipping through the branches, and humidity adds a new flavour to the air.

I realise we're in front of the newest villa. Its huge black gates are a couple of metres ahead, set within the wall of trees. The rest is out of sight, but still a presence, like the feeling of being watched but not wanting to turn and confirm it.

'Why did you run away from me?' There is hurt in Nate's voice. He continues to crouch beside me, his long legs folded awkwardly, his *Segreto* apron hanging undone around his neck.

'Why did you chase me?' I counter.

'To explain!'

I extend my spine. 'Then explain.'

'Will you believe me?'

I promise nothing, though his wounded expression brings an involuntary pang to my chest.

He trails his fingers in the pine needles. 'My mate asked me to look out for his sister – Hanna – while she was in Lake Garda.'

Some job you've done of that, I think, but I keep listening.

'She asked me about working here. I knew Gordon had been looking for someone for this week. A woman. I assumed he was falling back on his old tricks, making the place look good for when VIP guests arrive. I wish I hadn't told Hanna about it. As soon as I did, she wanted me to recommend her. She said it didn't bother her, it would be a quick way to earn some money before she moved on to the next destination in her travels. Eventually, I gave in . . .'

'Nate!' I say, breaking my silence.

'I know. I'm not proud of it. But she was fully in the picture and I didn't see the harm . . . Until she arrived. It was the first time we'd actually met in person, it had all been texts and phone calls before then. As soon as she walked into *Segreto*, I got this uneasy feeling. Everyone's been running round after the guests in that big villa all week. I started wondering why they suddenly wanted another Mannequin, what was planned for today . . .'

'Exactly what I've been wondering.'

He nods, looking past me for a moment. 'I felt like the shittiest friend in the world. So I told Hanna she should leave. I even gave her some money to make up for the lost earnings. She was a bit bewildered but she took it and slipped away. I think she'd started getting nervous about the whole thing once she was on *Il Mandarino* turf, anyway. I . . .' He reaches out to me, tentatively touching my shoulders. When I don't pull away, he shuffles closer and draws me into a cautious hug. 'Please don't think badly of me,' he murmurs into my shoulder. 'I don't want us to part on bad terms . . .' He holds me closer, and I feel my body giving in, sinking against him, wanting to accept his explanation.

My cheek presses into the warmth of his chest. His fresh, familiar scent: citrus and mint and sunshine. I feel the brush of his curls, the weight of his chin on top of my head, and I close my eyes. The cicadas' chorus seems to build in intensity all around us. Nate's heart pounds in my ear, almost as fast and hard as mine. Should I lift my chin and kiss him? All of a sudden, I'm frightened again. I draw back and he looks at me questioningly, worried I still don't trust him. I can't meet his eyes because I'm not completely sure, I just know that I want to, that my heart is still going wild for him.

By way of a distraction, and a peace offering, I fish my leather bracelet out of my pocket and hold it out to him. 'I wanted to give you this.'

He takes it and closes his fingers around it. When he looks at me, I'm surprised to see his eyes are moist. A lump comes into my throat. This isn't the goodbye I imagined, but for a moment everything else recedes, all the chaos, and something pure seems to pass between us. I try to hang on to it, forcing back any doubts.

'There's something else, Amy,' he says, breaking the spell. 'I need to tell you something else.'

He's anxious again, squeezing the bracelet. The white noise returns to my brain and our bubble is well and truly burst.

'I wasn't going to,' he goes on. 'I just wanted you to leave tonight without anything to divert or upset you. But . . .'

'What?' I ask. 'Tell me what?'

'It's about Olivia.'

31

Joanna

'I've never been to Lake Garda.' Joanna didn't know how many more times she could say it. 'I've never even heard of this *Il Mandarino.*' Her bewilderment became hot, frustrated fury, searing into her voice. 'Why am I the one defending myself all of a sudden?'

Callum stared into her face. 'The booking had your name, and it said Derby, England—'

'What *booking*?'

'The villa.'

'I don't understand any of this.' Joanna cupped her hand to her forehead, touching her own nervous sweat.

'Let's sit down,' Callum said, pointing at the bed. 'And talk.'

'I just want you to leave.'

'Maybe we've got our wires crossed.' He sounded reasonable for a moment, until his expression darkened again. 'But I don't think so. I *saw* your name. That's the reason I'm here. There are no other Joanna Greenfields in Derby, or not that I could find . . .'

She shuddered at the word *find*. How had he tracked her down? Why? The 'why' kept boomeranging back and nothing was making it any clearer. She glanced again at her phone, remembering him kicking it out of reach. That wasn't the action of someone who just wanted to talk about crossed wires.

'What do you want with me?' she asked.

'Just . . . information.' But the word had a cold, hard quality as it came out of his mouth. His eyes widening with expectation.

She couldn't give him what he wanted. She had no information. She didn't even have understanding. Her fear filled in the rest: *If you don't have what he wants and you can't make him believe that, what might he do?*

'There's an Italian guidebook on your shelf.' He pointed without turning his head, seeming to already know where it was.

'I told you I'd *wanted* to go to Italy. But I never have.' Something rose and then burst at the back of her mind as she said this. It was swallowed by the loop of her previous thought: *He doesn't believe me. He's not listening. What's going to happen?*

She couldn't wait any longer: she lunged towards her phone. Callum blocked her and she heard him gasp with the pain. 'Jo, don't phone the police! It could be bad for you too!'

'I've done nothing wrong!' She dodged around him and managed to scoop up her phone. Callum tried to snatch it back. It was as if something was alive in their hands as they wrangled.

Joanna knew what she had to do. Other options were running out. But it was so counter-intuitive to her, even in these circumstances, like overriding her whole personality.

She took a breath, lowered her eyes, then pushed her palms into Callum's ribs. He cried out and staggered backwards. She kept her head ducked to avoid seeing his pain – even now, she just couldn't – and sprinted past him out of the room.

Her feet skidded on the stairs as she descended in three long strides. Her phone was still in her grasp, but she didn't dial anyone for now. The knowledge that she *could* seemed enough, that Callum knew she could, too. Her other hand stretched towards her front door, fumbling with the latch. At last, she felt fresh air on her face. Spots of cool rain. She allowed herself a moment to gasp it in and then she bolted down the street, putting distance between herself and her house guest. Glancing back, she saw he wasn't following. Her phone buzzed in her palm, his name on the screen. She stabbed to reject the call and kept moving, her neighbours' familiar houses and cars fuzzing past. She headed for the station. Even if he followed, there would be people around. When a sign for the Roundhouse Hostel caught her eye, she slowed. The place Callum had been staying. Was this also the street where he had been run over? Had it happened outside his accommodation? Joanna came to a halt, spinning around as if she might see car debris or blood still on the road. Of course, there was nothing. But suddenly his accident was clear in her mind – tyres screeching, Callum knocked flying; the driver roaring away, having done what they'd planned. Because Joanna felt sure, now, that it had been a deliberate act. Someone had targeted Callum, as he had targeted her. And she had to find out why.

Catching her breath, she ducked inside the hostel. The woman behind the reception desk stared at her. Joanna knew she must look red-faced and dishevelled, perhaps still wild-eyed with fear, though her adrenaline levels were starting to sink. She wasn't sure of her next move but she felt safer, now, and a different need was claiming urgency – a need to understand the situation she was caught up in.

'I . . .' She swallowed, panting. The receptionist was still staring at her as if she'd crashed through the roof. 'I think my friend has been staying here. Callum Foley? Could you check for me?' As she said it, it occurred to her that it might not even be his real name. She'd never seen any proof. But wouldn't the hospital have checked his identity? *Just like you should have done,* a voice in her head chided.

'I can't share guest information with you,' the receptionist said bluntly.

'I just want to check I've got the right hostel. Is he on your books? Have you seen him in here? Tall, curly hair . . .' Joanna trailed off at the receptionist's unfriendly expression. There was no way this woman was going to confirm whether Callum had been living here, so close to Joanna, for weeks prior to their first meeting.

Watching her? Following her home? Getting himself a job in the pub where she sometimes drank.

Another chill came over her, cementing the sweat against her skin.

'Okay.' Joanna stepped back from the desk. 'But do you mind if I stand over here for a moment, and send him an email to check?'

'It's a free country,' said the receptionist, losing interest as she unwrapped a Twix.

Joanna tucked herself in a corner and began searching the internet, trying to recall the details Callum had mentioned. Lake Garda, *Il Mandarino*, Amy Wynne.

She typed them all in, her phone flooding with results about a luxurious, family-owned holiday resort. She saw villas like white castles; attractive people drinking champagne in front of fountains and lemon trees; posed shots of an immaculate couple, the owners, sometimes with a teenage girl and sometimes, in older pictures, with two children in matching dresses. She saw a panorama of the resort from a distance, occupying its own mountain above its own bay.

Among the reviews and promotional pieces, news articles in a very different tone leapt out.

Resort in Turmoil After Devastating Loss.

Witnesses Questioned in Relation to Tragic Lake Garda Death.

Inquest Reaches Decision of Accidental Drowning for Twenty-One-Year-Old Amy Wynne.

Sickness crept back into her gut. The daughter of the resort's owners had drowned last year. She stared at a photograph of a young woman with tousled hair and a wide, natural smile. It was one of those pictures that made Joanna sad, even without much context. Because she was dead, she supposed. And because she looked so happy in that moment.

But what did this woman have to do with her?

She kept searching and scrolling until an image made her freeze.

Callum.

Slightly younger, dressed in a crisp white shirt and a black apron. It was an article from almost two years ago, about the opening of a new 'flagship' cocktail bar at *Il Mandarino.* Their 'dynamic cocktail artist': Nate Fraser. He had an orange cocktail in his hand, shimmering with flecks of gold.

Now Joanna had a new search term to use. The name Nate Fraser brought up a stream of results that made the nausea course all the way through her.

32

Leah

Verona to Gatwick.

Sunday 30th June 07:40.

Click here to manage your booking.

Leah sat alone on the moon-washed terrace at the side of the family villa, staring at her phone. It was silent and cool out here, a relief after the busy heat of the party and the claustrophobic shadows of the landing upstairs. Gordon was still up there as far as she knew, blocking her opportunity to use the office keys. Leah felt heavy all over, as if dread had calcified in her bones.

She shook away flashes of the last few hours and concentrated on her flight, willing herself to disobey Gordon. She couldn't quash an irrational fear that, the moment she did, he would know.

Stop being a coward. Otherwise, there would only be tomorrow – no, today – to find out the truth.

Gordon's warning wasn't the only thing stopping her. A voice in her own head urged her to get on a plane, soar away. But then she would think about Amy's pleas in the voicemail. Staying was the only way to belatedly answer her niece's cry for help.

She tapped to cancel the flight. The screen buffered and

a notification told her the connection had been lost. Leah growled beneath her breath, then stood and wandered in a restless circle, searching for an internet connection. The office keys pressed against her skin inside the corset of her dress, the metal now warm and slightly moist.

She drifted towards the wall that overlooked the pool and the guest annex, and her mouth opened in an almost-scream.

There was a swirl of plum-coloured chiffon in the water.

Leah hitched up her hem and charged down the stone steps.

'Char!' she yelled, her heart in her throat. Stud lights glowed from the bottom of the pool, turning it a blinding electric blue. She stumbled over something lying on the tiled surround, fear resurging as she saw it was one of Charlotte's sandals.

Then she realised, with a dive of her pulse, that she was shouting at nothing but a dress. Still, her stomach churned at the way it floated like a face-down body. She ran to the guest annex, seeing that one of its windows was open, and hammered on the door.

'Charlotte? You in there?'

There was a silence. Leah could hear the swishing movement of the dress in the pool behind her. She glanced back and saw it had twisted over now, coiling in on itself as the night breezes shunted it about.

She raised her voice further: 'Charlotte?'

A faint reply came from within: 'Leah? Is it just you? Come in.'

Relief made her legs weak as she opened the door. Charlotte was in the super-king-sized bed, white sheets pulled up to her chin, wincing as Leah let in the glare of the pool lights before she closed the door behind her. Charlotte's face seemed older, her make-up scrubbed away, dark half-moons beneath her eyes that might've been mascara residue or shadows of exhaustion. Did she have a migraine? Why was she in here again?

Charlotte shuffled to sit up. She was in her bra, both straps falling down her shoulders. 'What's the matter, Lee?'

Leah was thrown to be asked, when Charlotte was the one who looked ill, whose clothes were strewn around outside. '*I'm* fine,' she said, sharply. Shock was giving way to frustration and anger. 'Your dress . . .?' When Leah pictured it now, the plum shade became redder, like a streak of blood in the water.

Charlotte put a hand up to her face. 'Oh, God, how embarrassing. I was tipsy when I got back from the party, and felt so hot I just ripped it off and chucked it before I'd even got inside. And that was where it landed. I thought it was sort of funny at the time. Now I see it might've freaked you out.'

'Just a bit,' Leah murmured, cracking her knuckles. She stared at her sister, trying to comprehend her mood. She'd seemed so carefree only a few hours ago. Flinging off her clothes before she'd even got inside was classic Charlotte from her younger days. But now she looked exhausted and sad.

Leah walked closer to the bed and perched on a chaise longue that hugged one wall. Glancing to her left, her heart skipped to see a photo of Amy on a small side table. She hadn't expected it. There were none anywhere else, after all, apart from in Amy's room. Yet here was her smiling, sunlit face, propped up in a delicate wooden frame.

Leah looked at her sister and Charlotte looked silently back. Her dark eyes were glassy. Leah groped for the right thing to say, but all that came out was: 'How often do you sleep in here?'

'Often, these days.' Charlotte sighed, but her tone was flat as she added: 'My marriage is basically over, Lee. But it would be the last straw for Olivia if she thought the family and the business were breaking apart. So, we keep up the pretence.'

'I . . .' Leah thought of saying she was sorry, but somehow it didn't seem appropriate. 'Olivia was in a bad way at the party.'

Charlotte blinked and looked away. 'I shouldn't have let her get like that.'

'She *was* worried you'd be cross.'

Her sister's head turned back. 'Was she?'

'She kept saying she'd let everyone down . . . again.' Leah recalled how often the word *again* had surfaced through Olivia's sobs. *I fucked up again, let everyone down again.*

Seeing that face again.

'I didn't mean I shouldn't have let her get so drunk because of . . . of how it looked in front of the guests,' Charlotte said. 'I didn't mean that.'

'Then explain it to me, Char. You and Olivia. You and Gordon. This place. *Amy.* I want to understand.'

Her sister looked taken aback. She twisted the bedsheets between her fingers, her eyes darting. 'I've got a lot of things wrong, Leah.' The formality of *Leah* instead of *Lee* landed strangely.

Leah's heart fired. Was Charlotte going to speak honestly at last? Or would she flit onto talking about how many moths there seemed to be this year, or the wine she had lined up for today's lunch?

'I'm sure you can see it,' Charlotte went on. 'Olivia isn't a normal teenager. And that's our fault. We've trapped her in a . . . a deluxe prison.' She raised one hand, gesturing at her surroundings. 'And made her think she loves it more than anything. All because Gordon wanted to create a place that's admired and talked about, and I wanted to *be* admired and talked about . . . And we put so much into it, year after year, bigger and bigger, that it took over everything, even our family . . .'

'Olivia does seem to devote a lot to *Il Mandarino*,' Leah said. She'd never heard such self-awareness from Charlotte. She didn't know whether to be relieved it had finally arrived, or fearful of what might come next. Amy seemed to watch them from her frame; Leah wondered if she could hear them, wherever she was. 'Is there . . .' Leah paused. 'Does she have a problem with her eating?'

Charlotte's lips tightened. 'What do you mean?'

'She doesn't seem to eat much. And a couple of times, I've seen you . . .'

'Seen me *what*?' Charlotte sat up straight now, her chin high. Leah felt a roll of unease.

'Gesturing . . .' She enacted what she'd seen Charlotte do at the lunch table: a kind of stop signal. 'For Olivia not to eat anymore.'

'You think I starve my daughter?'

'*No*, I—'

'You think I'm that kind of mother?'

'No, no . . .'

'Why would you ask these questions? Why are you look-ing at me like I'm some sort of monster?'

Leah sprang up, but then felt as if she was looming over her sister, and saw Charlotte draw herself up in response. The duvet fell away and she knelt on the bed in her under-wear, radiating defensive anger.

'After Amy died –' her eyes flicked towards the photo – 'Olivia stopped eating. It's only in the last three months that she's really started properly again, but if she has too much, it makes her ill. That's why I remind her not to overdo it. Not some vanity thing! Okay, I may have influ-enced her to be a little too obsessed with her looks, but I would *never* encourage her to . . .' Her hands went to her face. 'Never . . .' Her shoulders began to shake, and it took Leah longer than it should've done to realise she was crying into her palms.

'Sorry, Charlotte, I'm sorry,' she said, clambering onto the bed.

'I *am* a bad mum,' Charlotte cried, clammy with tears and stale alcohol, just as Olivia had been an hour before. 'A bad person. I've done some awful things.'

'You're not,' Leah said. 'You . . .' She was going to add 'you haven't', but the words dissolved because she still wasn't convinced, in her gut, that Charlotte hadn't made any catastrophic choices.

Charlotte pulled back as if reading Leah's thoughts. Her

pupils contracted as pale light from the half-shrouded windows hit her eyes.

'Could you go, please?'

Leah shuffled back, giving her space. 'Do you want some water?'

'I just want to be alone.'

Leah slid off the bed, but hovered, not knowing what to do. Her sister lay down again and pulled the covers over herself, turning away on her side.

'Go, Leah,' she said to the wall.

Leah backed out of the annex and stumbled away, trying not to look at the dress still floating and twisting in the fluorescent pool.

33

Joanna

The search results for 'Nate Fraser *Il Mandarino*' were like pieces of a nightmare queuing up on Joanna's screen. Speculation that he had been questioned in relation to Amy Wynne's death, that they had been seeing one another in secret. An anonymous, leaked eyewitness account claiming to have seen them arguing on the day of her drowning. Old tweets full of vitriol, voicing concerns or outright accusing him, complete with their own #JusticeForAmy hashtag.

NF is more than ten years older than Amy was. Bit of a drifter, knew she was rich . . . Not hard to see a motive. #JusticeForAmy

Amy Wynne's a friend of a friend. I heard she'd not been seeing her best mates much lately. Was Nate keeping her all for himself? #JusticeForAmy #RIPAmy #IlMandarino

Anyone know who saw them arguing and what it was about? #JusticeForAmy

Police are trying to stop speculation about Amy & Nate Fraser but they're not offering any other answers #JusticeForAmy

Who's seen the #IlMandarino statement about the inquest decision? No mention of Fraser. As usual Twitter's got itself in a spin without any facts. #Trolls #WhyDoIStillUseTwitter

The hostel receptionist was positively glaring at her now, as she continued to hover in the lobby, bent over her phone. Joanna avoided her eye. She didn't dare leave this place, even though it smelled of sweat and fried onions and there were patches of damp on the walls like spilled tea.

A text from Callum – *Nate* – flashed at the top of her screen.

I didn't mean to scare you.

She swiped upwards to dismiss it, along with a lurching flashback of being in her room with him. Whether he'd meant to or not, he'd scared her more than she'd ever been scared before.

Another text followed.

I'm so sorry. I've gone about this all wrong. Don't blame you for running away. I'm going to try to explain. I know texts aren't the best way but it's all I've got at the moment.

She watched, dry-mouthed, as further messages trickled in. They were even harder to scrutinise for truth than if she'd been able to see his face. But they were also easier to absorb now there was distance between them, her immediate panic subsiding.

Amy was the daughter of my employers. And one of the best people I've ever known. There were rumours we were having a relationship but we weren't, we were just close.

She drowned in Lake Garda last September.

There was a short pause after this one, and Joanna tried to picture him – collecting himself as sadness came over him? Or calculating his next lie? She could only see him against a blank background; it was too painful to sketch her house and belongings into the scene. And Roxy. Where was she? Joanna hoped she was roaming the streets, getting into mischief with dead mice and other cats, rather than at home with Callum or Nate or whoever he was.

People became convinced I had something to do with her death. The police soon dropped any inquiries into me, but I had to leave, the rumours and trolls were unbearable. I got rid of my phone, hardly brought anything with me. Even when I reached the UK I was paranoid I was being followed, so I started using a different name – an old friend's name, and his date of birth too, whenever I had to fill out anything official.

Acting like I was on the run without having done anything wrong.

I would NEVER have hurt Amy.

Joanna had to hold herself back from responding, asking more questions, trying to drive his story forward to some lightbulb moment of understanding. What if he could somehow work out her location from her messages? His basic phone might be just another ruse. The door to the hostel opened with a chime and she jolted with anxiety. A woman in an oversized T-shirt and a denim skirt came in and Joanna's posture slumped back down, her eyes returning to her phone as a stream of further texts came through.

Amy was supposed to make a break for it that evening. Leave Il Mandarino for the life she wanted.

**I was desperate to see her do it. She deserved it, she
wasn't happy. But something or someone stopped
her, I'm sure of it. She turned up dead in the lake,
even though she was supposed to be in a taxi heading
to Riva.**

**And in the last conversation I ever had with her,
she was standing outside Il Mandarino's biggest
villa, trying to get in. Trying to do the right thing,
fight against the bad, like she always did. But that
time, I think it got her killed.**

Joanna pulled in a breath, closing her eyes. When she
opened them, her screen was full again.

**Before I left, I promised myself I'd find out who'd
been staying there. I think they might've been the last
person to see her alive, the missing piece of the puzzle.
I owe Amy that, at least – truth, justice. For me, too,
I guess, but mainly for her. I let her down that day.
Handled everything so badly. Just like I'm doing now.**

**I managed to get a look at the booking system while
I was signing off paperwork to terminate my contract.
Everyone was so distracted at the time, it wasn't as
hard as it might've been.**

**And it said Joanna Greenfield, Derby. There was
even a signature and a passport number.**

**When I looked you up, you were the only one who
fit the bill.**

'But – no!' The words escaped her lips and the receptionist swivelled her way.

'Are you sure I can't help you with anything else?' she
asked, in the least happy-to-help tone Joanna had ever heard.

She shook her head. Ducking back to her phone, she searched for: *Joanna Greenfield Il Mandarino.* It felt strange. She'd never googled her own name before. There were no results that linked it with the resort, but she wasn't sure what that proved. She checked the date of Amy's death. *What was I doing, that day, that week?* She opened her phone calendar, fighting off an uneasy sense that she was providing an alibi.

'This *is* a waiting area for *guests* who are checking in or out,' the receptionist said, pointedly.

The words 'guests' and 'checking in' mingled with Joanna's confusion. She imagined someone signing her name as they checked into a luxury villa. Surely all she had to do was prove it hadn't been her, then this could end. More texts came through from Nate, explaining how he had found her, planned to slowly get close to her, how his accident had only accelerated the plan. Apologising, begging her to come back to the house so they could talk. Joanna didn't want to hear it anymore. She stayed focused, navigating to last September in her phone.

She stilled as she read the entry in her calendar for that week. Something dropped at the back of her mind, like a jigsaw piece trying to slot into place, but getting stuck, dangling clumsily. Her free hand went up to her mouth and she closed her eyes, hoping that when she opened them again, there would be nothing there. Nothing written in that week to send her thoughts and her heart charging again.

34

Leah

Leah ran back into the main part of the villa and up the spiral stairs, dress now hitched above her knees so she could move more quickly. She stopped outside Gordon's office, touching the outline of the keys inside the corset top. Was he in there? She couldn't hear anything. The whole landing was silent, but her head was far from it – snippets of her argument with Charlotte kept blasting back.

Why are you looking at me like I'm some sort of monster?

I've done some awful things.

Leah shook her head to banish its noise, then pushed into her room, stripping off the dress with a sigh of relief. Being back in her own clothes gave her a new energy. She imagined herself climbing a dizzily high rockface or a practice wall, regulating her breathing, concentrating on the positions of her feet and hands. *Don't think about the bad things that might happen. Just think about your strategy. Higher and higher without looking back.* She clung to the mantra as she checked her phone and saw there was still no word from Francesca.

As she was tucking the phone into her pocket, trying to form a plan, she heard a door open and then close. It had come from further down the landing, around the corner of the L: Charlotte and Gordon's room. Gordon's footsteps were distinctive, turning the bend. Leah stayed motionless behind her door as he approached. He seemed to pause right outside – for one, two, three of her short breaths – then carried on past. Once she'd heard him descend, she darted out of her room and across the landing to the balcony, where the resort lay in velvety darkness below. Moments later, she saw him emerge from the house and stride off down the snaking path.

He was gone. There was no way of knowing how long for, but this might be her only chance.

Creeping back along the landing, Leah paused to double-check Olivia wasn't stirring and nobody else was around. All was quiet. She retrieved the keys from her pocket and slipped them into the lock of Gordon's office door.

Then she was inside, trying to think quickly and clearly about how to approach her search. Her dad's voice popped into her head, saying 'if you were a SIM card, where would you be hiding?' in the way he always did when he'd lost something. A yearning swelled in Leah's chest, but she hardened herself against it. She had to treat this like a work problem or a puzzle to be solved.

While the computer was booting up, she ran her eyes over the desk and rifled through its drawers. They were neatly stocked with expensive stationery, but nothing that seemed meaningful, and no sign of the SIM. Leah inspected the paper in the printer. It didn't look like the paper the photos had been printed on. As the computer hummed to life, she leaned over the keyboard and tried the same password as for the WiFi. Incorrect. She tried an older WiFi password, recalled from a past visit: also incorrect. Afraid of locking the computer with too many attempts, Leah turned her attention to the filing cabinets instead.

The smaller key on the tag slotted in. Her heart lurched as the first drawer opened with a loud, metallic clang. She grabbed it before it could fly off its hinges, and listened for any signs of having alerted someone. A creak, nothing more. Maybe Olivia turning over in bed. Leah tried to speed up, but her eyes blurred as she thumbed through the many divided sections of the cabinet's deep drawers. Financial documents, supplier contracts. She pulled out a few papers, flinching at every too-loud noise she accidentally made.

Rushing on to the second cabinet, she found this one full of printed booking records. Most of the villas were named after Italian fruits and herbs, but there was one folder simply marked 'New', which she took to be the large, exclusive villa, its lack of name another thing setting it apart. She tugged out its booking records, seeing Alec Huxley's name on the current one, with notes such as, *Financial Times daily/otherwise DND unless requested.* Leah leafed through to last September. The booking for the week Amy had died was under the name 'Joanna Greenfield'. There were a lot of notes associated with it, handwritten in looping fountain-pen script.

Two guests.

Premium package, all extras.

Business facilities needed throughout week, highest confidentiality.

SATURDAY (completion): Moët case (2015 vintage); canapés (NO SHELLFISH); company (in recruitment).

Saturday. The day Amy had died. Clearly, something special had been planned for the VIP guests. Was it relevant? Leah's eyes settled on 'Company (in recruitment)', something tapping at the back of her head.

Then she froze. Footsteps. The groan of that uneven floorboard, which she herself had stood on when eavesdropping a few days ago.

Whose footsteps? At this hour? She strained to identify them, forming excuses in her head for if she was caught. They got closer, louder, then a male voice said: '*Pronto?*'

It sounded like one of Gordon's advisors. Acting on instinct, Leah pushed the computer chair aside, dropped to her knees, and crawled into the dark space beneath the desk. A smell of mahogany reminded her of the boardroom at work, and of something else, something troubling – maybe the interior of the big villa from the night of the storm.

As she drew the chair back into place in front of her, she heard the voice again, speaking in Italian. It paused, continued, paused, continued. A phone call. Leah waited, her heartbeat seeming to vibrate the shadows around her. She pressed her fingertips against the soft carpet and tried to take quiet breaths.

'*Grazie,*' said the voice. '*Sì, sì, arrivederci.*'

Leah recognised the sign-off, and braced herself for what he would do next. She couldn't hear a thing except a rasping in her throat and the faint hum of the computer's hard drive. Then there was movement, and she sank forward in relief because it was movement *away*, footsteps receding, the click of a hard sole on the lacquered stairs.

Her back leaked sweat as she clambered out from her hiding spot. Any sense of calm or strategy had unravelled. She had to finish quickly and leave. Her hands fumbled through the rest of the cabinets but there didn't seem to be any physical CCTV tapes. The recordings were probably kept on the computer: should she try one last time to access it? Attempting to guess a password was a near-impossible task, though. Better to keep her focus on the printed paperwork.

She paused again when she reached the very back of the last drawer. There were a number of letters addressed to Charlotte, marked *Private and Confidential*. Leah opened one and pulled out its contents, reading rapidly.

Subject tracked to Heathrow. Stayed one night in a hotel. After that, trail goes cold but am following up leads. In touch again soon.

Leah tugged out another.

Potential lead in Derby. May or may not be subject. More soon.

Then one that was dated around three weeks ago: *Job terminated, as requested. Please find final invoice enclosed.*

Leah glanced at the invoice. *Samuel Letherington, Private Investigator.* An extortionate total, and a short summary: *Client requested early termination of job.*

As she stood frowning, trying to understand, another creak came from somewhere outside. She'd been in here too long. She shoved the letters back into the drawer, committing their contents to memory as best she could. With a final glance around, she turned off the computer, listened to check the coast was clear, and slipped out.

Her thoughts spun as she locked the door. Why had Charlotte hired a private investigator, but terminated his services early? Who had she been tracking?

Other fragments were trying to connect and clarify in her mind.

The voicemail, the villa, the cameras. Had Amy found out something she shouldn't? Was that what had killed her, not the weather and the waves?

'Excuse me, Miss Hannell?'

Leah whirled around, her breath trapping in her throat. It was one of Gordon's advisors. From his voice, she guessed he was the same one she'd just overheard on the phone – why was he roaming around the family villa in the early hours of the morning? He glanced at the office door, at the keys still in her hand.

'If it's not too inconvenient . . .'– his eyes lingered on the keys –'your legal expertise is required again. For our guest, Mr Huxley.'

'Oh.' Leah pressed her arm into her side. All her instincts were yelling at her not to go with him. 'Well, I'm afraid I'm busy at the moment. Packing. And then I need to get some sleep. It's almost four in the morning!'

'I realise that. I'm told it's urgent. Sorry to interrupt . . .' His gaze flicked towards the office door again, but his face remained blank.

'I'm really not the best person to assist him, anyway. Can't your own lawyers help out?'

'You've been requested.'

Leah stood her ground, even as her legs shook. 'I'm sorry. I can't.' She turned and walked to her room.

Inside, she expelled a long breath, and listened until she heard the man leave. Silence gripped the villa. She couldn't make out anything from Olivia's room, now. She felt she should check on her, but she was reluctant to step out again too soon.

Think, Leah, think.

She wished she'd managed more sleep over the last two days. Wished she didn't feel as if a clock was ticking, as if all the responsibility was piled on her shoulders.

Her phone buzzed and she scrambled for it, hoping it would be Francesca. Instead, it was an email. Leah read it in growing confusion.

Auntie Lee, it's Olivia. I'm in the big villa. Please come. I need you. I'm scared.

35

Amy

Last September
Two and a half hours before sunset

'She—' Nate seems to pull himself up short before his sentence has begun.

'She what?' Concern prickles over me. 'Nate, come on, what *about* Olivia?'

He sighs and scratches his chin. 'I didn't want to bother you with this.' It's a repetition of his earlier sentiment, filling me with impatience. 'I wanted you to stay focused on leaving.'

'Bother me with *what*?'

'When Olivia came back to drop off the empty pitcher . . . something didn't seem right.'

'How do you mean?'

'For one thing, she looked as if she'd been crying . . .'

'Olivia did?' I used to hate it when she cried when we were younger. It's been a while since I've seen it, since she's trusted me enough to show me her feelings. Sometimes I catch the momentary crumple of her face if Dad snaps unthinkingly at her, and it always makes me want to hug her, to put us briefly back on the same team, but I never seem to get the chance.

'And . . .' Nate's eyes slide. 'There were . . . marks on her arms.'

Alarm catapults through me. '*What*? What kind of marks?'

'Like . . . bruising.' He flinches. 'Finger marks, almost.'

'Shit, Nate—'

'I don't want you to get worried, though, Aimes. There's probably an explanation . . .'

How can I not be worried? Crying. Bruising. *Finger marks?* I spring to my feet and so does Nate, watching me as I try to collect my thoughts.

'What time was this?' I ask.

'About an hour ago.'

The sequence of the day rolls backwards through my mind. Then I fast-forward, thinking about how long I've got left, what I need to do, my rucksack and phone still in my room. And too many threads left hanging, or so it feels.

'Did she say anything?' I ask.

'No. She dumped the pitcher and left. I tried to talk to her but she hurried away.'

'Back to the villa?' I glance towards its gates, a liquid feeling swilling in my stomach. Above the criss-cross of tree branches, the clouds are beginning to clump together, pile themselves up tall.

'I don't know. Don't let this divert you, Amy. You *can't* miss your taxi. And I've got to get back for my customers . . .'

Precious customers, I think, but I know it's just my anxiety making me short-tempered.

'I'll fetch my phone, call her . . .' My brain starts ticking, hands patting my pockets to double-check I didn't bring it with me.

'Aimes, you know you're on a tight schedule with your journey.'

'It's under control, Nate.'

'I recognise that expression.' He gestures at my face. 'You're plotting.'

'Plotting? She's my *sister*, and I'm just trying to make sure she's okay. It's not a fucking plot.' But as I say it, dread hits me again. *Is* there a plot? Why does it feel like there is, here, today, and I'm failing to work it out?

'You know what I mean. I just don't want you to . . . I shouldn't have said anything about Olivia. Shouldn't have alarmed you.'

'Well, you did, and how can I ignore it now?'

'Because you have to!' He steps close to me again, hands lifted. 'You can't solve everything!'

'Surely you knew I would react like this!'

'I just thought—'

'What if—'

'*Amy!*' A third voice sails into the middle of our spat. 'Nate! What is going on here?'

We both whirl around. The black gates have opened – just a small amount so far, clearly not enough that we noticed, but enough to have allowed Mum to emerge.

'I could hear your raised voices from inside the gates,' she says. 'It's really not appropriate to be arguing here!'

'We weren't arguing,' I say defensively, wondering if she heard any of what was said. She looks between us, taking in my dusty clothes from my earlier tumble, my grazed knees, Nate's apron hanging loose and our matching flushed cheeks. The cut on my finger has started bleeding again. Maybe it got knocked when I fell, or when we hugged. I press the dressing to try to stem it, but a thin trickle of red makes its way across my palm.

In contrast, Mum is flawless in an emerald green dress, her perfume altering the scent of the humid air. She looks as if she has more to say about the state of us, or about causing a disturbance, but I get in first: 'Is Olivia in there?'

She's momentarily thrown by the topic change, then irritation scrunches her face. 'She *should* be. Or contactable, at the very least! She's supposed to be overseeing things there today. I don't know where she could've got to. And she left this on the floor inside!' She holds out her hand and I see part of a broken acrylic nail in the middle of her palm. Dark red. One of Olivia's. Something tilts inside me as I look at it, shining against Mum's skin.

'Not like her to be sloppy,' Mum continues. 'Still, it's been a busy week. And they've got their cigars now, so they're happy.' She closes her fingers around the nail and stares into the trees.

'It isn't like her to go AWOL on guests, either,' I say. 'Do you think she's okay?'

Mum snaps to. 'Oh, I'm sure she's fine. She's probably got caught up elsewhere. There are more guests than those two, although it's easy to forget that.'

'Should we look for her?'

'Actually, Amy, I've been looking for *you*.'

That stops me in my tracks. 'Me?' For a second there is a pitiful pleasure in having her attention, until I remember what that usually means: checking up on me, or attempting to tidy my appearance, or quieten me down when I talk too loudly about controversial things. And yet she told me, once, that she was in the debate team at school. 'Only because it complemented drama club,' she added hastily, as if she had to excuse it. I sometimes wonder if she would've become an actor, or something else, if she hadn't married Dad and bought into his *Il Mandarino* dream. I don't know whether she has regrets about her life. I just hope I'm on the verge of leaving mine behind.

'Why?' I ask, trying to sound casual.

'A call came through to reception. For you, apparently. Something about a taxi.'

Shit. I told the taxi company only to call my mobile. But then, stupidly, I left it in my room.

I hear Nate shifting behind me, the snap of a twig beneath his feet. Mum's eyes drift to him, then to my bleeding finger as my other hand falls away from it in my distraction. Her eyebrows draw together. I'm not sure what to explain away first – my cut, why Nate and I are here, why a taxi firm is calling for me.

'I ordered one to take me to Francesca's party,' I say. I hope she won't object to this; she thinks of Francesca as one of my more acceptable friends because she's known her family a long time.

'Aren't you going by boat? It takes twice as long across the top road.'

'But it's going to rain.' I point at the sky, silently thanking the slate-grey clouds.

Mum seems to think about this, still frowning. I take the opportunity to walk briskly past her. 'I better go and call them back.'

'You're bleeding,' she calls suddenly after me. 'Amy? Are you alright?'

I'm stalled by the concern in her tone. Most of the time, stressed and absorbed by this place, she forgets to be motherly. But there are moments when it breaks through and catches me unawares.

I consider turning around and telling her all the ways I'm not okay. Perhaps she would listen if I gave her the chance. Understand. Maybe we would realise we're not that different after all.

'I'm fine,' I throw over my shoulder instead. I walk even faster, leaving them both behind, imagining I can see them in a floating rear-view mirror, shrinking and fading into the pines.

Hopefully Mum won't call the taxi company or Francesca's parents, verifying my story as if I'm fifteen, not twenty-one. Two hours left in which to hold off suspicion and find Olivia. I still feel protective towards her, despite the gulf that has opened up between us. I feel guilty that I let her shoulder all our parents' expectations, even as I want to scream at her for doing just that.

Bruises. Finger marks. Her nail on the floor of that villa.

I can't leave without knowing she's okay.

36

Joanna

Joanna left the dubious sanctuary of the hostel and the disgruntled gaze of the receptionist. Out in the street, she looked in all directions, feeling immediately exposed. Dusk was falling and the streetlamps had started to glow. Smells of other people's Friday night meals brought a longing for normality, fish and chips, a glass of wine. As she marched past cosy-looking windows, every car engine or set of footsteps seemed to be coming for her.

The idea that had germinated in her mind when she'd checked her calendar was rooting deeper by the second. Obvious one moment, impossible the next. And with it, so many questions, driving her onwards.

Luke had been away the week Amy had died. In Italy, no less – supposedly in Milan with work. Joanna grappled to recall what she'd known about his trip. She'd been caught up in her own stresses at the time, so her memories were mixed in with those. They'd been completing their house purchase, and Luke had become so busy with a new, demanding client that all the admin of the house had fallen to her, even though it had been his dream to buy it. Her irritation had been greater than her interest when he'd announced he was going off to Italy at the click of that same client's fingers. Especially as it had been the start of a new academic year and she'd been swamped with preparations. But apparently, as always, Luke's work was more important.

Why do you need to be in Italy? she recalled asking grumpily, as he'd packed. *You do most of your work from home.*

She remembered him vague, preoccupied, saying his client was going through an important merger and wanted to hunker down somewhere with no distractions to see it through. It seemed he'd needed Luke at his beck and call to ensure the PR around the deal was flawless. Joanna had *hmphed* about that, then felt bad for being sulky, and kissed him as a peace offering.

He's paying me ridiculously well, Luke had said. *He's basically buying our new house.*

As if Joanna earned nothing, contributed nothing. That had turned her grumpy all over again, so much so that she'd claimed she was too busy to take him to the airport.

He'd said Milan, though, not Lake Garda. Could it be nothing more than a bizarre coincidence?

This was what she had to find out. The quickest route was back past her own house, but she couldn't do that, so she took the long way around, skimming the station where commuters poured out to cushion her inside a crowd. Callum tried to phone her again but she ignored it. As the crowds thinned out, she felt vulnerable once more, jogging through a dank underpass.

When she finally turned onto Luke's street, her heart sank. *Mandy.* She was at Luke's door, knocking in her naturally demanding style. There was no way Joanna could talk to Luke with his sister there. She was about to back away when she saw Mandy knocking again, for a prolonged period, then pushing Luke's letterbox to peer through. Mandy stepped away from the house and stared up at it; then turned, and spotted Joanna.

'Jo! What are you doing here?'

Resignedly, Joanna walked towards her. She wondered whether she looked as jittery as she felt. Whether Mandy would be able to tell she'd had the most surreal evening of her life. Its events seemed to ebb away now, as if they might not even have happened, yet another puzzle had crashed down in front of her. Might Luke have the answers? Would he tell her if he did?

'I . . . just need to talk to him.'

'Oh?' Mandy blinked, and Joanna waited for the inter-rogation, or the performance of not-one-to-pry restraint. Instead, Mandy gestured at the house. 'Well, I don't think he's here. He's not been answering my texts or calls. He was supposed to see Mum and Dad this evening but he didn't turn up.'

Joanna's butterflies renewed their dance. 'I'll try calling him,' she said, pulling out her phone. It rang until Luke's voicemail clicked in, while Mandy resumed banging on the door. 'When was the last time you heard from him?'

'Wednesday,' Mandy said. 'I rang him during the day. He seemed very quiet, like I was saying to you when we were out.'

'I saw him,' Joanna blurted.

'*Did* you? When?'

'I popped round after our drinks.'

'Right.' The short word was loaded. Mandy peered at Joanna in an almost suspicious way. 'How did he seem?'

'Pretty upset, actually.' Maybe it *hadn't* just been paranoia or generalised guilt. Maybe it was all linked to something much bigger than an unexplained break-up.

Mandy chewed her lip. 'He's obviously not in. We're wasting our time here.'

'Perhaps he's out with his friends,' Joanna said uncertainly. 'It's Friday night.'

'He was supposed to be at Mum and Dad's!'

'I could check some of the pubs I know he likes. And text a couple of his mates.'

Mandy tilted her head. 'It's odd he's gone AWOL right after you two saw each other for the first time in ages.'

Joanna bristled at the accusation creeping back into Mandy's voice. 'We don't know he's gone AWOL,' she snapped.

'He normally *always* answers the phone to me. What happened between you two? Did you argue? I thought I made it clear he's been delicate recently.'

Joanna ground her teeth. 'To be frank, Mandy, it's not really any of your business. Nothing that went on between me and Luke ever *was* your business, though you've determinedly made it so. I'm sure you're only trying to be helpful . . .' She paused, because she wasn't actually sure of this, but she let it pass. '. . . But leave us to it, will you?'

She felt a little breathless after her unplanned, cathartic speech, and didn't stick around to watch Mandy's shocked expression develop into anything else.

* * *

For the next hour, she felt as if she was on a journey back through time. She walked from bar to bar in search of Luke, visiting places they used to go together. The student pubs they'd favoured when they were seventeen, brandishing fake IDs and ordering sugary alcopops. The craft ale bars they'd moved onto later, sitting at long wooden benches drinking expensive beers with quirky names. The little cocktail place they would visit for aperitifs before going out for Thai – which now seemed to take on a new resonance, an invisible connection to a cocktail bar on the shores of Lake Garda.

In one of the pubs, she came across a group of Luke's friends, including Dev, whose presence – then Luke's – had so thrown her on her first and only date with Callum. They were drunkenly pleased to see her, encouraging her to sit and have a pint. Joanna found herself getting flustered as she tried to fend off their tipsy hollers of 'How have you been?' and 'Things aren't the same without you around!'

'Has anybody heard from Luke?' she eventually shouted over the top.

A surprised silence fell as they seemed to realise this wasn't just a chance meeting. Joanna felt a twinge of regret because, in different circumstances, it would've been nice to have a drink with them. They'd been her friends, too.

'He's not at home,' she forged on, 'not answering calls, and apparently didn't turn up at his parents' tonight.'

The group exchanged glances, frothy pints hovering.

Dev spoke up. 'We thought he might join us here as usual, to be honest. He hasn't been answering my texts either.'

Joanna thanked them and hurried on.

As she strode through the Cathedral Quarter, where she and Callum had meandered and chatted during their date, her thoughts moved with her feet. She and Luke had lived a normal life. That was what was so dumbfounding. They'd become adults together, found careers, made homes, bought grown-up things like a slow cooker and a range of barely used power tools. They'd had friends round for dinner, splashed out on nice wine.

And last summer, they'd been at the peak of it all, or so it had felt. Until Luke's declaration in November. *I can't do this. Can't give you what you want.* Joanna remembered saying to family and friends, during what had felt like a prolonged post-mortem: *It's as if a switch in him has been flicked.*

Now the timing haunted her. The switch had flicked after Luke had visited Italy with his client. After Amy Wynne had drowned.

The watch guy. That had been his client. She remembered photos of sleek, silver watches plastered around Luke's study at the time. Sketches of people wearing them; dozens of slogan ideas on scattered Post-its. Pausing in the doorway of a closed shop, she googled 'posh watches' until her memory was jogged: Brookmyre. They made expensive watches for men, women and kids. *Where prestige meets family values. Timeless quality and style for every generation.* Had Luke come up with those words, that marketing angle? Had he suggested the photos of well-dressed parents and children with matching watches and desirable lifestyles?

She brought up Luke's website and went to his list of clients. His early contracts had been with small businesses who'd hired him to help build their brand. Joanna felt nostalgia for those days, when Luke had been starting out and had been grateful for any clients rather than aiming for the major players. There was a noticeable upwards curve to his client list, and Joanna looked for the peak, the culmination ... but there was no mention of Brookmyre. She scrolled up and down, noticing that his more recent clients seemed smaller again. But Brookmyre wasn't listed. It had either been removed, or never there.

Her heart punched against her ribs. Now she was diving into her WhatsApp conversations with Luke, scrolling back to last autumn. It was still painful to see their exchanges from when they'd been together. His texts had definitely got briefer and cooler after the end of September, and she'd noticed it at the time, along with the other changes in his behaviour, but she hadn't even contemplated the idea that their relationship might end. That they could ever *not* be Joanna and Luke. There were still flashes of affection among the messages – 'I love you,' he had sent out of the blue, one Monday in mid-October, and she'd reciprocated with a string of kisses.

Finding the week he'd been away, she scrutinised the texts they'd exchanged. Hardly any, actually. Luke had been fairly uncommunicative, apart from to tell her he was very busy.

Seen anything of Milan? Joanna had asked at one point.

No time, Luke had replied, and she'd responded with a sad-face emoji.

He had sent a goodnight message at around midnight every night. Long after Joanna would've been asleep, but she did remember waking up to them each morning and smiling, forgiving him for being out of touch during the day. Now she saw, with a stop of her heart, that there was one missing. He hadn't sent one on the Saturday. She checked and double-checked, dread cloaking all her actions. No contact from Luke on the day Amy had drowned.

Oh, God. Please let this all be a horrible misunderstanding.

She put her phone away and began walking again. A damp wind whipped her face and drizzle shimmered in the spilled light from restaurants and bars.

Hold it together. Get to the bottom of this. Put it right.

Just as the rain got heavier, she took a turning out of town, shedding the crowds and picking up her pace once more.

37

Leah

For a few moments Leah didn't move, still processing the email she'd read. Please come. I need you. I'm scared. Then she jumped up and hurried down the corridor, nudging the door to Olivia's room and confirming it was empty, the sheets on the bed rumpled around her absent shape.

Caution stopped her from immediately dashing out of the house. But of course she had to go. She'd never forgive herself if she ignored another niece in need.

Outside, the sky was in limbo between night and dawn. The lake was milky and opaque, stained pink at its edges, the mountains turning from featureless silhouettes to cratered moonscapes. Leah's nerves were a new bind, determined to slow her stride as much as the dress she'd now taken off. She pumped her arms, visualised the power in her muscles, weary as they were. As she took the fork away from the centre of the resort, the pine trees were spiky silhouettes against the pale sky.

Now there was the matter of getting inside the villa. She looked around for an intercom, but there wasn't one, only a camera – of course – pointing at her from the top of the gates. She imagined somebody inside, examining her face, and she stared into the lens: *Let me in.*

A green light on the camera winked on. Leah's breath scratched in her throat. To her surprise, the gates whirred and swung open, like a slow reveal, slower than last time it seemed. It reminded her of sailing around the rocky outcrop to see *Il Mandarino* gliding gradually into view. The ornate inner gates followed suit, and Leah walked forward, suspicious of how easy it had been.

In the pre-dawn light, the villa looked even vaster. The front porch was like a stage, with orange drapes pinned in sweeping loops between the pillars. The pool smelled freshly chlorinated and she saw outdoor gym machines under a kite-shaped canopy.

She headed for the front doors, her pulse pounding through her body. They were open a crack, so she edged inside. Behind her, she heard the main gates closing. Then the interior doors clicked shut, too, darkening the foyer. It reeked of cleaning products. The mirror she'd seen last time gleamed out of the gloom.

'Olivia?' she called, but there was no answer, only her voice echoing back.

Her phone vibrated in her pocket. She reached for it, wondering if it would be another email, but instead found the message she'd been waiting for. Francesca.

But not at all what she'd been expecting her to say.

Sorry I haven't replied until now. I was a bit freaked out. I got a letter yesterday, hand-delivered. It was from Il Mandarino, asking me to stop 'causing distress' and 'attempting to reopen a painful case that the family considers resolved'.

I thought it must be because I talked to you. I wondered how they knew. But then I saw – and this was what was so strange – it had your signature on the bottom. 'Legal representative for Il Mandarino and the Wynne family', it said.

'What?' The word came out of Leah's mouth, too loud in the empty foyer.

Her eyes ran back over the message. It didn't make any sense. She hated the idea of Francesca receiving this formal warning, thinking it was from her. Who had sent it? Why use her signature rather than the regular *Il Mandarino* lawyers'? Leah thought of everything she'd signed since she'd got here. Receipts at *Segreto* to charge her drinks to the family account – Leah had wanted to pay, but Bram had said Charlotte wouldn't dream of letting her. The contract she'd checked for the current guest of this villa.

Now she was frozen, like one of the many ornaments dotted around the room, half of her motionless reflection visible in the mirror. She twisted to look over her shoulder, confirming what she already knew: the doors were closed. She went to check whether they would open, but they were sealed and unbudging.

There was no going back, and so she went forward, through the next set of doors into the room with all the sofas. Empty. The doors on the other side stood open, revealing the office space where Leah had helped Alec. Also now deserted. The papers gone from the polished desk. Beyond it, through another open door, she could see a room so sparkling white it looked carved from ice. She inched towards it, glancing around for something she could use as a weapon. The room came into focus and she realised it was a giant kitchen with white surfaces, as bewilderingly beautiful as a snowy landscape reflecting the sun.

Gordon was sitting on a high stool at a huge marble island, with nothing on it but an empty fruit bowl. As Leah walked in, he whipped off his glasses and looked at her without smiling.

'Gordon,' she said. 'I . . . was told the guest here needed some further assistance.'

'Actually, he checked out yesterday.'

Fear rolled through her core. 'Is Olivia here?'

'No.' Gordon rapped his knuckles on the island. 'I sent that email. Sorry about that.' He didn't sound sorry, and Leah wanted to throw a stool at him. 'I just needed to get you here. Knew it was the only way to persuade you.' He gestured to the seat next to him. 'Sit down, will you, and let's have a talk?'

38

Amy

Last September
One hour before sunset

Olivia isn't answering her phone. Every time I get her voice-mail message (which is ultra-professional and mentions *Il Mandarino*, even on her personal number), my worry cranks up another notch. I search for her all over the resort, and even check with some of the ferry captains if she left on a boat. Eventually, I reach the conclusion that there's only one place she can be. Back inside the big villa. And so I find myself back there, too.

I've always thought it overkill, the security around the place. It's just a way of making the guests feel like they're staying somewhere special. But now its locked-away nature feels menacing. Not to mention frustrating. I push the gates, knowing I'm wasting my time – it's not as if they're going to swing conveniently open. Glancing up, I see a security camera watching me from the top, and I tilt my head slowly left, slowly right, half-expecting it to move with me, like one of those paintings where the eyes follow you. Beyond it, the sky looks swollen to the point of bursting, and the sun is low and faint. I check the time on my phone and see I've only got half an hour before my taxi. While my mobile is in my palm, it starts to ring – Nate again. He's called many times while I've been looking for Olivia. As my eyes scan the gates, I answer the phone.

'Amy.' He sounds stressed. 'Where are you? Tell me you're waiting for your taxi.'

'Not yet. I've got half an hour.'

'Twenty-five minutes,' he corrects. 'Where are you?'

'I've been looking for Olivia. Can't find her anywhere.'

'But where are you *now*?'

'Back at the big villa. She *must* be in there.' I start to walk with the phone at my ear, following the curve of the trees around the perimeter of its grounds. Peering through where I can, seeing flashes of colour but no way in.

'Tell me you're not trying to get in there,' Nate says, as if he can see me.

I don't reply, and in the pause that follows I hear the hubbub of pre-dinner cocktail hour at his end.

'I've got to go, Nate,' I say, though I don't really want to, I want us to keep talking. Not about Olivia but about all our usual things, our conversations that would continue over days and weeks, by text and in person, like a thread running through my life. I have to keep my focus on my sister, though. If I could just see her, even briefly, it would put my mind at rest.

'You need to head back up and get your stuff, Aimes. I'll make sure Olivia's okay, I promise. I'll text you when I see her.'

'I think there's something bigger going on. Something not good.'

'None of it's good. That's why you're leaving, remember? Don't get sucked back in at the last minute. Put yourself first for once.'

'Do you know if there's another entrance apart from the gates?'

Even an opening in the trees might do. I could slither through. Crawl if I have to.

'Amy, you're not listening to me!'

I spot a larger gap between branches but it's high up, out of my reach. I leap in the air, trying to at least see through it, but it's too high. As I crash back down I almost twist my ankle, and Nate's voice becomes frantic in my ear.

'Aimes? I heard a thud. Are you okay?'

'I'm fine.'

'What are you doing? Amy—' But I hang up, feeling guilty for doing so, yet knowing we're going round in circles. His name sticks on my screen for a second, then disappears, and I swallow a pang of loss.

I stand still, listening. It's eerily quiet, the usual sounds of the resort muffled, with no evidence of life coming from the villa itself. A weird thought strikes me: maybe there's nobody staying there, and it's all a stunt, an illusion. Like those plays in which a character is suggested so strongly that the audience doesn't realise they haven't actually seen them, that they may not exist.

For a moment, I imagine I'm the only person on this mountain. There are times when I've wished that were the case, but now I'm frightened by the idea. I turn back to my phone and, on impulse, dial Auntie Lee. She always helps

me when my own thought processes won't. She rarely insti-
gates heart-to-hearts, but just the act of talking while she
listens often leads me to a solution. I don't think she even
realises. Don't think she knows that it was a conversation
with her, over a year ago, that encouraged me to finalise my
plan to leave.

My body deflates with each ring. She's probably still at
work, or on her way home, scribbling out Sudokus on the
bus rather than falling asleep like the other commuters. I
long to hear her steadying voice. She hates the phone but
she makes an exception for me. I hang up when I hear the
first syllable of her voicemail message, and pull myself
together, slapping my cheeks. *Stop wasting time you don't
have.*

I break into a run, back towards the front of the villa. A
traitorous voice in my head agrees with Nate: *Give up, Amy.
Just leave it, now.*

And then I see her.

Olivia is standing at the closed gates, staring up at them
just as I was doing a few minutes before. Except she surely
knows how to get in, and yet she isn't moving. I drop down
to a walk, my footsteps softening. She's holding a wooden
box of cigars against her chest. *Partagas*, it says. *Limited
Edition.* A spot of moisture drops onto the 'P', but it isn't
rain. Olivia is crying.

'Liffy?' I say.

She jumps, almost dropping the box.

'Why are you creeping about?' she snaps.

'Why are you crying?' I ask in return.

'I'm not.'

'Liffy, you are.' I speak more gently, step nearer. 'What's wrong?'

She picks at the corner of the box. My eye is drawn to the finger with the broken nail, short and chipped compared to the others. She's changed clothes since earlier. The skirt with the slit has been replaced by dark linen trousers and a high-necked top with billowy sleeves, masking any bruising or marks that might be on her arms.

'Nothing,' she says, but her face crumples.

'Liffy.' I'm surprised when she lets me put my hand on her shoulder. The material of her blouse scrunches like crepe paper under my fingers.

'I've got to deliver these,' she says anxiously, nodding at the box. There are tearstains all over its lid now, and she starts trying to blot them with her sleeve.

'I think Mum already took them some,' I say, hoping this will reassure her.

She freezes in her blotting. 'Mum? When?'

'I saw her come out about an hour ago.'

'What did she say?'

'Nothing much. Just that you must be busy, and they'd be happy now they'd got their cigars.'

'I should've . . . I was supposed to . . .' Her whole mouth trembles, her expression seeming to break up, like cracks in face paint. She whispers something I don't catch. I ask her to repeat it and, finally, I make out her words: 'I don't want to go back in there.'

The dance in my chest goes still. Becomes something solid and heavy.

'Why not, Lif?' I take hold of one of her wrists. I'm not

sure if I'm trying to comfort her or anchor her, afraid she'll run away before she's told me the whole story.

Part of me knows what she's going to say. I feel it coming like the vibration of a wave. With the cigar box over her face, she mumbles: 'He . . . he touched me.'

39

Joanna

The smell of her mum and dad's house was so comforting Joanna almost disintegrated. It smelled of cherry blossom from the plug-in air fresheners her mum dotted every-where, which always made Joanna jump as they puffed out breaths of scent. Tonight, it also smelled of the spaghetti bolognese her parents had every Friday, a recipe from an Italian cookbook her dad had been faithful to since 1986.

It was a true sanctuary, a better one than the hostel. Joanna was tempted never to leave, but she reminded herself that she wasn't here to hide. She was here to make a proper plan. She felt like her best self in this house, where her mum had recovered and Joanna's attempts to care for someone had had a good outcome.

'It *must* be a mistake,' her mum said, after Joanna had struggled through an abridged explanation of the events of the last week, watching her parents react to each small reve-lation along the way. 'This man must have the wrong Joanna Greenfield. The connection with Luke has to be a coincidence.'

Joanna wriggled her toes into the thick living-room carpet. Her mum was stuck where she had been a couple of hours ago: in denial. But Joanna was beyond that now. So much so that she had broken her silence with Callum, and messaged him: **Does the name Luke Jacobs mean anything to you? Or Brookmyre?** There had been no reply so far. Now that she wanted to reopen communication, he had gone unnervingly quiet.

'Luke wouldn't get mixed up in anything bad,' her mum said. 'I know he wasn't perfect, and I'll never forgive him for hurting you ...' Maggie's mouth tightened with the expression that clenched her features whenever she talked about Luke breaking Joanna's heart. 'But, he was *Luke!* Our Luke.'

'Luke aside ...' Her dad spoke up for the first time. 'This man is still in your house? The one who called himself one name but actually has another? The one on the run, with no fixed abode?' He was painting a picture, using his 'parental guidance' voice, as Joanna and her brother used to call it. These days, she understood that it sprang from worry, a desire to protect, but it still made her feel childish and rebuked.

'Yes, he's still there, as far as I know.'

'Then perhaps we should go back there?'

'We should phone the police!' Maggie said, looking pained.

Joanna shook her head and held up her palms, her parents watching her in surprise.

'I need to understand it all first,' she said. 'What if Callum – Nate – can explain how Luke fits in? It feels like an answer I've been waiting months for. And my name on the booking? I just need to—'

'Okay.' Her mum put her hand over Joanna's. 'Okay, love. But you're not going back alone.'

Joanna nodded, closing her eyes, wondering why she hadn't confided in anybody before now. She had nothing to be ashamed of; she wasn't the bad person in this story. She just wished she could be sure of who was. Perhaps the most disquieting part was not knowing where the real danger lay. Miles away in a country she'd never been to, or here in the tangle of her own life?

She sent another text to Callum, trying to sound assured, now, to show him she wasn't going to cower the next time they were face to face.

I think I know who was staying in the villa.

If he was as desperate for the truth as he seemed to be, maybe this could be her leverage.

'How do you want to play this?' her dad asked as they sat outside Joanna's house in his car.

Joanna squared her shoulders, digging deep. 'You wait here. I'm going in.'

'Jo,' her mum said, 'I really don't think—'

'I have to talk to him. It'll be okay. I promise.'

'We'll be here,' her dad said, clearly trying to mask the extent of his concern. 'Take your phone, be *careful.*'

Maggie protested once more, but Joanna jumped out and walked towards her house. She focused on the hanging baskets she'd planted and nurtured, the small fence she'd recently varnished, the cooling rain against her face.

Then she paused, frowned, and looked back at the street. Her eyes fixed on the stretch of empty curb opposite her front garden, next to her mum and dad's car.

In her distraction, she hadn't clocked it when they'd first pulled up. *Her* car was gone.

Darting to the edge of the pavement, she peered up and down the street. No sign of it. She turned and raced into the house, where the hall and living-room lights were on but the whole place was silent. Roxy came streaking down the stairs and Joanna scooped her up, pressing her face into her soft fur.

'Callum?' she shouted, wandering around, still clinging to the cat. 'Nate? Are you here?'

His trainers were gone. Her car keys missing from their hook. She stormed around, checking whether anything else was missing. Upstairs, the bedroom had been tidied, the chair righted, books back on their shelf. Her laptop was in the spare room drawer. Roxy squirmed in Joanna's arms but Joanna didn't want to let her go. She ran back downstairs and checked the cabinet in the living room, finding all Callum's belongings still there.

Roxy leapt away in fright when Joanna's phone vibrated from her pocket. This time, when she saw it was Callum, she answered immediately.

'Have you taken my car?' she shouted, at the same time as he said: 'Jo. Thank God.'

After their voices had clashed, there was a beat of confused silence. His breathing was loud and ragged. She could hear rain and wind at his end, sounding stronger than the drizzle spattering against her windows.

'Where are you?' she asked. 'Where's my car?'

'Jo, I need you to come. Right now.'

Joanna's heart galloped. 'What do you mean? Come where?'

'I'm somewhere in the Dales. Near Cromford, I think. Please—'

'The *Dales*?'

'I don't know what to do. We need your help.'

'*We?*'

'I – I read your texts.' He was having to shout over the weather at his end now, only adding to the confusion. 'And then I saw him, and everything slotted into place. But now . . . Shit . . .'

Joanna paced the room. 'Saw who?'

'The person I should *actually* have been looking for all these months.'

She stopped in her tracks and dread trickled through her. The cold creep of understanding.

'Cal— *Nate*. You need to explain.'

'When you get here. He's on a ledge, Jo. I didn't mean to . . . I think he's going to jump.'

She put her hand on the wall but it seemed to slide away from her. 'Are you talking about Luke?' she asked, her voice a croak.

'Yes. I can't get through to him. This wasn't supposed to happen. Please, hurry.'

40

Amy

Last September
Half an hour before sunset

Anger sears up through my core. I try to keep my cool for
Olivia, for the sake of listening, but already I feel murderous.

'Tell me what happened,' I whisper. 'It's okay. You can.'

She shakes her head, her face still covered. I try to lower
her hands and relieve her of the cigar box, but she resists.

'Liffy,' I say. 'Who touched you?'

There is another long pause. I make myself wait, my
blood beating hard. Her words are muffled when she finally
speaks again. 'Mr Brookmyre.'

I think of what Dad said. *Brookmyre could make or break
us.* My muscles are so tight that spasms shoot up my legs.

'He's the guest there?' I nod towards the villa.

'Our first really important one. Brookmyre watches,
Amy! That's major. Everything was supposed to be perfect.'
This, of all things, makes her cry harder. She lowers the
cigar box to her stomach. 'I took the lemonade earlier and
they were closing on the merger, all pumped up, everything
going through—'

'They?'

'He's got an assistant with him. A PR guy. They thanked me for all our support, said everything had been faultless, they couldn't have done it without *Il Mandarino*. I left on such a high. But then . . . then Hanna let us down . . .'

'*Hanna?*'

'The woman that was at *Segreto* when you—'

'I know who she is.' I can't get my words out fast enough. 'What's she got to do with this?'

Olivia hesitates, and I think she's going to close down. She's avoiding my eye, chewing her lip. Then she starts talking again. 'Mr Brookmyre wanted a proper celebration once the deal had been closed. He asked for champagne and food to be brought to their villa. And . . . a woman.'

The hairs on the back of my neck stand straight up. My hand rises to my face but in slow motion, as if through water, and I press it flat against my forehead to stem an onslaught of horrible thoughts.

'Olivia,' I say, still pressing my head, 'are you saying what I think you're saying?'

'No!' She rushes to protest. 'Not for anything untoward! Just someone pretty and fun to have a celebratory glass of champagne with them, wear one of their watches, liven things up. Honestly, Amy, that was all it was supposed to be! And Hanna knew that. There was a proper contract and everything. She was fine with it. But it seems like she got cold feet on the day.'

'It sounds vile, Olivia—'

'It's just business! It's just *image*, isn't it? Mr Brookmyre and his PR guy having a drink together doesn't exactly spell celebration, after all their hard work. They just wanted to relax and toast their success with a bit of female company. Dad was even going to chaperone, but then Hanna disappeared and he was stressed and everything went . . .'

'Went what?' I try to get a handle on my outrage, steer the conversation back to Olivia's ordeal. A hard mask has returned to her face while she's been defending their intentions, but I see it weakening. The shake of her chin, the downturn of her mouth.

'I stepped in,' she says. Perhaps she sees my dismayed expression because the explanations start tumbling out again: 'Dad didn't know, I did it off my own back. I knew it would ruin the whole week if their celebrations became a damp squib. Everything would be undone. Brookmyre would badmouth us rather than praise us. So, I put on the watch that Hanna was meant to wear, and a bit of extra lippy, and I had a drink with them . . .' Her shoulders jerk in a shrug, as if she's reliving her rationale: *No big deal. Just a drink.* 'But it . . . things turned . . .' She seems to lose her breath and her words, staring at the floor.

I touch her arm, fighting my own face as it tries to scream. 'Tell me.' My voice comes out very quiet, as though it's either that or the opposite.

She swipes a hand across her nose. 'Mr Brookmyre kept topping up my glass and his. Flirting, standing close to me. Then he asked his assistant to go and call for more drinks . . . And as soon as we were alone, he kissed me. I tried to laugh it off. He's still a guest, after all, and I wanted to stay polite. But then he grabbed my hips and pushed me into the wall . . . and that's when I got really scared.' Now it's her voice that's quiet; I have to hold my face close to hers. She must be able to feel me trembling. A drop of rain falls onto my face and I smear it down my cheek, finding it as warm and sticky as the air.

'I told him to stop but he pressed himself against me. Put his hands up my skirt. If we hadn't heard his assistant coming back, I don't know what might've happened. I just ran out of there, I could hardly think straight . . .'

'That *bastard.*' I press both fists beneath my chin, feeling the shake of my jaw. 'Bastard, bastard, bastard.'

'I shouldn't have—'

'No!' I release my hands, holding a finger in the air. 'Do *not* blame yourself, Olivia. This is on him. And he's not going to get away with it.'

Her eyes widen. 'But I don't want anyone else to know!'

'That's what *he* wants.' I'm speaking too roughly again, anger making me tactless. 'The world should know what a pig he is!'

'No!' She raises her voice, too. 'No, Amy! It would become a whole big thing. It would be in the press. Would ruin this place.'

'Who gives a *shit*, Liffy?'

'Everybody except *you*, that's who! This is our family business. That means much more than some stupid . . . grope. They'll be gone tomorrow and I can forget it.'

I pace in a tight circle, eaten up with rage. 'He can't assault you like that and get away with it.'

'He didn't assault me.'

'Of course he did!' I want to punch something. All I can do is drive my knuckles into the palm of my other hand. Then I see Olivia wiping away tears, and it jars me out of my outrage. She needs support, not a tirade. But when I try to hug her, she shoves me away.

'Forget this!' she yells. 'Forget I said *anything*!'

'How can I? Liffy, you've been—'

'This is not one of your campaigns!' Her hair comes free from its clips as she shakes her head repeatedly. It shimmers over her shoulders as a dark waterfall, flecked with rain. Then she's right in my face, her breath hot and sweet-smelling, and she grabs me by the shoulders. 'You can't tell anyone about this, Amy.' She shakes me so hard my teeth knock. 'You *can't*. I won't let you destroy everything, humiliate me. Not this time.'

41

Leah

Gordon shifted on his stool, loosened his tie.

'Leah,' he said. 'Why were you in my office?'

Leah's stomach plunged. How did he know? It must've come from the advisor on the landing, who'd seen her with the keys. She said nothing, and slid onto a stool, trying to create an illusion of nonchalance. It made her feel awkwardly perched, her feet flailing above the white tiled floor. The kitchen glimmered around her like sculpted ice, as dawn light seeped in through the almost-closed blinds.

'You've been doing other things, too,' he said.

'What do you mean?'

'Your visit to Malcesine.'

'I usually go when I'm here.'

'Asking questions of my staff.'

'It's not a crime to talk to people.'

'But it's not just chit-chat, is it?' He leaned forward. 'You've never been one for that. What on earth do you think you're doing, Leah?'

Jutting out her chin, she took a leap into the zone of Unmentionable Things: 'There's a lot about what happened to Amy that doesn't fit.'

His shoulders stiffened. 'That's not your concern. It was a police matter, and a family matter, and it's resolved.'

'I *am* family.'

He nodded curtly. 'Amy was very much attached to you, and you to her. I understand it must be difficult . . .'

Leah laid her forearms on the worktop and raised herself up, hovering just above her seat. The contraction of her abs was familiar, reassuring. The building of heat in her muscles. 'What happened to her?' Her forearms trembled. 'And *don't* lie.'

She saw Gordon's chest inflate as he drew in a breath.

'Sometimes things don't make complete sense,' he said. 'I've learned that over the years. And learned to accept it. Life is not all neat endings and explanations.'

Leah kept herself tensed. Her heart beat furiously as she realised she wasn't going to stop, wasn't going to hold herself back this time. 'Why did the police ignore statements and evidence that contradicted the accepted story? Did *you* tell them to?'

'Careful, Leah.' He splayed his fingers on the shining surface. 'Careful what you say.'

'Amy was a risk, wasn't she?' She was aware, almost distantly, of being frightened, but stronger than that was an explosive need to make Gordon tell the truth, whatever it took. 'To this place. Especially on that day . . .' It was a stab in the partial dark, but it seemed to hit a target: Gordon's eyes reacted before he could shutter them.

There was a creak as he slid off his stool and walked towards her.

Leah kept going, even as he loomed. 'Amy was never going to Francesca's party. You knew that. And the voicemail—'

He grabbed her wrist and Leah almost slipped off her stool, but managed to stay balanced, her spine twisting. The more Gordon leaned into her, his breath in her face, the further she arched away.

'You don't know what you're talking about,' he said. 'And you need to stop what you're doing.'

'Why?' Leah stared into his face, now flushed purple with a band of sweat at his hairline.

He grabbed her other wrist and tilted her stool onto one precarious leg. 'If you knew the reason, you *would* stop. Go back to your life, forget this.'

'How the hell can I do that?'

'Just do it.' He tilted her even further. She felt the stool leg slip and scrape beneath her. If he let go, she would crash onto the tiles. Yet still it wasn't fear she felt most strongly, it was anger. She wanted to hit him, spit at him, but he had all the power and she had only his grip on her wrists for support.

'No, I won't *just do it*,' she said. 'Why was a private investigator involved? Who was he trying to find?'

She saw the skin tighten around his eyes, so close she could map every line and pore. 'That was Charlotte's obsession for a while. Chasing Nate. Chasing closure, revenge. But she was opening it all up again, for the wrong reasons, so I had to put an end to it.'

'Like you're trying to with me? And Francesca? Did you send her a warning? Did you steal the SIM card, leave photos in my room?'

'Now I don't know what the fuck you're talking about.'

'Don't you want closure and revenge, too?'

'Not at the cost of—'

'What?' Spittle left her lips. 'The cost to your business? Your reputation?'

'*No.*' The emphatic word, yelled into her face, brought another stagnant blast of his breath. 'I'm trying to protect my *family.*'

Leah was starting to feel sick, her neck aching from the angle. 'You have some twisted ideas about protecting them.'

'You know *nothing* about it.'

'You made Amy feel like a misfit, you're dismissive and controlling of Charlotte, and Olivia's in a constant losing battle for your approval.'

He jerked her wrists so she lurched sideways on the stool, and the leg slipped further, almost giving way. 'I may be hard on Olivia sometimes, but it's because . . . it's *precisely* because . . .' Abruptly Gordon swung Leah upright, all three legs of the stool smacking onto the floor. As he released her wrists, she grabbed the worktop to steady herself. She was panting. Her wrists were sore, ringed with vivid red marks, as if they'd been in hand-cuffs. And now she could hear a noise, a distant whirring – the gates opening?

Gordon grabbed her by the shoulders. 'Haven't you realised by now? I thought you were smart.'

'I've realised Amy was too good for this place. But I knew that already. She deserves better. I'm not going to stop until she gets it.'

'And what about Olivia? What does she deserve?'

'Better, as well. Better, better, better.' She tried to shrug his big hands off her shoulders but they were like clamps.

'If you keep digging, keep pushing, you're going to ruin Olivia's life, too.'

'I know it'll upset her, having all her illusions shattered, but it's better that she knows—'

'For fuck's sake!' Gordon half-shoved her away. 'Don't you *get it?*'

He turned and strode across the room. Leah rolled her shoulders and her wrists, shaking with anger as she watched him bend down to retrieve something from the corner of the kitchen. When he came back, he was holding a laptop bag. He drew out a silver laptop and placed it on the worktop, all his movements jerky and sharp. While it booted up, he opened a drawer in the island and suddenly he was holding a knife. Leah stifled a cry, but he held up his free hand to show he meant no harm. Still, she kept her eyes glued to the blade, her heart in her throat, as he made a slit in the lining of his laptop case and slipped in his hand. It emerged holding a USB stick.

'What's that?' Leah asked, but he didn't answer, just inserted it into the computer and typed in numerous passwords to access its files.

'Watch.' He pushed the laptop roughly towards her.

Leah bit down on her lip and stared at the screen.

The first thing she saw was Amy. Her face, her moving image, like a wound to the heart. *CCTV footage*, Leah thought, recognising the grainy quality, similar to the stills left on her bed. She watched on with her stomach in knots. Amy was arguing with somebody. Her palms were raised as if to fend them off or try to surrender. After a few seconds, the other person came into view: Olivia. Now shaking Amy's shoulders, screaming viciously into her face.

Leah glanced at Gordon. He looked grey, watching over her shoulder, though he'd clearly seen this before. 'Is this from the day . . .?'

He nodded. 'Some of the cameras really were affected by the storm. But not all of them.'

Leah put her hand over her mouth. She'd never seen the sisters like this before. Cool with each other, yes, but never violent. It was hard to watch. After a few moments, Gordon reached over and switched to another tab, then fast-forwarded through various mundane images of the resort: Amy's last day alive speeding past Leah's eyes. Distantly, she thought she heard another noise from outside the room, the bang of a door. But she couldn't rip her eyes from the screen, as Gordon stopped on another image and pushed the laptop even closer to her.

It was darker and blurry with rain, difficult to make anything out, but this camera must've been nearer to the shore, capturing the glimmer of the lake and the lights of the dock. A figure streaked across the lens, bushy ponytail flying. Amy? She was followed by another, with long, loose hair, both running towards the water. The two sisters, again. Olivia's arm strained towards Amy, trying to grasp hold of her clothes, her hair. Amy glanced behind her for a second, just long enough for the camera to capture her eyes, wide and shining with fear. Gordon paused the footage on the freeze-frame of her terror, and Leah had to look away, feeling as if she was going to be sick.

'Do you see?' Gordon said quietly. Then, much louder, almost shouting: 'Do you *see*?'

'I don't know—'

He slammed his hand onto the worktop. 'Olivia killed Amy! Everything I've tried to keep hidden has been for her sake. Not for mine, not for the business, for *her*.'

Leah stared at him, shock ringing in her head as if she *had* fallen from her stool and hit it. For a second she wanted to laugh at the absurdity. The next second she wanted to cry, and beg Gordon to take back what he'd said.

Olivia? Bile rushed up into Leah's throat and she struggled to breathe.

At the swing of another door, they both turned, and Gordon flipped the laptop closed. Footsteps approached the kitchen. Orange and white polka dots were the first thing Leah registered, also seeming absurd. People who killed their sisters didn't wear polka-dot dresses. They didn't get excited about smoothie bar celebrities, or tipsy on cocktails, didn't sob like little children in the bed of the person they had killed.

It wasn't true. It couldn't be.

Olivia stood before them, wobbling on her heels, showered and seemingly ready for the day, but with something strange about her make-up. One eye was much heavier with mascara, giving the impression, from a distance, that the other was missing. She was wearing mismatched earrings, too, one stud and one dangling, oversized pearl. It was as though the grooming routines that were so important to her had broken down. Along with, Leah feared, everything else.

42

Amy

Last September
Half an hour before sunset

Olivia backs me up against the gates, her fingers making imprints in my upper arms. Tears are spilling down her face and her words are increasingly garbled as she repeats, again and again, that I can't tell anybody what happened.

I'm crying, too, sobs jumping in my throat as she keeps shaking me. My body has gone limp and I've bitten my tongue. I hate that Brookmyre has done this to us. That *this place* has done this to us. I feel one of her palms against my sternum. My head bangs into the gates and they reverberate with a shuddery clang.

'Liffy, stop it,' I say, 'I only want to help.'

'You're not helping. You're meddling. You don't understand. You think I'm so stupid for loving *Il Mandarino*, but it's all I've got.'

'I don't think you're stupid! I love—' My words slide away as I feel my body slide too, as if the ground has pitched.

It takes me a second to understand what's happening. The gates are opening. Olivia and I are tilting, heading for a slow fall. I flail for something to grab onto, my hand tangling in Olivia's hair. We overbalance and land in a breathless heap on the ground.

Chalky dust rises around us. I stare up, blinking in mild shock. The sky is dim, but it's hard to tell whether it's twilight or just the ever-thickening storm clouds. Olivia groans and wriggles. Our arms are touching and for a moment I hold her hand, and she lets me.

Then a shadow falls over us. I register breathing that isn't ours.

Two faces. Two men.

'What the fuck?' says one, as they peer down at us.

I scramble to sit. The men look amused, exchanging a glance, offering us a hand. I haul myself to my feet without accepting their help, then pull Olivia up, too, before either of them can touch her. My gaze wavers over them. The one with fair hair is the younger and shorter of the two, wearing a noticeably cheaper suit, though I'm disappointed with myself for being able to tell. He's neatly turned-out and his brown shoes gleam, but his eyes look tired as they dart between Olivia and me, then back to the other guy, as if expecting him to take the lead.

The other guy. He projects an aura, somehow. He is tall with long limbs, probably in his early forties, his dark hair close-cropped and his eyes made almost turquoise by tinted contacts. His grey suit has developed a metallic sheen in the rain, and it moves with him as he slides on a pair of designer glasses to inspect us more closely.

'I didn't know there was female wrestling on tonight.' He smirks. 'Right outside our villa, lucky us. We thought we were going to have to make our own entertainment.' He laughs smoothly and his companion joins in a beat too late.

A taste of vomit floods my mouth.

'You think that's funny?' I rasp.

'Amy,' Olivia says warningly, under her breath.

The two men swap another glance. The fair-haired one looks confused. What I really notice, though, is the brief flash of discomfort in the dark-haired man's face. It's him. Brookmyre. I look at his wrist and clock the silver watch, which somehow manages to glint in the fading sun. The gates are juddering, trying to close but we're in the way, so for the first time I can see straight into the villa's grounds. I see thick pillars rising behind iron railings, smell cigar smoke and hear a robot cleaning the pool.

As I recover my breath, anger floods me again, like an injection of energy. I step towards Brookmyre. 'You,' I say, more confidently, though my legs are trembling. 'You're making jokes? After what you did?'

'*Amy*,' Olivia says through clenched teeth, pinching my elbow. 'No.'

I brush her off. 'You think you can get away with assaulting my sister?'

At this, I see the assistant's eyes widen. Either he doesn't know what his boss has done, or he's alarmed that *I* know about it. He's the PR guy, Olivia said. And this is surely the worst kind of publicity. Meanwhile, Brookmyre's mouth twitches slightly. It seems to take over his facial muscles for a second or two, before he brings it under control.

His whole thing is control, I can tell. The precise lines of his very short hair, the way it has been shaved cleanly above his ears, the way his jacket sleeves are just the right length to reveal his watch when he gestures with his speech. The gestures of a trained public speaker, and maybe a practised liar. He takes a step to the left, nudging his assistant with him, and for a moment I'm confused, until I realise: he knows where the camera is. He's keeping them both out of its range.

'I beg your pardon?' he says. 'I think there's been some mistake.'

'Ignore her,' Olivia cuts in. 'She doesn't know what she's talking about.'

I watch Brookmyre smoothing the lapels of his jacket even though they're flat. There's a swishing noise as his hands glide over the fabric. 'Well, that much is clear,' he says. He doesn't even look at Olivia, which makes me even more incensed.

'You're a *pig*,' I fling at him, wishing I could be more articulate. All that's spilling out is insults and clichés.

He scowls now. 'I think you'd better watch your tongue.' Finally, he looks in Olivia's direction, as if expecting her to agree with him. I sense that maybe she's going to, so I leap in again: 'You *won't* get away with it.'

He weighs me up, as though considering me a real problem for the first time. His eyes are freakishly vivid and I wonder, at one remove, if he has contacts in different colours, if changing his eye colour is something he does for fun. 'Throwing accusations like that around can get you in a lot of trouble,' he says. 'Especially as I'm a guest here. A *high-paying* guest with a lot at stake . . .' He glances at Olivia again, and her whole body flinches at the reminder. 'And you have no grounds on which to—'

'I have grounds.'

He blinks at me twice. 'That isn't possible. Because nothing happened.'

'Right,' Olivia says, her voice tiny.

I feel terrible that she's so distressed, but cogs are turning in my mind. I slide my phone out of my pocket, slowly, buying time. 'I have the whole story right here.'

'I doubt that.' He looks increasingly uneasy, though. He runs a finger beneath his crisp collar and I notice a gold wedding ring. Beside him, his assistant doesn't seem to know what to think. He keeps looking around him, as if his main concern is who is witnessing this showdown, and then glances at Brookmyre with nervous expectation.

Brookmyre wipes any semblance of concern from his own expression, and regards my battered phone with disdain.

He thinks he's untouchable.

It emboldens me.

'I have a recording of my sister's testimony.'

Olivia gasps. 'You have *what*?'

'I recorded you, Liffy. I'm sorry.' I'm wracked with guilt as I watch her mouth open in horror, but I have to make this believable. Have to smash through Brookmyre's arrogance, make him slip up, admit something he shouldn't. 'It's all on there. Enough to open an investigation, at least.' My voice doesn't feel like mine, but I'm aware of it growing stronger. 'And there are plenty of details the police could corroborate.'

'This is absurd.' Another fault line cracks in Brookmyre's face. He glares at his assistant as if it's somehow his fault, then takes a step towards me.

'Amy,' Olivia whispers. Her wide eyes fix on my phone and I can almost see her peddling through her thoughts, trying to work out whether I really recorded her. I didn't, of course. It was the last thing on my mind as I listened to what she'd been through. But she looks too panicked to make a judgement either way. 'You're not going to show that to anybody, are you?'

Brookmyre looks at her sharply. It's the first time she's come near to admitting that anything happened. That there might actually be something on my phone that neither of them would want made public.

'For fuck's sake,' he says. 'Give that to me, now.' He thrusts out his hand like he expects me to acquiesce.

I clamp it to my chest. 'Why would you want it, if there's nothing on it?'

'You could've faked something for all I know. You seem unhinged enough.'

'Why don't we let the police decide? And the press?' I fling a glance at the PR guy to see how that will land, but he just looks overwhelmed.

Brookmyre lunges. 'You silly girl!' He makes a grab for me and I feel the cold scratch of his watch. 'Luke, don't just stand there!' The assistant stirs and moves forward, seeming dazed. Brookmyre grasps at my arm again but I twist and duck and then I'm running, skidding in the wet, finding my legs and the adrenaline I need. My phone is in my palm and all three of them are chasing, shouting, the white path vibrating with their footsteps as the sky ahead turns burnt orange with the sunset and the storm.

43

Leah

'What did you say?' Olivia asked, staring at her dad as she came further into the kitchen. Thick smears of concealer shone beneath her eyes as she passed under the strip lights.

'Liffy,' Gordon said: a family nickname Leah hadn't heard him use in years. 'What are you doing here?'

'I came to see if everything was okay with Mr Huxley's check-out. And then I just heard you say to Auntie Lee . . .'

'Liffy—'

'My name's Olivia,' she said, with a sharpness she didn't normally aim at her father. 'Nobody calls me Liffy anymore.' A footnote dangled, unsaid: *That was Amy's thing.*

'Okay.' Gordon held up his palms.

'What were you talking about?' She stopped on the other side of the island, looking from her dad to her aunt, her eyes snagging on the closed laptop.

Leah felt the burn of panic in her blood. *This can't be happening.* There was a blockage in her brain, a shutter slamming down, but behind it, so many questions pulsed. How had Olivia killed Amy? Why? The CCTV images flickered in her mind's eye and she held her stomach to stop herself from heaving.

'I've told her, sweetheart,' Gordon said, his tone gentle.

Olivia's chin tremored. 'Told her what?'

'What you did.' He seemed to struggle against his emotions, something Leah had never really seen him do before. 'It's okay. She won't tell anyone.' There was an implied threat in his last sentence, his gaze sliding towards Leah.

Tears hovered in Olivia's eyes. 'You said . . . you told her I killed her.'

Gordon went around the kitchen island to his daughter. He put his arm carefully across her shoulders, drawing her in towards him. 'It's okay.'

'You actually used those words.' She began to shake. 'I just heard you.'

'I shouldn't have blurted it out like that. But Leah wasn't going to stop until she knew. And she loves you, as I do. I haven't let anything bad happen to you, and I still won't. She'll understand when we tell her the whole story.'

Olivia turned her head to look at him. The rising sun peeped through the blinds and outlined the two of them in sharp gold.

'We haven't even talked about it ourselves, Dad. Not properly. Not since that night.'

Gordon scooped Olivia's hands inside his. 'I know, but we have an understanding, don't we? No need to keep talking about it. Better not to, in fact. I dealt with the police, the witnesses, the remaining CCTV. Anything that might've pointed towards you. And I'm still making sure. All the time, I'm protecting you.'

Olivia pulled back her hands. 'But I . . .' She looked lost, casting her eyes around the room. 'Did I commit a crime?'

Gordon's eyebrows jerked. He glanced over at Leah, but all she could do was keep holding her stomach, blinking hard.

'Well, yes, sweetheart,' he said to Olivia, as if he was talking to a young child. 'I know you didn't intend to. And I know you must've done it to protect *Il Mandarino*, because of how much you care. But murder ... even manslaughter ... I could *never* let you be charged with that. I never will. Amy was my daughter, and I miss her every day – I know you do, too. But that doesn't mean I want my other daughter's life ruined. You made a mistake, Liffy. I still love you. I realise I haven't always been the best dad ... but you're my baby girl.'

A silence fell after his speech. It seemed to have knocked the breath out of him; he sagged, his eyes closing. Olivia stared at him again and a tear ran down her cheek.

'Murder?' Olivia said, 'Manslaughter?' She shook, but not with tears, now: with fury. Her face was transforming with it. Her shoulders drawing up around her ears. 'You – you think I killed Amy?'

'Well ...' Gordon looked as if he'd been hit. 'Well, yes, Liffy.'

'How could you think that?'

'I found you on the dock.' There was less certainty now, less of the coaxing, calming tone. 'You were soaking. And so distraught you couldn't move. You were just standing there in the rain, staring into the lake. And don't you remember what you kept saying?'

'No. I was in shock.'

'You were saying, "she shouldn't have meddled". And, "it wasn't my fault". But then, after I'd got you inside and dry, you switched to saying it *was* your fault. I didn't know what you were talking about, I thought you were delirious . . . but you had bruises on your arms. You wouldn't explain how they'd got there. Then somebody spotted Amy's boat. The helicopter found her body. And you stopped speaking altogether. Stopped eating –'

'So from that, you assumed I *killed* her?'

'You just . . .' He seemed bewildered now, as if he couldn't believe he might've got this wrong. 'You seemed to know she was dead before anybody else did. And then later, I saw some things on the CCTV . . . They only seemed to confirm . . .'

Olivia lurched forward, seized the large empty fruit bowl from the centre of the island, and smashed it against the worktop. Fragments of porcelain exploded around her, bouncing high.

'Is that really what you've thought all this time?'

A few pieces had catapulted across the island and landed in Leah's lap. She realised she had ducked, and was still scrunched down on her stool, hands in front of her face. She forced herself to unfold, and stand, brushing away the white shards.

Walking around the kitchen island, she arrived at Olivia's side. Olivia looked at her as though she'd forgotten she was even there. She was still trembling, and Leah was, too, as their eyes locked.

'Olivia.' She touched her arm. 'Tell us what happened.'

'I'll show you,' Olivia said, grabbing Leah's wrist. 'I'll take you through it all. But only you, Auntie Lee.'

44

Joanna

Joanna was behind the wheel of her mum and dad's car, accelerating along a rising road with rain lashing at the windscreen. Dark hills reared up either side of her, flinty with rocks and covered in the black shapes of scrubby trees. She searched for the landmarks Nate had mentioned as he'd tried to describe where he and Luke were. The village of Cromford. A road climbing to the right. A large boulder, a ledge above it . . . Joanna squeezed the steering wheel and pushed the small Fiesta to its limit.

She was thankful, at least, that she'd managed to persuade her parents not to come. Especially her mum – Joanna still thought of her as fragile, not to be subjected to stress. There had always been a battle between them about who was looking after whom. Despite the earlier relief of finally telling them what was going on, she'd had to play this part down, saying she just needed to borrow their car to go and see Luke.

She tried not to think about what might happen if she failed to find him in these hills.

Whizzing through the village, then swinging up an even steeper road, she scanned for the boulder Nate had mentioned. The dark landscape all looked the same, all looked so bleak. But then she saw something up ahead: pinpricks of light. *Headlights.* They got bigger and brighter, until she could make out the shape of her own car, lights on, parked at the foot of a huge boulder that shimmered silver in the wet moonlight. Luke's car was there, too, abandoned at an angle. Joanna bumped across the rough grass and parked beside them. The wind whipped her hair across her face as she leapt out, strands catching in her mouth. There was nobody in the other cars, so she half-ran, half-scrambled up a path that wound around the back of the boulder, towards what looked like a rocky ledge high above.

Time stalled as she took in the scene. Two male figures were visible against the storm-lit sky, with their backs to her: one who looked as if he was levitating, nothing beyond him but dark clouds and a veiled moon, another standing a few feet behind, with his hands on his head as if they were playing a game. She moved closer and saw that it was, of course, no game. Nate's hands clutched his head in panic; Luke wasn't levitating but teetering on a ledge, with only sky to step into. A black valley curved underneath. It was as if all the landscape had been scooped out, apart from this point on which they stood.

Nate turned and came rushing towards her.

'Jo!' He seemed to stumble and buckle in relief. 'You found us. I've been trying to talk to him but—'

'What the hell happened?' She had to raise her voice over the rain and wind, keeping her eyes on Luke a few metres away. 'Why are you both out here?'

'He came to the house.' Nate raked a hand through his wet hair. 'My mind was already whirring, realising you were onto something – not you in that villa, but someone *close to you*. Then there was a knock on your door. I thought it might be you so I opened it. And I recognised him. I must've got a glimpse of him around *Il Mandarino* that week. He started asking for you, saying he was your ex, seeming agitated. I suddenly knew he must be the link. The final piece. So, I—'

'You what?' She made a frantic gesture to hurry him, sidestepping in Luke's direction. '*What* did you do?'

'Confronted him.' Nate's eyes were wild. 'That's all. But he freaked out. Ran away. I got into your car and followed him, just wanting to *talk* to him. I'd come so far looking for the truth, I couldn't let him leave! But he just kept driving and driving. When he finally pulled over, he was in a state. He ran up here and I followed . . .' He waved his arms around, suddenly manic. 'I didn't know he would go to the edge, threaten to . . . I never intended—' But Joanna didn't wait to hear the rest of Nate's guilt trip. She moved towards Luke, calling his name into a fierce gust of wind.

45

Leah

Olivia led the way out of the kitchen. Leah threw a glance behind her as she followed. Gordon stood gripping the marble corner of the island, gazing after them. Leah was reminded of the first day of her stay, when it had struck her how much he had aged. His stature seemed to shrink now, as if they were moving away at a much higher speed than they were.

She focused back on Olivia, could hear her crying as they walked. Yet still her niece couldn't curb ingrained habits: she paused to straighten a picture on the wall of the villa's reception room, to swipe a fleck of dust from a surface.

'You really care about this place, don't you?' Leah said.

'It's the only thing I'm good at.'

'I don't think that's true.'

'Mum and Dad drilled it into me, when they had it built – how important this villa was. The level of service its guests would expect. It was like a new challenge. I loved stepping things up.' She stopped and looked around her. 'I picked these chairs.'

'They're nice.' Leah's face ached with the effort of keeping her tone light.

'Amy thought I was so sad, getting excited about furniture. Running round after VIPs. But I lived for it. I still do, even after what happened with Mr Brookmyre. How messed up is that?' She ripped her eyes from the decor, then they were on the move again, striding towards the villa's exit.

'Who is Mr Brookmyre?' Leah asked, but got no answer.

Olivia pressed a release button and the two sets of gates opened, one after another like traffic lights changing in staggered sequence. The sun was still on the rise above the whispering trees, streaking the sky ruby, and there was a scent of wild herbs in the air. Olivia took off her heels and strode barefoot. They reached the main path and the lake came back into view, a mirror to the flame-coloured sky.

Then Leah heard her name being called from somewhere behind. She turned and saw Matilde hurrying towards her from the direction of the family villa. 'Leah!' she said again, sounding distressed. 'Can I talk to you?'

Leah looked back to where Olivia had pulled ahead, disappearing down the slope, seemingly oblivious to Matilde. 'I can't right now,' she replied, anxious not to lose her niece.

Matilde rushed up to her. 'Please. I have to speak to you.'

'Later? I've really got to . . .' She gestured after Olivia, without wanting to give too much away.

To her shock, Matilde burst into tears. She swiped them roughly from her eyes, shaking her head. 'I'm so sorry, so sorry.'

'Matilde, what's wrong?' Leah shot glances between her and Olivia, who was getting further away, almost out of sight. 'Has something happened? Is it Charlotte?'

'No, no, it's not that. I don't meant to alarm you—'

'If it's not urgent, I promise we'll talk later.' Leah squeezed the housekeeper's arm; she was still in mysterious floods of tears. 'Whatever it is, we'll sort it. But right now I *have to* –' She edged away, feeling guilty, worried, but doubly scared about letting Olivia disappear in this state, losing her chance to hear the truth about Amy.

She didn't look back as she sprinted after her niece. Kept her eyes on Olivia, tried to block out everything else. Olivia was winding down the slope, past signposts pointing towards the spa and the restaurant and *Segreto*. She didn't seem to be taking note of her surroundings in the way she usually did, though. No longer looking for things to add to her job list. Leah fell into step next to her, trying to move seamlessly back into their conversation, perhaps the most significant one they would ever have.

'Who's Mr Brookmyre?' she asked again.

'Do you know who *anyone* is, Auntie Lee?'

'Nope,' Leah said. 'You'll have to enlighten me as usual.'

'Top-end watches "for all the family". Probably the most powerful person we've had staying.'

'Something happened with him?'

'Well . . .' Olivia's voice faltered. 'It was kind of ironic that his company was all "prestige meets family values". He didn't have very wholesome values himself, as it turned out.'

Leah allowed herself a moment to take this in. Pictures formed in her mind but she shuddered and thrust them away.

'Was he who you meant when you talked about "seeing that face again"?'

Olivia nodded. 'He was on a bit of paper among Mr Huxley's things. They're on some board or committee together, I think. It was just a shock, seeing his picture. Especially there, in the villa. I still feel like he's in there sometimes.'

They had reached the bottom of the mountain and were approaching *Il Mandarino's* dock. Apart from the soft slap of water against the jetty, the morning remained hushed. A pair of gulls circled overhead, but so high up that they were just M-shapes, line-drawn birds from a child's picture.

Olivia walked to the end of the dock, curling her bare toes over the edge. Leah hurried after her. 'Be careful.'

'Let's go out on the water.' Olivia pointed at the boats that were moored to her right, bobbing softly.

'I'm not sure . . .'

'I can't tell you the story here.' She glanced around. 'This place hears and sees everything. I don't feel . . . I've never been able to . . .' She touched her throat as if to indicate that there were things trapped, things she needed to get out.

It was the first time Leah had heard her say anything negative about *Il Mandarino*. She agreed, of course, thinking of the images in the envelope, and turning to peer up the mountain, half-expecting Gordon to have followed them. She couldn't see him, or Matilde any more. Then Leah realised Olivia was pulling at the rope of a boat, lowering herself off the dock.

Leah darted forward. 'Olivia! Is this a good idea?'

'I need to be away from here, away from the CCTV cameras. And I need to show you where it happened.' There was a thud as she dropped into the boat and it wobbled, creating a flurry in the calm.

'*Olivia.*' Leah scrambled to get in with her, scraping her arms in her rush. Her niece was untying the tether rope with impressive speed. 'Why don't we just sit here, finish talking?' But Olivia's mouth was set in a determined line. Leah grabbed onto one of the stilts supporting the dock, keen to keep them near dry land. Her hand slipped off the wet wood as Olivia jabbed an oar against the same post and pushed them off. The water parted like a zip and they were away, Olivia rowing fiercely, seeming to head for the huge rising sun on the horizon.

46

Amy

Last September
Sunset

I race towards the main path with burning legs and lungs. If I can get myself to the centre of the resort, there might be other people around; they can't keep chasing me then. But the light is disappearing and it's raining harder, so there aren't any guests or staff milling about. I could head for *Segreto*. Nate would help me. But what if he still just wants me to drop this and leave? Or what if Mum or Dad is there? What if I can't make any of them understand?

Brookmyre's voice carries from behind. 'One of you stop her!' The wheeze to his words makes me feel better. I'm clearly fitter than him. But he keeps yelling at the others: 'Get your sister under control! *Luke*, get that phone off her or we'll both be in the shit.' I even hear the two men shouting to one another about the CCTV cameras. Aware of them, swerving them, even in the middle of a chase. Olivia seems to be closest to me – at one point I feel her fingertips grasping at the ends of my hair. I fling a glance over my shoulder and see her contorted, almost unrecognisable face, then I turn and run even faster, powering away from her with stars in my vision.

I hurtle downhill, propelled by my own gravity. The chasing footsteps are like rumbles of thunder – or maybe that's *actually* a rumble of thunder? I'm not sure anymore. Everything's confused. I tug at threads of thought: I need to get to someone who will take this seriously. The police in Malcesine? Francesca? As I stumble onto the dock, a white glow beckons me, until I realise it's lightning over the far side of the lake – a warning, not a welcome. I can't turn back now, though. They're closing in and there's nowhere to go except onto the water. I can only hope the eye of the storm is as far away as it looks. Moisture feathers around me as I swerve towards the boats that are knocking against each other in the wind.

'Amy!' I hear Olivia's voice one last time, then I become conscious that there is only one set of footsteps now. I don't want to turn to see who it is in case I slip or slow myself down. I try to act confident, surefooted, as if I really do have evidence that I'm planning to take across the lake to somebody who will listen. Perhaps I even start to believe it myself, as I search the row of boats for one with a fuel cannister attached. Finding one, I leap in and untie its rope, fingers clumsy, the dock booming with a heavy vibration that might be someone running along it or might be the beat of water against its stilts.

A tailwind catches me, pushing me out. Then I'm slicing through the water, the last throws of sun swallowed by its choppy surface. I row with one oar, attempting to start the boat's engine at the same time, but the choke keeps dying, the pull cord escaping from my hand. Finally, I give it a ferocious yank and it splutters into life, the boat spurting forward with a reassuring kick.

I stab at my phone, praying for a signal. One miraculous bar flickers in the top left corner. I bring up my contacts and a longing for Auntie Lee's voice seizes me again. But what could she do from so far away? I need someone who can help me now. My boat pitches and I grab the side, almost catapulting my phone into the water. Clamping it to my ear, I call Francesca.

It rings and rings. *Please, please, please.* I hear a greeting and I gasp in relief, until I realise it's her voicemail. My mouth opens, words pour out. I'm conscious of the wind snatching them, but I keep going anyway, praying something will reach her.

'It's all gone wrong, Fran. I was trying to leave but I don't know if I can. Now I'm trying to get to Malcesine . . . There might be someone following me. And the storm is getting worse. Please tell someone. The watch guy, Brookmyre. He's bad. He hurt Olivia. I think the whole thing's bad – that villa. Can't let them get away with it . . .'

As the wind gets even louder, I give up and drop my head, exhaustion overwhelming me. Olivia's face is in my mind. I see us as children, drawing mermaids in the sand, hers with beautiful long curls and mine with raised fists and eels for hair. I join our two mermaids' hands in my mind, remembering the brief moment, earlier, when Olivia and I lay on the path after falling through the gates, and she let me clasp her fingers.

I straighten up, knowing I can't rest. Can't give in. I'm close to the outcrop and the water is flinging itself against the rocks with great hisses of spray. I push my engine almost to its limit, wrestling with the rudder. I can make it around the outcrop. It isn't far. Then Malcesine will be in sight.

Two lightning bolts rip downwards, closer and brighter than before. The jagged shapes of the mountains are briefly backlit – and something else is illuminated at the edge of my eyeline, too. My heart thuds as I turn to squint at it. Another small boat looms out of the spray, like a mirror image of mine, lurching towards me with a silhouetted figure on board.

47

Leah

'I always wished I could be more like Amy,' Olivia said.

Leah watched the swish of the oars through the pink-tinted water, trying to let their motion keep her calm. Nothing bad could happen at this steady, rhythmic speed, on such a gentle morning. She ignored her niggling awareness of how quickly the weather could change out here. Ignored the fact that Olivia was gripping the oars with a kind of quiet violence.

'Did you?'

Olivia nodded. 'She had principles. I've never had principles.'

'I bet you do. They're just not as obvious as Amy's were. But you're a good person, with your own values.'

'Am I?' Olivia left the question dangling, staring towards the mountains on the other side of the lake.

Leah swivelled to peer at *Il Mandarino*, already surprisingly far away. It had taken on the look of a toy town. As her eyes dropped to the dock she saw a figure there, also miniature and model-like, but recognisable. Charlotte was standing on the jetty in her distinctive red robe. Looking for them? Leah felt an urge to strain towards her. For a strange moment, she was Amy and Charlotte was Olivia. She felt a thread pulling taut between them, threatening to snap as she got further from the shore.

'She made me feel so *ashamed*,' Olivia said, with a forceful stroke that made the boat surge.

Leah twisted back to her. 'I'm sure Amy never meant that.'

'She acted as if I was letting her down because I didn't want to make a scene over what happened with Mr Brookmyre. Letting the side down.'

'It's hard with sisters sometimes.' Leah flung another glance over her shoulder. Charlotte was even tinier, *Il Mandarino* stacked up behind her looking almost unstable, as if it might collapse and bury her. 'But I'm *certain* she wasn't ashamed of you.'

Olivia's eyes clouded with more tears. Her rowing faltered in rhythm but not speed, the boat zigzagging.

'You know, your mum and I are really different, too,' Leah said.

That earned a moment's pause. Olivia's interest seemed piqued, her rowing calmed. For a moment they drifted at an angle, reflections and shadows striping the surface around them.

Leah kept with the theme. 'We've often struggled to be honest about how we feel. I didn't even tell her that I'm signed off work at the moment. For yelling at a client.'

Her niece gazed at her. 'I can't imagine you doing that.'

'Well, I did. And I was too ashamed to admit it, even to my family. But, actually, I don't think your mum would've cared! I think she would've understood that people do out-of-character things when they're having a tough time.'

Olivia stopped rowing altogether, the oars resting across her lap as she seemed to sink into a reverie. Leah kept silent, though her head was abuzz with questions. A small noise left her mouth as one of the oars began to slide. She lunged to catch it but she was too late, it splashed into the water. Olivia seemed to have shut down, barely reacting. Leah strained for the oar but it bobbed away from her fingertips, so she grabbed the other one from Olivia and steered towards the escapee. There were a lot of weeds in this part of the water. A thick knotted mass sucking the oar down. As Leah plunged her arm in after it, she felt the boat tilt, and her head snapped round to see Olivia wobbling to her feet.

'Olivia, what are you doing?'

Olivia stood tall, rocking. Tears ran down her cheeks. 'This was where it happened, Auntie Lee. This was where she died.'

'*Please* sit down.' Out of the corner of her eye, Leah could see that the oar was submerged. 'Let's keep talking.' The boat lurched again and she tried to shift her weight to balance out Olivia's movements. 'How do you know this was where it happened? Sit down, tell me.'

Olivia covered her face with her palms. 'They found her here, tangled in the weeds.'

Leah clenched the remaining oar, fighting off a mental image of Amy anchored by plants, unable to swim to the surface, unable to breathe.

'You weren't on the boat with her?' she croaked. 'You didn't see it happen?'

'No. But it was my fault.'

'Tell me. It's okay.'

'She said she'd recorded everything I'd told her – *in confidence* – about what Mr Brookmyre did. She said she had it on her phone and she was taunting Mr Brookmyre with it. Then she ran off and we were all chasing her, me and Brookmyre and his PR guy, Luke . . .' She waved her arms around as she spoke, the boat undulating, water sloshing over the sides.

'Olivia.' Leah thrust out her hand. '*Please* sit.'

'She got into a boat and I knew she was heading for Malcesine to go to the police, or maybe the press. Everything I'd begged her not to do! Mr Brookmyre yelled at Luke to go after her, saying he'd have a career-ending shitstorm on his hands otherwise. I didn't stop him. I even pointed out which boat he could take to follow her. But I didn't think . . .' She choked on her own words. 'I didn't realise what he was going to do.'

There were black spots in Leah's vision. Her heartbeat was heavy and huge. 'What did he do?'

'I don't know exactly. But Luke went out there. I waited on the dock . . .' She pointed towards it. Charlotte had now disappeared. 'He came back without Amy. Grabbed my arm really hard and said, "We were never here, okay? We were never here." And then he ran away and I just stood there in shock. I think I knew something very, very bad had happened, but I couldn't seem to move. That was when Dad found me. And a few hours later . . . we were told Amy was dead.'

Leah's shivers were uncontrollable. She felt as if her skin was wet, drenched even, but when she clutched her arms, they were dry. A cold anger was snaking through her. It had nowhere to go because she couldn't picture their faces: Brookmyre, Luke. They were shadows in her mind's eye.

'What happened after that?'

'By the next morning, Mr Brookmyre and Luke had gone. And I was too scared and ashamed to tell anybody what had happened. People started saying stuff about Nate, and about Francesca's party, then the verdict came back as accidental death. All the time I said nothing. I was sick with guilt but I was relieved, too, that all the theories were so far away from the truth. I had no idea *Dad* was diverting them, controlling it all. That he thought ... How could he think *that*?' She broke down, the boat rocking wildly. 'How could I have done that to her?' It wasn't clear whether she was talking about what Gordon thought she'd done, or what she actually had. The two seemed to bleed together.

And then it happened. Leah couldn't tell if she'd meant to, but the next moment Olivia was in the lake. The water and the weeds were swallowing her up, and she was gone from sight as if she'd never been there at all.

48

Joanna

Luke turned at the sound of her voice, and Joanna's heart catapulted into her throat as she feared he would lose his footing. He watched her inch closer but she couldn't read him, didn't know this version of him. She had been on suicide prevention courses at work, but all advice disintegrated now that there was a life at risk in front of her. A life she cared about hugely, no matter what Luke had done. She wondered what the lecturer who'd saved Rohan had said to him. Joanna had admired his bravery, felt guilty for not being there to play her part. Now here she was in a parallel situation and she was terrified. The stakes were too high.

'Luke, it's me.'

He looked bedraggled and hopeless. It took everything she'd got not to charge straight at him. His eyes seemed to beg her, yet there was a frightening blankness to them, as if he was already too far gone to listen.

'Please come away from the edge.'

He shook his head, twisting back to face the drop. The wind pushed at him, billowing his clothes, and Joanna thought of Amy in her storm.

'Can we talk somewhere else? Luke, please – I'm

freezing.' She tried to appeal to his protective side. 'We can sit in my car. Find a way through.'

'There's no way through.' He sounded broken. 'I've been trying to live with it but it's impossible.'

'Live with what?'

He fell silent again. Joanna tried not to dwell on how high they were, or how many sharp rocks would break their fall. She imagined they were having this conversation in a normal environment, where things could be predicted, controlled.

'Is this about Amy?' she asked cautiously.

The silence went on so long her teeth began to chatter. She glanced behind and saw Nate watching with his knuckles in his mouth. The rain formed a curtain between them, as if Nate was the audience and she and Luke were enacting a play behind a hazy screen.

She swivelled back as she heard Luke shifting his feet.

'I fucked up,' he said, stamping one then the other, still teetering on the edge. 'And everything fell apart after that. Me. Us. I didn't feel like I deserved our life. I don't think I deserve any kind of life, but I've been muddling through, pretending. Not anymore, though. Can't go on like this.'

'Tell me what happened. Whatever it is, we'll find a solution. Don't do anything you can't undo.'

'I already have.'

A streak of horror went through Joanna. But she couldn't let it show. She had to keep her reactions calm, be the unshockable counsellor, everything she'd wanted to do for Rohan and others, even for Luke when he'd lost his way at the end of their relationship. Could she be that person, in these circumstances? There was no choice; everything was dwarfed by the immediacy of needing to keep Luke alive.

She moved a few steps closer, avoiding staring into the black bowl of the valley. She thought she heard Nate call something from behind, but she kept her focus on Luke and on her balance, feeling like a reed in the wind.

'You were in Lake Garda, weren't you, when Amy died? At her parents' place – not Milan. You and Brookmyre used my name on your booking?' She hoped that, by showing him she'd already figured out part of the story, he would see that they were halfway to his confession already, and she wasn't condemning him.

But Luke seemed to recoil at her words. The action took his left foot over the edge, stones skidding and falling. Joanna grasped at his coat, and he brought his foot under control, back onto solid ground. She cursed herself. She'd questioned him too soon. But then, to her surprise, he started talking.

'He had a big merger to close and he wanted privacy. At least, that's how he framed it. I'm not sure, now, if that's really why he chose that place. He told me not to tell anybody our specific location, so it was just easier to say Milan, even to you, Jo. For the same reason, he instructed me not to put the villa in his name, or anybody's associated with his company. He said use a woman's, it attracts less attention. I didn't really get that, maybe it should've set off warning bells, but I used yours without thinking too much about it. It didn't seem a massive thing at the time – he said he didn't want rivals or press interfering until the merger had gone through. But I . . . I wish I hadn't dragged you into it.' His voice splintered. 'I really do.'

Joanna felt a wave of anger, thinking of the fear Luke had caused her, bringing Nate into her life. But she swallowed it, for now. Stamped it down, if not out. 'It's okay,' she managed to say, and inched forward a little more, assessing the positions of his feet, trying not to startle him with sudden movements. Taking a risk, she reached out and grasped his hand. He jumped at her touch and her stomach plunged, but he left his hand in hers, stiff and cold.

'How did Amy become involved?'

'It was all so confusing.' He pushed his hair out of his eyes with his free hand, then left it there, cupping his skull. 'She started making accusations against Brookmyre. Shouting at him about assaulting her sister. I didn't know what was going on, who was telling the truth. I was exhausted from a week of trying to keep up with his demands, keep his image spotless. He was my biggest ever client and it felt as if our future was riding on him. Now here was this girl threatening to ruin him. And me, maybe, by association. Next thing I knew, we were chasing her. Then she took off in a boat, in a storm . . .' His chin tilted towards the sky, as if he was making the connection for the first time between this storm and that one. Joanna wondered if Amy had felt as scared as she did now. Luke's words were eroding her composure: *assaulting, chasing*. She tried again to detach herself from them. As long as he was talking, he wasn't jumping.

'Brookmyre yelled at me to go after her. Said he'd take me down with him if I didn't get this mess cleaned up. And

I believed him, in that moment. It had been such an intense week – that *villa*, there was just something about it – and I felt like my little livelihood was all bound up with his massive empire.' His fingers spasmed, and Joanna felt the tension flowing along his arm and up hers. 'I wasn't planning to hurt her, Jo! I didn't *have* a plan, I just rowed after her with my head full of Brookmyre's threats. When I caught her up, I shouted to her to give me the phone. But it was all so chaotic – the weather, the whole thing. She tried to row away from me, I tried to keep up with her. I could tell I was scaring her but I had tunnel vision: get the phone, make it stop. Our boats collided. Hers capsized. And she – she disappeared under the water. I saw her arm, flailing. And then . . . gone . . .' His chin came down hard and he began to cry. Joanna wanted to pull her hand out of his as she pictured Amy going under, and him doing nothing, or so it seemed. She made herself hang on tighter instead, maybe too tight, channelling her anguish into her grip.

'It was an accident,' she said desperately, unsure if it was a question or a statement.

'But I left her. I panicked and I left her.'

'Maybe there was nothing you could've done.'

'But I was *chasing* her.' Luke bent at the waist, racked with sobs. 'I was such a coward. I did what I was told, and I fucked up, and then I ran away from the consequences. Looking back, I *knew* Brookmyre was a bad guy. I saw how he spoke to women, how he came on strong with Amy's sister that day. Yet I chose to be loyal to him. And he's *still* keeping me quiet. Contacting me with threats, warnings, making sure I'm not going to tell anyone. I was so worried

he'd got to you, too, Jo. Mandy said you'd seemed preoccupied recently and I was terrified Brookmyre had started
harassing you.'

Another reel of thoughts passed quickly through Joanna's
mind. Last night at Luke's made sense, now. As did their
break-up, all of it. And what about Nate's hit and run?
Could that have been Brookmyre, too, targeting another
person who might be getting too close to the truth?

It was a horrible web. She had to keep herself present,
keep control. Luke was rocking now, one hand over his
face, blind to where he was putting his feet or the momen-
tum he was building up. Joanna dragged down on his hand
to anchor him. At the same time, she cleared a path in her
mind. Luke's guilt was a liability, the thing that had brought
him to the edge, but could she also use it as a tool? What
else did she have to try?

'But . . . jumping off this ledge won't make things better
for anyone, Luke.'

The rocking slowed. He straightened up halfway and
looked at her.

'If you come back with me, there might be things you can
do for Amy's family. You could give them closure. An apology. Not this – what good will this do?'

She sensed him thinking about it. Luke was a rational
person most of the time. He responded to logical arguments
if he could see past his own fixations. And he wanted to make
people proud. He put pressure on himself to do so, maybe
too much, maybe that was why he'd panicked when he'd
found everything he'd worked for under threat. And perhaps,
even in these circumstances, Joanna could play on that.

'You know your death wouldn't cancel out Amy's,' she forged on. '*You* dying in a storm won't lessen her family's grief. Maybe it would even make it worse – losing their one chance to meet the person who was there for her final moments. Even if you can't bear what happened, you could give *them* something valuable.'

She felt the tension start to leave his arm. His weight swayed forward, his body soft. More little stones tumbled over the drop.

'You know it would be the brave thing to do, Luke.'

Her gut lurched as he released his hand from hers, raised his arms over the valley and let out a guttural sound. Joanna's own hands shot out, poised to grab him but knowing it would be futile, really, if he jumped. Her tongue met the roof of her mouth, anticipating her cry of 'no!'

Luke's palms fell to his head, dragged down his face. She watched, muscles flexed, as he folded over again. But this time it was a deflation. A plug had been pulled.

Joanna stayed vigilant. He seemed more malleable, now; she was able to turn him, bit by bit, away from the ledge. As he crumpled to his knees and curled into a ball on the wet ground, she placed herself between him and the drop. Everything seemed to become about logistics: where he was, where she was, where the safety zone began, how to shuffle him there. How to hold it together until she didn't have to anymore.

Nate ran forward to help her. As he looked at her over the top of Luke's head, his face stricken with relief and guilt and gratitude, Joanna could only stare numbly back. Sensation returned in pieces: the rain and tears making her eyelashes sticky; the sting of her cracked lips in the wind. And Luke's weight as they guided him to the cars, the reality of what could've happened and what hadn't happened and all the things that already had.

49

Leah

'Olivia!' Leah hollered. A faint echo bounced between the mountains, but her voice was minuscule in the vast space, seeming to plop into the water.

She peered over the edge of the boat. She could only see dark, drifting weeds. A flicker of movement made her swing to the left. 'Olivia?'

There was another motion below the surface, the rug of weeds bulging. Leah pulled off her sliders and leapt in.

The weeds swirled around her legs and clung to her skin. She tried to cast them off but they followed wherever she swam, attracting further strands. Holding her breath, she ducked under the surface at the point where she had seen motion. She opened her eyes but it was murky and dark, flailed her hands but met sticky, clawing plants. How could Olivia have disappeared? Leah's panic tried to persuade her she couldn't swim. Her limbs thrashed and she was Amy again, struggling in the weeds – but with a clear sky above her, that was the difference. She grasped at that: there was no storm. She could see land, lift her head above the surface and breathe.

She plunged under again, letting her breath out through her nostrils as she swam in a loop. With a leap of her heart, she spotted Olivia through the underwater haze. She wasn't far below the surface, but looked encased in weeds, as if she had deliberately dived into the thickest mass. Her hair was floating and swaying like part of the plants. There was something almost beautiful about her: upright, entangled and motionless.

Leah swam towards her and began to hack at the weeds that bound her ankles. Each time she loosened one she discovered another, twisted into an even tighter bind. Olivia's face was white, her head sagging forward, but the weeds kept her floating almost vertically, as if suspended in a cage. With another sear of panic, Leah felt something circle her own wrist. She jerked it free. Her breath was running out. She swam upwards, broke the surface to gulp the air, then descended again, fingers reaching for the next knot to untie. The weeds pawed at her. *Stay calm,* she chanted to herself, trying to view her task as a mental and physical challenge, the kind she normally rose to, rather than a terrifying one of life and death.

She hadn't known it was possible to scream underwater, but something like a scream left her body when a large weed clamped around her thigh. She couldn't move. It was a sucking tentacle, snaking down into the depths of the lake. She yanked at it and kicked her legs, imagining she was climbing or running, trying to believe in her own strength.

Finally, Leah released herself, and broke the surface for another gasp of air. As she returned to Olivia, her hacking and pulling switched from methodical to frantic, water bubbling into her nose and stinging her eyes. She wrapped her arms around Olivia's waist and pulled her sharply into her body, as if performing the Heimlich manoeuvre. There was a tangible feeling of release, of snapping weeds. She tried again. The third time, she realised Olivia was untethered. Leah kicked harder than ever in her life, finding more reserves of power. She kicked and thrust and dragged her niece with her, then they were above the surface, and Leah was wheezing and spluttering, heaving Olivia towards the boat.

Grabbing the side, she struggled for breath, panicking again as she couldn't seem to get enough into her lungs. There was a crushing pain in her chest. Olivia was a dead weight in her arms, and Leah clasped beneath her chin to keep her mouth out of the water. Her lips were blue, her skin icy. An urge to howl flooded Leah's body. She couldn't lose another niece. Her sister couldn't lose another child, her parents another granddaughter. No, no, no.

But she felt wrung out. No energy left to even drag herself into the boat, let alone Olivia too. She gritted her teeth. She had to do this. She'd come this far. And her body *could* do it – suddenly it was as if all her training had actually been for this. Tilting the boat, she clamped her left arm around Olivia's torso and stretched her right arm across the slippery wood. Her muscles were like cloth. Her head swirling with stars and splodges of black. She couldn't get any purchase on the boat, couldn't hoist herself and Olivia up with nothing to push off from. After grappling for what felt like forever, panting and crying with frustration, she managed to drag them halfway on. They lay awkwardly, the boat almost on its side, their legs still in the lake. It was enough – just. Leah turned Olivia's head and water gushed out from between her lips. She stuck her fingers down her throat, scooping out leaves. Olivia was limp and unresponsive, but hope rose as Leah felt her wrist: there was a pulse. No breath, but a heartbeat, a sign of life. Leah pinched her niece's nose and began to breathe into her mouth.

She'd delivered three long breaths when she heard it. In the distance, but coming closer: the purr of a speedboat. Help was surely on its way. The thought brought another small burst of adrenaline. She managed to shuffle Olivia further up the boat, exhaled into her mouth one more time, then held her close, praying for the warmth of breath.

Nothing. The engine noise swelled and she saw the boat now, bouncing towards them with two people onboard. As it got closer, she could make out the figures: Charlotte and Matilde, wearing orange lifejackets, their boat throwing out foam as they drove it as fast as it would go. Leah spun back to Olivia as she heard a sound that made her cry out in relief: coughing. Olivia was spluttering and convulsing, ejecting more water. Leah scrambled towards her and supported her head. Olivia's eyes rolled, her hand flailing to her throat.

'It's okay, darling,' Leah said, sitting her up further. 'Don't panic. Keep coughing. Help's coming.'

The other boat reached them. 'Olivia!' Charlotte screamed, straining towards her daughter. Olivia's chin lifted briefly at the sound of her mum's voice, then she sagged forward again and vomited, while Leah rubbed her back.

'The emergency services are on their way,' Matilde said, through tears. 'We knew we'd be able to get to you sooner, though.'

Charlotte's gaze raked frantically over her daughter. 'Matilde told me she suspected you were heading out onto the water. When you were gone a while, we got worried. Matilde found some binoculars . . .'

'Thank you,' Leah said, her eyes brimming as she continued to watch Olivia, to check her breathing, her pulse, the temperature of her skin.

'It's the least I could do,' Matilde said.

Leah looked at her questioningly.

'We'll talk about that later.' Charlotte's voice was shaky. She glanced at Leah. 'Matilde has . . . things to tell you.'

'I have things to tell you all, too,' Leah said. 'When Olivia's . . . There's so much to . . .' It overwhelmed her again, everything she'd learned. Everything that had happened to her family.

Charlotte's face crumpled. 'But now all that matters is—'

As she said it, there was a noise from above. The whirr of a medical helicopter, its propellors spinning against the powder-blue sky. The sun had fully risen while Leah had been pulling Olivia out of the lake. Like the opposite of Amy's awful, unnecessary death as the sun had sunk. The helicopter hovered above them, a loudspeaker urging them to stay calm, and Leah felt a dam burst in the backs of her eyes. She clung to Olivia and released all the tears that had been bottled inside her for months, let them rack her body and salt her face and mingle with the lake-water all over her skin. And as she looked up, she saw her sister leaning against Matilde and doing exactly the same.

★   ★   ★

They'd been in Verona Hospital for two hours before they got a chance to catch their breath and return to the conversation they had danced around in the boat. Olivia lay in bed in a high dependency ward, pale and sedated. The medics had repeatedly praised Leah's actions, but they'd made it clear that Olivia was still in danger. There had been a lot of anxious discussion about possible lung damage, brain damage, or infection, which shouted louder in Leah's mind than any praise.

She herself had a pounding headache, a throat that felt full of glass, and a hacking cough. But the doctors had deemed her well enough to vacate her own hospital bed and sit beside Olivia's with her family. Charlotte wept quietly and Gordon's face was grim, his eyes bloodshot.

Matilde sat in the corner, clutching a tissue. Eventually, she couldn't seem to hold it in any longer. 'This is all my fault.'

'No, it isn't,' Charlotte said. 'You got caught up in –' she glanced at Gordon, then down at her hands – 'things that should never have happened.'

Gordon pinched the bridge of his nose and stared at the corner of the room, seeming haunted. Did he deserve sympathy? Leah wasn't sure. But she couldn't help sparing him some, as she saw how alone he was, not knowing where to put his pain.

Matilde came over to Leah with her mobile phone, and silently handed it to her. Leah looked at it in confusion. On its screen was a series of messages, from a number with no contact name attached.

Keep an eye on Charlotte's sister, the first one said, dated a couple of days after Leah had arrived in Italy.

Text this number if she starts asking questions about Amy. You don't want to find out what will happen if you don't.

Leah's mouth fell open and she stared back at Matilde. Matilde seemed to swallow more tears, motioning for Leah to keep reading. The next message was a day later.

I'd advise you to stop ignoring me. I know where you live and where your two children go to school. Believe me when I say I have a lot of contacts. Locate CCTV images of the sister. She's been getting around.

Matilde had replied to this one: **Who are you? Please leave me alone.**

Someone with a lot more power than you, read the response. **My sources tell me Leah has an envelope. Get rid of whatever's inside it. Leave her a warning that somebody's watching – I will forward specific instructions. And don't call the police. Your children seem to spend a lot of time in that gelato place next to Malcesine Castle, I've noticed.**

'I . . .' Leah turned freezing cold, as if back in the water. She shook her head in disbelief as she met Matilde's eye. 'Do you know who it was?'

'No. The threats kept arriving and I got more and more scared. I wanted to tell you, warn you. I tried, but . . . I didn't know what I was dealing with. I am so, so sorry, Leah.'

'We'll tell the police, now,' Gordon said, his voice gruff. 'It's okay, Matilde. You'll have our support.'

This made Matilde break down again. Charlotte covered her face and Leah blinked hard, struggling to process it all.

Someone with a lot more power than you. Why did everything seem to come back to power?

A murmur from Olivia pulled their attention back to the bed. She was stirring. Her eyelids fluttering, hints of colour seeping into her face. A cry escaped Charlotte's mouth and two dots of pink appeared in her own cheeks. She leapt to her feet, almost knocking over her chair, and ran to her daughter. Gordon stood up, too, hovering anxiously. Olivia's eyes opened properly for the first time in hours, taking in her family gathered around her. Leah shifted to the edge of her seat, waiting until it was her turn to go to her niece, trying to grasp on to hope and shake away her lingering fears.

SIX MONTHS LATER

50

Joanna

The final stretch of Joanna's journey had to be taken by boat. She waited on 'the dock with the golden railings', just as her confirmation email had instructed her to, feeling like a lost soul hoping to be scooped up and taken to where she needed to be. Except she was also unsure of what she'd find once she got there. Nothing about this trip was what she'd imagined when she'd dreamed of visiting Italy in the past.

It was the off-season, so it was quiet and there was a chill in the air. But it was also just before Christmas, so there *were* people milling around the pretty town of Malcesine, visiting its festive market, smells of cinnamon and chocolate on the wind. Joanna was the only one who boarded the ferry when it arrived, though. She closed her jacket as they steamed out onto the water and a wintery breeze cut through to her skin. Staring at the ripples made by the accelerating boat, she couldn't fend off other images. Luke pursuing Amy, watching her fall in, disappear.

She became aware of the boat's captain trying to make conversation. Joanna had chosen a seat too far back and it was difficult to hear. She stood up to move forward – not in the mood for chitchat, but not wanting to be rude – just as the boat changed direction and she staggered sideways, grabbing the railing. As she recovered and looked up, she saw they were sailing around an outcrop, and an entire mountain straight ahead of them was twinkling as though it was showered in stars. Joanna began to distinguish shapes amid the constellation. White villas, green trees. All sparkling like a vast Christmas decoration.

'Welcome to *Il Mandarino!*' the captain said, as they drew up to a dock strung with coloured lights and sprigs of holly.

Joanna shouldered her rucksack and stepped into the resort. There were golf buggies waiting to take guests to their villas but she decided to take a slow walk up the mountain, to help herself believe she was actually here. As she passed the row of buggies, she noticed the drivers were wearing Santa hats. From what she knew of this place, she hadn't expected a jaunty festive vibe. She felt marginally soothed, but there was still a knot in her stomach as she climbed higher.

With every bend of the white path, her preconceptions about the resort were dented further. She recalled looking at the photos online, that day she'd hidden in the Roundhouse Hostel, and seeing champagne fountains, people in smart linen suits, seafood arranged on clean white plates. She remembered feeling intimidated, even beneath the horror of the things she was discovering. For that reason – and others – she had deliberated for a long time about whether she *should* stay here for these few days, for the trial she felt compelled to attend. In the end, she had decided to brave it. She'd guessed that the only way she'd get to see *Il Mandarino* was if she booked in for real this time. But she'd anticipated feeling completely out of place.

And yet.

Instead of perfect people sipping champagne, she saw families. Instead of the tennis courts she'd seen an aerial photo of, there was an adventure playground, with kids shrieking as they hurtled along a zipwire. And the big white yurt, which she was sure had once housed a spa, was now a Santa's grotto with a queue outside.

There were moments when she doubted she was even in the right place.

When she was almost at the top of the mountain, she asked a member of staff to point her towards her accommodation. She turned her collar up as the trees thickened around her, was glad of the fairy lights threaded among the pines, bringing some light to this darker corner of the resort. Two lamps glowed either side of an open set of gates, and she made her way towards them, her heartbeat outpacing her steps.

The 'big villa' had been converted into apartments. That was the only reason Joanna could afford to stay there. The rates had been much more reasonable than she'd expected when the idea had first taken root. The idea of staying in the building that had turned her life upside down.

She glanced at the crescent-shaped pool, covered for winter, then looked up at the enormous building, feeling as if she couldn't take it all in at once.

'Hello! Welcome!' called out a receptionist, as Joanna walked hesitantly into the foyer, trying to reconcile the warm terracotta walls and yellow beanbags with the images she'd had in her head.

She was led to her apartment on the upper floor, where she gazed out of the window at the resort cascading to the quiet lake. She released a long breath, clouding the pane, then rested her fingertips on the glass and wondered what the next few days would bring.

51

Leah

Leah leaned her elbows on the balcony railings and kneaded her neck with her fingers. She could feel the hard knots of tension, a reminder of all the things she had to get through this week. After months of slow recovery, now Brookmyre's trial and the meeting with Luke Jacobs were hanging over her head, bringing everything clamouring back.

She breathed in and felt a stabbing pain in her chest. Her lungs still hurt when she took deep breaths, especially in the colder weather. Charlotte wanted her to stay in Italy for the whole winter, and Leah was tempted. She'd spent so much time here over the last six months that she'd learned how to do her job from a distance. And *Il Mandarino* no longer felt like a place she wanted to keep away from. There were memories, yes, memories that woke her in the night and reared up at unexpected moments, but she was learning to deal with them, instead of hiding.

Leah looked down over the resort and contemplated its transformation. It blew her away, what they'd achieved in just a few months. The project had given them a focus, something to throw themselves into as the repercussions of the last year-and-a-quarter had threatened to destroy them. There had been times when they'd almost buckled under guilt and grief, but there had always been something to pick themselves back up for: a charity event in Amy's memory, the launch of the new playground, the redesigning of the website to make *Il Mandarino* seem more welcoming to everyone who wanted to come.

This had been Charlotte's ultimatum to Gordon. They would make changes, otherwise they would sell. And to be fair, he had agreed without protest. The events of last June had hit his conscience hard, too. Now he was living in Limone, separated from Charlotte, witnessing the transformation of his much-loved resort from afar. The resort he'd wanted to make beautiful, so obsessively that he'd been blind to any ugliness he'd created.

Leah's eyes rested on *Segreto*. The circular bar was still there, and all the tables, dusted in frost. It was the one place they still hadn't decided what to do with.

'Lee?'

Leah turned to see Charlotte stepping out onto the balcony, wearing smart trousers and a crushed velvet jumper. She seemed to move slowly these days. To smile more cautiously. She was struggling to forgive herself for everything that had happened, but a spark was starting to come back into her eyes – some days, at least. There were still the times when she closed herself inside the annex, and Leah would leave her alone for a while.

'Come and see, Lee,' Charlotte said now, holding out her hand.

Leah took it and allowed herself to be led inside. To her surprise, they went to Amy's room. Most of her clothes had now been donated to the local women's refuge, but her books had been kept and her cacti still lined the windowsill. Today, the room smelled different. It smelled of pine, making Leah's stomach twist in some deep-rooted association with the big villa. She shook the thoughts away, realising the source of the scent. Olivia was decorating a Christmas tree in the corner of Amy's room.

Leah and Charlotte stood and watched her. Her movements swung between uncertainty and confidence: sometimes pausing to consider the appropriateness or placing of a decoration, then seeming to make a decision, hanging it on a branch with a satisfied nod. Like Leah, she had the remnants of a chronic cough. And like Leah, she frequently relived so many moments from the past. Brookmyre pinning her against the wall. Amy jumping into the boat that night. The little she remembered of her own near-drowning in the lake.

But she had done astonishingly well. She had woken in hospital with a new determination: she'd wanted to tell the world what had happened to her and to Amy. To face Joseph Brookmyre and Luke Jacobs. They'd found out that Luke had already turned himself in, but her cooperation with the police – and his, apparently – had led to Brookmyre's arrest, and to six other women coming forward with accusations against him. He'd eventually admitted to threatening Matilde as well, coercing her into sending warnings to Leah and Francesca, stealing evidence, even forging Leah's signature from credit cards found in her room. Matilde was another person left traumatised and struggling to forgive herself. But at least Brookmyre's days of wielding power, abusing women, and hiding behind his company's 'prestige meets family values' image were over. Olivia had been so brave. Leah and Charlotte made sure they told her that, often.

Now Charlotte said, 'That looks wonderful, Liffy,' and Olivia's cheeks flushed.

The tree did look perfect. The bold-coloured pinwheels and unusual-shaped baubles were somehow very Amy. The angel on the top had its wings spread wide, as if she was about to do what Amy had never managed, and fly somewhere new.

The next morning, the mood was changeable as the three of them prepared for the day ahead. It took Leah back to how they had been a few months ago, in the wake of all the revelations: sometimes drawing together, dealing with the fallout; other times stumbling over what to say, how to behave, how to be a grieving family who actually shared their feelings.

Uncharacteristically, Leah changed clothes three times. There seemed no appropriate outfit for the kind of meeting they were about to have. In the end, she asked Charlotte's advice, knowing it would soothe her sister to help her pick out an outfit. They ended up looking weirdly matching, and Leah tried not to habitually compare.

Matilde came out of the kitchen to see them off and wish them luck. Leah was glad that the housekeeper's eyes no longer skittered away from her in shame. Glad that she'd stuck around. Matilde kissed them all and told them they looked smart, that it would be okay, as they fidgeted like nervous children.

They walked down the path with Olivia in the middle, taking the fork towards the big villa, or 'Forest Apartments' as it was now named. Sounds of laughter and children's shrieks echoed in the air. The atmosphere was so much freer, and not just because the heat of the high season was long gone. Leah's nerves returned as they approached the gates. Gordon was already outside, pacing the path. He hugged Olivia, then smiled tentatively at Charlotte and watched for her response, like an anxious suitor. She smiled tightly back and Leah mumbled a hello.

Once they were in a private room at the back of the building, the tension solidified. Leah exchanged a glance with Charlotte, and sensed they were both thinking the same thing: that maybe this hadn't been the best choice of venue after all. They'd had the option to meet with Luke Jacobs in the UK, or in a solicitors' office or police station elsewhere in Italy. It had been Olivia who'd said he should come here, face them on *their* turf, where it had all happened. But now that they were sitting in a silent row, behind the large desk that was one of the few things they'd kept, everything seemed heightened.

Leah felt Olivia grope for her hand beneath the table and she clasped her fingers in return. A clock ticked from the wall. The woman who sat with them, ready to supervise, shuffled her papers.

Finally, the door opened and Luke Jacobs came in.

He was an average-looking man, with sandy-coloured hair and wary grey eyes. He blanched to see the family sitting in a formal line on one side of the table, the air around them vibrating with expectation. As he sat down opposite, he seemed to look at Olivia in particular, who stared back and squeezed Leah's knuckles extra tight.

The supervising woman cleared her throat. 'Hello, everyone. I'm Eve, a Restorative Justice Facilitator. This meeting, as you know, was requested by Luke Jacobs –' she gestured – 'and you, the Wynne family, agreed on specific terms. It's happening with permission from the Derbyshire and Lake Garda police forces. Mr Jacobs would like to explain and apologise for what happened on the day Amy Wynne died, and answer any questions you might have. This is separate from any legal proceedings involving him or Joseph Brookmyre.'

Luke leaned forward, wringing his hands. 'That sounds so formal,' he said. 'It wasn't really how I meant it to be. But it's up to you how we . . .' He floundered, sweat shining at his temples.

Nobody spoke. They barely moved in their family line-up. Leah felt far away from her sister, on the other end of the row. Gordon was cracking his knuckles in his lap.

'I think we all have the same question.' This was Charlotte, her voice thick. 'How exactly did our Amy die?'

There was another pause. Olivia's grasp was now so tight that Leah's fingers began to tingle. She was glad of it, in a way. A sensation to focus on.

'I've explained everything up to when you left the dock,' Olivia spoke up, quietly. 'And the police have told us what you told them. But I . . . we . . . need to hear exactly what happened on the water. When you went after her. When I . . . let you.'

Luke's eyes swung to her again. He took a sip from one of the glasses of water that had been poured for all of them, and moisture clung to his upper lip.

'I would've gone after her whether you'd let me or fought me,' he said. '*I* made the choice.'

Later, Leah would realise this was a sort of kindness. It would take a while, there was so much to process, but at some point she would acknowledge that Luke had tried to lift a burden from Olivia. Now, though, all she could feel was the blow of the word, *choice*. So many people's choices, big and small, had led to Amy's death.

'Why?' she said, before she'd realised she was going to.

Luke's eyes were red. 'I've asked myself the same thing, lots of times.'

'And?' chimed in Charlotte.

'I've got no excuses.'

'But we need to know why. And how. And what you . . . whether she . . .' Charlotte's words broke up and Leah wished she was nearer to her. She saw Gordon attempt to comfort her, but Charlotte shrugged him off and accepted a tissue from the facilitator.

Luke straightened, as if realising he needed to do better. His gaze flickered along the row and then back to his water glass.

'I followed her onto the lake because I was scared of Brookmyre, scared of losing my business, or worse . . .' He glanced up. 'Shit-scared and weak. I didn't intend to do her any harm. But that's not the point because I—'

'Did you touch her?' Gordon cut in, his voice taut. 'Push her?'

'No. But I kept pursuing her even as she tried to get away. I shouted at her, wanting her to hand over her phone. I think I made her lose focus.'

'She was good on the water,' Olivia said. 'She knew how to handle a boat. She might've made it, if you hadn't interfered.'

Luke nodded, eyes down. 'I could tell she was strong. She didn't give up easily.'

'Was she scared?' It was another question Leah hadn't planned to ask. Hadn't known she wanted an answer to.

Luke faced her. 'I don't know. I'm sorry. I – I don't even know if this is helping you.'

'She would've been *angry*,' Olivia said, unexpectedly. 'That was what drove Amy. Anger at injustice. And that day, anger for me.'

The idea simmered and then settled in the room. Maybe it was preferable to think of Amy fired up with anger, with the energy of rage, rather than terrified at the end. And Leah noticed Olivia had said anger *for* her, not *at* her, which was a subtle shift in her thinking, but an important one.

After Luke had left, they sat in the meeting room in heavy silence. Hearing about Amy's last moments directly from Luke had been much more vivid. Leah closed her eyes and swayed in her chair.

Then Eve, the facilitator, cleared her throat again. 'If I may . . . there is somebody else who'd like to talk to you as well.'

Olivia and Charlotte looked faraway, and Gordon's face was grim, so Leah was the one who answered. 'Who?'

'He's in the area for Joseph Brookmyre's trial, but he realised this meeting was taking place, and asked if he might be able to see you. I said I would ask.'

'Who is it?' Charlotte woke up. Gordon and Olivia began paying more attention now, too, and Leah leaned forward, her hand still entwined with her niece's.

'It's a Nate Fraser?' Eve phrased it as a question, but of course they all knew the name well, and they collectively stilled.

Leah let her eyes slide sideways to observe her sister. Charlotte's face had blanched. She was running the delicate chain of her necklace through her fingers and it looked as if it might snap.

'Is he here now?' she asked.

'I believe he's waiting outside.'

Leah, Olivia and Gordon all glanced at one another, but Charlotte wouldn't look at anyone, bringing her palms onto the desk.

'Well, I don't see why not,' Gordon said, trying to catch Charlotte's eye.

'That's great,' Eve said, 'I'll just—'

'Wait!' Charlotte said, and the facilitator paused in surprise, halfway to standing. Charlotte didn't seem to know how to continue. Everybody stared at her. A vein began to pulse in Leah's brow.

'Shall I invite him in?' Eve checked.

'Could we have a moment first?' Charlotte said. 'In private?'

52

Joanna

Joanna was sitting on the beach when Luke emerged. Her hands were pink with cold because she'd touched the edges of the water as it had lapped the shore. She didn't know why; she'd just felt the urge. On the far side of the lake, the mountains were snow-capped and veined with white.

She'd asked Luke to come here after his meeting with Amy's family. There were things to be said. They had spoken a few times over the last few months, but Joanna had kept him at arm's length, kept a protective shield around herself. She had got him down from that ledge and she was thankful. But she also had her own life to set back on an even keel.

And it had been a rough ride. She realised that, now she was away from home with space to reflect. At times she had felt relieved that everything was out in the open, that she knew, finally, what had caused Luke to change so much, to leave her. But at other times she had struggled to come to terms with it all. The Luke she'd loved so much. The Luke who'd left a woman to drown.

Now he was walking towards her along the *Il Mandarino* beach, looking exhausted but somehow lighter. It struck Joanna that he'd been hanging his head and hunching his shoulders for over a year. She only realised now she saw him walking more upright.

He stood over her and let out a long sigh. 'It's done.'

Joanna got to her feet. 'How was it?' she asked. 'How were they?'

'It was really, really hard.' She could see he was close to tears. 'I never thought I'd be in a meeting like that. Puts every other meeting I've ever prepared for and worried over into massive perspective. I can only hope it helped them.'

'It was the right thing to do.'

He nodded vigorously. 'I know. And I'm so grateful – you know that, don't you, Jo? You made me put things right, or as right as they can be. I think only you could've done that.'

Joanna swallowed, unsure whether that was true, and turned to gaze at the grey water. 'You should've told me when it first happened, Luke.'

'I know.' He joined her in looking out, and Joanna wondered what he was thinking, whether he saw Amy each time he saw the lake, or whether he didn't need to be physically here to relive it. Most likely he did so every day, wherever he was.

Luke hadn't been charged with any crimes in the end, only required to cooperate with proceedings against Brookmyre. There had been murmurings about conspiracy charges, but the police had soon realised Luke hadn't conspired to harm Amy; he had acted poorly in the moment, made terrible choices. There was no way of proving whether he had directly caused her death. But Joanna knew Luke would be putting himself on trial for a long time yet.

'I wanted to help you *before*, Luke,' she said, 'When I sensed there was something wrong, last autumn, but all you did was push me away. You left me without answers, and Amy's family and friends, too . . .' She didn't mean to add to his guilt, but there was a lot she needed to get off her chest. 'Now you have to promise me something. Promise you'll get help. Counselling to deal with your guilt. I know you might think it's self-indulgent, like you don't deserve that kind of care, but you do, everybody does, and it's not just for your benefit, it's for all the people who still care about you and have been affected by all this.'

There was a silence. The water sloshed against the shore and the stilts of the nearby dock.

'I will,' he said, eventually. 'I'll do it, I promise.'

She nodded, feeling her chest loosen. Her belief in how much people could help each other was still a force inside her. It had been flattened for a while, in the aftermath, as she'd felt a weird shame about who she was and everything she thought she knew. Nate had tricked her into believing he needed saving. Luke hadn't let her save him until he'd been literally on the edge. What was the point? Who was she to think she could or should help anybody? But gradually, it had come back. Stronger than ever, she was surprised to find, and with a new perspective: she would stop acting out of perpetual guilt or fear of being blamed for things she couldn't control. She would trust her gut, trust herself. But she wouldn't be the one to help Luke, from now on. Somebody would, not her.

'I better go,' he said, wiping his eyes. 'I'm supposed to stick with my minder.' He gestured up the stone steps to where a woman was waiting for him, holding a folder and watching their exchange. 'I guess I might see you at the trial?'

Joanna nodded, although she was starting to think maybe she wouldn't go to Brookmyre's trial after all. It didn't feel like her place. And being here, in *Il Mandarino*, was proving enough to help her process things. Last night, she'd sat on the balcony of her apartment, awestruck by the incredible number of stars that were visible, and felt tiny and consoled all at once. She'd huddled into a blanket and composed an email to her boss on her phone, sending it before she could lose the sense of clarity and perspective that the night sky here seemed to bring. I want to be with the students more, it had said. I'll continue to manage the team, but I need to be able to do some counselling again, too. Otherwise it feels meaningless.

Otherwise I'll go mad, she had thought, but not written.

'Are you going to be okay?' she asked Luke now.

'Yes.' He was clearly trying to sound convincing, either to her or to himself. 'You?'

She nodded. She would.

Her throat was full as she watched him go up the steps, his fair hair ruffled into familiar patterns by the wind.

53

Leah

After the facilitator had left them alone in the room, Charlotte sat fidgeting in her chair, lips moving silently, as the rest of them watched her.

'Charlotte?' Gordon said, 'What's wrong? Don't you want to see Nate? I know you've suspected him in the past, but surely now we know the truth . . .'

'He's not bad, Mum,' Olivia said. 'He genuinely cared about Aimes.'

Charlotte folded her arms on the table and laid her forehead on them. Leah saw her torso swelling up and down as if she was either hyperventilating or beginning to cry. She was about to go to her but Olivia got there first, crouching at her side.

'Mum, it's okay. I know you thought it was all his fault. I know that's why you hired Boring Bram, who I'd have no chance of getting a crush on! You're so scared of history repeating itself. But . . . it was nothing to do with Nate, or any secret affairs. We know that now, don't we?'

Charlotte raised her head. Her face was chalk-white and her mascara was smudged. '*I* thought it was him,' she whispered.

'But it wasn't, sweetheart,' Gordon said. 'So, maybe this is a way of putting all that anger behind you.'

'Anger,' Charlotte echoed, nodding to herself. 'I had so much anger.'

Leah's heart began pounding. She wasn't sure why: an inkling, a dread. Charlotte looked straight at her as if she could hear its thump, then her eyes went back to her husband. 'And you wouldn't let me do anything with my anger, Gordon. You just wanted the whole inquest to go away.'

'Because—'

'Yes, I know why now.' Her gaze darted to Olivia, still kneeling next to her. 'But at the time, I felt so alone. You wouldn't listen when I said I'd seen Amy and Nate arguing. And that I sensed something between them – a secret. I had to resort to spreading rumours, trying to give him a trial by public opinion. Then when he disappeared, and I hired Samuel, you even stopped that too. Or at least, you thought you did.'

Leah heard Gordon's chair creaking as he shifted his weight. This felt like the airing of grievances that Gordon and Charlotte had needed for a long time. But it was heading somewhere unexpected.

'What do you mean, I "thought I did"?'

Charlotte lowered her voice. 'I kept Samuel on. He found Nate for me. And I didn't know what else to do. You were blocking all the official channels, Gordon. I was desperate. So . . . I went to England. Took matters into my own hands.'

'*England?* When?'

Leah had rarely heard Gordon sound so shocked. Under other circumstances, she might've felt smug that Charlotte had wrongfooted him. But now she just felt scared. She'd thought their ordeal was over, that she'd got the remainder of her family back. The prospect of more damage was like a band tightening across her chest. She could tell just by looking at her that Olivia's mind was careering along the same track.

'I didn't have a migraine while Leah was staying with us. I was . . .' Charlotte flung a guilty glance at Leah. 'I was in the UK. Derby.'

Leah was staggered. Her sister had left the country while she'd thought she was shut in the annex? How could she not have realised? For how long had it been planned?

And what exactly had she done? The question dangled unsaid, and nobody seemed to want to ask.

Eventually, Charlotte answered it herself. 'I ran him over.'

Gordon let out a low groan.

'Not to kill him,' she rushed on. 'Just to – to hurt him. Scare him, like Amy must've felt so scared. Then I panicked and rang an ambulance once I was a few streets away. And I didn't feel any better, of course. I felt much, much worse, but I couldn't take it back.'

Gordon kneaded his forehead. Olivia had pulled back from her mum and was rocking on her heels.

'It's going to be okay,' Leah said, without even knowing who she was talking to, or if it was true, or what good it would do. It seemed to snap Gordon back to himself.

'Right,' he said. 'Did you hire a car?'

Charlotte nodded.

'In your own name?'

'Yes. But I got it repaired. I charmed a garage into doing it off the record – not that I was feeling remotely charming, but I did what I had to do.'

'Might anybody have seen you? Seen the number plate?'

'I don't think so. I've heard nothing. And believe me, I've been waiting.'

Gordon seemed to chew the inside of his cheek as he thought. Leah realised she'd been doing the same, her mouth soft and swollen. She caught her sister's eye and a flush of shame spread across Charlotte's face.

'I'm so sorry,' Charlotte said. 'All of you. How could I have put us through this on top of everything else?'

Gordon got out of his chair and crouched alongside Olivia, grabbing her and Charlotte's hands. 'I won't let there be any repercussions from this. I'll take the blame myself if I can.'

Charlotte's eyes were bright with tears, but she shook her head and pulled her hand away. 'Gordon, there've been too many cover-up jobs already. We can't keep doing it.'

'But I can't lose you.' His voice broke. Leah looked away out of habit, then immediately looked back. Her heart hurt as she watched her family struggling again. She wanted to be with them this time, rather than against. Whatever had happened. Whatever it took.

'You already lost me, Gordon,' Charlotte said. 'We lost each other, and lost our way, years ago. And because of it, we lost Amy.'

'But Mum,' Olivia said, laying her face on Charlotte's arm. '*I* can't lose you either. I really, really can't.'

They pulled apart at the sound of a voice with an Italian accent outside the room: 'They are just in here. Sorry, I did not realise you were waiting to see them!'

The door opened and a woman smiled into the room – not the facilitator, but a member of *Il Mandarino* staff. 'Sorry Mrs Wynne, Mr Wynne, I only just saw you had a visitor in the foyer.'

Gordon sprang to his feet. 'No, no. There's been a mix-up. We're not . . .' He trailed off when he spotted, as they all did, the figure behind her.

Nate Fraser. With shorter hair and a scar running along his jaw.

There was a lull as he stared into the room, and they stared back.

54

Joanna

Joanna got a thick hot chocolate from *Il Mandarino's* restaurant and walked with it towards her apartment. She was planning to grab a scarf and head back out on a ferry to Malcesine, wanting to feel the lake breeze in her hair again, to climb up high and be alone with her thoughts.

As she took the turning into the pine trees, she stalled in shock.

Was that . . .?

Yes, it was Nate coming down the path, looking lost in thought, so much so he hadn't yet noticed her. Joanna froze, unsure whether she wanted to speak to him. She hadn't known he was going to be here, but maybe he was a witness in Brookmyre's trial. She ducked behind a tree and watched him get closer, painfully aware that this wasn't the only time she'd observed him from a hiding place.

It was this parallel that made her pull herself together. She was done hiding from Nate Fraser. She drew up tall and stepped out, startling him.

'Jo!' After the initial shock, he actually smiled.

Her own reaction was more complicated. Her feelings about him and what he'd done were another thing that had lurched up and down over the last six months. She knew he felt guilty. That he was grieving, too. And to give him his due, after that night in the Dales he had offered to confess to the police about his deception of her, but she'd no longer wanted him to. An unspoken agreement had formed: it was all about Amy now, about justice for her.

That didn't mean Joanna had to let him off the hook entirely.

She was the first to speak: 'I didn't know you were going to be here.'

'I didn't know you were going to be here, either.'

'I just . . . wanted to see the place. Are you here for the trial?'

'Partly.' He exhaled through puffed-out cheeks. Joanna tried to read him as he appeared to collect his thoughts. 'I just met with Amy's family.'

'You as well?' she said before she could stop herself, but he didn't show any surprise; perhaps he knew Luke had been talking to them today, too.

Nate nodded. 'I wanted to see them again, now that they know I had nothing to do with Amy's death. I thought it would bring some kind of closure . . .'

Closure. The word kept coming up, like a hallowed answer to everybody's problems.

'And did it?'

He looked down at his trainers. The same trainers that had occupied a spot in Joanna's hall for almost a week, nudging up against her own shoes. It seemed crazily intimate now.

'Not really,' he said. 'It was very strange.'

Her interest was piqued. 'Strange how?'

He blinked at her. 'Sorry, it's probably really inappropriate to talk to you about this. I just . . .'

'Go on,' she said, 'What happened?'

'There was a weird vibe from the moment I walked in. It was like they were hiding something. They stared at my scar and they were tense and quiet, even when I tried to explain that I just wanted to talk about Amy, explain about our friendship. That was all I *did* want to talk about, initially, but I felt it coming off them in waves . . .'

'What, exactly?'

He contemplated. 'Fear, I suppose. And guilt.'

Joanna frowned, but understanding was beginning to dawn as Nate pattered his fingers along his scar. He had never had any so-called *closure* about who had run him over.

'The hit and run?' she ventured. 'You think it was them?'

'In some form . . . maybe.'

She squeezed the lid of her hot chocolate. It was still warm and little drops oozed out from under the rim. 'But . . . Olivia knew what had happened to Amy all along, didn't she? And Gordon thought it was Olivia . . .' She trailed off. That left Amy's mum, Charlotte. Joanna thought of the photos she had seen, and the images on the news: an elegant, anxious-looking woman. Could she really have broken Nate's ribs, left him bleeding in the road?

Nate looked at her, nodding slowly, as if knowing she'd made the same deductions as him.

'What are you going to do?' she asked.

He let out another weary sigh. Being here didn't seem to be having the same therapeutic effect on him as on Joanna.

She felt a sudden rush of sympathy, especially as a memory came to her: the last thing he had said out in the Dales, when they'd made it back to their cars. *Storms smell different here.* Then he'd leaned against her car bonnet as if something heavy had landed on his back.

'I don't think I'm going to do anything,' he said. 'I don't think I can.'

'There might be evidence, if you decided to go back to the police. I know it might raise some questions about you using a false identity in hospital, but . . .' She petered off, his face confirming what she'd already half-known: that this wasn't what he'd meant by *don't think I can.*

'They were on edge, but they were also so sad,' he said. 'And they were sitting really close. I've never seen them cluster together like that before. And . . . Olivia. I kept looking at her and thinking about everything she's been through.' He shook his head. 'I feel like Amy would've wanted me to leave them to heal.'

Joanna nodded and closed her eyes, focusing on the smell of the pines and the sound of the birds. A murmur of voices made her open her eyes. A family had appeared further along the path, and Joanna's breath hitched: it was the Wynnes. Nate had his back to them, still buried in thought, but Joanna watched as they paused and huddled, not speaking but patting each other's shoulders and hands as if checking they were all still intact.

It was an intimate moment in the wake of the two meetings Joanna knew they'd had. As the family started to move again, Joanna whispered to Nate: 'The Wynnes are coming, just in case you don't want to bump into them.'

'I'm not sure they'd want to bump into me,' he whispered back, and slipped behind a tree.

Joanna didn't hide this time. She stood to one side and smiled tentatively at Amy's family as they walked past her in two rows. Olivia and her dad led the way, with the two older women following – Charlotte and her sister, Leah, whom Joanna had also seen on the news. She knew Leah had unravelled the truth about Amy's death. As she caught her eye, Joanna felt a flicker of kinship. *She* had played a tiny part in piecing together what had happened to Amy, too, though Leah probably had no idea who she was. They exchanged a polite nod and Joanna's heart skipped as she glimpsed a strong flash of resemblance. Amy's aunt looked just like her. Like she would've done if she'd been allowed to age.

And Joanna felt it again: a strange but powerful regret that she'd never met Amy Wynne. It was a ridiculous thought, really, but she felt sure she would've liked her, that in some alternative universe they could've been friends.

Acknowledgements

Once again, I have a huge number of people to thank for helping this book into the world. Second books are notoriously difficult to write, but I've adored writing this one (most of the time!), and that's largely because of all the amazing people who have supported me.

As ever, an enormous thank you to my superstar agent, Hellie Ogden, for her encouragement, advice, belief in me, and for always helping me to see the bigger picture. It's so reassuring to know you're on my team!

It's not an overstatement to say this book wouldn't exist in its current form (and maybe not at all!) without my incredibly talented editors, Kimberley Atkins at Hodder and Danielle Dieterich at Putnam. I've been so grateful for your editorial insight, your thorough and collaborative approach, and your passion for my story and characters.

Thank you to the brilliant and hard-working teams at Hodder and at Putnam, including Amy Batley for all your support in so many ways; Natalie Young and Madeline Hopkins for such thorough and thoughtful copyediting; Niamh Anderson and Kristen Bianco for publicity; Nishtha Patel and Callie Robertson for marketing; and everybody else who has helped to shape this book and get it into readers' hands. It's been a pleasure working with you all.

Thanks also to the people who have helped me with research and queries while writing this book, including Stuart Gibbon and Adrian Deegan for advice on police and legal procedures, and Phillip Irving for helping me work through some wording, grammar and general writing dilemmas in its later editing stages. Any errors are mine!

Hugs and gratitude to all the new author friends I have made since my debut novel was published, especially the fellow Hodder authors I've got know, and everybody in the Debuts 2021 online groups. Your friendship has kept me going and your excitement for this book has been so motivating. And a heartfelt thanks to all the members of Leicester Writers' Club, who have been so supportive, not just with super-insightful feedback on chapters of this novel but also in terms of my writing in general. You're all wonderful.

Speaking of wonderful, I'm lucky enough to have a long list of friends and family members (too long to print them ALL here, sadly!) who support me tirelessly, both in my writing and in life. Thank you to all of you who have been by my side, both physically and virtually; who have kept me going and reminded me to be proud of myself. Special mention, as always, to Mum, Dad, Gramms, Christine, Yassin, Idris, Aryn, and the girls from the Whānau WhatsApp group.